by

YVES LF GIRAUD

2018 Lonestar Ventures, LLC.

Kahnu

1st edition
Edited by Misty Huffman and Yves LF Giraud
Cover illustration by Yves LF Giraud

WWW.YVESGIRAUD.COM

Published in the United States by Lonestar Ventures, LLC.

ISBN: 1727319761
ISBN-13: 978-1727319767

DEDICATION

This book is for my grandparents
Yvonne Legoff, Auguste Giraud and Marthe Giraud.

CONTENTS

ACKNOWLEDGMENTS

While this book is a pure work of fiction on my part, I would like to thank several individuals who have made this journey possible, either by landing their ears and knowledge on the various ideas and subjects this first novel covers, or by giving me the moral and encouraging support I needed to see this work to completion.

Of those, I'd like to thank my parents, Pierre and Monique Giraud, as well as my brother, Christian Giraud, for their love and continued support throughout my chaotic life as a writer and musician.

My friend Robert Cayol, my best and worst critic.

My ex-wife and best friend, Carol Via for believing in me, even when I did not.

Most importantly, I want to thank my wonderful friend, agent and manager, Misty Huffman, for all her support, dealing with my artistic personality, and without whom this book would have never seen the light of day.

Prologue

Kahjuna, the blue planet

A gigantic flash of light suddenly lit the entire sky. Bright as the mid-day sun and piercing through the cloud cover at over 30,000 kilometers an hour, a giant blazing ball cut through the thin atmosphere, igniting the blue sky behind its path in a long straight blaze of fire. As the object streaked from one end of the sky to the other, the shadows of trees, rocky outcrops, and other tall features below seemed to run across the alien landscape in the opposite direction. A few seconds later, the thundering sound of the tremendous pandemonium caused by the spaceship shook the ground below.

Inside the cockpit, bathed in a hazy purple hue, several beings were seated around a circular platform. Flashing lights and alarms were going off everywhere. The ship's occupants, fighting the effects of the vessel's speed and the planet's gravity, were in obvious discomfort.

Sitting in the center of the group, Silargh, the largest of them, his heart pounding furiously in his chest, slowly raised his arm with great effort due to the extreme pressure the rogue ship was putting on him, and finally able to get his hand high enough, made a waving gesture in the direction of the circular platform in front of him. A perfect sphere, about two meters in diameter, appeared in the center of the pad. The shiny object, hovering just above the platform, slowly started spinning. As colorful rays of light, appearing and disappearing at random, began creating beautiful waveforms above its off-white surface, the sphere also began to glow from within.

"*Silargh, forty-nine seconds left before impact!*" said Tehe, one of the female passengers, without making a sound. She was sitting to his right, hands clutching her armrests, struggling to bear the enormous pressure that was pinning her to her seat. Her head turned toward him, she was waiting for a telepathic response. But, although he had "heard her," Silargh didn't reply. He was concentrating all his efforts on re-initializing the ship's gravitational generator. He knew doing so while in flight was a dangerous maneuver. At their current speed, the shock would be tremendous, but he also knew it was their only chance to stop their ship before it crashed on the fast approaching ground below. The task was taking all his concentration. Regaining some strength after the previous effort, he slowly managed to raise his arm once more, and with another elaborate move of his hand in the air, made the hovering sphere rotate on itself to expose a small hole beneath. Inside, a bright light flashed an instant, responding to his telepathic command, and everything went completely dark.

Almost in the same instant, an enormous change in velocity sucked the air out of everyone's lungs on board the spaceship. In less than three seconds, the vessel's speed had dropped down to 1000 kilometers an hour. Any human would have been killed instantly by the sudden deceleration. The passengers, used to a strong gravity on their home planet and physically much stronger than any life form on Earth, were capable of withstanding much greater forces. Even so, not all the occupants made it through the maneuver unharmed.

"*Tehe, Berhis is hurt!*" said a voice in Tehe's head as the lights in the room came back on.

Without hesitation, Tehe unfastened her invisible restraint with a wave of the hand and rushed out of the room. Running through the corridors as fast as she could on her massive legs, her heart pounding with fear, she reached the cargo bay in seconds where she knew Berhis was stationed. She saw him as soon as she entered the room. He was awkwardly seated on the floor, his large elongated head resting uncomfortably against the back wall. To his left, a few containers were strewn about on the floor. Three other passengers were leaning over him. She could see he was having difficulties breathing. Her heart jumped in her chest when she looked at Lishieru's face. She was the most qualified doctor onboard, and from her deeply concerned expression, Tehe knew it was bad.

"*Berhis!*" she called out mentally as she ran toward him. Lishieru stopped her before she was in reaching distance.

"*Don't touch him, he's in pain and is having difficulties breathing. I'm afraid he may have serious internal injuries.*"

Looking at Berhis with distress, Tehe said telepathically, "*I'm here, Berhis, I'm here. You're gonna be OK.*"

She was struggling not to grab his hand or touch him in anyway. Most of all, she was desperately trying not to cry or show him the fear and despair she felt inside her, seeing him in such a state. A difficult challenge since her people could read minds. He looked up at her and tried to give her a reassuring smile, but he was in excruciating pain.

Lishieru opened the box sitting in front of her on the floor and pulled out a handful of round objects called Rodas that resembled hockey pucks. With a slow movement, she tilted her hand and all the small disks started gliding out and approached Berhis' injured body, slowly hovering in place under his arms, legs, back and attaching themselves to him. Lishieru then stood up and with a slow hand motion over Berhis, made the small hovering devices slowly raise his body, ever so gently.

A few moans and grunts came out of Berhis' mouth, a part of the body he very rarely used, but within seconds he was asleep. The Rodas, now supporting his body above the ground, were designed to induce the injured patient into a deep state of trance that completely numbed the person's sensory system, eliminating pain, and allowing the caretaker to perform any surgery without additional anesthesia.

"*How is he?*" asked Tehe with desperation in her eyes.

"*I don't know yet, we need to get him on the scanning platform*," answered Lishieru hastily. Every second counted and she was already rushing to the medical quarters, Berhis' body floating in front of her through the ship's corridors.

"*Attention, everyone! We are about to attempt a landing. This is going to be rough. Secure yourselves! Impact in less than two minutes*," announced Silargh telepathically from the cockpit.

Lishieru, still controlling the hovering "package" in front of her, entered the medical lab in a fury, Tehe and two other occupants right on her tail. The lights came on automatically as they entered, and a hovering medical bed approached them to receive Berhis' body. With one more hand gesture from the doctor, a white cocoon like pod quickly materialized all around him, enclosing his entire body.

Tehe was about to rush again to Berhis' side when Lishieru called her, "*No time Tehe! He'll be OK for now. We need to secure ourselves down. We're about to land... TEHE!*"

Tehe, seemingly confused at first, finally came back to the reality of their situation and rushed to a seat nearby to anchor herself in, as everyone else was doing on the ship.

In a few minutes, they would land on an alien world, a rocky and completely foreign landscape, covered by a wild and lush vegetation and inhabited by strange creatures and monsters they had never seen before; a dangerous and uninviting world, full of unknowns and deadly things. A new world, nonetheless, they now would have to call home. It was known to them as Kahjuna, the blue planet. Seventy million years from now, man would inherit it and call it Earth.

PART I

Chapter I

The welcome mat

The sky was still overcast, but the rain had stopped. Walking through the large Amsterdam airport, Dedrick was looking for his passport. He had just used it at customs and hoped he had not left it there. He stopped in front of a big map of the city on the wall and put his bag down. Searching every pocket, he finally found it in the left one of his Swede jacket and slipped it into his carry-on bag. After closing the zipper, he took a look at the map. The Schiphol airport where he had just landed was just southwest of the Netherlands capital, in the municipality of Haarlemmermeer. Staring at that name with interest, Dedrick was counting the multiple letters in it when a voice behind him called out, "Mr. Sokolov? Dedrick Sokolov?"

Dedrick turned around to face a beautiful short hair brunette staring at him through her glasses, holding a sign with his name on it.

"Yes?" he replied a bit hesitant.

"My name is Sylvia Kaarzeev. I work for the Mars First foundation. I am your guide. Welcome to Amsterdam. This way, please." Her Dutch accent was barely noticeable.

Pointing towards the exit sign, she added as she started walking beside him, "Do you have any other luggage to pick up?"

"No, that's it. Would you mind if I grab something to eat before we go, though? I'm starving!"

"There will be a meal waiting for you at the base when we arrive. The drive is not long."

Feeling there was probably not much room for discussion on the matter, Dedrick followed her to the exit. After crossing an automatic double glass door, they walked straight to a black limousine parked along the sidewalk. A man wearing a dark suit was already holding a door open for them. Sylvia gestured for Dedrick to step inside the vehicle and followed him in.

A few minutes later, the black car and its passengers were flying down A1, in route for Amersfoort, about thirty minutes southeast of the airport.

Sitting across from Sylvia in the back seat, Dedrick couldn't help looking at her. She seemed lost in thoughts, looking out the window at the scenery, her legs and hands crossed. A very attractive woman, probably of Asiatic descent, he thought. She looked sharp and professional while still very sexy. Her legs looked fit under her long skirt and her suit jacket was shaping her upper body nicely, without revealing hardly any cleavage. Sensing the Russian's obvious stare, she slowly brushed her medium-length hair with her left hand, revealing a gold hearing dangling a couple of inches from her ear, then turned her eyes on him. Dedrick turned away immediately. She smiled.

"How was your trip?"

"Good... good," he replied, trying to hide his embarrassment.

"I don't like traveling in those big airliners much," she then offered. "Or I have to fly first class. People drive me nuts."

He was glad to see he wasn't the only one thinking so. "Actually, me too. I can't stand some of these people. Not that I am complaining, of course. Your company paid for my trip and I'm grateful for that," he added quickly, not wanting to sound rude or ungrateful.

Looking down, he noticed her thin ankle chain.

"Trust me, Mr. Sokolov, the company I work for doesn't mind. You are an asset to them now."

"Yes, I guess. Me and forty others."

She just looked at him for a moment but did not reply. As she turned back her attention to the scenery outside her window, Dedrick thought he had noticed a faint smirk on her face and wondered what she knew that he didn't.

For the next several kilometers, neither one said anything anymore. The two passengers lost in thoughts, seemed to focus their attention on the flat landscape rolling outside.

Dedrick knew very well this wasn't Russia anymore. Of course, anyone observant enough would have quickly noticed the different vegetation, rolling hills, and European style architecture that was so distinct and differed from the buildings and houses he was used to back home. Yet, he was also thinking of how similar the world could be from country to country. Although several thousand kilometers apart, cities like Amsterdam and Moscow were essentially identical in their overall layout and function. People gathered and lived in them in pretty much the same way. Arteries of roads and highways often connected the different suburbs and places of interest to the town's center while the essential amenities, water, electricity, and communication lines were made part of their intricate design. Some eco-friendly balance was almost always considered as well, allowing space for enough parks and "green" places, sufficient trees, walking trails, flower filled medians, especially in heavily populated areas. Mars would definitely be a new experience, no doubt.

"*No trees or rivers there… I hope we know what we're doing*," he thought, thinking of the other candidates as well.

Dedrick wasn't much of a talker and even less so in front of such a beautiful woman but the small confinement of the car eventually made him want to fill the silence, so he asked, "Do we have far to drive?"

"No, not far, we'll be there soon," she replied without looking at him.

About forty minutes later, after having crossed several small towns and made several turns, the limousine finally came to a stop in front of a guard house. A few signs were visible but Dedrick couldn't read any of them since he did not know Dutch.

After showing his passport and a few checks were made by one of the guards over the radio, the gate was lifted, and the limousine let through.

They drove another kilometer or so through a dense forest of pines before entering a clearing several hundred meters in diameter. The grass looked freshly mowed. A few lonely trees stood in the open space, randomly scattered around. In the distance, a dense forest partially encircled the area, making for a dramatic contrast. A wide, two-story building stood in the center of the field. Dedrick quickly estimated the structure was fairly new and covered a good 10,000 square meters at its base.

"*That's a pretty big space,*" he thought to himself. Another white building had just come into view behind the first one. A large dome adorned its roof. "*There must be one heck of a telescope in there.*"

Connecting the two buildings, a tall glass gallery was flanked by manicured vegetation and beautiful flowers of all sorts. The car came to a stop near the entrance of the larger building.

"Here we are Mr. Sokolov," said Sylvia getting out of the vehicle. "You can leave your bag in the car. I'll have someone take it to your room, but first, I'd like you to meet Mr. Bruininck before I show you around. This way, please."

Dedrick followed the woman along a narrow, gravel path. Two large glass doors opened automatically as they approached the building and four armed guards appeared from inside.

"Hi, ma'am. We've been instructed to check everyone's ID. I'll need to see yours too, sir."

"Don't worry, this is typical these days. We've received several threats in the past few weeks. Lars takes security very seriously," she informed Dedrick.

"*The welcome mat, I guess…*" he thought to himself.

A few minutes later, both entered a small office at the end of a long hallway. The man seated behind the desk looked tall and thin, in his thirties with a receding hairline, and a friendly smile. Behind him, a three-dimensional reproduction of the Mars First station, laid in front of a photo of the red planet. It included a couple of astronauts and two rovers.

"Hello Dedrick. I'm Lars Bruininck. Welcome to Mars First," said the man smiling while vaguely pointing at the walls around the room. His heavy accent left no doubt as to his Dutch roots.

"Thank you, sir. Glad to be here," replied the young Russian as he moved forward to shake Lars' extended hand.

"Please, call me Lars. Have a seat. So, how was your trip?"

"Very good. Sir, Thank you." He thought of mentioning how long the trek had actually felt, but refrained.

"Have you seen the complex yet? And your quarters?"

"I haven't taken Mr. Sokolov around yet. I wanted him to meet you first," replied Sylvia before Dedrick could.

"Oh OK, good. Well, I'm glad you made it here without a glitch, and I have a feeling you're going to enjoy your stay with us. I think you'll like the place. The complex offers great amenities, including a large gym, an indoor pool, and we also have a wonderful training lab in the east wing of the building. Wait 'til you see it. You're gonna love it!"

"I'm sure I will, Sir- I mean, Lars," Dedrick replied with a nod and a smile.

"Great! Well, I'm sure you're tired and impatient to check out your room, so I'll let Sylvia take you there. Enjoy the rest of your evening and get some rest. We have a long day ahead of us tomorrow. We'll have an orientation briefing in the morning, and you'll get to meet the other members of your team, but Sylvia will explain all that to you in details. Good to have you on board, Dedrick!" Lars finished as he shook his hand and sat back down in front of his laptop.

"Thank you, Lars. I'm looking forward to it!"

"Good," he replied as Sylvia and Dedrick left the room.

After visiting a few key places, including the recreational area, the centrifugal room, and the 590mm reflecting telescope, that last stop at Dedrick's request, Sylvia finally led the Russian to his quarters, deep in the east wing of the main building.

"This is your room. The cafeteria is at the end of the hallway, on the right. Dinner is at seven thirty…that's in about twenty minutes. If you need anything, just ring the front desk by dialing pound one on your interphone. Make yourself at home, Mr. Sokolov and I'll see you in a few in the cafeteria."

"Thank you, Sylvia," replied Dedrick, daring to use her first name to keep things informal.

She just glanced at him with an approving smile and left.

The apartment was decent in size. The first thing Dedrick noticed was the giant flat screen TV on the wall across from him. Below it, a fake fireplace, vaguely reminding him of the one at his parent's house, looked surprisingly new. "I wonder if it works," he thought. A great bay window, almost as wide as the wall it covered, offered a clear view on the lavish forest beyond the compound. To the left, a small office area was filled by an armoire partially hidden behind a desk and chair, on top of which sat a computer. He stared an instant at the "Mars First" logo, moving slowly across the monitor. Beyond, a clear glass door opened into a modern bathroom with an all-around shower and Jacuzzi bathtub. Dedrick walked to the inviting bedroom. The room was uncluttered, with a single queen bed in the middle, a dresser and one chair near the window.

After removing his jacket and hanging it in the closet, Dedrick took off his shoes and walked to the small kitchen area to make himself some coffee. The kitchen was one step higher than the rest of the apartment, in an interesting split-level design. Turning around, his back to the percolating coffee machine, he stared a moment at the retro looking dark green couch that was sitting caddy cornered, facing the large TV. Not really to his taste but nonetheless classic. After pouring himself a well-deserved cup of warm coffee, he looked up at the low ceiling while taking a sip. Dedrick was a tall man at one meter ninety-two, and the ceiling offered only another half a meter or so of room above his head, giving him a strange feeling of confinement but that slight disappointment was compensated by two large skylights that offered a beautiful view of the open sky. In fact, every part of the complex, Dedrick would later learn, was designed to receive as much natural light as possible, a choice that he fully approved. It wasn't the home of his dreams, but he would make the best of it. He had to. He was going to spend the next eight years here.

Coffee in hand, Dedrick walked to the small table in the middle of the living room, grabbed the remote, sat on the green couch, and turned the TV on. After scanning through a few local channels, he found a documentary on the Ajanta caves of India. He could not understand Dutch, but was nonetheless immediately captivated by the amazing images of temples carved right out of the mountain. For a few minutes, he watched, pondering on the challenges of such an undertaking. But after the excitement and exhaustion of the trip, even his fascination with ancient monuments was not enough to keep him awake for long, and he was soon deep asleep in front of the screen...

He was suddenly awakened by a loud noise outside his room, forty minutes later. At first a bit disoriented, he slowly reached for the remote and turned the TV off. After getting up uneasily, still groggy and walking a few steps, he reached his front door and opened it just in time to see Sylvia slap a young man and walk away.

"I guess I deserved that," said the man, turning to Dedrick, one hand on his left cheek.

"François! Good to see you, my friend. I see you've met Sylvia," said the Russian with a smirk.

"Yeah. Nice girl," replied the Frenchman.

"Come on in. When did you arrive?"

François stepped into the room and Dedrick closed the door behind them.

"Want something to drink? Let me see what we have," continued Dedrick, heading to the small fridge in the kitchen, while François let himself fall back on Dedrick's green couch and rested his feet up on the coffee table in front of him.

"Sure. Thanks. I just got in a few minutes ago."

"I see you've met Sylvia?"

"Yep. I guess I'll have to find my room later. She was about to take me there, but I don't think she liked what I said."

"What did you say?"

"Oh, nothing worth getting so out of shape about. I just commented on how hot she looked and that I hoped my room had a strong enough bed because I intended to rock her body all night. Ha, ha. Yeah, I know..." he replied with a laugh.

"Wow! Leave it to the French! Yeah, I guess that's a bit forward for a first meeting," replied Dedrick, laughing as well.

Dedrick and François were among the first of two hundred thousand plus applicants to sign up for the Mars First project back in 2013. After a pre-selection process that had reduced that number to a mere few hundred the following year, the two friends were now among the lucky final twenty-six scheduled to begin astronaut training.

They had met online after exchanging multiple emails through the Mars First website. Dedrick had been selected as a candidate a few weeks before François, but it was François who had contacted the Russian applicant first, asking for his help with a female Russian applicant he was trying to impress. He needed help translating some emails and a poem the Frenchman was certain would sweep the woman off her feet. Dedrick had kindly obliged and translated the documents in Russian, but not without laughing when he had read the so called "poem." Of course, François had sent the letter enthusiastically anyway, and as Dedrick had predicted, the young woman had politely declined the Frenchman's advances and stopped corresponding with him soon after. That incident also explained why Sylvia's reaction to François' clumsy courting tactics earlier had not really surprised the Russian. Nonetheless, the two men had become good internet friends over the past year, and they would now have plenty of time to get to know each other even better.

Over the next several years, they were going to train, eat, and live together, day in and day out. Their social skills and team spirit would be tested to the breaking point and so would their determination and morale. But with a little luck, their friendship would last and even extend beyond the boundaries of Earth, all the way to the planet Mars.

Vera

A few weeks into the program, a special celebration was about to take place, and the man behind Mars First enterprises was getting ready to speak as guests and co-workers mingled in the large conference hall.

Mars First was the creation of Netherlands Entrepreneur, Lars Bruininck. A man with a unique vision, Lars had made his money in the early 2000's with a company named Syspam, where he had developed a new technology to harness and combine photovoltaic (solar) and wind energy. By 2011, he had sold his share of the company and started Mars First, a non-profit organization that envisioned not only to send people to Mars, but also to establish a permanent human colony there, and begin the slow process of colonizing the red planet. The ground-breaking idea that the astronauts sent to Mars would settle there permanently had never been proposed before. Not needing to bring the astronauts back to Earth eliminated the most challenging and costly portion of the mission, the return home. Without the extremely expensive and technically challenging aspect of the journey, the return to Earth, sending a manned mission to Mars was a feasible enterprise, even for a private company. Mars First was the first company to present a feasible plan to colonize the red planet years before any other organization, even beating NASA to the punch. The other innovative aspect of the concept was that the future astronauts would be selected from a large pool of civilians who had volunteered for the chance to be one of the first people to walk on the red planet by simply applying online. The contest had been open to anyone in the world, regardless of age, as long as the applicant was at least eighteen years old, sex, ethnicity, religious beliefs, or professional background.

The critics had been ferocious, some calling the endeavor suicide, even murder. But three years after the launching of the project, and a remarkable 206,507 applicants from all around the globe, the dream was beginning to feel very real. Lars was now standing in a room filled by some of the most dedicated and respected scientists in their field, fully passionate about the company's mission and their role in it. Alongside them, the final twenty-six future astronauts who had made it this far in the selection process were just as excited and enthusiastic.

He could not have been prouder.

The room was quite large with a high ceiling, and a good eighty people were gathered for this celebration. Lars and the Mars First team had made the unofficial announcement that same morning: they had just reached the first of their six billion-dollar financial goal for the project. Thanks to public and private donations, Mars First was now ready to begin the designing and construction of three cargo ships, four habitats, two rovers, and advance to the next stage of the candidates' training. The rest of the investment would come, it was expected, through marketing ads and the media related revenues generated by the TV coverage of said training.

Lars had discovered a few years prior the astronomical amount of money the media had been able to raise during the Olympic games. Between the sponsors and the advertisement from major corporations and trademarks, Lars had immediately realized the monetary potential of television. Mars First would create a new form of reality show; One that would follow the future astronauts during their eight-year training and would be broadcast all around the globe. The entire world would want to watch such an undertaking.

The project's timeline had been clearly outlined. In 2019, a first ship would land on Mars, unmanned, and meant not only to put to the test the reliability of the technology used, but also to begin creating an outpost on the red planet before sending anyone there. At least three cargo ships would be launched over the following three years. Along with them, two large rovers would begin constructing the outpost. This first small base, made of several interconnected pods, each the size of a small room, would also begin creating the oxygen, water, fuel, and other resources the team would need to survive once there.

The first manned mission and its four astronauts would arrive on Mars in late 2025. By then, several habitats would await them, cone-shaped containers that were once spaceships, put in place by robotic rovers. The technology to supply essential needs for the survival of the Martian colonists, such as oxygen, water, power, and other needed resources, had already been studied and deemed reliably achievable within the given time frame, using minerals and chemicals in the Martian soil and atmosphere.

Of course, many had criticized the whole project, calling it unrealistic, too risky, and too early in the race to deep space. We simply didn't know enough yet about the effects of low gravity on the human body, nor did we have any idea how much radiation the astronauts would be exposed to in Mars' thin atmosphere, let alone during the voyage there. The risks were enormous, the dangers even greater. Growing food in greenhouses had never been tested on another planet, not even on the Moon. The probability of success of such a bold proposal was simply too low for many. Some had even called it pure suicide. They may have been right, but Lars also knew every great advance in human history had involved taking risks. Although still limited, the information available on the effects of space and low gravity on the human body had been studied and well documented, ever since NASA had started the space program, and gave the Mars First company confidence that the mission would be a great success.

Either way, they now had the money they needed to cover the cost of research, the building of several test outposts, and purchase the necessary manufacturing resources to do much more.

So tonight, the company was celebrating, and everyone involved was in attendance in the big reception area.

A voice resounded through the loud speakers in the room.

"If I could have everyone's attention, please!" the conversations started dying out.

"Hello, can everyone hear me?" as the room turned quiet.

A thump reverberated through the sound system and Lars, standing in front of the microphone began his speech.

"My dear colleagues. I want to personally thank you all for being part of this great vision that has become the Mars First project. Five years ago, a few friends and I began an amazing journey to bring to life a dream. A dream to put humans on Mars, not only to…"

Lars' speech went on for several minutes before he finally raised his glass.

"…and so, my dear friends, I would like to make a toast. To all of you and all those not here tonight who have contributed in some way in the realization of a vision, a dream I had almost four years ago. Thank you! Thank you all and Mars, watch out! Here we come!" he finished loudly, raising his glass high with the rest of the room. A few "ooooh ooohs, yay!" and shouts of approval followed.

A moment later, the main lights dimmed, and as the music started reverberating against the colorfully decorated walls of the large room, the crowd began mingling and dancing under spinning spotlights of varied colors, syncing their movements to the tempo.

Dedrick wasn't much of a social bee. He preferred to keep to himself, and was standing towards the back of the gathering, munching casually on appetizers, when he noticed her.

She was definitely looking in his direction. He was leaning against a file cabinet, and a wall was right behind him so there could be no mistake. There was no one else around. For a few moments, his glances kept meeting her gaze, causing him to look away each time, but he eventually gazed back at her long enough for the exchange of a few smiles and a toast from a distance.

By now, Dedrick knew her name, Vera. She had been in training with him and two other applicants for almost a week already. She was from Chicago and she had a sister... Katy or Cathy. She liked cats and preferred white wine over red, had been a flight attendant for a major airline until her selection for the astronaut program, and had never been married. That was all he could remember at the moment. She was beautiful, and she was smiling at him. He gave her a weak smile in return and turned his eyes away once more. He found it hard to look at her, particularly tonight in her black dress with low V-neck, cleavage cut that left little to the imagination. To make matters worse, her beautiful shoulder length blonde hair and bright blue eyes would have made any man melt. After staring at his wine glass for a few more seconds, he took his courage back and glanced in her direction once more. Now, she was walking straight for him. As a wave of panic grabbed his body, she quietly stopped right next to him and turned around to face the rest of the room.

"Hi Dedrick," she said smiling while looking at the dancing attendees.

"Hey Vera. How are you?" he replied a bit shy.

"I'm good, thank you."

After a few seconds passed…

"Nice party."

"Yes. It's great!" he replied, shaking his head in approval with a bit too much enthusiasm.

"What are you drinking?"

"Oh, huh... It's Chardonnay," he replied.

She looked down at her glass and then back at him. He followed her eyes and suddenly realized her glass was empty.

"Oh, let me get you another one," he said, feeling a bit clumsy as he walked to a table a few meters away and grabbed another wine for her.

"There you go."

"Thank you!" again smiling at him.

A few moments passed.

"So, what is the name of your hometown in Russia again?" she asked seemingly genuinely interested.

"Tambov. It's a mid-sized town in the region of Tambov Oblast, in East Russia," he replied modestly. "My family has been there for four generations, now. I'm the fourth generation."

"So, you mean, three generations then."

"Three?"

"Well, yes. You see, since you're leaving to go to Mars, you can't be counted on Earth as well. You're either an Earthling or a Martian. But you can't be both."

He did not realize right away she was having a bit of fun with him and responded as if seriously intrigued by her statement.

"Mmmh. I guess you're right. I didn't really think about that."

It took him several seconds to notice the funny smirk on her face that said, "*Really? Can't you see I'm messing with you*?"

He chuckled.

"Ha, yes, of course. You got me there."

"I'm from Boston, by the way, but I was born in Charlottesville, Virginia," she suddenly offered.

"Ah... Nice. I've never been to Boston. In fact, I've never been to America."

"That's too bad. It's beautiful. You should visit, sometime," she added with a little smirk on her face.

He felt a slight tinge in his back. "I would like that," he replied with a smile.

Dedrick took another sip of wine and finished his glass.

"So, looks like things are going just as planned with the program. I can't wait to start the next phase of the training." He vaguely looked at the podium where Lars was standing earlier.

"Yes, so it would seem," she replied without much enthusiasm.

In all truthfulness, she was more interested in the two of them than the boss' speech.

A moment of silence passed…

Leaning close to his ear, whispered, "You want to go to the pool?"

"The pool?" he whispered back in surprise, as he turned to her.

"Yes. Come, I'll show you," she said smiling, as she grabbed his hand and pulled him towards the exit.

The music was still resonating through the hallway when they reached the indoor pool area. The door squeaked and reverberated as they entered the large tiled room. The pool was almost exactly in the center of it. The water was barely moving, its almost perfectly flat surface reflecting occasional rays of light from the neon lights above as the steam rose from the warm water. The only hint of color was coming from the red overhead exit signs above the four doors around the perimeter.

"You're sure we're allowed in here this late?" asked Dedrick.

"No, we're not. That's what's exciting!" she replied with a mischievous look in her eyes.

She began undressing as she faced the pool, turning her back to him. Her skirt fell to the tiled floor, followed by her top, underwear, and bra. Without hesitation, she plunged, head first, in the water below. Dedrick stayed still for several seconds, watching her body move through the ripples. She turned around, facing him while maintaining her floatation by waving her arms and legs in the water.

"Are you coming?"

He suddenly felt his member get aroused as he started to take his clothes off. He dove in, reappearing after a few laps underwater right next to Vera who was now standing in a section of the pool only one and a half meters deep. She slowly walked to him and brought herself right against him. As he felt her beautiful, sexy body press against his briefs, he tried in vain to keep his erection under control while she slowly wrapped her arms around his neck. As he watched her lips get closer to his, her beautiful sparkling blue eyes entranced him, and they kissed passionately. He grabbed her hair and the back of her head in his hands, and her body started to slowly pulse against his. In the distance, the crowd screamed in unison as the AC/DC song "Shook Me All Night Long" echoed through the complex.

The journey had begun, and it was off to a great start.

Team One

The first six years of the Mars First program had gone on without hardly any incidents. The very first year had been the most exciting and the easiest in many ways. Aside from the centrifugal accident of Petrea Stonovich, one of the women candidates, during which the subject had had a mild heart attack, forcing Mars First to remove her permanently from the program, most of the twenty-six applicants picked by the committee had proved up to the training expectations. Of course, there were a few resignations from uncertain candidates who, realizing the true magnitude and demands of the mission after the real training had started, had chosen to leave Mars First of their own accord. The company had expected that much and a smaller group of applicants had also been selected as replacement for such situations. Overall, the program was a success and on schedule.

By 2020, the Mars First engineering team was now comprised of some of the best on the planet. After the explosion of interest in the reality show, "Mars First Now," Lars' company had created to finance the whole endeavor, the company had acquired some well-deserved recognition in the media as well as the scientific community, and the entire planet was watching. By that summer, the eight members comprising team one and two were in a race to be the first team to land on Mars. Their lives were broadcasted almost twenty-four, seven in twenty-nine countries around the globe. Most of the world's news was keeping up with the daring project as well. The decision to give the future astronauts a few hours of privacy at night had been reached after the psychiatric advisory board had made it absolutely mandatory. The candidates were left alone from 2100 hours to 0600 hours, military time, every night, unless a special situation prevented it. The rest of the time, a small crew of two, a cameraman and a sound technician, followed them around from their bedroom, to the cafeteria, to the test labs, and especially to the simulation facilities where most of their physical conditioning and training took place.

Occasionally, a TV host was added in the mix to help explain the technical and scientific mumbo-jumbo related to the tests and training of the astronauts, but had otherwise been deemed unnecessary. Most people understood well enough what was happening and were much less interested in the technical aspect of the program than they were in the human interactions and conflicts that occasionally took place between the participants. But those were few and far between and most days were about the clockwork regiment of the tasks at hand. Of course, if something went wrong during an exercise, the media never missed to inflame the incident for good drama effect. For the applicants, being watched constantly presented its own challenges. Privacy was often non-existent, but the fortunate selectees were quick to remind anyone who asked that the discomfort of being watched by millions all the time was a small price to pay for a chance at becoming the first man or woman to set foot on another world.

For Liu Xing, a twenty-six-year-old physics teacher from South Korea, science and discovery was everything. She was a member of crew number two. A fierce rival of Dedrick's team, her group had high hopes to be the first to go to Mars. Liu, however, secretly hoped her team would not get their wish. She, for one, preferred to land on Mars after someone else had made it there safely, already tested the unknowns of the six-month trip and spent even more time on the red planet itself. It was true that the risks were enormous, and although being the first to land on Mars guaranteed a place in the history books, she figured being on the next flight would probably make history just as well. Either way, she preferred getting there alive.

For now, the public was showing a preference for crew one. Each crew was comprised of four individuals, from four different countries. Two women and two men had been the preferred arrangement from the get go. Lars had insisted on it and to his pleasant surprise, most of the administration and board members had agreed, for the very same reasons he had presented. One, of course, was the non-discrimination of genders. He had quickly argued that this was the 21st century and an evenly mixed team was best. He had also explained that the four astronauts should come from different regions of the world, and preferably be of different ethnicities. Age discrimination, racial profiling, and religious favoritism would have to be avoided as well. In short, diversity in background and personality of those selected was essential to the success and global appeal of the project.

By the end of 2021, Team One, comprised of thirty-year-old Russian candidate Dedrick Sokolov as commander and mission leader, thirty-one-year-old French candidate François Menardais as mission engineer, twenty-eight-year-old Guatemalan candidate Sabrina Lazano as chief biochemist and science officer, and thirty-eight-year-old American candidate Vera Via as medical officer, had become a favorite. The public votes had placed them in the lead to be the first team to reach Mars. This was of course not unrelated to the recent news of Dedrick and Vera's romantic involvement, which had immediately become a subject of great interest to many. The two candidates had somehow managed to keep their romance private the first few years, but the public had finally caught on regardless, and since the Mars First Corporation had not opposed it, they had finally made it official.

It had also been decided early on that the first four to go to Mars would be voted by the public. Of course, that was what everyone had been told. The final decision would still be made by the Mars First project team leaders. The general voting would be considered of course, and it was obvious telling the audience they had full power in the final selection making would generate more interest in the project. The voting system had become so popular by the end of 2018, that it had barely made a dent in the number of votes when the company had announced the decision to charge a small "fee" for every vote made. It had certainly paid off. Mars First had raised over $700 million during the past eight months alone.

No one was complaining. It was a win-win situation. Dedrick and his team were more than happy as well, and as it was, their crew had a few advantages over team two. François' French accent and bad boy image had managed to charm more votes than any of the candidates. Vera was close behind. Her physical attributes and social skills had a lot to do with it, and she was certainly not shy in front of the camera. Dedrick was a favorite among the scientific community for his logical thinking, self-discipline, and natural leader abilities. Sabrina was in a league all her own. Although she came last in the official reports, the Latin community around the world was more supportive than any other demographic group, and had it not been for the fact that some of the voting countries had been temporarily suspended from the list for senseless political reasons and unwarranted foreign tensions, her votes would have tallied higher than any of them.

All in all, 2021 was going extremely well for the four and the grand endeavor was well on its way.

The next couple of years had only showed great promises for

the astronauts. Ladli O'Connor, the Medical officer on Team Two, had become the first woman in history to withstand 9.4 G-s during a centrifugal exercise before passing out. The thirty-five-year-old Irish woman, it was true, was more athletic than most of her male colleagues. A body builder in her early teens, she was physically fit; a trait her team's mission engineer, Tendai Nyandoro, found particularly attractive. The Zimbabwe man was known to love a good challenge, and there again, Tendai had met "courtship resistance," as he often called it.

In Ladli's defense, her past had a lot to do with it. Ladli's early childhood had not been easy. After losing her parents and three siblings in a house fire at the age of ten, Ladli had found herself in an orphanage. The tragedy of losing her entire family had made her stop talking. She had eventually been placed in a foster home a year later. From day one, that arrangement had been challenging for the quiet girl. Both parents were verbally abusive and treated her like an inconvenience, a situation that had only worsened over the years. Her foster dad in particular had been an "abusive bastard and an evil monster," as she had often mentioned in therapy. After Miss Richards, her school counselor, had learned from Ladli herself that both her parents were abusing her sexually, she had been removed from that terrible environment at the age of fourteen and forced to attend mandatory therapy sessions after school. The following two years of therapy had helped the child regain her speech and cope with her past to some degree. Unfortunately, as luck would have it, her second foster family had turned out to be just as difficult to deal with for the teenager. Her new mother was overbearing and pampering while her husband was an absolute control freak, and the dysfunctional nature of her second foster home had given Ladli ample reasons to leave as soon as she had been legally able to. The string of bad relationships that had followed until her recruiting by Mars First had given the Irish woman even more reasons to be guarded.

Those were all important facts that Tendai would learn much later. Regardless, the two had eventually become involved.

Practice makes perfect

Jumping off his bucket seat, Dedrick plunged forward and grabbed François' right arm, stopping him in his tracks. "What do you think you're doing?"

"What? I'm opening the cabin door, like I'm supposed to?" replied François.

"I would not do that if I were you." Dedrick was pointing at a bright red light slowly pulsing to the left of the door.

François immediately removed his hand from the handle, but it was too late.

All at once, the simulator's four alarms suddenly trumpeted in unison, and all the lights in the room came on, full bright.

Dedrick, shaking his head, let out a heavy sigh.

Behind one of the glass panels surrounding the room, Dr. Arnold's silhouette was starting to emerge, as the computerized black tint was quickly fading away. The lab director was leaning forward, both hands on the console in front of him for support and staring, with pure rage in his eyes. Putting his hand back in his pocket and turning slowly towards him, François simply said with a tone of mild indifference, "Sorry". Then, glancing at Dedrick with a smirk on his face, the culprit gave his colleague a wink and exited the room.

Everyone stood there without a word, watching him disappear down the corridor, a cameraman on his tail. Dedrick didn't move for a few seconds, stoic and silent, while the cleaning crew hastily entered the pod to reset everything.

"*Seriously?*" he thought to himself.

A few minutes later, the Russian astronaut, crossing a doorway that looked more like a submarine hatch than it did a door, entered a small red and white room, his every movements followed by two cameras secured to the ceiling.

François was lounging on a small couch in front of a round table adorned by a basket of fruits.

"So, what is it exactly that's wrong with you again? Because there's definitely something wrong with you, my friend!" Dedrick's tone conveyed an equal part of serious irritation and one of absolute amazement.

"I just don't understand why you do it. I don't even understand what it is you're trying to do. If it's to have us both fired, then you're doing a fine job! What do you think the guys back at headquarters are gonna say? We only have one job to do, ONE! Now Dr. Arnold is going to have a field day with this latest stunt of yours and one more reason to try and replace us. What were you thinking?"

"I don't know. I was just distracted I guess…"

"How can you be distracted during a test? You know they are watching us and evaluating everything. Trust me, all they're thinking now is one distraction like that on Mars and we're all dead in seconds."

"Yeah, I know. I'm just tired of these simulations."

"Come on, François! You know how important this is for all of us. Can't you take at least one thing seriously, once in your life?" Dedrick was losing patience.

The two were now engaged in a serious back and forth conversation, as they often did, with Dedrick pacing around the egg-shaped room, babbling to no end, and at times almost shouting in frustration while François, lounged in a reclined position against the soft cushion of his seat, eyes closed and smiling, was enjoying some grapes from the fruit display in front of him.

"I really don't see what the big deal is," he finally said to the Russian.

"What? Are you for real? We barely got out of Dr. Arnold's office alive after you pulled that 'Karaoke' stunt last week, and you don't see what the big deal is?"

It wasn't so much what François had done or was saying that infuriated him, it was the way he always seemed to rejoice in those moments that drove Dedrick mad.

The Russian commander grabbed a fork from the counter nearby, and still talking, started poking around at a couple of apples on the table in front of François.

The Frenchman, his eyes still closed and not noticing his friend had moved so close to him, was just about to grab a few grapes when he felt the fork brush his fingers.

"Hey! No need to get violent, Mr.!" he said teasingly. "What happened? You didn't get lucky last night?"

Dedrick was about to say something back when a feminine voice behind them said, "You two sound like an old couple!"

Both immediately shifted their attention to the doorway where their team's biochemist was standing, holding a tea cup in her left hand. Pale vapors of smoke could be seen rising against the poorly lit corridor behind her.

Sabrina was a little over one and a half meters tall, slightly overweight for her height but still sexy. Sporting long dark hair resting evenly on her shoulders, and eyes of a bluish tint, she had a Latin complexion, and as François liked to say, a nice rack. Dedrick preferred to mention that "she had a smile that could melt any heart."

And although, in her red and white outdoor PLS suit, the feminine curves of her body were not readily apparent, the feminine scent of her perfume and the way her hips swayed when she walked both confirmed without doubt that she was all woman.

She started walking towards Dedrick.

"Hey Sabrina, come on in, love. Grab a drink from the cooler, and come join me."

"Stop calling me love, François. You are going to get me in trouble." She was holding her index up and pointing in his direction in a reprimanding gesture.

François, his legs crossed under the table and both arms up behind his head, simply reclined even further back in his seat, a big smile on his face.

"How could he ever be mad at her," he thought to himself. She was so cute and sexy when she was mad like that, and that Spanish accent, "*I love that Spanish accent of yours, Sabrina Cherie*," he thought.

"Plus, I already have a drink, if you didn't notice, Mr. Columbo," she continued, raising her cup. She then walked to the other side of the room, put her coffee down on the table, and sat next to Dedrick.

The three were now quiet. Dedrick, looking out the only small window in the room, far into the darkness of the desert outside, was thinking about his dog, Rita, who he had been forced to leave behind with his brother back home when he had received his acceptance into the Mars First project six years earlier. He truly missed her. For a moment, he imagined Rita in a space suit and smiled to himself.

Sabrina was slowly stirring her coffee while trying to decide if she should add another cube of sugar in it or not, when François suddenly bolted out of his seat.

"OK, you really want to know what my problem is? I'm tired of doing the same thing every day! Yeah, that's what my problem is, and you know perfectly well what I'm talking about. How many times have we done this simulation? How many times do they want us to get it right? We know it so well, we couldn't screw it up even if we tried! No, I'm telling you man, I think they're just buying time, that's what they're doing. Stalling while the 'big guys' fuck it up with their stupid politics and their budget concerns! I'm telling you, Dedrick, we're ready. I'm ready! I just want to go!"

Sighing heavily, "I don't know, I just don't know anymore," finally said Dedrick, shaking his head. "Something's definitely wrong with you."

Will you marry me in space?

Liu had managed to decline every advance teammate Najib Shamsi had attempted on her and cursed herself for it. In truth, she liked him a lot but was too shy to act on it. Of course, the opportunities to meet anyone were limited. Outside of their daily training, the future astronauts were confined to their own quarters, with no other distractions than an indoor pool, a recreational area, and a beautiful but gated compound. But the Indian man had finally worn her out, eventually tricking her in accepting his invitation to a challenging game of ping pong. His "group" competition had turned out to be just the two of them. Of course, he had later admitted that it was François who had given him the idea. The Frenchman had heard through the grapevine that Liu was a ping pong champion back in her home country, and he had a feeling she would be hard-pressed to turn down a chance to play. He had also warned the Indian the petite woman had been known to be a fierce adversary. On that last point, Najib would later wonder if the Frenchman had spoken from personal experience that day. Regardless, he had been right. Later that same week, Liu was talking to Ladli about her new-found love and she was radiating.

Ladli O'Connor, an Irish woman from Dublin who had discovered at an early age her sexual attraction to both men and women alike, had taken her teammate's joyful news with mixed feelings. Although Ladli had never openly admitted it, the Team Two crew medical officer felt a strong attraction for her South-Korean female colleague. She had struggled to keep her feelings hidden during the early years of training, but Liu's new-found happiness wasn't making things any easier for the buffed redhead.

Nonetheless, Najib and Liu's relationship had grown, and one summer night, while the two were gazing at the stars and talking about their future on Mars, the Indian had asked the unexpected question: "Liu, will you marry me in space?"

The brown eyed Asian had been completely taken aback, not only by the proposal itself, but also by the last few words of Najib's question, "in space."

"Wh...what?" she had first replied, looking at him somewhat at a loss.

He repeated the question, still staring at the starry sky, "Will you marry me in space?"

"In space?"

He turned to look at her, "Liu, will you marry me?"

Her eyes filled up with tears and with a huge smile on her face, she wrapped her arms around his neck and kissed him passionately, "Yes, I will."

After the initial euphoria of the moment, the south-Korean leaned back and asked what Najib meant by "in space." Najib envisioned the wedding taking place soon after their launch to Mars, during the flight there.

"That's still years away and there is no guarantee we will be on the team selected to go first anyway. I don't think we should wait that long."

He knew she was right. Dedrick's team was already the preferred choice by many, which probably meant they would have to wait until 2027, if everything stayed on schedule, before the next ship left Earth.

Three months later, the two lovebirds were getting married on the ISS, thanks to Lars who had managed to convince his good friend Sir Richard Branson, owner of Virgin Galactic, to fly the couple to the international space station. Lars would later admit that convincing the famous entrepreneur had not been hard once both Branson and the ESA, the European Space Agency, had realized how much the publicity alone would benefit them. Branson had insisted on performing the ceremony, and Ladli had come as maid of honor, and Lars as witness. The event had been highly televised, and the newlyweds had been said to have loved the experience, even if Liu had felt a bit space sick for part of it.

Mask Art

"Did you ever think you would be here today?"

"Honestly, no. I really liked the idea, but I never thought they would pick me. It's still surreal…"

Both men were seated, legs crossed on the floor of a small terrace overlooking the hillside. Arms around their knees, they were reflecting, staring at the distant panorama.

"Did you?" asked Dedrick.

"I don't know… I think, in some way, maybe… I had a feeling 2013 was going to be special for me, you know?"

"Do you miss anything?"

"What do you mean?"

"I mean, like your family or friends? A woman?"

"A friend, maybe…" François cracked a smile. "Yeah, my friend Christophe. We had some fun times together."

"Where is he?"

"Still in L.A. I believe," seeing the questioning look on Dedrick's face, François added, "Los Angeles, California."

"Ha, yes, I've heard of it, of course. Never been, but I would like to visit, some day."

"It's OK, you didn't miss that much. It's just another city," he paused a moment. "Well, actually, I'm lying. L.A. was cool. I think I had the best three years of my life there. Christophe and I used to work at this place, "Mask Art." We printed t-shirts. They had this cool technique where they had us bleach black shirts, and then print on the bleached part of the fabric. It was a real bitch to use bleach, though. It got everywhere, on our boots, our pants, our hands. I had holes everywhere. It was a nasty job. But the printed shirts looked really cool, I must say… I remember my last day there as if it were yesterday." François' thoughts wandered back to the distant memory…

The business was on the first floor of a two-story building, smack in the middle of Hollywood, Los Angeles, the famous Californian movie capital. The large space was mostly filled with screen printing equipment, dozens of paint cans of various colors sitting on shelves, freshly painted shirts drying on their hangers, and stacked up boxes of shirts waiting to get their turn on the quad screen machines.

About half a dozen employees were busy pressing down screens on stretched out shirts and sliding squeegees across mesh applicators. A few others were setting t-shirts in place or filling mesh screens with a thick colored ink, lining up squeegees, and getting ready to start a new batch. François had just reached the last step of the building's only staircase, an outdoor concrete stairwell that showed more cracks than the dry beds of the Black Sea in late July. He entered the doorless room with a smirk on his face.

It's not every day you see someone tell their boss 'I quit!' with a big smile on their face, but it's even less likely you would ever hear them add, 'I'm moving to Mars!' Yet, that was exactly what François Menardais had just said to his employer, Paul Wemlock, the man behind the only desk in the room. Christophe, standing in front of his quadcopter machine at the other end of the room, almost lost his balance when he realized his friend was serious. He knew he had applied for some crazy online astronaut program, something to do with Mars, but until today, he had never expected François would hear anything back. Plus, this whole going to Mars talk of his was simply ludicrous. Who in their right mind would spend billions of dollars on a space program, and then put it all in the hands of someone like François? Of course, he loved his friend, but he knew him too well. The nineteen-year-old Frenchman was disorganized, had no job experience whatsoever, no career aspirations, no real accomplishment of any kind to his name, knew nothing about being an astronaut, and hadn't even finished high school. François Menardais was a wannabe musician who had come to Los Angeles from France just a little over a year ago, seeking fortune and fame, and now worked part-time for a small screen-printing company that sold images of famous people and movies printed on bleached t-shirts. In fact, it was Christophe who had helped François get this job in the first place. And now, he was talking about flying off to some distant planet. If the endeavor was genuine, Christophe was happy for his friend, but in his opinion, selecting such a volatile character was not giving much credit to the company behind the project."

Paul was staring at his French employee with suspicion, "What do you mean, you quit? Why? And you're going where?"

For a moment, he even thought he had misunderstood the young man. It happened a lot, especially since Paul was British and François still had a fairly heavy French accent.

"Mars. The red planet... You know," he replied, pointing at the ceiling with one finger and a big smile on his face.

Paul stared at him a bit longer with a puzzled look. Then, realizing there was probably an inside joke he was not getting, or that François simply didn't want to tell him why he was really quitting, he said, "Well, I guess, if that's what you want... OK. Sorry to see you go. But you must stay 'til the end of your shift, at least."

By now, most of the other employees in the shop had stopped what they were doing and were attentively following the conversation. François looked around the room and replied with little enthusiasm, "Yeah, I guess so. Can you give me my money before I go tonight?"

"Sorry, you'll have to come back on Wednesday. David writes the checks and he's not here today," replied Paul, mentioning his business partner.

That was not entirely true. Paul could have given him cash, but he was a bit upset at the moment. He never liked people quitting on him, even if François was far from being one of his best employees. Now he was going to have to rework everyone's schedule until the found a replacement.

François walked to Christophe's station and said, "Tu veux sortir une minute?"

The two made their way down to the parking lot where they often sat during their lunch break.

"Alors, c'est vrai cette histoire? Tu vas vraiment le faire? Partir pour Mars, je veux dire…" started Christophe. They rarely used English between themselves unless someone else was around, since both were much more fluent in their native language.

"Ouai! Ça vat ètre genial! J'ai réellement impatience!" replied François.

"Tu pars quand?"

"Je sais pas exactement. La lettre dit juste que j'ai été sélectionné et que quelqu'un me contactera dans les jours qui viennent. Y'a aussi des papiers à signer, trucs legaux. Des formalités, quoi."

"Cool... That's cool..." replied Christophe in English, without much enthusiasm.

Both were sitting on a parking block, looking at their feet, quiet and lost in thoughts. As the silence slowly became more obvious, both friends knew what the other was thinking... soon François would leave and probably never see his friend again. The sun was starting to set, and a tint of orange reflected off a car windshield, and onto the wall across from them.

François cracked a smile. In a few years, if all went well, his whole world would be orange.

"Hey, wanna drive up the PCH?"

"Quoi? Maintenant là, desuite?" replied Christophe.

"Yeah! Right now! On se prend une bouteille de Cisco au store du coin et on part faire un tour."

"Et Paul?"

"Who cares? Come on!"

A big smile came back on Christophe's face.

"Sacré Yvon. OK, let's go!"

Ten minutes later, the two friends were sharing a cheap bottle of Cisco, driving down Santa Monica Boulevard, on their way to the Pacific Coast Highway. François' old beat up, '87 Camaro wasn't the most attractive vehicle on the road, but the two couldn't have cared less at the moment.

They were drinking, laughing, and checking out girls on the sidewalk, enjoying life. The sun was starting to set over the horizon as they finally reached the coast. Heading north, François soon mentioned how disappointed he was by the famous Malibu Beach. He did whenever he drove through it. François knew his friend Christophe had already heard it countless times, but the Frenchman began his rambling anyway.

"I really don't see what the big deal is. If I was famous and had a lot of money, this is not the beach I would choose. I mean, you know I'm not big on France, but it's the people I don't like there, mainly. I love the topography, and the climate in the south is pretty nice for the most part. It's beautiful on the French Riviera. So much better than this rocky beach full of gravel and small bushes. It's just weird looking to me, almost creepy. And the water is cold as fuck most of the year. I'd like to live in Florida instead or on an island. Yeah, an island would be nice. A private one would be even better, with a helicopter pad and a yacht. Oh, and a recording studio with a grand piano, a white one," he paused. "One day man; one day I'll have all that. I'll be famous, and I'll have enough money to never worry again about anything. And you'll live there too. We'll build you a house next to mine. We'll have girls over all the time, hot ones, of course."

He cracked a smile. "You've got to hear this new demo I'm

working on. It's really good. I think this time-"

"Well, that's cool but I'm afraid you're gonna have to put your dreams of fame and your songwriting on hold for a while. I mean, with that Mars training program and all, looks like you're gonna be pretty busy," interjected Christophe.

"Yeah, you're right... hey, I could be the first human to write a song on Mars. Wow! That would be awesome!" suddenly thought François. "I better come up with something good, though."

"Yeah, I guess you better," said Christophe unconvinced. "Your training is what? Six years long? Eight? Well, at least you've got time."

They both laughed.

"Plus, you don't know if you'll make it do the end of the program, you know. There's probably a bunch of tests you're gonna have to pass, first."

"That's not a problem. I've got this. I can feel it. I'm meant to do this. I'm gonna go to Mars. Wow! Do you realize what that means? I still can't believe it. It's gonna be SO awesome!"

Once again, François' over-confident attitude was taking over his own rational judgment. But strangely, although most would have called him irresponsible, the young Frenchman always seemed to manage the impossible when he set his mind to it, and Christophe knew it.

"Yeah, pretty cool... I'm gonna miss you though, man..." said Christophe in a voice that trailed off under his breath.

François cracked a subtle smile and turned his attention back to the scenery in front of him. Racing west towards the coast, both young men watched in silence the last rays of sun disappear behind the horizon while the road carried them away in the night.

Almost eleven years later, the sun in front of the two men perched on the terrace of the Mars First training complex was also getting low. Dedrick, looking pleasantly entertained by François' story, was thinking of his own reaction when his dad had told him. Of course, in Dedrick's case, things had been quite different. For one, he had never applied to be a contestant on the Mars First astronaut recruiting program in the first place. His father had done so without telling Dedrick. That had bothered him more than anything at first.

Dedrick turned to François, "Did I ever tell you I never applied for Mars First?"

"What? What do you mean, you never applied? How did you get

here, then?"

"Well, you see, my father—"

Dedrick was brusquely interrupted by the abrupt opening of the door behind him, followed by the loud entrance of Liu and Najib, playing a game of mouse and cat.

"Shit! Oops, sorry, didn't know someone was here," she said looking a bit frazzled and tipsy.

"It's OK, Liu, no harm done," replied Dedrick.

"Sorry guys," added Najib with a smile as the two retreated the way they had come, the Pakistani-born Indian pulling the door shut behind them. As peace returned to the terrace, François got up and took one last look at the horizon.

"I think I'm gonna go lay down, buddy. I'll see you at dinner," he said before exiting the balcony through the same single door.

"Sure. See you there," replied the Russian, half under his breath.

Leaning back against the wall behind him, Dedrick aimed his gaze at the small sparkling lights past the dark forest in front of the complex. Thousands of vehicles, small as specs, were rushing along the string-like highways, barely visible in the far distance. He suddenly recalled the footage of a bomb striking a similar looking city on the news the previous night. A new war had just broken out between two Asian countries he could not remember the name of. There was so much unrest in the world. He was going to miss many things about Earth but that, not so much.

#

It was only after a long phone conversation that Lars was able to convince the other board members to authorize a leave of absence for the crews to go spend some time with their families. He had felt very strongly that the astronauts could benefit greatly from the break. After all, they only had a few months left before the big launch, and it would not be long before the whole complex would be locked down for obvious safety reasons.

To everyone's surprise, however, one of the crew members had preferred to stay put.

François, who had initiated the whole "vacation" idea, had been the first to turn it down. He had quickly explained he did not really get along with his family back in France and didn't see the need to go anywhere. Dedrick and Vera had chosen to go to their respective stumping grounds together. Vera who loved traveling was looking forward to seeing Russia, but most of all, her sister, Cathy, who had recently moved back to Boston with a new man. In fact, the younger sibling was dying to meet the famous Russian commander in real life. Dedrick, on the other hand, wasn't so sure he wanted anyone to meet his dysfunctional parents, but to his mother, he could never say no.

Sabrina had been hesitant to head back to her Guatemalan hometown at first for fear of her stepfather's wrath but had eventually agreed to it at the insistence of her mother. Going back would stir some painful memories of her sister, Sofia, who had passed away two years earlier from ALS, a lethal disease, but this would most likely be the last time she would see her mother in person. In truth, most were glad to spend these few days apart from each other, regardless of where they went. After more than ten years of constant proximity, only punctuated by rare personal time off the base, the change in venue had been a welcomed one.

However, things were a bit different for one of the future astronauts. Like François, Ladli had stayed at the complex. Born an orphan, she had left her second foster family on her eighteenth birthday and never looked back. The following years had been challenging for the Irish girl. Moving from job to job and having one bad relationship after another, she had also been left to deal with an abortion on her own when her fiancé had left her for a co-worker three weeks before the wedding; something she never talked about. That same year, she had met Patsy, her first lesbian experience. Several months later, Patsy had broken her heart too. That's when Ladli had thought of enlisting for the MSF, Médecins Sans Frontieres, an international humanitarian organization, in the hope to be sent to another country altogether, but she had abandoned the idea soon after. A chance encounter with an old high school girlfriend in a book store had been the catalyst for her interest in continuing her education. Eventually securing a good job as Lab Assistant for a large corporation, while taking night classes at the University of Dublin, Ladli had finally obtained her MA in 2013 and applied for the Mars First contest the very same year. After having been selected as one of the twenty-six in late 2014, she had sold her one bedroom flat and left Ireland for good. She had never returned to civilization after that, always finding a good reason to stay at the Mars First headquarters. This time, she could have gone with Tendai to visit his friends and family. He had asked her to, but she could not deal with that much social stimulation anymore and had preferred to stay put. For the past ten years, the Mars First complex and its residents had been her home and family, and the redhead, green-eyed woman had no real urge to go anywhere.

Chapter II

Twenty-three days before lift-off

Lars walked into the lobby, his daily report in one hand, a cup of coffee in the other. Don Arnold, Mars First's operation manager, was sitting in a low-back chair, facing the chief mission controller. The two men were deep in a technical conversation when Lars interrupted them.

"Don, I need to talk to you. Can you come to my office?"

With those words, Lars passed the two men without looking at them and disappeared through a door at the other end of the lobby. A sign, "Authorized Personnel Only" hanging from the door, squeaked a couple of times as it rebalanced itself.

"Sure Lars. I'll be right there! Sorry, I guess we'll have to continue this discussion later." He got up and left the room.

Don entered Lars' office with a smile.

"What's the word, boss?"

Lars was leaning back in his office chair, looking at Don with a frustrated look. He dreaded what he was about to say, in a way. He never liked lying, no matter the reason, but it wasn't the first time he had had to make decisions that didn't please him, or the people around him. It was part of the responsibility that came with his position as CEO of Mars First.

"I want to address a few things with you. Have a seat."

Don wasn't quite sure how to take the comment. Suddenly feeling a bit nervous, he turned to the small counter against the wall, where the coffee machine was. "Mind if I grab a coffee first?"

"Go ahead."

While he was pouring himself a cup, Lars began, "Don, I'm afraid we may be facing a few complications we had not counted on. I just talked to Robert Carone at the Swiss embassy. The mayor's office is putting some serious pressure on him to have access to our portfolio. I'm not sure why or what they are after, but we can't have our sensitive information fall into the wrong hands. I just don't trust anyone these days."

Still listening, Don came back to Lars' desk and sat down across from him.

"What do you mean?"

"I talked to our security adviser, Michael Blem. He is worried about the daily traffic we have with the media coming in and out, and employees changing shifts and doing the same. He thinks we need to lock down the facility sooner than we had planned."

"How soon?" asked Don, sounding concerned.

"Now."

His jaw dropped.

"You mean today? Right now? Then, I… I need to go home and tell my wife, see my kids. I mean, I can't just leave without telling my family what's going on. I need to take care of a few things first. It wasn't supposed to be for another two weeks, at least. What's going on, Lars?"

Don was getting worked up and somewhat alarmed at the possibility of being stuck inside for the next twenty-three days, the number of days left until the launch.

"I know. Believe me, I don't like it any more than you do, but we are facing some serious challenges and we cannot let anything go wrong. Too much is at stake. That's why I wanted to talk to you first. I know we can't just lock everybody in like this. I wanted to give you a head's up. I'm going to call an emergency meeting in the next hour. We have no choice, I'm afraid."

While talking, Lars was also observing Don's reaction and facial expressions without letting him notice. In fact, Lars and several high ranked board members believed someone was leaking very sensitive information and documents to the outside. The name, Don Arnold, had made it to the top of the suspect's list, and some board members were convinced he was a spy. If that turned out to be true, he was most likely working for one of the big corporations that had tried to get involved with the Mars First project, but had been turned down.

Of course, judging the man solely by his reaction would not be proof of guilt, especially given the situation, but unbeknownst to him, Don was now going to be monitored around the clock. Cameras had just been installed throughout the entire complex, and the small one right above Lars' head was currently feeding a live account of the conversation to the security office in another part of building. What Don didn't know either was that the "lock down" story was just an excuse to see what he would do next if he was given only one last chance to leave the Mars First complex.

As planned, Lars added, "I have arranged for the whole complex to be sealed by 2200 tonight. Make sure to be back before the curfew. I suggest you take advantage and take the rest of the day off. Go home. Spend a few hours with your wife. You won't see her again for several weeks. Send her my love. Just be sure to be back before ten, alright?"

Leaving the coffee cup on Lars' desk, Don got up, "Ok, thanks Lars," and exited the room quickly.

The trap was set.

As expected, the Mars First operation manager first went straight to his quarters. The place had already been bugged but he did not make a phone call, as expected. Instead, he hurried to grab some clothes, put a few documents in his briefcase, and exited the room, locking the door behind him. But rather than head towards the front of the building, as he would normally do to leave the building, he opted to go back to the training quarters in the opposite direction, making sure no one was following him.

Although no one was, he was being monitored by several cameras placed all around the complex, some barely visible, hidden in strategic locations by the security team.

Lars had also left his office, but not to follow Don. He had gone straight to the security office.

"Where is he?" asked Lars as he closed the door behind him.

"Looks like he's heading for lab number two," replied Michael Blem, a heavy-set man seated in front of a long, curved desk. He was facing an array of monitors on the wall in front of him and had his hands on a video controller, allowing him to switch various camera views in the building.

"Do you want to sit down, sir?" asked the woman standing to his left.

"No, I'm OK, Sylvia. Thanks."

Lars was staring at the central screen. The view from a camera above was showing Don ruffling through a series of drawers, clearly looking frantically for something.

"What is he doing?"

"I'm not sure, Sir, but he's obviously looking for something..." replied Michael Blem.

Lars walked around Sylvia and moved a bit closer to the screens, trying to get a better look at their suspect.

The man they were watching suddenly stopped his search, looking attentively at a couple of documents he had just found in a drawer.

"Can you zoom on that?" asked Lars.

"Sorry Mr. Bruininck, those cameras don't have that capability," replied Michael.

Don Arnold opened his briefcase and inserted the documents in a side pocket. He then closed the briefcase shut and randomly spun the rollers of the coded lock. After replacing the rest of the file, he shut the drawer and hurried out of the room, carefully making his way back the same way he had come, through the small maze corridors. Still attentively followed by the spying cameras, he soon reached the garage level.

Pressing the side button of his radio on his uniform, Michael Blem called out, "Unit two? The subject is leaving the garage in his vehicle. You should have a visual in a few seconds..."

"Yes, we see him," responded a man's voice.

"Please engage pursuit but keep your distance. We don't want to arouse his suspicion."

Leaving the garage in his blue 2021 Volvo Boog, Don was too preoccupied to notice the black 2023 Mercedes Sapphire SUV following, less than fifty meters behind. After passing through the guard's gate, the blue Volvo veered south. Following from a safe distance, the black SUV's crew started relaying its whereabouts to the security desk.

"Yes Sir, he just turned south."

"So, he is not going home... OK. Don't lose him!" replied Michael Blem.

"We need to find out where he is going, but we cannot let those documents leave his car," said Lars Bruininck, addressing the security chief.

"I know Mr. Bruininck. Don't worry, my guys have their instructions. They will not let that car out of their sight."

In the black SUV, the passenger next to the driver was following the Volvo with a long-range zoom.

"Looks like he's about to make a phone call on his cell."

Having heard what the man had just said through the monitors in the security room, Lars asked, "Can we hear the conversation?"

"Sorry, Mr. Bruininck, we don't have a tap on his cell, and we couldn't bug the car in time," replied Michael.

"What about tracing the call? Can we do that?"

"No, sorry, we don't have the capability to do that either. Only the police or the AIVD can."

"Darn! That's OK. Let's hope he takes us to his contact, then," replied Lars.

Michael Blem got back on the radio, "Unit two, what's your location now? Still on N227? Any change?"

"We just entered Doorn, sir. He is slowing down. Looks like he's about to turn right at the next intersection... Yes, he just turned on Dorpsstraat, heading west. Looks like he… Wait. Now he's turning left on a small side street. I think he's about to park..."

A few seconds passed…

"Well? Where is he now?"

"He just parked. We kept going to make sure he wouldn't spot us. We just made a U-turn a bit further down the road. We're coming back now. I still see him. He's still in his car and... He just got out. Hanz, park there. No, no, right there, so he won't see us..." he added, talking to the driver of the SUV, while pointing at an empty spot in the parking lot.

"Unit two, did you say he left the car?"

"Sorry, sir, we're parking. Yes, he's walking now. I have him in sight. He just reached the back of the building. We are pursuing on foot."

"Ok," said Michael.

"Are we gonna lose them?" asked Lars to Michael.

"No, they have in-ear communicators. They should be able to stay in contact with us and relay what's going on, as long as they don't venture too far from their vehicle."

A few seconds later...

"Huh... Mr. Blem? He just walked past the building where we parked. Now, it looks like he's heading straight for the big church in the back."

"A church? Why is he going to a church?" said Lars dumbfounded.

"I... I don't know," replied the security manager, just as surprised.

"Does he have the briefcase with him?" asked Sylvia Kaarzeev, who had just returned from getting herself a cup of tea.

"Yes, Ma'am!" replied one of the men in pursuit. "He just entered the church."

"What is he doing in a church?" asked Sylvia completely taken back, staring at Lars.

"No idea!" he replied, shrugging.

A very soft whispering voice came through the monitors a few seconds later, "We're inside. He is talking to a priest at the other end of the chamber. Wait... They just went through a small door in the back. What should we do?"

"Follow them!" replied Lars. "Don't lose him."

Quickly making their way to the other end of the large room as quietly as possible, the two men soon reached the door and entered a much smaller space that was completely empty, except for a small bench. Across, another door was ajar. They slowly made their way to it. On the other side, voices could be heard.

"Father, we have to act now. They plan on locking the complex down tonight. The security will be too tight if wait. You need to send your men in, now!"

"We don't have enough information. We still need the layout of the station. We can't just send them in blind."

"I got the plans! I had to act quickly, there was no time. That's why I'm here. I just left the compound, but I must return within the next few hours. Give these to your men. It shows all the security points of the complex, and how to access the lab. They need to act quickly!"

Don handed the documents to the priest.

"You've done well, my son. The Lord will be pleased. Walk safe and may Jesus be with you."

"Thank you, Father."

As Don turned around to head back, he came face to face with the two agents, standing in the doorway.

"Put the briefcase down, Dr. Arnold! And stay where you are, Father! I'll have the plans back now, please," said the driver of the SUV in a strong voice, while gesturing for the priest to give him the papers. Completely in shock and overreacting to the situation, Don tried to force his way between the two men, using his briefcase as a shield, but only managed to lose his balance and fall to the ground. Trying to take advantage of the confusion, the priest rushed towards the other end of the room, but the driver was on him before he had even reached the door.

"Don't hurt me!"

"I'm not gonna hurt you, Father, but I still need those papers." Taking the documents out of the priest's hands, he simply added, "Thank you."

A few minutes later, four police vehicles were stationed in front of the religious edifice and Don Arnold was taken into custody. The priest had pleaded not to be taken in with handcuffs in front of all the passersby and agreed to voluntarily follow the officers to an unmarked vehicle the police had dispatched and parked a few blocks away. Both he and the Doctor were taken in for questioning.

#

Two days later, Lars and several of his associates were gathered in the main conference room of the Mars First complex, talking via Skype to several members of the board.

"We do not know yet how much information was gathered by the group, but we know they call themselves the 'Goddelijke Rechtvaardigheid Broers' or GRB for short, a small group of religious extremists who believe that sending people to Mars is going against God's wish. It appears, from what was found in the church where both men were apprehended, that their intentions were to infiltrate our premises and place explosives around the base to destroy our labs. I had a long talk with my security officers this morning. We all agree that we may see more attempts in the future, not only by the same group of fanatics, but also by others like them. We have received numerous threats over the past few years. Now that we are only weeks away from the first launch, I'm afraid things will only get worse."

Sylvia, sitting next to Lars, was impressed by the calm in his voice. She was truly shaken by what had just happened. Don had not only been a coworker for years, but a close friend as well. This could have had a very tragic outcome. Someone could have died. And how could they be sure he was alone on this? What if he had an accomplice? Someone else on the base, maybe in this room right now! She scanned around the table, looking at every face, trying to imagine if one of them could be a traitor...

One of the board members responded from one of the screens on the wall.

"We agree, Lars, we think it's time to tighten security and limit access to the compounds to an absolute minimum. The board has agreed to your request for more security systems and guards. Get whatever you need. More equipment, cameras, dogs, whatever your team feels is necessary. We cannot take any chance now. Too much is at stake. We would also like to get a complete report on everything the police found on this religious group and Dr. Arnold's involvement as soon as possible. Have you decided on a replacement yet?" finished the man.

"Yes, Mr. Zakawi. We went through our list of candidates, and my team and I would like to bring in Doctor Ivaylo Kovachev, from Bulgaria. Dr. Kovachev has extensive experience with astronaut training. My assistant just uploaded his file to the system. You should have it. He worked for the Russian space program from 1992 to 2004, and then transferred to Antarctica's station Blokov, one of Russia's research stations, where he worked on survival studies in extreme environments. He applied to join our program four years ago. I had a phone conversation with him last night. He sounds highly motivated, and I feel confident he would be a great asset and a perfect replacement for Dr. Arnold's position," concluded Lars.

"Very well, then. Make the necessary arrangements to get him on board as soon as possible. We cannot afford any more delays. The launch window is too short, and time is money. Oh, and Lars, thank you, to you and your team for doing such a great job. Just make sure we have no more incidents like this one."

"Yes, sir. Of course, Mr. Zakawi. Thank you," replied Lars, knowing exactly what he meant.

#

Keeping the media out of the whole story had been impossible, but Mars First's legal department had done a great job at lessening the negative publicity the incident had fueled.

With or without enemies, Mars First had nonetheless managed to reach its goal of having the first go at sending humans to Mars. NASA was still eight years behind, at best.

By now, many of the early skeptics were on board, not because they had suddenly found the venture a beautiful one, or a great benefit to humanity, but mostly because the financial gains couldn't be ignored. "Mars First Now" had become the most viewed show in the history of television and the internet, combined. The ratings had gone off the charts.

For the men and women of the future Mars First colony, the public interest had been as intimidating as suffocating at times. So many had contacted them via email or through the countless social networks, blogs, and fan pages on the internet, that the astronauts had soon found themselves unable to keep up. The Mars First administration had eventually dedicated a small part of their PR department to handle all incoming correspondence.

Fourteen hours before lift-off

"...before. This adventure, you are all four about to embark on, is the most profound and the most daring journey ever undertaken by man. In less than six months, you will land on Mars, a planet no man has ever set foot on. A bare world, millions of kilometers away from our own Earth, where you will have the opportunity to establish a land post, a beacon for mankind, the first human foothold on another planet, and a successful first step toward interplanetary colonization. You will stretch the reach of our species millions of kilometers into space. Be proud and be brave. The whole world is watching you. You have our admiration, our support, and our love. May God be with you all." President Jarvis stepped off the podium and walked to the four astronauts to shake their hands.

Several thousand kilometers away, Makar Sokolov, was watching his son, Dedrick shaking the hand of the most powerful political figure of our time, the president of the United States of America. Makar had never felt prouder. His son was going to Mars. His name would be forever inked in the history books, Dedrick Sokolov would be remembered for generations to come. A few meters away, Dedrick's mother, standing in the shadow of the doorway, was crying silently.

#

The two black SUVs were almost at the entrance's check point. Inside the leading vehicle, François, feeling smug as he looked at the large "Bienvenue" sign, couldn't resist a smart remark.

"So, I guess you guys couldn't do it without the French. Good thing we're here."

Sabrina, seated next to him, rolled her eyes. Everyone else in the car ignored him as well. François was used to it. Team One had just arrived in Cayenne, French Guiana, that same morning, along with Lars. Without delay or rest, an SUV and escort had taken them directly to Kourou where the launch of MF1, the Mars First One spaceship, would take place in a few hours. Looking out the tinted windows, the astronauts watch the tall rocket in the distance slowly get closer as they approached. The two vehicles were soon joined by a military jeep and given priority access through a restricted area, leading the convoy away from all the media vehicles and reporters gathered outside for the event. Every major news media that had been able to secure a seat was there. Countless TV crews and journalists had come to immortalize the historic moment. Some family members were there too. Vera's sister had arrived the day before, and so had François' parents and brother, to his amazement. Sabrina's mother, still recuperating from an unexpected surgery, had been unable to leave Guatemala. As for Dedrick's parents, his dad, far too proud to let anyone know he had an absolute fear of flying, had turned down the invitation, blaming the whole thing on his wife for not feeling well, as he so often did.

The jeep soon left the two vehicles go on alone, and the convoy eventually arrived at the launch pad.

"So, this is it, ein?"

François, his head tilted back, was standing outside the SUV. They were stopped right at the end of the ramp leading to the launch tower. Only a few dozen meters away from him, the Mars First One rocket, MF1 for short, was towering above him and Dedrick. In a few hours, they would both be strapped inside the cockpit, along with Vera and Sabrina, ready to finally begin their journey to Mars.

"Yep! This is the real thing," replied Lars, looking up at the impressive machine. "She's beautiful, isn't she?" he said, with a radiant smile.

"It's big!" said Vera, stepping out of the vehicle.

"That's what she said," echoed the Frenchman.

"Oh, stop it, François. You're such an idiot at times," shushed him Sabrina.

The beautiful outer-casing of the enormous rocket, its black and white glossy paint shining in the bright mid-afternoon sun, was protecting one of the most brilliantly engineered pieces of machinery on the planet. Securely anchored down to the gigantic platform below, "la fusee sans frontiere," as François had called it, was standing proud and tall, majestic in its awesome grandeur, its nose aimed straight at the skies, as if ready to depart at any moment. Two tall scaffolds encircling the giant were occupied by twenty or so workers, busy at various tasks on different levels. Automatic valves were randomly releasing steam and smoke out of pipes and hoses connected along the frame.

"Follow me, please," Lars said, as he walked toward the small building to their left, the four astronauts of team one in tow.

After passing through a few doors and security check points, the five of them finally walked into the main control room of the small dwelling.

"This is where the last checks on the rocket are performed, before the ground crew leaves the platform. At T-minus two hours, fifty minutes, the ship will be filled with propellant, water, and oxygen. Once that stage is performed, at about T-minus forty minutes, you will be brought by a van to the foot of the tower, along with four crew technicians. After they have securely seated and strapped you all in your seats, they will close the hatch, come back down to the platform, and once mission control confirms all systems are a go, will head back to ground control at T-minus ten minutes, at the latest. That's where I'll be, witnessing your last moments on Earth, and your trip to the new world. Exciting! You will soon be flying to Mars. I envy you!" finished Lars with a tinge of regret.

"Wow! That doesn't leave much room for error," said François.

"You are right, but we have anticipated most scenarios, and are well prepared. We have several emergency vehicles on standby, as well as two large helicopters. Once the fuel has been dispensed, the least amount of time the ship stays on the ground the better. There are several good reasons for that, but we don't have time to go into it right now."

None of them said anything else. They were feeling both exhilarated and a bit scared, so close to the imposing machine, but the four astronauts also felt confident about their own role in the success of the mission, and that was what mattered most.

"Let's go to the top, shall we?"

A few minutes later, the exterior elevator transporting the five of them arrived at level four, the top level of the right scaffold. Lars opened the door, and they followed him across the bridge.

"This is the door to your living quarters for the next six months. I believe you are quite familiar with it by now. I want you all to see the real capsule for yourselves. It's identical to the one you have trained in for the past three years, but this is the real thing. It's gonna be your new home now, and if everything goes as planned, it will be for a very long time."

"*I didn't see Lars as a sensitive man, but I could swear the CEO is about to cry*," thought Dedrick.

T-minus four minutes

Team One was, strapped, secured and ready. They had all confirmed it multiple times. Over ten years had passed since that first day of training. They had prepared for this mission as much as any other astronaut would have. They knew their jobs inside out and had prepared for any scenarios the experts had thought of. At the same time, everyone knew the risks were countless, and a certain amount of nervousness was understandable, especially now, minutes from lift off.

For Vera, the fear was compounded with the disheartening news that Cathy had recently become engaged to Bruce, her steady boyfriend of the last six years, and that she wouldn't be there for her sister's wedding next year. She missed her terribly. Her mother would have been proud of her younger sibling. If there was an afterlife, she hoped she was watching over her.

"*I hope you're proud of me too, mom,*" she thought.

Even François, who loved to play the role of the calm and charismatic Frenchman, and whose phlegmatic personality always gave the impression he was in control of the situation, was now feeling the angst and nervousness of the anticipated ignition. "*Takeoff and landing; If we make it through those, we're OK. Of course, we got to hope all goes well during the flight too. It's going to get old real fast with the four of us in here too. Six months… Why did I get myself into this again?*" The challenges ahead were hard to imagine, but that was what made it all worth it. A man had once said: "Don't live lost in the past, and don't dwell long on the present. Always move towards the future for there you'll find all your answers."

The world was looking at them. They had a job to do and François hoped he was up to the task.

Vera was strapped tightly in her seat, her eyes glued on the dozens of switches and gauges filling the control panel above her, but she wasn't really looking at them. She was four minutes away from leaving Earth forever, and every cell in her body was trying to resolve the unbridgeable gap between her euphoric feeling of excitement, and her growing fear at the realization the next few minutes would be some of the most dangerous she would ever live.

Of course, they all understood the risks. They were aware of the countless dangers and innumerable variables that could play a catastrophic role in the outcome of their brave undertaking. Some would call that being foolish or irresponsible. Better yet, some would say they were complete idiots for taking such risks, but others would call them heroes, true explorers, frontier breakers to be admired and envied. Being a hero wasn't a goal for any of them, even if the public attention they had all received in the last few years had made them famous despite themselves.

To a lot of people around the globe, they were the new "Apollo Nine" of their time, and all the human pride and wonder that had followed the first Moon landing, were back in full force.

Either way, Dedrick Sokolov, Vera Via, François Menardais, and Sabrina Lazano were finally about to enter the history books, and in the process, so was the entire world, for this was truly going to expand the range of man's reach in the solar system. If the mission was successful, humanity would have begun its first step towards space colonization.

#

"T-minus 5, 4, 3, 2, 1, lift off!"

The fantastic roar of the enormous rocket engines came along with the powerful vibration from down below. In an instant, the nine-hundred-ton vessel pushed its enormous weight off the ground and began rising, exerting its tremendous G-Force build up on the four astronauts, pressing their bodies uncomfortably against the back of their upward facing seats.

It was a clear day, a beautiful day in French Guiana, and an ideal one for a launch. Leaving a huge trail of white smoke behind, the rocket rose without a glitch and reached the upper atmosphere within seconds. By then, the unpleasant effects of the acceleration had already lessened and given place to the much more comfortable feeling of weightlessness. Minutes later, the rocket's nose separated; releasing the MF1 capsule and its crew. The MF1 boosters engaged within seconds, sending the ship on its way to the International Space Station where it was to refuel. The crew was already preparing for the docking procedures. It would be the first and last stop before the long journey, to refuel and collect some needed laboratory equipment and cargo, sent ahead to reduce the initial payload of the launch. Outside the small window of their cabin, the day gave place to the purest of starry nights.

Forty-eight minutes later, the crew was saying its last goodbyes to Earth, and MF1 was off on the longest and most daring journey ever attempted by man.

One hundred seventy-five days after lift-off

"Twenty-eight – sixteen - zero – four – fifty-one," said Dedrick slowly, over-articulating.

"Twenty-eight – sixteen – zero – four – fifty-one!" repeated François as he entered the numbers on the keyboard pad in front of him. Vera and Sabrina were strapped in their seats, right behind the two men. Dedrick could hear Vera's fast breathing in his in-ear monitors. The ship was now only four kilometers above the Martian surface.

"Ship lined up with target. Fifteen seconds to retro-rocket boost," announced Dedrick. "Ten – nine – eight – seven – six – five – four – three – two – one – retro-rocket burn!"

"Burn confirmed," signaled François.

The red planet had been gradually slowing down the ship using what engineers called a "Ballistic Capture" technique, where the gravity of the approaching planet is used to reduce the velocity of the vessel, rather than the ship's rockets having to do all the work. Now, ready to enter Mars' atmosphere, the team was more alert than ever. The shaking vessel was on its final vertical descent, clocking at over 9000 kilometers an hour, and gradually slowing down. In the small cockpit, the four astronauts, experiencing the effects of several G's from the strong deceleration, were doing their best to manage the discomfort, while trying to contain their fear and excitement. Soon, they would set foot on Mars. They would be the first humans ever to set foot on the red planet. If they landed safely, that is. They had just learned the ship was off target by a few kilometers and had been forced to choose a new landing site.

Listening carefully to the on-board computer, all four closed their eyes and gripped their seats tightly as the artificial machine began relating their approach.

"15,000 kilometers to target landing site."

The shaking was now starting to subside, and all systems were still green.

"13,000 kilometers to target landing site."

François tried to look out the small porthole window to his left, but his range of motion was too limited to see anything but the night sky.

"6,600 kilometers to target landing site. Separation module release in five – four – three – two – separation module released! Detection confirmed."

Throughout the descent, Dedrick was keeping a close eye on the monitor in front of him, occasionally looking at the thin slice of orange landscape his window allowed him to see below the ship. All the numbers looked right. MF1 had traveled almost six months in space without a single glitch, and aside from a slight trajectory adjustment at the last minute, the landing on the red planet below appeared to be going just as smoothly.

A sudden jolt pushed the team members deep in their seat. They all clinched their armrests harder. The shock was strong enough to give Vera a short felling of panic.

"Stabilizing parachute deployed... parachute confirmed…all systems green…descent angle optimum."

"*Didn't need the confirmation on the parachute. I think we all felt that one!*" thought François.

"Two hundred meters – One hundred fifty meters – One hundred meters – Fifty meters"

François let a heavy sigh.

"Thirty meters – Twenty meters"

Sabrina swallowed.

"Ten meters – Five meters – Four meters"

Dedrick inhaled deeply and held his breath.

"Retro-rocket burn."

A tear began to slide down Vera's face. The ship was vibrating uncomfortably again.

"Two – One – Touch down! Ship leveled and stabilized. Engine shut down. All systems operational. Welcome to Mars!" finished the artificial voice.

For a few seconds, the four were silent. Outside, a small cloud of dust, picked up by a light wind, flew by.

"Oooh oooh!! Yeah!" suddenly screamed François, jolting the others in their seat.

Dedrick removed his helmet. "Welcome to Mars, guys. We made it!"

"Oh, my God! I can't believe we're here," said Sabrina as she loosened her harness and leaned over, trying to see outside the porthole window next to her.

Dedrick was already turning off a few switches overhead, while reading the data on the computer screen in front of him.

"How far off are we?" asked Vera seeing his troubled facial expression.

"Actually, only two point six kilometers," he replied. "That's not great, but it could have been worse."

"Sweet!" offered François with a smile.

Sabrina was now standing by the window, looking at the orange desert outside. She could see the edge of the plateau a few hundred meters away. Beyond, the giant cliffs of the Valles Marineris canyon seemed to go on forever.

"Can you guys believe we're really here? It's amazing! I bet everyone is celebrating back on Earth. Especially at Headquarters! I can see Lars now, jumping around his desk like a little kid." added Vera.

"Actually, no one on Earth is celebrating anything because no one knows yet, remember?"

"You are correct, Sabrina. They won't know for another twenty minutes or so. We've successfully landed on another world, and we're the only ones to know!" said Dedrick with a big smile. "How amazing is that?" He got off his seat, grabbed the Guatemalan woman in his big arms, and lifted her off the floor of the cabin effortlessly, laughing.

"Hey! Easy there, cowboy!" reminded him Vera, looking at the two with a teasing frown.

"Ha, ha! Don't worry, Vera. He's not my type," reassured her Sabrina.

Dedrick put her back down.

"What do you mean, not your type? Am I not the most handsome man on the planet?" as he winked at her.

"Now, you're starting to sound just like François. Give those two a chance to land on another world, and they think they're Gods of the planets!"

"Hey. Wait a minute…" began François.

"You know you're the only one for me, baby," said Dedrick to Vera.

"That's more like it." She gave him a playful smile.

"Oh, come on you guys, you're not gonna start this right now, are you? None of that romantic crap, OK? Come on, let's get to work!"

interjected François.

Dedrick looked at his French friend with lassitude and got back to his seat.

"Ok. We need to contact the station and give the rover our coordinates. Check on our exact location while I attempt contact," said Dedrick to François.

After making a few adjustments to several dials in front of him, Dedrick grabbed the keyboard and started typing a direct message to ARC 2, one of the two rovers waiting for the ship's arrival at the Mars First outpost.

"Hello ARC 2. This is Mars First One team leader, Dedrick Sokolov, requesting transport assistance."

A few seconds passed.

"ARC 2. This is Mars First One, requesting transport assistance."

"What's that rover doing?" asked François. "We have signal, right?"

"Yes. ARC 2. This is Dedrick Sokolov of Mars One First. Requesting transport assistance."

"Welcome Mars First One team leader Dedrick Sokolov. Please provide exact landing coordinates for transport assistance."

"Well, it's about time." said Dedrick out loud. "Ok, so where are we exactly, Sherlock," he asked François.

"I'm sending it to you right now," replied François as he looked over at Dedrick's screen.

"Got it! Thanks. Forwarding coordinates to ARC 2 right now."

"How long do you think before the rover gets here? Are we far from the station again?" asked Vera.

"We're exactly two point six kilometers away; not quite where we were supposed to land, but still within acceptable margin. I would say about fifteen-twenty minutes for the rover to get here, an hour or so to secure the ship, and another one to get back to the station. We should be home for supper!" finished Dedrick, with a wink.

Eight minutes later, the ship's door opened, and Sabrina emerged in her white and black spacesuit, one hand holding on to the wall of the cabin, the other casting a shadow over her glass helmet as she scanned the horizon.

"*Mars!*" she thought. "*I'm on Mars!*"

Vera was soon standing behind her, staring at the amazing view that none of the simulators or pictures could ever have done justice to. The two of them stood there for a while. Far in the distance, the orange horizon was meeting with the immense plains above the cliffs. The steep rocky faces surrounding the flat lands were a sight unlike any they had ever seen. And no other human, as a matter of fact, would see for at least another two years. Most of the immediate area around the ship was flat and predominantly desert like. Low dusty mounts, dirt, and loose rocks covered the ground. There were no clouds. The sun, low to the left, was adding a surreal tint of reddish blue to the alien landscape.

"Wow, check out the sun! It really looks smaller… I've seen countless pictures and videos, but now you can really tell. Crazy, don't you think?"

Vera did not reply. She was mesmerized by it all. Yes, the sun looked smaller from Mars, and several kilometers away, what had looked like small dried out river beds from space, now looked more like deep canyons with sharp cliff sides, taller than they had imagined. Being there was so different. The sensation was indescribable, and their hearts were beating faster than normal from the excitement. Yet, once one took in the immensity of the cliffs and their dark shadows; dust, dirt, and a reddish-brown ground was all that comprised the entire scenery, as far as the eyes could see. There were no oceans on Mars, nor rivers or streams; no trees, no plants, no grass. And this eerily silent, desert-like planet, a world completely devoid of life, was now their new home. The four of them had just spent the past six months traveling through space, crammed together in the confined space of the MF1 spaceship, in a space barely larger than a small studio apartment, and though their new habitat would only be slightly larger, they knew it was all worth it. This was the new frontier, mankind's next adventure.

There, just a few miles away to the right, Vera spotted the white glow of the Mars First station. "Look, Sabrina, the station."

"I see it!"

About halfway from there, a small trail of dust could also be seen behind the moving ARC 2 rover, clearly visible on such a nice day, even if still over a kilometer away.

"*This is it, our new home*," thought Vera.

After almost ten years of preparation and hard work, they were finally on Mars. The entire planet was now their new backyard, a barren world where they were going to spend the rest of their lives.

"So, are we going down or what?" asked François who had just come to the hatch to join them.

"We have to wait for Dedrick," replied Vera.

"Right!" he said as he pulled the lever next to him to release the outside ladder.

A few seconds later, François approached the small opening.

"Pardon me, ladies."

"Wait! You're not supposed to go down yet. Dedrick is still in the cockpit. We're all going down at the same time, remember?" voiced Sabrina as he started climbing down.

"What's the difference? Plus, we can't really all go down the ladder at the same time, now, can we? One of us will set foot on Mars first, no matter how we do this. I'm going down."

"Thanks, Pal! I thought you guys were gonna wait for me," said Dedrick who had just rejoined his colleagues at the door.

"There you are!" replied François, still climbing down.

"That's what we were just telling him," added Vera.

"I know, I heard you all in my helmet headset. Never mind. Let's go take a look at our new world. After you, ladies."

Sabrina started down the ladder.

"Go ahead, baby. I'm right behind you," offered Dedrick, gesturing to Vera.

A few seconds later, all four were standing on the bare rocky floor of the red planet, the Mars First One spaceship right behind them, its white shell shining in the orange glow of the mid-afternoon sun. They were now completely silent, taking in the fantastic view. François kicked up a small rock that went flying a few meters away.

"So… Where's the nearest bar?"

"Very funny," replied Dedrick, sarcastically.

"Should we say something? I mean, some profound line for posterity? You know, like Neil Armstrong did when he landed on the Moon: "A small step for-"

"Yeah, we all know the line, Sabrina. How about, 'Here we are!' blurted François, cutting her off.

"You can be such an idiot at times, really! I'm serious. Dedrick, wasn't there something headquarters wrote for you to say?"

"Actually, there is. Let's do it right. Take my hand."

Vera took Dedrick's suited hand in hers and turned to Sabrina who took hers. The four of them were now standing in a circle, hand in hand as Dedrick began.

"We, the people of Earth, have come to Mars on this Earth day of December 17th, 2025, in the name of all mankind. We come in peace and in humility, but also with great courage and strong spirit. May this day mark the beginning of a new era in man's exploration of the universe, a historical moment in the human colonization of Mars and the worlds beyond."

#

Two hours later, the strange convoy was driving slowly around a rocky bend when the Mars First station came into view.

"There! Look! Our new home. Isn't she beautiful?" said Dedrick excited.

"Wow! So it is. And it's about time. We only have another hour or so of daylight left. We still have to detach the landing module off the rover, and I don't know about you guys, but I'm exhausted."

"Did you listen to anything at all in training those past eight years? We'll setup the module tomorrow. We're to leave it on the rover for now and get the habitats ready for our first night on the red planet. That's our priority."

"Yes, boss!" replied François to Dedrick with a military salute and a smirk on his face.

The sky was even redder when they finally reached the station. An occasional wind draft was lifting orange dust from the ground around them as they stepped out from the vehicle. Transporting the module on the rover's bed had made the short trek a very long one, only able to go a mere six kilometers an hour on the flattest portions of the uneven terrain. Of course, once François had realized he could go faster on foot, he had simply taken off ahead of the convoy. But a few minutes later, Dedrick and the girls had convinced him to stop wasting precious oxygen and get back inside with them.

From a distance, the glittering white station was standing out like a sore thumb against the Martian landscape. The three modules comprising the entire habitat had been set up by the two rovers more than a year earlier. The small white pods, each only a few meters in diameter and spaced a couple of meters apart, were lined up in a straight row, their backs to a small Martian hill. Their only obvious features were the dark porthole windows, two per pod, and the brown streaks along the small jet outlets, left by the rocket boosters when the modules had landed. They were all identical to the one they had just flown in through space. Tomorrow, they would add the extra habitat to the small outpost.

"Ok, guys. Here we are. Vera, François, go check on the condition of pod one and two and activate the secondary life systems. Sabrina, you come with me," ordered Dedrick.

The four of them got to their respective duties. Once inside, Dedrick contacted Earth to let everyone know MF1 and its crew had landed without a glitch, and all the station's monitoring systems were checked thoroughly. They were busy another hour or so before finally retreating to their sleeping quarters for the night.

Tomorrow they would add their landing module to the row of habitats and connect it to the other pods. The real work would then begin. Mars First, the first habitable station on Mars, also included two greenhouses, already setup perpendicularly to the pods, partially buried in the Martian dirt mound behind the outpost. That's where they would now sleep. It made sense, the green plants would generate a good portion of their needed oxygen, while filtering the carbon dioxide the team released. All they had to do now was to grow them.

A few hours later, the new colonists finally laid down on their respective beds, and exhausted, quickly fell asleep. It was their first night on the red planet.

In the distance, a small dust storm was brushing up along a narrow corridor in the cliffs of Candor Chasma. Deep inside the canyon walls, in a large underground cave, a small purple light began glowing.

Chapter III

Martians

A few interesting events had taken place on Earth since the four had landed on Mars several weeks earlier. NASA had announced its intention to send a first manned mission to Europa, one of Jupiter's largest moons, within the next five years. Many scientists and highly respected experts now talked of the eminent opening of space travel and the future of space tourism. Several new private companies had also entered the "Race to Space" arena, working on their own projects, hoping to capitalize on this new trend.

Back on Mars, the small group was keeping up with Earth's affairs as much as they could, but their time away from their individual responsibilities was restricted. What made their solitude much more bearable, however, was their personal communication time with loved ones back home. Every night, each member took their turn in front of the webcam to send personal messages to family and friends back on Earth. The quality of the calls was surprisingly good, even with video, but the signal lag between the two planets was annoying, to say the least. Anything said on Mars took a little over twelve minutes to reach Earth this time of year, and the reply took just as long, making real-time conversation impossible. You simply had to wait.

Dedrick was a few minutes late when he finally sat in front of his computer. He awakened the touch screen, entered his password, and pressed on the "new message" video icon. A window opened, and the video message automatically started playing.

"You are a real hero, my son! Everyone is talking about you here."

His dad was talking loudly, a proud smile on his full face.

"We miss you terribly, sweetie. How are you doing, up there?" asked his mother.

"How's that greenhouse working?" asked his dad.

"Oh, your Aunt Sonya said yesterday's sermon at church included a few words from Father Kuznetsov about the 'travelers to another world.' She said it was very touching, and they all prayed for you. She asked me to wish you all the best," commented his mother.

"*Funny, she never seemed to care much about me until this Mars thing...*" thought Dedrick.

"We miss you terribly, sweetie," she repeated. "Are you eating enough?"

"Come on woman, of course he's eating fine. They've been training for this for almost ten years now. Don't worry, they know what they are doing. Right, son? That reminds me, I ran into Colonel Kuznetsov yesterday. He said you're a brave man and you're doing your country proud. I told him we always knew you were destined for great things. And I am very proud of you as well, son."

"Is that all that matters to you? Your son, our son, is lost on another world and all you care about is what Colonel Kuznetsov thinks? You should have never enlisted him in this crazy mission in the first place. It's all your fault if he's up there, now," she cried.

"What are you talking about, woman? Can't you see how important this is? What Dedrick is doing is helping all of mankind. And his name will be remembered many generations from now. The first man to set foot on Mars, Dedrick Sokolov- our son, my son."

"Who cares? First man on Mars? What good does that do me, now that he is so far away?" she finished, sobbing.

Watching both his parents argue on the screen was hard enough, but being unable to reply or stop them due to the lag time between messages was pure torture.

After a few more back and forth, they finally wished him good night and said they would await his reply impatiently.

"Hey Ma, hello Dad. How are you? You both look well..."

That wasn't quite true. Lately, they appeared to have aged significantly. Both in their sixties now, Dedrick realized he had not seen them in person for over a year already.

"To answer your question, yes, I'm doing good. We're all doing well. As you have probably seen on TV, we are ahead of schedule with our second greenhouse. Seems the new panels allow more light in, so the plants have been thriving. And yes, Mom, I'm eating well. Don't worry. I won't bore you with the technical stuff, but our meals have been planned according to our individual metabolism and are ideally calibrated for each one of us. We don't eat the most tasteful cuisine, but we are all healthy and fit. The greenhouses have become the focus of our current mission. We've started growing several vegetables successfully. We'll soon have tomatoes, cucumbers, carrots, potatoes, kale…even parsley and onions." He was counting on his fingers at the same time. "It will take a few more weeks before we can harvest anything, but we're pretty excited about it. As I said, the packaged space meals are not bad, but I think we'll all get sick of them eventually, and we're definitely looking forward to some real food mixed in for a change. Anyway, please don't worry, we're doing good. We've been on Mars for almost two weeks now, can you believe it?" he smiled. "François and I went on our third trip to the ridge this week. It's so grand and beautiful. I wish you could see the canyon for yourselves. The videos don't do it justice. Tomorrow, Vera and I are celebrating our eleventh year together. It's crazy. Eleven years already. Anyway, she thought we should take a trip to Lavida's crevice. There's this amazing view over the whole channel from the plateau above. I think it was in one of our videos last week, remember? Anyway, we're looking forward to it. We'll have a rover all to ourselves. It will be nice to get away from everyone for a few hours. That's what's weird here. We have this entire planet all to ourselves, just the four of us, yet we are together all the time, all cooped up in this small station. I'm not complaining, of course, we all get along nicely, but it's hard to have any privacy, you know? Well…tomorrow should be nice… Let me see, what else? Sabrina brought back some interesting samples of that rock slab she found yesterday in sector four. François is helping her analyze them now. There's very little chance this is anything more than an odd-looking boulder, but it's worth a check. That's why we're here, right? Who knows, maybe we'll discover something. Anyway, I miss you both and I look forward to chatting with you again soon." He reached across the desk and pressed the "send" button on the screen.

"*I should've asked them how they were doing… maybe I did… oh well…*"

He logged out of the video session and turned off the camera.

Olympus Mons

Weeks turned into months, and it wasn't long before the small Martian outpost had spent its first year on the lonely red.

By now, most of the world was following the "Fantastic Four," as the Chicago Tribune had renamed them, wanting it or not. Dedrick had been the first to mention how wrong the newspapers and media were, when they had mentioned the group had been on Mars seven months, since a year on the red world was almost twice as long as it was on Earth. François had been just as quick to point out that he could not call them months since that word was derived from Earth's Moon itself. Vera and Sabrina had rolled their eyes at them. Regardless, their names and faces had found their way into the marketing of countless products and commercial goods all over the globe. From coffee mugs and shampoo bottles to fast food chains and even car manufacturers, the four "Martians" were everywhere, and the Mars First Corporation was making money hand over fist, something Lars Bruininck had banked on from the very first day.

A few interesting discoveries by the colonists during their research experiments had made the news several times, but so far, aside from some promising new minerals, the search for liquid water had so far brought no results. The Mars First company wished the group had found some by now. It would make things easier for the future expansion of the colony. Although a bit concerned, they were now too busy preparing for the departure of MF2, less than a year away, to dwell on it. It would happen eventually, everyone was fairly certain of it. Dedrick and his companions would just have to keep digging further and deeper.

In the meantime, the day at hand was all about celebrating the group's first year on the red planet. Vera and Sabrina had managed to decorate greenhouse II with colorful bed sheets and clothes borrowed from everyone's living quarters. They had also garnished several plates with packaged sweets and dried fruits, and a homemade drink they had jokingly named "Olympus Mons" after the large Martian volcano, a punch of sorts containing "secret ingredients" the two women would not divulge. This centerpiece was by far the most talked about delicacy of the evening by the two men. François had brought out his ukulele and promised he would sing a song he had just written for the occasion later. Dedrick had hurried to turn on the computer's playlist he had put together at the insistence of Vera.

The Police's, "Walking on the Moon," came on through the speakers.

"Oooohoooo! Turn it up! shouted Vera in excitement. Her and Sabrina were making their way to the center of the room, dancing. François joined in. Dedrick walked to the table and poured himself a glass of Olympus Mons. He then turned around to face his three friends, leaned his butt against the edge of the table, and watched them dance away with a big smile on his face. Here they were, millions of kilometers from Earth with nothing but rocks and dust all around them, alone on a desolate world, and life was wonderful.

Back on the blue world, flat screen TVs and computers were re-transmitting the small celebration. That night, as countless candles were lit across the globe to commemorate the anniversary of MF1's historical landing on Mars, the people of Earth felt more as one than they had in a long time.

The following morning, the "Fantastic Four" woke up with a mild headache, but not all in their own bed. François had spent the night in one of the passing tubes leading to his pod, still wearing the top half of his spacesuit.

The day started off for most of them, dragging their feet when their 5:30 AM alarm got them up. No one was saying much. Dedrick, being first in pod one, was checking several containers of scientific equipment for today's mission when Sabrina entered the room.

"Morning!"

"Morning!" he replied.

"Have you seen François?"

"No. Why?"

"He wasn't in bed when I woke up. I don't think he came in last night."

"He's probably lying somewhere. We all had a bit too much to drink, I'm afraid. What was in that drink anyway? Did you check the greenhouse?"

"Yes. He wasn't there either"

"Weird…"

She was about to turn back when the Frenchman made his entrance.

"Hey! What's up, guys?"

"There you are. Where were you? I've been looking everywhere for you."

"Me? Well...eh...I..." he attempted to say, pointing at the passage.

"Yeah, OK, whatever. I'm going to help Vera clean up the greenhouse. We'll talk later, mister."

"Wha...What did I say?" He turned to Dedrick with a puzzled look on his face.

Grabbing one of the container's handle, Dedrick simply replied, "Wanna help me load these in?"

After shrugging his shoulders, he walked to the Russian and grabbed the other handle. One convenient feature in the design of the rovers was that their back could connect to the outside hatch of the pod, allowing access to the vehicle without the need to go outside or wear a suit. The two men finished loading up and climbed on board. After closing the hatch behind them, they slid into their suits and François turned on the dashboard computer. A line at the top left of the screen read: Captain's log, star date 21342.7 - 09:28

One of François' program improvements. He had always been a fan of the American TV show Star Trek. Luckily for him, his teammates were as well. The Russian commander called Vera from his headset.

"Vera, ARC 2 here, ready to move out. Can you confirm status on your end?"

"Guess where I woke up this morning?" asked François to Dedrick.

"I don't know... On Mars?"

"Ha ha, very funny. No, in tube three. Man, that Montagne Olympique drink was strong!"

"Olympus Mons," corrected Dedrick.

"Right. What did the girls put in that thing, anyway?"

"I don't know, and I don't need to know. Come on, we have a job to do. Give me a complete status check."

"Yes, commander!" replied the Frenchman sarcastically.

"Ok, hatch sealed. Oxygen levels – Check! Cabin pressure – Check! I'm undocking us."

After a sharp "clunk" and a slight jerking of the vehicle being released, François continued, "Batteries fully charged and solar panels out. We have at least three and a half hours of playtime. I think we're good to go, captain!" he finished with a smile.

"Ok Vera. We're ready here."

"Everything looks good in here too. I have a strong signal from both of you. Life systems are green. Weather is nice and calm out there. I don't expect any problems today. ARC2, you're cleared for takeoff."

"Ha ha, yeah, taking off in this thing would be funny to watch. Maybe if we had wings…" François looked at the Russian commander.

"Make it so, number one!" said Dedrick with a fair imitation of actor Patrick Stewart's voice. François looked at him with an approving nod and began to roll out the rover, adding: "Engaging impulse engines, Captain!" with an equally surprising imitation of Brent Spinner, including his laugh. The two men cracked up at their own silliness, and a new work day on the desolated red planet had begun.

"You know that's the android, right?"

"Yeah, I know. I can't do the other guy. Did I ever tell you I ran into Patrick Stewart, once?"

"Really?!" replied a shocked Dedrick.

"Yeah, in L.A. when I was a messenger. He was walkin-"

"A messenger?" asked Dedrick intrigued.

"Yeah, it's a type of service companies use to get packages from place to place faster; Big industry in the movie business. Anyway, as I was saying…"

As ARC 2 slowly disappeared beyond the slope, Sabrina turned to Vera in the monitoring room of the Martian outpost. She had just switch off the audio.

"What was that all about?"

"What, those voices? Never seen Star Trek? Never mind. You're too young," answered Vera to the clueless brunette.

Never going back

"Do you ever miss it?"

"What?"

"Earth."

He looked up at a bright dot in the dark reddish sky. It was so familiar by now, yet, it was still so strange…

"Not really. You?"

"Sometimes..." replied Sabrina thoughtful.

François was seated next to her on the back of the rover, looking at the small white spot out in the distance. The sky was not that different from Earth's on clear nights, and one could easily see the blue planet, even if it only appeared as big as a bright star. But it took a trained eye to spot it on a night like this. Of course, all four of them were pretty good at it by now.

"It's strange but I don't think I do. I mean, it would be nice to have water, walk on the beach, feel the wind on my face, but I don't miss the traffic, or the noise. I feel at home here, more than I ever did on Earth, I think."

She turned to face him.

"Don't you miss your family? Your friends?"

"Not really. I've never related well to my folks anyway, you know that. I love them, but I don't think they ever got me. We are too different. My dad has always done things by the book. He's honest and loving, but too set in his ways for me. There wasn't much room for socializing when I was young. Having friends at home was never easy, and he was capable of losing his temper at any time, for just about any reason. Screams and verbal abuse were common. I know he loved me but growing up in that house was really not comfortable. I guess I was scared of him when I was young. He could get quite obsessed about things. I left home as soon as I got the chance. My mom is kind and very pampering, but over the top. She worries way too much about anything. It can get suffocating. I mean, I love them both, but I never felt I belonged there anyway, you know? I just wish I could've helped my brother experience life more. I wish he had left too, moved to another town, at least, or traveled the world. He still lives with my folks. Never left my parent's house, never got married... He spends his time between his work and home. I don't even think he has many friends; at least not friends he hangs out with. It's the life he chose. Of course, he'll tell you he had no choice. He won't admit it, but it's fear of the unknown that keeps him from making a change. Like so many others out there. They are scared they'll fail. We talked about that many times. I try to make him see that there is always a choice. It's just not always an easy one, and most times, it's quite nerve racking. But it can be very rewarding… It's too bad. I'm afraid we don't understand each other either..."

He paused for a moment, looking out at the giant features of Valles Marineris. The bare ridges reminded him of the rocky formations on his occasional drives to Nevada, when he still lived in L.A. Back then, it didn't take much persuasion to get him and his friends to jump in the car and go. Life was fun, and the world was big. His mind wandered around the fond memories for a while. The vague memory of an old flame crossed his mind. "*What was the name of that girl?*" He could almost see her. She had reminded him of Elaine Benes, one of the characters in Seinfeld, an old American TV sitcom. "*That's right. Celina. And what was that place we used to go to all the time? Ah, yes, the 'Fame Café'. That's it. Strange, it seems so long ago…*" He turned his attention back on her.

"What about you?"

"I miss Sofia. Today would have been her 28th birthday..."

She turned back her attention to the amazing view of the distant cliffs.

"I'm sure she would have been very proud of her older sister."

"I hope so... It was hard leaving her. I was always there, you know? I know mom was doing the best she could for her, but she was so busy with work… And she had Paulo to worry about. He's a real jerk. Sometimes I hate him. He can be violent with my mom, and I wish she would leave him. I don't know why she stays... But I love my mom. She's always believed in me. Although, I'm not sure she understands why I'm here. Yesterday, in her transmission, she said she was sorry I felt the need to leave, and if I ever wanted to come back, there would always be a bed waiting for me at home. I don't know how to take that. It makes me feel lonely. It's so strange sometimes when I think of all this... All this space, this entire planet, and just the four of us. We are more alone than any human has ever been in a way, and yet, I feel at home here, you know what I mean? And I don't think she gets that."

"I don't know that too many people do. We've chosen to do something that most people consider weird, if not crazy. You've got to admit, we're a bit nuts," he giggled.

"Yes, I know... I guess there are some things I don't miss, though. Politicians, lawyers, murderers... Wars, religious fanatics, rapists, you name it. It's a long list. Nope, I'm not missing them... This is my home now, with you guys. And I like it like that. Some days, it's almost hard to believe we used to live back on Earth, doesn't it? It seems like ages ago when I think of the day I applied for Mars First. Do you remember when we landed? That's when it really hit me. We were finally on Mars. We were really here and there was no going back..."

A sudden draft blew sand up the slopes below, and a quick cloud of dust flew past them.

"Does that scare you?" she asked.

"What?"

"Never going back."

"Honestly, no. I never felt like I belonged there. I know it's a bit extreme to say this, but I don't really liked people, generally speaking. I mostly find them loud and obnoxious. Even back in school, I was never the popular guy. I was a bit weird, actually."

"You, weird?" she said with a teasing smile.

"Yeah, I know. I was an introvert, though."

She looked quite surprised. "You? An introvert? Yeah, right!"

"Oh yeah, big time. I was shy and quiet. The kid who doesn't say much in the back of the class room. I think I feared people, in a way. That's probably why I got into music, actually. It was my way of trying to overcome that fear of crowds. I also had to prove to myself I could do something big with my life."

"Well, I think all of us here have had the same drive. Either way, we're on this planet for good. This is our home now, and I'm glad I have you with me, François." She looked into his eyes with love.

The dark patches of mineral-filled rocks down in the valley below were slowly shifting from their usual black-gray volcano look to the charcoal-blue texture they had come to love. A spectacle that was like nothing anyone had ever seen on Earth, a true treat when the sun reflected on them in this season. A thin wall of dust flew close by again, pushed along the cliff wall from winds blowing upward along the face of the steep slopes below. A couple of small dust tornadoes appeared and disappeared just as quickly. Far away, the other end of the gigantic canyon was barely discernible against the background, due to its considerable distance, giving the illusion they were covered by a hazy veil of pale orange. Further out to the left, the sun had almost finished its descent behind the plateau. Within the next few minutes, millions of stars would begin to glow in the dark skies. And before the cold reached temperatures unheard of on Earth, the small group of humans would soon close the door latch behind them, settling for the night inside their Martian outpost. Yes, Mars was home.

Mount Shamsi

The following months were fairly uneventful. Most of the team's daytime activities centered around countless experiments and routine maintenance of the station. That last part was in itself a full-time job. Of course, the station computers were constantly checking all systems, habitat integrity, oxygen levels, and performing countless other diagnostics, but human supervision was still required. By now, the small group of four had grown to eight. MF2 had made it safely to Mars, landing on September 8th, 2027 without a glitch. Back on Earth, Mars First Headquarters couldn't have been happier, especially after the near mishap of the previous year, when a cargo shipment, sent ahead of the second team's arrival, had almost been lost on landing due to a sensor failure in one of its main landing gears. The second crew, comprised of Indian commander Najib Shamsi, South-Korean Biochemist Liu Xing, Irish Medical Officer Ladli O'Connor, and Zimbabwean Technical Engineer Tendai Nyandoro, had easily adapted to their new surroundings, thanks to the legwork of Team One, who had by now figured out all the kinks and quirks of their daily routine.

The station now counted five modules and three greenhouses. The latest addition, a garage to house two of the three rovers the colonists now had at their disposition, was designed in a similar way to the greenhouses. About ten meters in length and almost six in width, it was however, substantially larger. Although the huge additional cost had been frowned upon by Mars First investors, several incidents had called for a protective habitat for the vehicles. One of them had almost caused Tendai's life, his first year on Mars.

Back on that fateful day, two rovers had been deployed to separate locations, leaving only ARC 3 at the station. At the time, it had seemed perfectly acceptable to get two teams to work at the same time. Four members in one vehicle and two in the other, the two could do research in different quadrants of the "grid", and cover a greater area, speeding up the work.

Water was the focus of most outings. They had developed a grid system of several square kilometers and explored a new block daily. Starting in a low section of Candor Chasma, they were gradually moving towards the top of the range. Candor Chasma was a region of Valle Marineris, a giant canyon stretching several hundred kilometers south of the station. The area they were exploring was so large and the canyon so deep, that they knew they would never cover the entire region, no matter how many years they spent at it, but they didn't need to. They just needed to hit water once.

Back at the Mars First station, Vera and Tendai had stayed behind, monitoring the two rovers outside.

"ARC 2, ARC 2, this is Mars First. Please come back, over."

"Mars First, this is ARC 2. What is it, Vera?" answered Dedrick.

"Looks like it's about to blow something serious over here. The numbers are pegging like I've never seen before, and outside visibility is already down to zero."

"Crap! Are you in need of assistance? Should we come back?"

"I don't know that that would do much good. You probably don't want to get caught in this. I just wanted to give you a heads-up. It just appeared so quickly... We had absolutely no warning from the computers. It came out of nowhere. I just hope it won't mess up our instruments outside. I'll let you know if we start losing signal."

"How do the internal systems read? Any problems?"

"No, so far, so good. All the life support checks are in the green. Tendai is keeping an eye on the radar and satellite info. At least you shouldn't be affected where you are."

"What about ARC 1?"

"We're here. Nothing to report on our end. Sabrina and I have been monitoring your transmission. The two of us are ready to head back right away if you need our assistance, Vera. We are closer to you than ARC 2. Are you sure you can ride this thing?"

"Thanks François. We appreciate your concern. For now, Tendai and I are fine. Trust me, if we need you, I'll let you know. For now, you guys are safer where you are."

For the next twenty-five minutes, all three teams kept in close communication while the storm was active. It eventually let out over the small outpost and veered to the north, a direction Vera was glad to see it take, since the two rovers were southeast of the camp.

She was still monitoring the computers when Tendai, already partially suited up, called her on the intercom from the greenhouse.

"Vera, the storage unit outside of greenhouse III looks loose, I think I need to go anchor it before another gust of wind damages it further."

"What? You want to go out now? I know the storm seems to have calmed down, but it could pick up again at any moment. Can't this wait? I'd rather you did so later."

"I know, but it's pretty quiet out there right now, and as you said, that may not last. I need to go secure that thing while I can. I'll take ARC 3. It shouldn't take long." Tendai sounded determined to go.

"OK, but please be careful!"

"I will"

A few minutes later, ARC 3 was approaching the storage unit outside the greenhouse.

"Vera, I'm almost in front of the-shhhhhhhhhhhhhhhhh…" The radio had just turned to statics.

"Tendai? Tendai, can you hear me? Tendai…? ARC 3...!"

"Shhhhhhhhhhhhhhhhhhhhhhhhhhhhhhhhhhhhhhh…"

"Shit!"

Outside, ARC 3 and its passenger were at a standstill. The vehicle had stopped abruptly without any warning, and everything in the rover was shutting down. Soon, nothing was showing on any of the dashboard monitors anymore. No lights, not even a bleep from the onboard computer. The whole thing was dead.

"What the f… OK, now what? Vera? Vera, are you there?"

It was no use. He had obviously lost all power. "*When was the last time they had checked ARC 3? The vehicle was connected to its solar charger this morning, that much I'm sure of. Regardless, the computer should have alerted me that something was wrong with the batteries…!*" He tried to recall who had done the last system check …

"*Either myself yesterday morning, or maybe François last night…*" The Frenchman often spent the last hour of his work day working in the garage. He loved taking care of the vehicles. His aptitude in robotics had been discovered early on at the Mars First Headquarters. François had a knack for figuring out problems and fixing things. He was almost always working on some technical project in his free time, if he wasn't playing his Ukulele.

"*Either way, there's no point dwelling on that right now. What I need to figure out is what to do next. I can't get out without a suit. On that particular point, Dedrick is going to be pretty mad, I have a feeling. And he will be right. I should've checked the cabin before I left. I guess I have only myself to blame for that too. I'm the one who forgot to put the suit back in its place yesterday… Ok, so I guess my only choice is to stay put until someone comes to get me. I hate waiting…"*

Inside the station, Vera had already contacted the other two rovers. Both were on their way back. Dedrick had ordered her to stay put. He had formally forbidden her to leave the station. The storm had picked up again, not as bad as before, but visibility was still pretty much non-existent. Dedrick couldn't let Vera take the risk of getting lost. The thirty meters or so that separated her from Tendai were completely filled with flying pebbles and a dark brown dust, an impenetrable fog that was not to be reckoned with.

"Tendai should have enough oxygen for at least another hour. The power may be down, but the oxygen left in the cabin will be sufficient for ARC1 to get to him in time," thought Dedrick. At least, he hoped so. He really had no way of knowing that for sure, but he couldn't let Vera take any risk. Unfortunately, to make things worse, the storm had also extended south of the station, which was slowing the return of the rovers.

François and Sabrina reached ARC 3, just as Tendai was starting to lose consciousness.

"*Stay with me buddy, hang in there just a bit longer,*" François thought to himself, while heading back for the main hatch, the other rover in tow. ARC 1's backup suit was in its compartment, but there was no way to get it to Tendai without entering the vehicle, which would have exposed him to the outside air and killed him.

"Vera! Tendai is out cold. Get the defibrillator and oxygen ready. We're on our way. Meet us at the main hatch! Hurry!"

A minute and a half passed before François and Sabrina, their precious cargo in tow, reached the station. Already suited up, the Frenchman jumped out of his vehicle and rushed to the other rover. Accessing the external command panel, he deployed the rover's cab extension and connected it to the station's door. He then rushed to the next hatch and stormed inside the station, Sabrina right behind him. Inside, Vera was impatiently waiting behind the other hatch for the air in the pressurizing compartment of ARC3 to get back to normal.

The warning lights finally turned green, the hatch opened, and Vera rushed into the rover.

François, racing through the pod tunnels was already on her heels.

"François, give me the oxygen feed, quick!" yelled Vera as he approached.

"Here!"

Oxygen bottle in hand, she leaned over the unconscious man.

"Tendai! Tendai!" But the dark-skinned Zimbabwean wasn't responding. She quickly placed the oxygen mask on his face.

"How is he? Any response? Did you check his breathing?" asked François standing behind her.

"No, there's no pulse… Come on Tendai, come on! Guys, the defibrillator, now!"

Sabrina squeezed by François, the EBP machine rolling behind her, and extended the two pads to Vera.

"Remove his shirt, François. Hurry!" Vera grabbed the pads from Sabrina. François obliged immediately. She briefly brushed the two pads together, placed them on Tendai's bare chest, and yelled: "Clear!" François barely had time to step out of the way. Sabrina pressed the switch, and Tendai's body jerked up and back violently. Vera leaned down and placed an ear on his torso.

"Nothing. OK. What's my charge?"

"Almost there..." replied Sabrina looking at the machine's gauges… "OK, green!"

"Clear!"

Sabrina pushed the button again, causing Tendai's body to convulse once more.

"Still nothing. Shit!"

Vera let go of the pads. They swung back on each side of the EBP and dangled at the end of their accordion cords. She climbed on top of Tendai and began performing mouth to mouth, adding several hands-crossed pressures on his chest every so often. Finally, Tendai's lungs welcomed the forced air and soon, the man was opening his eyes.

"Tendai! Are you OK? Look at me. Look at me! Do you know where you are?"

He seemed a bit disoriented at first, staring silently at Vera for several seconds. Then, he began to smile, looking around at each one of them.

"Well, that was close. You had us seriously worried, you know?"

He smiled weakly at François and managed a soft "Sorry".

Vera's back slowly slid down the wall behind her. She sat there, shaking. She tried not to cry, fighting the overwhelming sense of fear. They had almost lost a member of their small group.

"Vera, you're OK?"

"I'm fine, Sabrina, I'm fine. Just a bit tired," she replied with an unconvincing smile.

The whole group soon regrouped, and the three helped Tendai into greenhouse II, where he could lay down and get some well-deserved O2 from the plants. Dedrick's rover and its passengers arrived half an hour later to find Tendai seated at a table, surrounded by Vera, Sabrina, and François, all laughing loudly, a glass of Olympus Mons in hand.

The worst had been avoided. But the lesson had been learned. After that incident, only one rover was allowed to leave the camp at any time, and all three ARCs were checked every morning and evening, and their backup suits had to be in the vehicles at all times. The breakdown was eventually attributed to a simple relay malfunction. A small short in it had caused the battery to drain overnight. Why the computers had not registered the malfunction was another mystery altogether…

After another incident, a few weeks later involving one of the rovers left outside, it had not taken long for Lars to request that a garage be added to the station. Luckily, since the successful landing of MF1 and its crew back in 2025, funding requests for the project had become much easier, and in 2028, a supply ship had delivered the kit-style garage, for the colonists to assemble.

White Veil

It was a particularly beautiful day. Dedrick and Vera had taken a trip to their favorite spot for some alone time. Bathed in the crimson light of a beautiful sunset over the Laguna plateau, the Russian had finally proposed, and the emotional woman had said yes.

The news had created some "disturbance in the Force," as François had put it. Dedrick had vaguely mentioned the possibility of proposing the previous evening after a few too many drinks, but the Frenchman had attributed it to the Olympus Mons taking and dismissed the comment altogether. Needless to say, he was quite surprised when his Russian friend had made it official. What had made things bad for François was Sabrina's envious reaction to the news. The next few weeks had been all about how wonderful marriage was, and how she hoped she would get asked too, someday. Her not-so-subliminal hints had been difficult for the Frenchman to ignore.

Regardless, Dedrick and Vera had finally tied the knot in May 2030, in front of the whole world watching from Earth. Ladli had been more than happy to be the bridesmaid for the second time, and Sabrina and Liu had helped decorate the small Martian outpost as best they could. Since Vera did not have a wedding dress, the two women had managed to fashion one out of several white and pink cloths, normally used to cover plants in the greenhouses. Regardless of the unusual look of her dress, Vera was radiant and couldn't have been more thrilled. The forty-seven-year-old medical officer had become the first woman ever to get married on another world, and she loved it. Dedrick had asked François to be his best man, a role the Frenchman had been a bit reluctant to accept at first, considering his interest in weddings, left alone participate. But truth be told, he was touched nonetheless, and eventually agreed. Performing the ceremony had been entrusted to Najib. Commander of MF2 and team two leader, the Indian man had promised to do a great job. The occasion had also been a wonderful excuse to throw a party. Life on Mars could get quite monotonous at times. The need for some occasional play time was understandable.

"Vera Via, do you take this man to be your husband?"

"Yes, I do."

Dedrick Sokolov, do you take this woman to be your wife?

"I do."

"With the power given to me, I pronounce you husband and wife. You may kiss the bride." A small explosion of applause and yells by their colleagues filled the greenhouse. Tendai reached down the bag he was holding and pulled out a full fist of confetti which he threw high across the room. Countless small pieces of colored paper came flying down everywhere, while the newlyweds walked the center of the room. Ladli moved to the control panel and pressed play. The song "On Mars", written and recorded by François a few days earlier for the occasion, came on. As the music echoed through the station, Dedrick and Vera started to dance. The dark ballade wouldn't have been Vera's first choice for their first dance, but Dedrick had convinced her it would mean the world to François. She had eventually given in.

Leaning against one of the support poles, Francois was watching the newlyweds with a satisfied smile. He turned to Ladli.

"I wrote that one just a few days ago. It's brand new," he whispered.

"Yeah, I know," she replied, unimpressed.

"I used a recording program I created when I was still at Mars First, back on Earth."

"Yep. I remember." Ladli didn't seem the least interested. But Francois went on.

"Listen, right there. Can you hear that?"

"Hear what?"

"That sound, in the background, like water."

"What are you babbling about, Francois?"

He shrugged his shoulders at her. "The bubbles. You don't hear that?" He had an arm extended toward the control panel Ladli had been at moments earlier.

"Oh, that? Yes, sounds like something under water."

"It's one of the Blobus Viscus tanks. I placed a couple of mics next to it when I was recording the song. I like it in the background, gives it a whole new dimension. What do you think? Pretty cool, right?" Francois seemed quite satisfied with himself.

"That's great. Good for you. I'm gonna grab a drink. Want anything?" Ladli did not give the Frenchman time to respond. She was already walking away.

Francois leaned back against the pole. Sabrina approached, drink in hand. She was giggling, looking at Francois with a mischievous look.

He instantly knew she was already feeling the effects of the Olympus Mons. That could only mean one think. He was in trouble.

"Hey baby." Sabrina rubbed her hand along his chest. "What are you up to, French guy?"

He moved her hand back to her side.

"Nothing, just hangin'. What about you, hun?"

"Just looking at Dedrick and Vera. They look so happy, don't they?" She leaned her forehead on his shoulder, still watching the newly married couple dancing.

"Yeah, sure. I guess. You know me and parties. Not quite my thing… I think I need another drink. Want anything?"

"Hold on, there, cowboy, What about us?"

"What, what about us?" Francois feared he knew too well what she meant.

"You know…" she replied, looking at him with love.

He knew it was coming. They had been a couple for almost fifteen years. She rarely mentioned it, but he knew she loved the idea. To the Frenchman, marriage was not something he was against, he just did not see the point. Anytime the subject was brought up, Francois was always quick to argue that getting married was not a guaranty of love or happiness. Plenty of people got married, only to get divorced just as quickly. Those discussions rarely went well. Tonight, he would have to expect a long talk on the subject. Sabrina was in one of her nostalgic moods. He would just have to do his best to stand his ground. Secretly, he wished himself good luck.

On Mars

By François Menardais

Gm
I always knew you would come back in time
D11/A
To tell us of the beauty you have seen
Ebma7/Bb
And how you find your soul inside a dream
Cm9
Falling

Gm
Far away, a storm rages on Venus
D11/A
Lightning bolts are crashing to the ground
Ebma7/Bb
And it rains on Mercury, 'cause you don't want me to see
Cm9
The real You

Ebma13/Bb *Gm7*
But it's love you'll find, when you expect it least
Dm11/A *Ebma13/Bb*
And your heart and mind can no longer resist
Gm7 *Dm11/A*
The flames of Mount Olympus will burn
Gm
On Mars

Gm
Welcome to the carnival of chimes
D11/A
Would you spare a vision for a dime?
Ebma7/Bb
No, I can't tell the future, but I'd offer you a smile
Cm9
If only, you were mine

Ebma13/Bb *Gm7*
But it's love you'll find, when you expect it least
Dm11/A *Ebma13/Bb*
And your heart and mind can no longer resist
Gm7 *Dm11/A*
The flames of Mount Olympus will burn
Gm
On Mars

The small colony now counted two married couples, and one very concerned Frenchman.

The accident

"Najib? Dedrick? Guys, I'm having trouble hearing you. Can you repeat the last transmission?"

Vera had been monitoring the small group from pod one since they had left the garage, two hours, forty minutes earlier. She had just figured out that this outing was her seventy-ninth spent at the station, while her colleagues were out in the field. Dedrick had asked her many times why she so often volunteered to stay behind. Mars was out there, and the excursions were the best part of the day to most of them. Wasn't she tired of being cooped up inside all the time? She always responded the same way. She loved the station and preferred staying home.

Sabrina figured she worried too much about all of them to feel comfortable letting someone else monitor the group. So most of the time, Vera preferred to stay in contact with them from the station, especially ever since the incident with Sabrina's suit a few months earlier. It could have been tragic, had she not been only a few meters outside the station. That had given her just enough time to get back inside before losing all her oxygen.

Today, the mission was exploring sector 421, a rocky and treacherous area, but a promising segment of Candor Chasma for potential water deposits.

"Dedrick? Can you repeat?"

"I said, we're coming back. The cave didn't lead anywhere. We did some probing down three of the lowest areas. The samples all came back negative. Looks like that fissure was not made by water after all. Or if it was, there is no trace of it now."

The members of the group were slowly emerging one by one, from the narrow passage out of the cliff. A week earlier, François had noticed the depression at the foot of a cliff while driving by the area. Judging by the shape of the embedded ridge, the team had speculated that water could have carved part of it.

"That's alright guys, it was a nice try. I'm glad you're on your way back. We have a storm coming from the west. If you hurry, you should be here before it hits us. By the way, Dedrick, can you pick up some milk and a dozen eggs on your way home, I wanna make pancakes in the morning."

"Of course, Hun. Need any maple syrup?" he replied with a chuckle. "OK, guys, come on. Let's go."

Ladli and Liu were still standing at the mouth of the cave, waiting on Najib. The Bangalorean commander, a geologist by trade, never missed a chance to study any new mineral he came across, often bringing back small samples to the station's lab.

"We're waiting on Najib," replied Liu. She was staring at the dark tunnel inside the cave, a fairly wide passage that led to a wide-open chamber, full of rocks and crevices, undoubtedly the work of some ancient seismic activity. She couldn't see more than a few meters in. The rest was in complete darkness.

"*What is he doing? He should be here by now...*" she thought.

"Najib? Najib?" she called out through her headset.

"Where is he?" asked Dedrick walking back to them.

"I don't know. He was just behind me," replied Ladli with apprehension.

"Najib?" called out Dedrick.

"Najib!" called Liu even louder. Still no response.

"OK, you both stay here. I'll go see what's the hold up." He walked right between the two women and started down the slope into the black tunnel. About thirty meters in, Dedrick noticed a light illuminating a spot on the ceiling of the chamber from the ground below. The light seemed fixed as if Najib was staring at something above him. Unable to see his colleague, he called out while still approaching.

"Najib? Najib?" No response. His first thought was a possible problem with Najib's radio.

"What's going on, Dedrick? Everything OK?" came Ladli's voice in his helmet.

"Najib? Hey buddy, are you OK?" simply continued Dedrick without responding to her.

Liu's voice came in next. She was rushing back inside the passage. "Najib? Najib! Dedrick, what's wrong? Did you find him? Why isn't he answering?"

A knot formed in Dedrick's throat. Something was definitely wrong. He was now only a few meters from the light, but he still couldn't see him or notice any movement. "*What is he doing?*" Rushing to the area, his fears materialized when he spotted Najib's body lying still on the ground.

"Najib! Shit!" Now he could see the crushed helmet and a huge crack in his facial glass visor. Najib's face, blotted and still, his eyes wide open and full of blood, betrayed his painful last moments as his mouth, partially agape, and his purple skin left no doubt he was already gone.

"Oh God," said Dedrick as he kneeled down by the body. Najib had fallen from a small niche a few meters above. Scraping traces along the ledge where Najib had slipped, and the small pile of rocks around the body, told the obvious.

"No, no, NO!" screamed Liu who had finally rejoined the team leader.

"Najib! Oh, my God, Najib! We have to take him back to the infirmary. Come on, Dedrick, help me!" she screamed frantically, as she rushed to Najib's inert body and began lifting his torso.

"Liu… Liu," said Dedrick as he gently grabbed her arm. "It's too late. He's gone."

"No! You don't know that. We must take him back to the station. Vera will know what to do," she replied harshly, as she pushed Dedrick's hand away and kept tugging at the dead body.

"Liu… I'm sorry. There's nothing we can do… It's too late… Liu?"

Finally realizing the reality of Najib's condition, she began to cry and fell back on herself, still holding Najib in her trembling arms.

"No, please God, no, not like that." And the tears kept flowing. Her world had just been shattered.

"*Najib is gone. My Najib. Please God, no*," she thought. "*Don't leave me. Najib… Please, not now…*"

She felt like a thousand daggers had stabbed her heart. All of her being was crying out in pain. The feeling was excruciating. Her entire world had just collapsed, and suddenly, so did she.

#

A few hours later, Liu woke up in her bed in pod four. At first disoriented, the images of the earlier events came rushing back at her, as she jumped up and screamed. Vera and Sabrina tried to calm her down the best they could.

Two pods over, the three men were talking about Najib's accident.

"From what I saw when I got there, I think he tripped and fell face first onto a sharp rock. The oxygen escaped instantly. The Martian air did the rest. He died in seconds," said Dedrick.

"What I don't understand is why you didn't hear anything. He must have screamed or something…" puzzled François.

"I just checked his helmet. His radio was broken; probably from the impact when he fell. We had no way of knowing... Crap. I should've stayed with him," finally added Dedrick, feeling guilty.

"It's not your fault, buddy. It was an accident. There was nothing you could have done. He knew the risks; we all do," François replied, trying to make his friend feel better.

Dedrick stared at the unforgiving landscape outside the porthole window, lost in thoughts. "By the way, I guess you realize we're gonna need to talk to headquarters tonight about how to handle this. I was hoping we would never have to, but we all know the protocol in such a situation. We have to close the EPM." François reached over and entered a command on the touch screen next to him.

"We are now restricted to the private Mars First channel for all communications with Earth. No talking to anyone about this until we are advised further. We need to tell the girls."

"What about the cameras? They've been filming us the whole time. No?" asked Tendai.

"Mars First headquarters purposely has a half hour delay on the re-transmission of the main feed they receive from us before the images go live. I'm sure they've already pulled the plug before anyone could see what had happened. They probably blamed it on the storm to avoid questions from the media," replied François.

Outside the complex, fast winds were lifting sand around the small outpost. The dusty brown fog was now covering several kilometers. The storm had been raging for hours and was showing no sign of letting up anytime soon.

That night, they all gathered around in greenhouse II and observed a long moment of silence. Liu did not attend. Vera had given her a sedative to help her sleep.

#

Back in pod four, Vera and Ladli were sitting around Liu the next morning. Like everyone else on the station, the two women were devastated by what had just happened the prior day, but Liu was obviously the most affected. Her relationship with Najib had begun years ago back on Earth but had grown even stronger since their arrival on Mars. At the moment, she was a mess, and her two teammates were seriously concerned. She had stopped crying, but now her silence was even more worrisome. Staring straight in front of her at nothing, she was unresponsive to both Ladli and Vera who kept asking her if she was OK.

"Liu?" asked Vera again as she put a hand on her arm. "Liu, please, say something."

Ladli was beginning to worry seriously about her friend as well. She knew how much Liu loved her husband. She still remembered, as if it was yesterday, how happy she was when he had asked her to marry him. Only a few days ago, Liu was still gleaming from the talk both had just had about having a child. Now, Liu looked as if she had aged twenty years. She was silent. Her eyes, glossy and foggy, were still puffed up from all the tears, and she looked white as a ghost. She didn't flinch when Vera inserted a thin needle in her arm and injected her with "Corxa", a relaxant, to help her sleep. She normally had a serious aversion to needles of any kind and was always a difficult patient. Now, she didn't even seem to notice.

A few minutes later, Liu was sleeping again peacefully in her bed when Ladli and Vera left the room.

Dedrick was lying on his when the two women entered the pod.

"How is she?"

"She is sleeping, for now," replied Vera.

"I think I'm gonna go back to my room. I'm exhausted. I'll see you guys later." said Ladli as she turned and proceeded to climb through the next passage, leaving the two to themselves. Continuing to the next pod, she lowered herself down into pod two, where Tendai and she spent most of their nights. He was seated in front of the computer.

"I just remembered why I can't check my emails. François said we're locked out of the system for now. Security reasons," he offered without her asking.

"I know. I just left Liu. She's OK for now, but Vera had to give her something else to help her sleep. Oh, Tendai, it's so awful what happened to Najib," she said as she sat on his lap, wrapped her arms around his waist, and leaned her head against his chest.

"I know, baby. I know…" he replied, holding her in his arms.

Outside their small window, far in the distance, the winds were picking up again beyond the plateau. Deep into the cliffs of the canyon, a small purple light was glowing inside a dark cave.

A needle in a haystack

François' hand was wrapped around Sabrina's left breast. The two were lying in a spooning position, when the alarm suddenly resounded, breaking the silence in their pod. Surprised by the loud noise, he jumped out of bed and rushed to the controls. Searching for the cause of the mayhem, he quickly located the red beacon on the panel. Someone had just opened the outside door of pod four.

"Merde! Liu!"

Rising slowly from under the covers, Sabrina, still half asleep, asked, "Hu... What is it, baby?"

François did not answer. Rushing out of the pod in his underwear, he rushed past Ladli and Tendai, and threw himself into the next tunnel.

"Dedrick! Dedrick! It's Liu! She's out!"

"Who? Wh…what?" mumbled the Russian, awakened by the sudden intrusion.

"Liu! She's gone! She left the station."

"What? How? What time is it?"

"Almost two in the morning. I just heard the alarm. She got out through her hatch. I've tried to find her with the outside cameras, but you can't see shit out there! It's still a mess with that storm."

"Fuck! We got to go after her," replied Dedrick, rushing out of bed.

"Oh my God! No. What is she doing?" Vera had just woken up. "Wait, I'm coming with you!"

"No. You stay here. It's too dangerous. François and I will go."

Dedrick grabbed his boots and, putting a hand on François's shoulder, added, "Come on, let's go!"

Within minutes, the entire base was on alert. Vera was trying to stay in contact with Derick's rover. But the storm was messing up the signal.

"I had her a second ago. She was moving north-east towards Mount Shamsi. I think she's heading for Najib's block."

"Ok, thanks. Don't worry, we'll find her."

Vera wasn't so confident. They all knew it, in that storm, it would be hard to see anything past a few meters, and she already had several minutes on them. They also knew she had only a few hours of breathable air in her suit, if the tanks were full.

#

The visibility was almost zero. The rover and its two passengers had been driving for over two hours now, forming wider and wider circles around the station, but with the storm still raging, finding Liu was like looking for a needle in a haystack.

"Fuck! I can't see shit in this crap. What was she thinking? And the batteries are getting low, we're gonna have to turn back soon. Still nothing?" asked François, trying to look at the radar screen in front of Dedrick.

"No. I got nothing. But the instruments are having a hard time with all this stuff flying around. How long do we have left?"

"We're down to thirty-eight percent power and forty-one percent oxygen. We can't stay out much longer."

"Damn it! We must find her. We HAVE to!"

Dedrick didn't need to spell out why. Both men knew her suit had enough oxygen for three hours at best."

"Maybe we should… Wait! I've got something! Turn left!"

The suit Liu Xing was wearing was equipped, as were all their suits, with a transmitter that the rover's radar system could detect, that is, up to a certain distance and weather permitting. Usually capable of detecting a signal over several hundred meters, the current weather conditions had drastically reduced that to a mere few dozen.

A weak beep suddenly appeared again on Dedrick screen as François veered left. Pushing on forward through the thick wall of dust, the two men were frantically looking in all directions around them, hoping to spot Liu in this foggy mess. Dedrick was also keeping an eye on the unreliable but helpful infrared camera.

"We're close! She should be right in front of us."

"I don't see anything," replied François.

"It's this damn storm. It's messing with the instruments. She can't be far. I have a strong signal now."

Slowing down to a crawl, François was moving in short zigzags, trying to cover as much ground as possible.

Suddenly...

"There! There she is! I see her!" screamed François, pointing slightly to their right with one hand, while turning the wheel with the other.

"Liu! LIU!" screamed Dedrick in his suit radio. After checking that François had his helmet on, he jumped out of the rover still moving.

She was walking in a straight line, her back turned to them, apparently unaware of the edge of the cliff ahead. Her slow but steady walk gave her a robotic stance, dragging her feet, as if on auto-pilot. Dedrick reached her within only a few steps of the precipice and grabbed her arm.

"Liu! Stop! LIU!"

Barely fazed by Dedrick's hold, she turned around and looked at him through her helmet with a dazed look that sent chills down his spine.

"Liu, where are you going? You can't be out here. It's not safe."

But the South-Korean woman was not responding. He could clearly see she was not herself. She did not even seem to "see" him.

"*Probably the sedative Vera gave her,*" thought Dedrick. "Come on, Liu, let's go home."

"Home?" she repeated in a weak voice.

"Yes, come on, let's go home."

"Home," she whispered again, so low, Dedrick barely heard her.

Turning around in the thick haze, Dedrick radioed François.

"Ok, I have her. We're walking back to you. Can you flash the headlights or something, I can't see a thing?"

"François, did you hear me? François?"

No answer. Dedrick's grip on Liu Xing's wrist tightened a bit. Looking frantically around, trying to spot the rover's dark shape through the impenetrable fog, Dedrick called out again.

"François! FRANÇOIS!?... Fuck!"

Having released his hold on her, Liu began walking away again, in the wrong direction. Dedrick turned around just in time to see the frozen edge of the plateau a few feet away from her. He threw himself forward and forced her to the ground, only centimeters from the sheer drop. The cold ground cracked slightly in a few places around them, and the Russian had just enough time to roll the two of them off the collapsing corniche. A large chunk of rock gave out and fell down the abyss. His heart beating furiously in his chest, he rested there a moment before getting back up on his feet. Pulling Liu Xing to his side, he began walking slowly back against the wind, in the general direction, he was fairly certain that he had come from, looking for the rover.

"*I don't understand, he was right here. What happened?*" wondered Dedrick.

A mere hundred meters away, François was driving in circles.

"Crap, where are they? I can't believe this."

"Dedrick? Liu? Merde!"

"Fran...ctttcrk..."

"Dedrick? Dedrick, where are you?"

"Crrrckkk...sssssshhhhhh..."

"Damn it! Lost them again."

Driving blindly through the dense dust cloud, one eye on the occasional beacon light appearing on and off on the dashboard screen, François suddenly heard something hit the side of the rover. He stopped the vehicle immediately.

A hand appeared on the passenger side window.

"Dedrick! Thank God!"

"I know, I thought you'd turned back without us!"

"Don't be stupid. How could you even think-?"

"Open the hatch!"

Liu Xing was of no help. Dedrick had to lift her carefully into the cabin of the vehicle and remove her helmet for her once the pressure had stabilized.

"So, what happened to you? Where did you go? You had me scare there, for a moment."

"Yeah, sorry. Right after you stepped out to grab Liu, I almost drove off the edge of the plateau. I had to roll back. I started looking for you, and... But that doesn't matter now. Listen, we better hurry up. We only have 21% oxygen left."

After seeing how sad and depressed Liu looked, neither men had the heart to reprimand her for her actions, even if she had put more than her own life in jeopardy. Dedrick tried to say a few comforting words, but none seemed to even reach her. She spoke none to him.

The morning after

The morning sun was slowly making its way along the ridge the Mars First station rested on. There was a good 200 meters or so of plateau between the Martian colony and the edge of the cliff. Close to the precipice, Vera was contemplating the beautiful landscape of the giant canyon in all its rust-orange splendor, a site she could never get tired of. François approached her and sat to her left on a flat rock.

Far in the distance, the immensity of Valle Marineris appeared without end. As far as the eye could see, the great cliffs bordering the giant canyon kept on, fading eventually in a foggy haze beyond the horizon. The magnificent geological feature was several thousand kilometers long. If nature had carved it across the United States, the canyon would have reached from one coast of the country to the other.

"She's OK, by the way; exhausted but OK. I gave her a stronger dose and we're not leaving her side this time. She's not going anywhere," affirmed Vera. "Ladli has taken the first shift."

"I hope not. That was a close one. We were lucky to find her in that mess out there."

"I know. None of us expected that. I should've been more attentive to her. Najib's death was a real blow for her. She loved him, you know? Poor girl… a few days of rest should do her some good though."

"Look! There."

He was pointing at an object in the early morning sky. About twenty degrees above the horizon, a spherical body was flying quite rapidly in the far distance. Phobos, the largest of Mars' two moons, was tracing across the Martian sky, as it did every seven hours or so. Although quite dark and small, the natural satellite could easily be spotted due to its close proximity to its parent planet.

"They say Phobos will eventually crash into Mars in about fifty million years or so."

"Really? Why is that?"

"It's due to its orbit. It goes around us faster than Mars' own rotation speed and that causes the planet to pull it even closer. The process is very slow of course, but Phobos is getting faster and closer every time it goes around us. Eventually, it will get swallowed by the planet."

"Now that you say it, it sounds familiar. I think I heard about in training," conveyed Vera.

"Now, the other interesting thing is that the other large moon of Mars, the smaller one of the two, Deimos, goes around Mars much slower. Its orbit is about thirty hours, therefore much wider. Eventually, that one will be sent out into space, away from us."

"I see..." Vera was looking at him a bit surprised. She wasn't used to François having a normal conversation, without his usual cracks and rude comments.

"Am I boring you?"

"No, no, on the contrary, I like when you are not constantly goofing around. I'm just not used to it, that's all," she offered with a smile.

"Hey! What do you mean, goofing around? When do I--"

"Guys, can I see everyone in greenhouse II? Thanks," Dedrick's voice left their helmet headsets as quickly as it had appeared.

#

Half an hour later, they had joined Ladli and Tendai in the greenhouse. Dedrick was addressing the small group.

"OK, Mars First headquarters finally got back to us. Apparently, they had to figure this one out. They are going to make an announcement to the media in the morning. That's in about four hours from now, for us. They asked if we could wait until then to do the ceremony. They've also asked that one of us film the whole thing, mentioning their intension to broadcast a worldwide salute to Najib. Anyway, I guess we can wait a few hours."

"So…where should we…bury him?" asked Sabrina hesitantly.

"That's why I wanted you all here. What do you think?"

"Do we really have to talk about this now?" asked Ladli, almost in tears.

"I'm sorry, Ladli. I know how you feel, but we need to address this."

"He's right. What about Mount Shamsi?" offered Tendai.

"That was my thought as well," replied Dedrick.

"Yep, I think that's a good idea. He would have liked that," added François.

"I miss him," said Sabrina. She was now crying.

They all got quiet for a moment. There wasn't much anyone could say.

"Ok, I guess I'll go get ARC 1 ready, then," finally said François.

"I'll come with you," offered Vera

"Wait for me," added Tendai.

#

There were seven of them now. It seemed an odd number to Tendai who was somewhat superstitious, although he would never admit to it. He was a logical man, a scientist by nature, and had a need for balance and stability. Eight was always preferable to seven; it was an even number. It felt safer to him. Odd numbers seemed…chaotic and unpredictable. In some cultures, odd numbers often represented danger and evil. He was a bit obsessive that way, always worrying about numbers and their significance. But they were all used to it.

Liu was walking along Vera who was holding her against her side, an arm wrapped around the poor woman. They were walking right behind the three men carrying Najib's body, still in his suit. There was no coffin. The Mars First outpost offered many amenities, and the colonists had many essential resources at their disposition, but a coffin wasn't one of them. Dedrick was in front, holding the stretcher with both hands, his back turned to the rest of them to face the way up the hill. François and Tendai behind him, one on each side, were carrying the other end of the load. Ladli had fallen a bit behind but was slowly catching up, while Sabrina was following the group from the side, a camera in hand.

They were all silent. It was a sad procession to see, for sure. The sun had already begun its descent towards the Martian mountain range to the west. Cast by the amber light of dusk, rocky shadows were slowly growing all around, and the late evening sky was adding to the dark mood, bathing them in shades of deep reds and somber oranges. Slowly making their way to the top of the hill where they all had agreed Najib should be laid to rest, their convoy finally reached the summit. After each one of them had taken their turn to say a few words about their friend, the teammate and co-worker, the loving brother, the often funny, always wonderful, most honest, hardworking, true loving soul they all would miss terribly, Najib's body was lowered carefully in the hole François and Tendai had dug earlier. They then shared a few minutes of silence. Seated in a circle around Najib's final resting place, each began absorbing the reality of the tragedy.

François was now the one behind the camera. He followed the small group around with his zoom. Looking at his colleagues through their helmets, he tried to imagine what each one was thinking.

It was obvious Tendai was praying. He was the most religious of them.

He paused a moment on the Asian member of the group.

"Poor Liu. She's not taking it well. I've never seen her this way. I guess she really loved him." He slowly turned his attention to his Russian team mate.

"Now, I bet Dedrick is eaten away by the feeling he screwed up, somehow. Najib was under his care. He keeps mentioning he was his responsibility. I wish he wouldn't put so much on himself. It was an accident... Bad luck... Ladli... Hmmm... I'm not sure what Ladli is thinking. What is she looking at?"

Following her eyes, François easily spotted the large boulder near the ridge, just a few dozen meters behind them. "*Najib's block.*" It was by far the biggest rock on "Mound Shamsi," and had been the very first Martian feature to be named after one of the colonists. The oddest thing about the rock was obviously its shape. It was almost perfectly cubic. Seriously battered by the elements of time, and half buried, the artificial looking block had managed to go unnoticed, until, only days after his arrival on Mars, Najib had tripped over the protruding top, on his very first outing. He had spent the next several hours trying to convince the rest of them to help him "unmars" the unusual boulder. Two days later, the colonists had managed to reveal most of the rock.

François carefully took another look at it, zooming with the camera. It was an unusual rock, no doubt. But eventually, they had all agreed it was probably a broken piece from the plateau above, that a lucky set of circumstances had shaped that way, nothing more. Najib kept coming back to the site every time he got the chance, regardless. He always hoped to find something else nearby, something just as unusual that would vindicate him and his theory.

"Another object would multiply the odds, you see," he had argued.

Najib was convinced another intelligent civilization had lived on Mars. He was a huge follower of the "Face on Mars" movement. Decades earlier, a NASA photo showing a large rocky feature on the red world resembling a humanoid face, had sparked a worldwide debate on the subject. The belief by some that the monument had been made by an ancient Martian civilization, had been rekindled in 2021, when another NASA photo, taken by its rover, Mars Explorer II, had clearly shown a pyramid shaped formation in the Cydonia region. Several dark spots along the ridges of the pyramid, believed to be entrances, had proved to be the most controversial argument. With NASA unable, or unwilling, to send the rover back to the area, the public's interest had quickly died down. In the end, the pictures had brought up for some, more questions than it had delivered answers, but Najib had his own opinion on the subject. In fact, he hoped Lars and the board would eventually allow him to go check the area. He had suggested it to them many times. The place also offered some very intriguing features. Strange geometric formations, seemingly grouped intentionally, that had many question the possibility of random coincidence. Here again, he felt the sharp geometry of his NS1 boulder was more than a natural formation. He has scoped the surrounding area many times. Unfortunately, he had never found anything else unusual.

"*Either way, I'm glad we got to name the place after you while you were still alive, buddy…*"

"Mound Shamsi" and its Najib block had both been suggested to the Mars First committee by the Martian group, in honor of the Pakistani's discovery. Now, it would also be where the first human casualty would rest, a sad reminder of how fragile life can be.

And although, he would have agreed Najib's life had ended too soon, François found comfort in knowing that his colleague had lived his dream of going to Mars. A feat only seven others had ever done, in all of human history. And for that alone, Najib Shamsi would be remembered for posterity.

#

Later that night, the Mars First public relation's department issued a lengthy statement to the press about Najib's untimely death, calling the incident a regrettable and tragic accident, but also clearing any wrong doing or negligence on the part of the Mars First company and the colonists. A commemorative event would take place that weekend in Bangalore, Najib's home town in India.

And all over the world that same night, thousands of small communities and large cities alike joined in large groups outside to light candles and observe a night of silence in memory of a human being who had gone further than most ever could. A funny and loving man many had come to admire. They had followed his training and subsequent landing on Mars on MFN, the media channel Mars First Now, for almost fifteen years. That night, astronauts watching Earth from the International Space Station, reported a significant increase in brightness in many parts of the world.

Regardless of the worldwide sympathy, the tragic event had genuinely jeopardized the whole Martian endeavor and stopped any future missions, at least for a while. The reality of the dangers the Martian explorers were exposed to day after day had suddenly become a great concern across the globe. Alone on a distant planet, far away from any help or anyone, and left to fend for themselves, what chances did they really have to survive? Some felt spending billions of dollars to send people to such an unforgiving place was absolutely irresponsible and even criminal. The incident had refueled serious questions about the whole program. "Did Mars First have the right to send these poor gullible souls to their certain death?" as some news media had phrased it. The company's responsibility in Najib's death was being seriously questioned, and it would take another four and a half years to defend.

"Do you still maintain that sending these unqualified, everyday citizens to that hostile and desolate world, millions of kilometers away, is not pure murder? What life can these young men and women possibly expect on a frozen piece of rock, itself devoid of life, where the air is not breathable, the temperature can plunge to minus -133 Celsius, and solar radiation is deadly?" had asked a reporter.

"First off, let me correct you on a few points, if I may. The Mars First applicants ARE qualified. Their astronaut training program takes almost eight years to complete and is as extensive and rigorous as NASA's won program. Our team members go through countless evaluation tests, and we make sure to provide them with the tools necessary to insure the highest chance of survival possible. They do not get to go to Mars unless our team of experts certifies they have met or surpassed all physical and mental expectations. I would also like to remind you that the first two teams sent to Mars have done very well, in terms of adapting to their environment. And if I may, regarding the temperatures on the planet, -133 Celsius is an extreme, and Mars' average temperature is closer to -55C. And did you know that temperatures on a summer day can easily reach a comfortable 27 degrees? Of course, this is somewhat irrelevant, since no one can be on the Martian planet without a suit. Now, it is true that certain conditions can be difficult to work in. You mentioned radiation. Over time, radiation bursts from solar flares can have serious consequences on the human body, but as the Martian colonists have demonstrated on several occasions, they can shelter themselves from those rare events, in the isolating the underground booth designed for that purpose."

Lars was always good at handling reporters and TV journalists without sounding annoyed or losing his temper, even when some seemed biased against the project. He was used to it. But after Najib's untimely death, many more such accusations would test his patience to the limit.

Regardless, the company had been forced to reschedule the departure of the Mars First 3 ship, to let some of the initial steam fizzle down. The legal actions that had followed, and the amount of time and energy Lars' organization had had to spend defending and maintaining the integrity and validity of the program, had put a serious financial toll on the whole enterprise. Sending a spaceship to Mars couldn't be scheduled hastily, and the time window for the launch was precise and short. Departure had to be synchronized when Earth and Mars were lined up on a precise curve, allowing the ship to travel the least amount of time and distance. Even so, the shortest trip to Mars still took about five months, and that window was only available every two Earth years or so, since Mars revolved around the sun significantly slower than its blue cousin.

At first, hoped to be just a step back until the next planetary alignment, twenty-six months to be exact, the ramifications of the Najib's death had proven to be a much longer ordeal than anticipated, and the entire project had been put on. Luckily, the discovery of liquid water in underground lakes in 2033 would finally change the public's opinion in the program's favor, and the green light would eventually be given later that year. MF3 would finally launch in early 2034, five years late.

Part II

Chapter IV

H2O

The fast winds were blowing dirt in all directions around the small group of explorers, and their suits were looking dirtier by the minute, but the brown dust flying all around was not enough to make them pack and go back to the base yet. Although the winds could blow at much higher speeds than they did on Earth, for the most part, small Martian tornadoes and occasional winds storms were comparatively weak, due to the thin atmosphere of the planet. Nonetheless, they were certainly annoying conditions to work in. Especially because they meant reduced visibility and clogged everything.

"How deep are we so far, Tendai?" asked Dedrick.

"Almost eight meters. Still nothing."

"Ok, let's bring it back. I don't think the drill will go much-"

"Wait! I have a new readout. This is different. Look!" said Tendai with excitement.

"What is it? Let me see," said François who was closer to the screen than Dedrick.

While the Russian commander was making his way to the two men standing next to the machine, Tendai stopped the drill.

"Look! The numbers are climbing. No doubt about it. Unless this analyzing probe is defective, we've got liquid water down there!!" said François.

"Let me see." Dedrick as just reached the two men.

"Yes! YES!" he exclaimed, his two gloved fists up in the air. "Awesome job, guys! Lars is going to be ecstatic. Wait 'til we tell him about it! Wow! Finally," he added, letting out a big "Fewww! Ok, Tendai. Let's get this baby back up. François, come help me with the GA sampler. We need to bring some water back with us for analysis. We're gonna have one hell of a reason to celebrate tonight!"

As Dedrick and François, walked to the rover, the two shared a well-deserved high five with a big smile on their faces. They had been drilling the area for almost two weeks and made eleven holes in promising spots, but none had yielded any results until now. Number twelve had finally paid off. They had found liquid water on Mars. This meant a lot more than a new geological discovery to them. It meant a new source of H2O for the colony, one of the most needed resources for their long-term survival on the desert planet. Although they didn't know the quality or quantity of water below their feet yet, they knew it had to be large enough for the water to be in liquid form. That also meant there had to be more underground reserves like this one elsewhere on the planet. This was an amazing discovery, a life changing moment for them and all future colonists.

While François guided the plunger down the hole to begin retrieving a sample of Martian H2O, and Tendai busied himself packing up the rest of the equipment, Dedrick got into the rover and called the Mars First outpost. Ladli appeared on the small screen in front of him.

"Hey guys. How's work going?"

"Ladli, turn off the satellite feed for a minute."

"What? The whole feed? Why?"

"Please, just do it."

"OK. Give me a sec… OK, Done. What's going on?"

"You're sure it's off, right?"

"Yes! I just did. I swear. What's going on?" she replied with apprehension.

"We did it! We've found it! We've hit water!"

"WHAT!?" she screamed, as her face lit up. "Oh, my God! I can't believe it! Vera! VERA! Oh, my God. Wait until I tell the others. That's fantastic!" added Ladli.

"I know."

Vera stormed the control pod. "What? What is it?"

"They've found it. They've found water!"

"Ahhh!!" Vera screamed ecstatic. The two women jumped in each other's arms and started dancing around the room, jumping up and down like two little kids.

"Vera. Vera?" called out Dedrick.

"Yes, yes, what? Oh, my God, oh my God! Heee!" she giggled, looking at the screen while still hugging Ladli.

"Calm down, love. Listen. I asked Ladli to turn off the satellite feed. I want to surprise Lars and the Mars First team back home during our conference call tonight. Can you guys turn it back on once you've regained some composure, and make up some story about having some technical difficulty, or whatever? Can you do that?"

Ladli spoke first. "How are we going to explain you asking me to cut the feed just now? I'm sure they heard that."

"Good point… Tell them we had some technical difficulty and didn't want to alarm them until we got things under control… I don't know…"

"Hmm, right. Ok, don't worry. We'll figure out something."

Vera agreed. "Yes, sure. We'll think of something. Oh, my God! I can't believe it!"

"I know, we're pretty excited here too, believe me. We're packing. We should be back at the base within the hour. See you soon," finished Dedrick.

"Ok," replied Vera. She turned to Ladli and the two started giggling and smiling again at each other like two kids in a candy store.

#

"Good evening, Lars," said Dedrick in front of the flat screen monitor.

Dedrick was sitting right up front, with Vera leaning over his shoulder, her hand around his chest, smiling. The others were standing around them. François and Sabrina were seated on top of an emergency oxygen tank container, with Ladli and Tendai standing to their left. Liu was standing just outside the camera shot.

Although Dedrick and his team were using the latest technology to communicate with Earth, it would take fourteen minutes for their message to reach the Mars First team leader back on Earth; a delay that made any conversation extremely tedious, to say the least.

"How's everything back on Earth? Anything exciting to report? We have some news of our own we'd like to share. First of all, Vera is doing very good. The pregnancy looks healthy and we are all quite excited, I tell you. Another few months and we should have a new member on the team," replied Dedrick with a big smile on his face. "It's still hard to believe I'm gonna be a dad, the first Martian dad, to think of it."

He paused for a second.

"Also, we celebrated Sabrina's birthday yesterday. Ladli made a pie that almost tasted like one. What was in it, again?" he asked her.

"Hey, you liked it, don't lie," she replied, feeling teased.

"I know, I know, it was really good, actually."

"I agree," added François. "That woman can cook," he finished, giving her a lustful look.

"Oh, please," said Sabrina rolling her eyes at him.

Dedrick giggled a bit and went on.

"We have something else to tell you. Something wonderful has happened. But I'd like to keep the suspense going. Why don't you let us know how things are on your end first?"

He terminated the recording and pressed "Send."

About thirty-five minutes later the team was back in front of the screen to watch Lars' reply.

"Good to see you all. The picture is very good here today, by the way. I'm glad to see you are all doing well. Wonderful, Vera! We are really excited as well! And I must tell you, the arrival of the first newborn on Mars is fueling the media like crazy! Everywhere we turn these days, someone is talking about it. Newspapers, magazines, TV, the internet… You name it. It has become the most anticipated event of the year! We are really happy for you and Dedrick."

He paused a short instant.

"So, what's the other news you mentioned? We figured something was up when the video feed we were getting from you guys went from your forage mission to Ladli talking about the new greenhouse setup. Not that it wasn't interesting, but I know you guys too well. I had a feeling you were hiding something. Now, you have us all intrigued. Waiting to hear back. Lars out."

Dedrick started a new recording session. At the top left corner of the monitor, the number 42.204 appeared, the first two digits indicating the Martian year, a dating system put in place by NASA back in 1955. This was the forty-second Martian year since, and 204 was what scientists call the Ls number, a degree system adopted to represent the time of year. Dedrick and his colleagues gathered closely in front of the camera.

He turned around to look at his team.

"Ready, guys?"

And, after a quick countdown, they all shouted in unison, "WE HAVE FOUND WATER!"

"We made the discovery late this afternoon, in grid 6-55-B, at a depth of eight and a half meters. We don't know yet how much there is, but we've analyzed it. Ninety eight percent H2O!" added Dedrick.

"Hoo hoo! Yeah man!" added François in a cowboy style scream.

"So, we are pretty excited here, as you can imagine. We intend to go back tomorrow and survey the rest of the pocket. We're also hoping to find more sources in the surrounding areas. We've mapped out the terrain. Fairly common levels of materials and minerals found almost everywhere else in this part of Valles Marineris. We're fairly confident this is just the beginning. François and Tendai have also begun introducing some of our plants to the new water. It will take several days before we know if they are any incompatibilities or reactions, but if that comes back negative, it will be very promising. We're crossing our fingers."

"Hey Lars, how about sending us some bathing suits?" asked François with a silly smirk on his face.

"Stop it, François! Don't listen to him. But we're still waiting on that bottle of tequila you promised us last year, remember?"

"I'm with Sabrina on that one. Some booze would be nice," echoed Tendai with a smile.

"Hey Lars, what about some coconut rum? And we could really use some Pina coladas as well!" said Vera, laughing.

"Yes, that sounds really good. And some salt for the margaritas!" added Sabrina giggling.

"Don't listen to them. They're already drunk… No, I'm just kidding. Anyway, we're gonna celebrate our own way, tonight. We can use a break. Don't worry about us, we'll make it a fun party regardless. Ok, looking forward to your reply."

Dedrick leaned forward and clicked "Send."

A few minutes later, back on Earth, Lars was getting ready to listen to the Martians' new message. He was joined by two of his heads of operations, Sylvia, and Dr. Kovachev.

"Do you think someone else is pregnant?"

"I don't know, Sylvia. That or they've found something at the digging site, today. They sounded pretty excited. That's why I wanted you both here. I have a feeling this is going to be good."

The past thirty-two minutes had seemed particularly long to the Mars First CEO. Dedrick wasn't one for theatrical approaches, but the small group had convinced him to make Lars suffer a bit for his money.

A huge smile exploded on Lars' face the moment he heard the team's unified announcement. After listening to the whole message, he began composing his video reply in front of his own camera.

"That's fantastic! Wow! Guys! This is going to change everything. Now, we have liquid water on Mars. This is huge! I'm so proud of you. We're ecstatic. Great job!"

Sylvia leaned over Lars and kissed him on the cheek, hugging him from behind. Staring at the screen, she also congratulated the Martian team.

"Thank you, guys! That's such great news. We are so very happy for you and wish we could celebrate with you. Vera, I'm so excited for you too, love. A baby girl; that's wonderful. My love to all."

Fifteen minutes later, the Martian group was listening to Lars' reply.

"… margaritas and Pina coladas? Ha ha, sounds like a fair request. I'll see if we can give team three some 'treats' to bring along with them. But I can't promise anything. Either way, I'm afraid you'll have to wait another seven months before they get there, but I'm sure you'll gladly wait. And it looks like MF3's landing will coincide with the baby's birth, so you'll have two reasons to celebrate. I can't tell you how thrilled we are here, guys, and very proud of all of you for your teamwork and your progress. You've done such a good job at adapting to the planet's demanding challenges. Thank you! You have surpassed our expectations, and I can't wait to make the announcement about today's discovery to the media. As soon as I talk to the board, I'll arrange a conference. NASA is going to be so pissed we got there before they did! Ha ha. Anyway, go ahead and celebrate, you deserve it! I speak for all of us, here at Mars First headquarters, when I say we wish you all a wonderful night! Earth signing out."

"You think I should've asked for ice cream?" asked Ladli to Vera.

"Darn! I bet they would have sent us some," she replied laughing. "We'll have to mention it tomorrow."

Everyone on both sides of the communication screens was gleaming. This was a day to be remembered, and they intended to. April 14th, 2034, the day they had found liquid water on Mars. The first important discovery made by the team since their arrival on the lonely planet. François had promised he would do something special for the occasion.

That night they gathered in greenhouse II, and the Frenchman broke out a bottle of special brew he had concocted the year before by fermenting a strange mix of ingredients he was determined to keep secret.

"The girls have their 'Mount Olympus' and now we have this," he had said proudly, still miscalling the Olympus Mons drink. He was holding the bottle and its blue content up high in front of them.

"Oh yeah? What do you call it? 'Sacre blue?'" asked Vera sarcastically, with a forced French accent.

"Ha ha, you're cute. 'Non.' I call it Eau d'Amour," he replied, in perfect French.

"Ouch! Wow! That's strong. What's in it? Whatever it is, I love it!" said Tendai with a big grin on his face, before pouring himself a full glass.

"So, we know we need confirmation from headquarters, but I'm assuming we can start working on setting up the extraction equipment. The weather has been very favorable to us lately, so we should be able to do some good work tomorrow. What do you all think?"

"Dedrick, baby… don't worry about tomorrow. Come and dance with me," said Vera, extending her hand for him to grab, while François was selecting the Stereophonics' song, "Maybe Tomorrow," from the music library.

That night, back on Earth, a Mars First employee was alone in his office. He picked up the phone and dialed. In his native language: "Yes sir. We have confirmation. The Mars First team has found water. Lars wants to make the announcement tomorrow… Yes, sir. I agree. It will be the perfect opportunity. I will take care of it… No need. I have someone… Thank you, sir. I'll be in touch." And he hung up.

#

Less than two hours later, Lars was reviewing the speech he was about to deliver to a room filled with cameras and reporters. Accompanied by Sylvia, Dr. Kovachev and several high ranked officials from the Mars First board of directors, he was about to report on the latest news from Mars, water and baby included. Key engineers and project managers were present as well. TV stations and internet social media were getting ready to broadcast the event live all around the world from within the Mars First Headquarters in the Netherlands.

They had all been invited with the promise of exciting news from the red planet.

Not too far from there….

"Good evening and welcome to Mars First," said the man in uniform to a young female journalist who had just passed through a life-size x-ray machine. Following the signs along multiple corridors, she eventually came to the door of the amphitheater and pushed her way in gently. A woman seated behind a low table greeted her with a smile and gave her the sign to approach.

"Gina Glenver," the visitor said quietly, as she reached the table.

"Let me see… Gina Glenver… There you are. Sign here, please," replied the woman, pointing at a long registry list in front of her.

After the reporter had signed her name, the woman added, "Here is your badge, dear. Please make sure to wear it at all times."

"Thank you. I will," replied Gina, as she turned away and started walking toward the large door behind her. She quickly found her seat among the crowded assembly and made her way to it quietly. At the other end of the room, the Mars First officials were seated in a row on stage.

Lars Bruininck, the man behind the podium, began his speech.

"Good evening. On Tuesday, April 14th, 2034, the Mars First team confirmed the discovery of liquid water on Mars. It is thought to be an underground cave containing at least several pockets of H2O. Water! The exact amount has not yet been confirmed, but the water is there. The team was able to…"

Twenty minutes and several questions later, Lars ended the conference.

"Thank you all for coming. Goodnight!"

As the large audience slowly made its way to the exits, Gina made hers against the flow of the crowd, and eventually managed to get Lars' attention.

"Mr. Bruininck? Mr. Bruininck? Lars!"

"Yes?" he replied, turning around.

"Gina? Is that you? Oh, my God! You look fantastic! How are you?" he added with a big smile.

Lars and Gina had met in New York back in 2012, at a conference hosted by Dr. Neil Tyson-DeGrasse, an American astrophysicist. A short-lived romance had kindled between the two, but life obligations and career responsibilities had ended it just as quickly. Almost five years had passed since they had seen each other.

"It's good to see you, Lars. Your speech was very impressive. Congratulations on your progress with Mars First. Water… That's big! And right before the launch of your next ship!"

"It is. We couldn't be happier."

But he did not really feel like talking about Mars right now. Seeing her again after all this time had suddenly stirred all kinds of emotions and feelings in him.

"But, what about you? What's new? Do you still live in New York? Still working for the New York Post? Do you want to get a drink somewhere? Or how about a coffee? Are you hungry?" He suddenly realized how nervous he was.

She smiled.

"Yes, a coffee would be nice."

"My car is outside. This way," he said, smiling back at her and pointing to the staircase behind him.

Lars had only one rule about inviting women back to his place. He simply didn't. Not that the opportunity presented itself very often anyway, but his work at Mars First headquarters didn't give him much time for anything else. Recreation was always at the bottom of the list for him. He had pretty much been a single man all his life, had never married and didn't care to. He was so secretive about his love life that some of his close friends suspected he was gay. He was not, and was in fact strongly attracted to the opposite sex, but didn't like to mix work and pleasure, and didn't care to be seen with a companion. Lars also had a bit of a paranoid personality, which made him suspicious of anyone he didn't know well. As for Gina, if the evening went as he hoped, he had a place in mind. A small studio apartment in Amersfoort that he rented year-round, and where he often retreated when he needed to clear his mind. Or in a case like tonight, have some privacy.

In the meantime, across the Mars First compound, in a quiet area only guarded by a skeleton crew that night, two employees were busy making their way along a small corridor to a restricted area. After reaching one of the labs, one of the two men entered a series of numbers on the pad, and the door opened with a light "click!" They carefully skittered along the walls, making sure not to be noticed by the security cameras, and finally entered a chamber with walls as white as snow filled with delicate machines and rocket parts. Hiding behind a large container, the taller of the two men aimed a device at the three cameras in the room and "froze" their picture one by one, while the other approached a large turbine. After removing a small cover from the side of the engine, he pulled a very small disc out from his pocket and placed the object under a row of electrical wires, before closing the cover back.

"Ok, done," he whispered. The tall man pressed the remote again while facing each camera, and the two men exited the room and quickly disappeared back down the dark corridor.

A few minutes later, one of them was making a call on his cell.

"Did you get the codes?"

"Yes. He didn't suspect anything. What about you? Did you do it?" asked a woman's voice at the other end of the line.

"Yes, it's done."

"Good," said Gina before hanging up.

The tiny device the men had just managed to hide would never be found before Mars First 3 departure, and they would use the access codes Gina Glenver had managed to steal from Lars to render Mars First's remote access to the ship's computers inoperable. The consequences would be devastating.

The next morning, Lars was surprised to find himself alone in his Amersfoort apartment when he woke up. Gina had left a simple note on the kitchen table, "*Thanks for everything.*"

MF3

Six days later, the crowds outside the launch area at the Guiana Space Centre in Kourou, French Guiana, was nothing compared to the number of viewers around the world glued to their TV sets to see the departure of MF3, the third manned ship to be sent to the red planet. The Mars First reality show, Mars First Now, and its constant coverage of the astronaut training since the mid 2010's, was greatly responsible for the public's interest. The team members of MF3, Italian commander Antonio Bardino, Swedish medical officer Ebba Andreasson, Danish mission specialist Jessie Bruun and Australian geologist Daniel Patel, had become celebrities, just as had all the others before them. However, the estimated ninety million viewers worldwide for today's launch paled in comparison to the 800 million who had watched the departure of MF1, almost exactly nine years earlier. The Mars First project had gained a great deal of notoriety at the end of that year, with an estimated two billion watching the historical landing on the red planet. This third mission had already become old news to some. Just like the first manned missions to the Moon, nothing had ever compared to the first landing. And by now, to those in a rapidly growing world, full of responsibilities and restrictions, Mars didn't sound quite as fascinating as it once had.

For the four astronauts who had just spent the last twenty years training for this mission, however, the moment was grand, and they were now waiting anxiously in their seat for the green light to leave Earth and rejoin with their Martian colleagues. This launching was going to be the most important day of their lives, at least until their subsequent landing on the red planet six months later. That one would be the grand mother of all prizes.

"Nervous, Bruun?" asked Daniel Patel, the mission's geologist seated behind her.

"Nope. Just impatient to be on our way."

"I'm nervous," offered Ebba Andreasson, seated next to Daniel. "I don't mind saying it. In a few minutes, we're going to soar into space and I'm anxious. I know it's gonna be beautiful once we're above Earth and look down, but I would lie if I said I wasn't a bit nervous."

"OK, I'll admit, I am too. But I'm mostly excited. We've been waiting for this for so long…" admitted Jessie Bruun.

"Personally, I'm too excited to be nervous," volunteered Antonio Bardino, the ship's commander.

#

Back at the Kourou spaceport, the launch director was looking at several reports in his hands. "What's the status on the crew?"

"Everyone is loaded in and secured, sir. And commander Bardino told me to let you know the sooner they leave, the sooner he will be able to send you a postcard from Mars." replied a man.

The director cracked a smile. "Ok, thanks."

"Alright, people, this is it. Let's do a complete check of all stations, please."

"Navigation?"

"We're go."

"LAS?"

"Go."

"PRS?"

"PRS is a go."

"CAPCOM?"

"We're go," replies Dr. Kovachev who had been brought in two days earlier to oversee the capsule's progress on this historical flight.

The flight director went on.

"System Module?"

"Go!"

"ART?"

A few seconds passed.

"ART? Are you a go?"

A few more seconds…

"ART is a go."

"Thank you, ART. Launch is a go, people."

Dr. Kovachev, who was looking at the giant screen on the wall in front of him displaying the countdown in large numbers, turned around to face the engineers in the room and said, "OK, people. Let's go to Mars!"

Back in the MF3 capsule, Jessie Bruun wondered if her defunct parents were watching from beyond, proud of her.

Less than a minute later…

"Ten, nine, eight, seven, six, five, four, three, two, one, engine ignition, separation, and lift off!" said a clear voice through the crackling speakers.

A few miles from the ship's launching pad, the spectators suddenly saw the immense cloud of white smoke forming under the MF3 spaceship, followed seconds later by the tremendous roar of the engines. And as all watched in awe the vessel rise and quickly gain altitude and speed, the impressive white tail of smoke caused by the huge consumption of fuel engulfed most of the clear blue sky below. Like a bright shooting star reclaiming its place in the dark night above, the blinding brightness of the ship's burning rockets, pushing through Earth's atmosphere with incredible force, soon disappeared into the darkness of the upper stratosphere.

Back on the ground, "Tanks separation in three, two, one, tanks have detached."

"MF3 engine burn in three, two, one, engine burn!"

"System check?" asked Dr. Ivaylo Kovachev.

"All systems green, sir," replied a man in front of a screen.

"People, we're on our way to Mars!" said the launch director loudly, a huge smile on his face. The entire room erupted in applauses and cheers.

MF3 was bound for the ISS, the International Space Station, the ship's last stop before the long trip to Mars.

Chapter V

Red lights

Rushing past the well landscaped lawn, the two black limousines came to a halt at the back of the white edifice. Three men in black suits came out of the first vehicle and hurried to take position on the steps of the wide staircase, scoping out the surroundings through their dark sunglasses. Four more men rushed out of the second one, two of them in military uniform. Swiftly moving up the stairs, the second vehicle's occupants rushed up through the stairs to the security desk and kept walking at a quick pace along the wide hallway beyond. After climbing another staircase, the two men wearing black stopped when they reached a small corridor, and the two in military uniform kept on. Bursting into the presidential study, the younger of the two said, "Mr. President, I think you're gonna want to see this!"

"Mike? John? What is it?" replied the man seated in the room, completely taken by surprise. Colonel Mike Spade rushed to the small TV set and turned it on.

"You still watch TV on this old thing?" the other asked.

"It still works. Why change it? It pre-dates President Obama. When I got into office, I promised myself I wouldn't replace it until it stopped working. I'm not sure why; call it nostalgia," replied President Jarvis.

The image of China's president, Xi Jinping appeared, while Colonel Spade adjusted the volume. All three men were now silent, watching the small screen.

"...as I have many times before. It is time for America to recognize China's power and remove its military presence in North Africa before the end of the month, or we will have no choice but to take military action against the west. It would be a mistake to underestimate China's resolution on this issue. We are prepared to stand our ground and take the necessary actions. For too long has President David Jarvis tried to find what he falsely calls a peaceful resolution to the problems China faces with misleading talks and one-sided propositions. For too long has America been treating China like a child and not listened to its demands. It is time for America and President Jarvis to learn that they are no longer the main player on the world's chessboard. The time has come for China to be recognized as the greatest economic and military power in the world. We will not accept any more interventions from the United States in China's affairs. If America's military troops have not left North Africa by the end of the month, we will take action, and the consequences will be on President Jarvis' conscience."

Xi Jinping's words were translated in English by his own interpreter, standing a few steps to his left and back. Even if they did not understand Chinese, the tone of his voice left no doubt as to the gravity of his address. Mike Spade turned the screen off as the TV anchorman began his commentary on the Asian leader's speech.

The President turned to General John Glenn.

"Not good… OK, John, what do you think?"

"David, this is serious. I think we have a real problem on our hands, here. My intel agrees. China is ready to strike, and they don't think he's bluffing. Some even suggest he'll go forward with his threats, regardless of what we do."

"I agree, Mr. President," added colonel Spade. "He means business, and it looks like he is simply looking for any reason to start a war. We should get our men out now. It's probably time to talk about our military defense position as well."

"OK, I'll arrange for a cabinet meeting ASAP," replied the American President. "John, you need get our guys out. I'm not taking any chance with this lunatic any longer than necessary." He then picked up the phone next to him and called for his senior staff.

As the two men were exiting the room, President Jarvis put his phone on his chest and called out, "How's your wife, Mike?"

"She is well, Mr. President. Thank you."

"When is the baby due?"

"Any day, now, Sir."

"Send her my best, will you?"

"Thank you, Mr. President. I will."

As the two men started back down the hall, John glanced at Mike, giving the young colonel an approving smile. It wasn't that surprising that the president had asked him such a personal question at a time like this. David Jarvis had been elected at a time when the

American people were in great need of a leader they could trust again; someone who truly cared for the well-being of the nation and its people. Too many times had the country witnessed the disappointing lack of change promised by those elected. Too often had the bashing between candidates become the focus of their electoral campaign, while the addressing of serious issues was pushed aside, unanswered, or altogether ignored. And, while vague, and even outlandish, claims were still made by some of the other Presidential candidates, the North Carolina politician had quickly become a favorite in the polls. A few weeks later, he had become the youngest American president at the age of forty-one, winning over his rival candidate with an overwhelming eighty-nine percent of the votes. Incidentally, he had also become the second president to ever win the elections running as a third-party candidate since George Washington, back in 1789.

Six years after his election in 2028, he was still a well loved and respected by most of the population. Now in his second term, he had managed to bring the nation back on its feet in many areas. Unemployment was lower than it had been since the 1970s. Real estate had regained strength, the economy was stronger than it had been in decades, and foreign relationships were better than could have ever been expected, all things considered. One country, however, continued to stubbornly challenge the world's peaceful balance. China had become a loose cannon in the global power arena. All experts agreed. Xi Jinping was now a dictator of alarming cruelty and thirst for power. China was on the brink of declaring war with the west, and this new threat was being taken extremely seriously by the United States.

A week later, 12,000 troops were moving out of Africa. It was estimated it would take another couple of weeks to get them all out, but it was believed the Chinese deadline would be met. Several plans were put into action to evaluate, and ultimately respond to, the threat the Chinese President had made. But even after China had openly invaded several small Asian countries soon after the address, some experts still believed Xi Jinping was bluffing. Attacking the US was obvious suicide for the Chinese. Only a mad man would. Regardless, the possibility of a world war was too great to ignore, and a team of elite snipers and marines had been secretly dispatched to the East by the CIA. The Black Sparta, as they had been named, would infiltrate China and assassinate Xi Jinping.

President Jarvis had given the OK for an immediate strike, and most of his advisors had agreed with his decision. In three days, the Black Sparta task force, it was hoped, would manage to enter China and put an end to the abusive regime of president Xi Jinping.

Meanwhile, in Washington DC

"Right now?" said the man standing in the doorway to the woman in front of him. She was accompanied by a young man dressed almost entirely in black. Both were wearing dark sunglasses, and it was obvious the two were not here to trick or treat.

"President Jarvis has asked for your presence at the White House immediately, sir. This is a level 5." replied the woman. She was tall and slim, in her early forties. Her sort blond hair was combed back, and the fit body under her clothes suggested she exercised regularly. A small birthmark just above the right side of her upper lip made her look very attractive to Dr. Robert Byrd, the man in the doorway.

"Dr. Bird? Sir?"

"Ha, yes... Sorry... Huh, please give me a few minutes to gather my papers and change my clothes. I'll be right there," he said, realizing he had been staring at her.

#

Three hours later, Dr. Byrd was seated at a long oval table in the center of a conference room, having a conversation with several other men, when the president entered with four Whitehouse officials in tow. President David Jarvis made a gesture for them to stay seated before any had a chance to get up.

"No time for that, gentlemen. Let's get right to it, shall we? Mike?"

Colonel Spade went to the end of the room where he could be easily seen by all and began. "As most of you may already know, three weeks ago, China president Xi Jinping made the public threat to declare war on us, if we did not recall our troops from North Africa by the end of the month. We had reasons to believe the threats were serious and decided to comply with his demand. We have already pulled out more than half our troops and expect to have them all out by early next week. However, two days ago, the CIA received credible intelligence that the Chinese are planning something regardless. It would appear they have mobilized several thousand military planes, and if our sources are right, they intend to launch an attack on the US within the next few days."

Everyone in the room was silent for a moment. Most eyes were scanning the faces around the table. President Jarvis spoke first.

"Gentlemen, I do not believe it is necessary to tell you how upsetting this report is to my staff and me. We have worked very hard for the past several years now to bring the Chinese president to realize how disastrous a war between our two countries would be, but I am afraid our efforts have failed. This is why we are all here today."

Pointing at the man in the military uniform to his left, he continued, "General Glenn believes we must act immediately, and strike China's military bases before those planes have a chance to leave the ground. What we do not know, however, is what these planes carry. The CIA report we were given this morning suggests we may be looking at chemical warfare, here. The copy of the report, in front of each of you, mentions several documents found in a highly guarded lab in Beijing. We were only able to retrieve a portion of the file, but we think we have enough to conclude the threat is very serious. Dr. Byrd, what are your thoughts on the chemicals mentioned on page eleven?"

The fifty-one-year-old bearded man brought his thick reading glasses to his nose and started reading. It didn't take long before his facial expression changed drastically.

"Oh, my God... Oh my God!" he repeated several times while still reading.

"Dr. Bird? What is it?" asked the President. The scientist was too

Finally, after several passes over the same two pages, Dr. Byrd slowly took his eyes off the report, and staring unconsciously at the center of the table, said almost too quietly, "They're going to kill us all."

"What do you mean?" asked the man seated to his right.

"I mean they are going to k..." He paused. Turning back to the president, he continued, "Mr. President. I have seen this paper before."

"You have? That's not possible. This is classified. We just received the intel this morning."

"I mean I know this portion of the report. I know it because...I wrote most of it."

Everyone in the room was taken by surprise. General Glenn was the first to speak.

"You... You wrote this?" The expression on his face was one of true disbelief.

"Yes, General. I'm afraid so... Let me explain. Almost five years ago now, two colleagues of mine and I were working on an anti-virus hybrid. We were looking for a cure against the Brown's disease that had caused so much devastation in south India the year before."

"I remember hearing about that terrible epidemic on the news," offered a stiff looking woman seated on the other side of him.

"Yes," he replied, briefly looking at her. "So, we worked on a cure for several months, and although we were unable to find a way to kill the virus completely, we managed to create an anti-virus that minimized drastically its strength and reduced the percentage of death greatly. Within a year or so, the deadly Brown's disease was under control."

He paused briefly...

"But during the months following our initial research, still trying to improve the strength of the anti-virus, we also came across a new hybrid, a new version of the virus, itself so potent and resilient, we eventually gave it the name Mortis Fortis. Our subsequent tests became quickly conclusive. This was the most dangerous virus ever engineered."

There, he paused again, grabbed his cup and gulped a mouthful of coffee, as he assessed the looks on everyone's face around the room.

"You see, the virus is airborne and attacks blood cells. It is highly contagious, very resilient, and can spread very quickly. At first, we were fascinated with it for its ability to kill just about any other virus known to man, but soon realized how hard it was to destroy. After weeks of tests, we only found one way to kill it. Extreme heat or cold. Those are the only two things that seem to have an effect on it. It can survive temperatures ranging from -80C to +420C. And it thrives like crazy between twenty and eighty degrees. We studied this monster for almost eight months, all in all. Every test subject died within hours of being infected. We never found a cure, or a way to even slow its metabolism. We eventually agreed to destroy every trace of it. We incinerated every sample we had. Even the research was destroyed. I don't understand how the Chinese got their hands on this. We had destroyed all our research; every last of it, including the lab itself. Only the three of us ever knew about this. This makes no sense."

The entire room was silent. Everyone was staring at him, trying to comprehend what they had just heard.

"Dr. Byrd, who were the other two scientists working on this with you?" finally asked the president, breaking the dreadful silence.

"Well, there was Professor Ram-"

Suddenly, a man burst in the room with several others behind him.

"Mr. President! We have a code red, Sir. We need to get you to Air Force One now!"

"What's going on?" asked the President dumbfounded.

"Chinese planes have just entered our airspace, sir."

Panic struck the room immediately.

"What?" said General Glenn, jumping out of his seat. "That's impossible!"

"Mr. President. There is no time. We need to go now, Sir!" repeated the man in the doorway.

"Very well," replied the president. Getting off his seat, he addressed the group around the table once more.

"Gentlemen, it would appear time is not on our side, after all. Dr. Byrd, I'm gonna need you to come with me. General Glenn, Mike, I'll need you as well."

"But, I-" tried to interject Dr. Byrd, but the President was already leaving the room surrounded by several security personnel, General Glenn, Colonel Spade, and his head staff in tow. One man made a quick gesture for the doctor to follow.

In the hallway, as all were rushing to get to the helicopter waiting for them outside, the President asked, "Mike, I don't understand. I thought you said the Chinese planes were still on the ground back in China. How can they be here already?"

"I have no idea, Sir. I am as puzzled as you are. My only guess is that those are different planes. Planes we weren't aware of. I am calling my men right now. Let me see what this is all about. Excuse me, Mr. President."

Colonel Mike Spade grabbed his cell phone and dialed a number.

#

Lisa was standing in front of her grandfather. He was struggling with her helmet. She didn't look very happy about having to wear "this big ugly thing", as she called it, but grandpa was absolutely adamant.

"All young girls must wear their head gear protection if they want to ride their bicycles with their grandpa. No two ways about it, young lady!" he had told her.

To make sure she would comply, he was wearing one too, although he didn't normally when he rode his bike by himself.

"Sara Frank never wears a helmet when she rides her bike!" had said Lisa moping.

"Well, Sara Frank can do what she wants. You are wearing a helmet if you want to ride. It's for your own safety. You don't want to hurt your head if you fall, do you?"

"Hey, you two! Don't be too late, I'm making fajitas for lunch, and there's a surprise for dessert. I think you'll like it, Lisa," shouted Lisa's mother from the porch.

"Chocolate cake?" asked Lisa, excited.

"Maybe. I can't tell you, it's a surprise," she replied with a smile.

Soon, Lisa was riding away on her bicycle, helmet on, and grandfather in tow. The streets of her California suburban community were quiet this time of day. The summer sun was already hot, but the trees provided nice shady areas all along the way. A few minutes later they reached the park. A few other cyclists could be seen on the trail ahead. Lisa approached a picnic table and stopped by the bench. She lowered her bike to the ground and sat down on the grass. Her grandfather was about to do the same when the phone in his pocket rang.

"Grandpa, what's that?"

"Hold on, sweetie, I'll be right there."

"Mike? What is it? The... What...? Slowdown, I can't understand a word you're saying. What planes...? Who...?"

"Grandpa!?"

"Not now, sweetie."

"What do you mean, under attack? The President...?"

At the other end of the call, Colonel Mike Spade was trying to be quiet, making his way to the back of the helicopter, trying to hide from the rest of the staff. Calling friends and loved ones was not part of the protocol in an emergency such as this one, but the colonel couldn't leave without trying to save his own family. He wasn't the only one breaking the rules. Walking into the cargo room, he stumbled upon the chief of staff, standing behind life size containers, phone in hand. She didn't need to say anything. Her deer-caught-in-the-headlights look said it all. She was calling her loved ones as well. They exchanged a quick look without a word.

"Dad, I'm telling you, we have Chinese planes in our airspace. You need to go home, get inside, and wait there. I'll have a car sent to you as soon as I can. Do you understand?"

"Yes… Yes, OK. I'll be at your sister's house, and Lisa is with me too."

"Ok, that's good. Wait for the car. Inside! I've got to go." And he hung up.

"Grandpa! Look!"

"Mike? Mike?"

"Grandpa! Look!"

She was pulling on one of the legs of his pants.

"Yes, what? What is it?" he replied a tinge annoyed.

With her arm extended, she pointed at the sky with one finger.

He looked up and noticed a triangular object in the sky. Quietly moving across the blue background, it looked completely foreign to him. His military background didn't seem to help him identify what he was looking at. It resembled no plane he had ever seen. Dark and unmarked, it looked surprisingly small and slow for a plane.

"*Could be a drone, I guess… But I have never seen one like that before,*" he thought to himself.

Somewhat triangular in shape and measuring no more than twenty feet in length, the object was gliding slowly above the open field without making a sound. Trailing behind the shadowy form, a thin yellowish fog was spreading wider and wider, slowly descending towards the ground.

"Crap! Time to go! Come on, Lisa." Grandpa grabbed the little girl in his arms and began running back towards the house, a couple of blocks down the street.

"Grandpa! My bicycle!"

"No time, sweetie. Don't worry, I'll get you a new one."

A few minutes later, the two were rushing into the house.

"Close all the windows! Right now!" ordered Lisa's grandfather to his daughter, while he locked the door behind him.

"What's going on? Why are you back so early? Everything OK, Dad?"

"Close all the windows! Right now!" he repeated, as he rushed upstairs.

She could tell the seriousness of the request in his voice. Heading for the nearest window, Lisa's mother began closing each one.

Half an hour later, she and her five-year-old daughter were sitting at the kitchen table while Jack Spade, Lisa's grandpa, was frantically trying to reach someone on the phone.

"Thanks Colonel. We will," he said as he hung up.

"*Damn it! I don't understand. No one knows what's going on. All they can tell me is that they are receiving thousands of reports of similar sightings all around the country, but they don't know much else. It doesn't make any sense. How did unmarked planes get this far inland? How could they have made it pass our military defenses in the first place? And where is that darn car?*"

"Mommy, I'm scared."

"It's OK, baby. I'm sure it's nothing to worry about. You're safe here in the house with us," said her mother unconvincingly, trying to reassure Lisa.

Jack looked at his daughter and granddaughter. He felt powerless.

"*Where is that darn car? And now, of course, I can't even reach Mike,*" thought Jack. He also hoped his son was OK.

Hundreds of miles away, seated in the main cabin of Air Force One, Colonel Spade was lost in thoughts.

"Colonel? Colonel?"

He finally came back to reality when he realized the President was calling him.

"Yes, sir?"

"I know you are worried about your family, Mike. I understand, trust me. We all are. I wish there had been more time. But we have to get to our destination. I'm sure they've been picked up already."

Mike wasn't sharing the President's optimism. The fact that all communication with land had been suspended for the time being, part of the code red protocol while Air Force One was in the air, didn't help reassure him. He wouldn't be able to call the outside for the next five hours. That was best case scenario.

Meanwhile, Jack was pacing back and forth in his daughter's living room.

So far, the news on TV had been of no help. All the channels were showing the same thing. Over most large cities across North America, the same scene was taking place. A handful of mysterious looking planes were spraying a strange yellow gas that seemed to rapidly spread across entire neighborhoods. All of them had appeared around the same time that morning along the west coast. The air force had managed to shoot down a few, but most were only being spotted after they had started releasing the unknown gas. Jack had also just learned from an old captain friend from his Desert Storm days that the foreign planes were undetectable by radar, and it seemed the air force was one step behind. Meanwhile, new planes kept appearing over all major cities. Some had already made their way to the central states. Within hours, they would reach the west coast. All they knew with certainty was that the planes were Chinese. Jack's friend had also offered to come get Jack's family to a military base nearby, but Jack declined.

"Thanks, Kirk. I'm sure my son's people will be here soon."

As the day went on, the news reports got worse, but all the media could advise was to stay indoors. They were very serious about reminding people of the curfew in place, and that no one should be outside. Also, due to the unknown effects of the chemical released by the intruders, and their rapid spreading all across the country, the government had issued an order to stop any evacuation. Of course, thousands of people were by now rushing through the streets of Sacramento, chaos was already evident, and for Jack, staying put seemed the best plan of action, for now at least. He just hoped that car would show up soon, otherwise, they would have to take their chance in the madness outside. But, to go where? That was the biggest question. It looked like no place was safe. His son had advised for him to wait for the car. So, wait they would. If no one showed up by morning, he would reconsider heading for the country side then.

As the hours passed, Lisa and her mother finally fell asleep on the couch while Jack desperately kept trying to find out whatever else he could, and hopefully a way out of their dire situation, but all the lines kept ringing either busy or dead. Eventually exhausted as well, he turned off the TV and opted to forego his comfortable bed upstairs to go lay down on the big living room chair, next to his daughter and granddaughter.

Four hours later, the loud siren of an ambulance screamed outside as it drove by the Larson's house. None of them heard it, they were already dead.

Over the course of the next few hours, many more sirens could be heard all across the capital city, but gradually, like a carnival fair slowly closing down for the night, their number steadily diminished, until finally, all city noises one expected to hear any other day, completely vanished and the city became dreadfully silent.

#

The following days were abominable. Everywhere in big cities across the US, people were dying by the millions. The terrible disease was spreading like wild fire. Other countries across the globe were watching, helpless, as North America was quickly losing an impossible battle against time. In a secret Alaskan underground bunker, the American President and his staff were trying to assess the dire situation.

"OK, John, what's the status on those planes? Are we taking the bastards down or what?"

"It's more complicated than that, Mr. President. We have reports that the planes we have shot down so far caused even more damage once they got hit. The virus is released instantly in huge quantity when a plane gets damaged. They must use a safety release mechanism that goes off on impact. Bottom line, we can't shoot them down."

"Damn it! OK, so what do we do?"

"We have secured three of our four headquarters, Base Two in Morocco, Base Four, our last security option, near the South Pole, and Base Three, right here, of course. Base One, in Montana, was contaminated before we could seal it."

"Yes, I know all that. I'm not asking you about us. What are our options to contain this epidemic and stop those Chinese bastards? How much of the population can we save?" asked the President in a demanding voice.

"I'm sorry, Mr. President. I'm afraid the situation has become much worse than we first realized. The Chinese unleashed a devastating chemical weapon on us, and it is spreading faster than anything we've ever seen. We're losing people by the millions each day! I'm afraid there isn't much hope to save most. Canada is already feeling the effects as well. We were able to get twenty or so planes to several safe locations here in Antarctica. Some of them contained supplies, but most were used for civilian transport. If everyone checks out clean, that's about twenty-five hundred people. I'm afraid there's not much we can do for the rest of the population at this point… This epidemic is moving way too fast. I'm sorry, David."

The President fell back in his seat, devastated. "Twenty-five hundred? That's it? This can't be happening…"

After resting his forehead in his hand for a moment, he looked up again.

"What about our military? What's our situation there?"

"Most of our ground bases have fallen. We have no one left there to man them. We pulled our units out as soon as we could. Those who made it are heading this way. We don't know how many yet but hope at least a few hundred."

"That's insane! Are you telling me the entire US population has just been reduced to a meager three thousand people overnight? This is a nightmare!" He stood up and began pacing, his hand roughing his hair. "What about the rest of the world? Why can't we reach anyone? What's going on with our communication satellites?"

"As far as we can tell, the Chinese have taken advantage of the chaos to shot down many of them already. A few are still operational. Unfortunately, our ability to communicate with them is dwindling fast, along with our resources. Power stations are shutting down all over the country. At their current rate, we'll probably lose all electric power plants in the nation within the next couple of days." He grabbed the glass of water in front of him and took a long sip. "I'm afraid there's not much else we can do at this point."

#

A few hours later, in the main chamber of the underground Alaskan bunker, eight men and women were gathered around for another briefing.

"As you all know by now, the bio-chemical the Chinese planes released over our territory yesterday, was originally stolen from us, or at least its formula. So, we know a great deal about it and its lethal potential; and although I'm sure the Chinese experts are just as competent as ours, it seems they have underestimated the consequences of their actions. The virus is not only spreading across our territory at an exponential rate, but we now know it has also spread over most of South America and reached Europe last night. Even China itself is far from safe."

"How?" asked the secretary of defense.

"The winds," continued Dr. Byrd. The virus can easily survive in the air for months, even years. Africa, Australia, even Asia and pretty much every country around the world will be affected. From the last report, we received about an hour ago, China has already begun reporting some effects. On our end, the virus has managed to kill most of our population in less than forty-eight hours. The casualties in China will be ten-fold by the end of the week. The entire planet is in a state of emergency. In fact, our civilization has never lived through something this serious before. The death tolls will be in the billions." He nodded to the man across from him.

Colonel Spade got up and asked for everyone's attention. Reaching for the large flat screen, he pointed at a set of round colored patches on a map of Earth. Everyone in the room was now silent.

"What the enemy obviously neglected to realize was that the number of deaths would be so great and would take place in such a short amount of time, that the rotting bodies, and I apologize for the visual, would accelerate the spread of the disease, and even give it strength. The devastation is not only going to affect all living organisms around the globe, but the ground and waters are also being contaminated as the virus keeps spreading across the continents, riding the winds and air currents through the atmosphere."

"What about the oceans?" asked someone.

"As far as I know, it can also thrive in water. I have to assume the epidemic is going to spread to them too. I'm afraid its growth is unstoppable. Within the next two months, every continent and ocean will have been contaminated."

"Are you telling us that nothing can be done to stop this? How long will this epidemic last? And how many casualties do you expect worldwide?" suddenly asked General Glenn with obvious frustrated.

Turning to the military man, Dr. Byrd took off his reading glasses and let out a heavy sigh, "I'm afraid it's worse than you realize, General. I don't expect anyone to survive this. Even us, in this room, it's only a matter of time. This is what we call a global killer. And it's not just us humans and our civilization that will perish. What I am saying is that within a year, maybe even less, every living creature on our planet will be dead, including us."

Voices erupted in the room.

"What?"

"That can't be!"

"Oh God!"

"That's impossible!"

After the calm had returned, Colonel Spade took over.

"I think you underestimate this place, Doctor. This bunker was built to resist a nuclear strike. We're two hundred fifty-five feet underground and have enough food and supplies for several hundred people to last down here for years."

"Even if we do, the world above is dying. It will take generations to come back from this, hundreds of years even. And that's a best-case scenario. Life on Earth may never recover from this." Doctor Byrd sat back in his seat. His face betrayed the same sense of defeat they were all feeling.

There was really nothing much they could do at this point. During the next few days, a few hundred more survivors made their way to the colder regions of continent. Aside from its few facilities in the Alaskan state, the country gradually ceased to function. One by one, power plants shut down and the American cities were plunged back into darkness.

Eventually, a satellite feeds were re-established, allowing the President and his staff to assess the extent of the damage.

Several satellite views were scrolling on the wall in front of the small assembly.

"What is that? These dots everywhere?" someone asked, pointing to an overhead view of Manhattan in New York.

"I'm afraid those are people; dead bodies to be exact," replied the colonel. "It's the same things everywhere across the country. The cities are littered with them. Same thing all the way down south America. We started to see the effects in Europe too. I'm sorry, Mr. President, I wish I had better news, but I'm sure how we're gonna make it through this one."

"How did it get to this? Man, the intelligent species. Millions of years of evolution, and here we are, eradicated by our own stupidity. I think I'm gonna throw up," commented the President in discuss. He fell back in his chair and the room went silent.

The last call

Days earlier, Lars had tried to bring the Mars First outpost up to speed on the latest world events. Staring at the small webcam on his computer monitor, he looked as if he had aged several decades in only a few days. His hair was a mess, it was obvious he had not shaved for the past few days, and the bags under his eyes attested to his lack of sleep.

"I don't know how to say this, but it's bad, really bad. The Chinese attacked America five days ago. From what I heard, hundreds of small planes entered the US airspace and released a chemical weapon over the whole country. Reports on the situation there are devastating. It's horrible. I can't even wrap my head around it yet. It all happened so fast... The entire country has stopped functioning. Every communication has ceased since Tuesday. The last reports say that more than half the population has been affected. Millions are already dead! The entire country is a disaster zone. No one knows for sure how far the virus will spread, but it's moving fast. Central and South America have been affected as well. Millions are reported dead there too. It appears nothing can stop this thing. God! What a mess..."

He brushed his fingers through his uncombed hair.

"But that's not all..." He paused a moment, staring at the ceiling, trying to hold back tears of despair. "They say the virus is a deadly lab experiment, some crazy biological monster, concocted by the Americans themselves, a few years back. Apparently, the Chinese got a hold of it somehow, and engineered their own supped up version. But they it appears they have underestimated how dangerous this thing is. The virus is going to keep moving across the whole American continent, but it is not going to stop there. It's spreading hundreds of square kilometers within hours, even over water. Last night, they were talking about Ireland being touched already. I just got off the phone with Miles Waffenson, an astrophysicist I knew back in college. He said London is turning into a giant graveyard, and he doesn't expect to make it through the night. From what they can tell, there's nothing anyone can do to stop this epidemic, and there's no time to evacuate. There's nowhere to go, anyway... At this rate, this horror will be on us by this afternoon. Within a week, it will have spread over the entire planet. We're all fucked! I'm sorry. I wish I had better news…"

He stared at the screen for a moment again, numb. Turning his attention to a picture of the twelve colonists taken before just before the launch of MF1 nine years earlier, he wished more than ever he could be there with them.

"I know this is hard to take. But it looks like you are the only ones safe from this carnage, now… This might be the end of our civilization. Maybe even of all life on Earth…" He paused once more.

"These freaking idiots! What a waste… The human race, modern civilization. What a joke! A sad joke. Power and greed got the best of us. I guess we got what we deserved…" Fear and sadness showed on his tortured face, even more so now.

"I guess I may as well tell you about MF3. They… before they left, there was a…" Looking at the ceiling again, he held back the tears best he could and tried to regain his composure. "We didn't know. We only found out aft-" He was suddenly interrupted by someone off camera view. After an apparent exchange of annoyed whispers, he gave a reluctant nod and spoke again.

"I'm afraid I have to go. I wish there was something else I could say or do, but I'm afraid you are on your own now. Obviously, there won't be any more cargo ships sent your way, so make sure to maintain the base the best you can. You've made it this far, I know you will manage. Dream big and build something grand! I wish I could be there with you… At least, I'll die knowing you are up there, creating a new world. A second chance to-"

Sylvia entered the room and rushed to his desk, a note in her hand. She placed it right in front of him. She looked frantic.

He took a glance at it and his face went pale.

"I… I will try to contact you again if I can… Good luck, my friends. God be with you." He terminated the call and the two rushed out of the room.

#

About twenty minutes later, on Mars…

"I don't understand. I mean, it can't be. He has to be wrong, right?" asked Vera, turning to Dedrick. He leaned back in his seat and brought his hands to his head.

"My God, what have they done?"

A sense of despair engulfed Vera as she looked at each one of her teammates. Liu had fallen to her knees, crying. Ladli was trying desperately not to.

"What do we do?" asked Tendai distraught.

"Honestly? I don't know... What can we do?" replied François at a loss.

The last nine years had been lonely but now, the emptiness and loss they felt was indescribable. They were all in shock. It was hard to grasp, it all seemed so surreal. They all had loved ones back on Earth.

"I guess that explains why we weren't able to get through anyone the last couple of days." François rushed to the control board. "No signal. Damn it!"

The Russian slowly rose from his seat. "I doubt you'll get any. Lars said all the communication satellites connections have been shut down. I don't know how he managed to get us this last message. Shit! How can this be happening so fast?"

"I don't get it either. I mean, everything was fine on Monday. What the fuck? And what was that about MF3?"

'I don't know... I don't know..." The Russian commander stared out in the distance through the porthole window. Far up above the horizon, the moon Phobos was passing in front of the sun. Although this took place four times a day, what made this transition unique was that Phobos' shadow, projected onto the planet's surface, was aligned just right for the station to be in its path. For a moment, the plateau around the base was plunged into darkness, as if the day had just turned to night, instantly. This short eclipse wasn't a first for the small group, but after Lars' tragic announcement, the eerie coincidence seemed ominous. This was by far the hardest blow the astronauts had faced since their arrival. They had always managed but... This time, Dedrick was seriously questioning their chances of survival.

The minutes turned to hours. Eventually, unable to do anything else, they sent messages to family and friends anyway, hoping some of them might get through. The colonists were using a special private channel in case of emergency. But no reply had come back through that one either, even days later.

While most of the group had given up hope after a few weeks, Tendai had kept checking the log several times a day. "Even if they can't respond, someone might be listening," he had argued. But over time, he too had resigned himself, forced to accept the gruesome reality that they were probably not going to hear from anyone for a long time.

And as the weeks turned into months, they eventually returned to their regular schedule. They had to. The station did not allow much slack in the maintenance schedule. Especially now more than ever, they had to keep the outpost in absolutely perfect running condition. If any of the systems were left unattended or worse, failed, they had no other supplies than the ones already with them on Mars. They had to be vigilant. Spare parts were scarce. A certain amount of deterioration due to usage had been expected and included in the planning of the mission, but had been deemed manageable as long as supplies would be sent along with a new crew every two years or so. Now, they had to suspect MF3 and its precious cargo, due to reach Mars in just a few weeks, would be the last ship to come from Earth, at least for quite a while.

Just a weird dream

With the arrival of the third ship and its crew approaching, the Martian colonists had begun to refocus their attention to their demanding tasks, which included preparing for Chasma's imminent birth. It had not taken long for the new MF3 team to catch up to the situation back home. As shocked and saddened by the horrible news as Dedrick's colleagues, they also felt very lucky to have left Earth before the breakout. They had lost all communication with headquarters several days earlier as well, but at least they were now in constant communication with the Martian outpost, and all were looking forward to the upcoming landing.

"Can't wait to see you guys!"

"Thanks, Ladli, we're really excited to see you too. I think we're all ready to stretch our legs and take a stroll out on the Martian ground. We've been cooped up in here for over five months now. But you know how that feels, you guys had to go through the same thing. How's Vera, by the way?" asked Ebba.

"She's doing great. Looks like she's gonna have the baby right when you get here. We'll have two reasons to celebrate!" said Ladli with a smile.

"That's great! I bet Dedrick is excited too."

"Oh yeah, he sure is. You should see him. He's constantly trying to find new chores to do. I think he's trying to keep his mind occupied. He just went out with François to grid 50-21. Did I tell you they found another pocket of water yesterday? They should be there now. Ladli is monitoring their progress from pod 1."

"Wow! How exciting! That's marvelous."

"By the way, everything still green on the ship's self-diagnostic?"

"Yes, don't worry Ladli. I'm telling you, the computers onboard have run multiple checks. Everything is in order. I don't know what Lars was trying to tell you guys, but we're fine and on schedule. Thanks for all your concerns guys, we do appreciate, it but we're good and sound. I promise. Can't wait to get there and join you guys on all the fun. Well, I better go and start my shift. I'll talk to you tomorrow, unless something important needs to be addressed before then. Be safe, love," finished Ebba.

"Mouah!" replied Ladli, blowing a kiss back at her through the computer screen. But she couldn't help it, she was still concerned.

#

Valles Marineris was a big place. It was called the largest canyon in the solar system for a good reason, with its several kilometer-deep trenches, covering over 4000 kilometers in length and 650 kilometers wide, the geological feature was a real wonder. For the colonists, it had become their backyard, their place of work and research, and the familiar site never ceased to amaze them. Ladli and Tendai had taken ARC 2 for their excursion up the high plateau a few miles south of the station, a time alone that the couple cherished any time their turn came to break away from the base. Even Liu, who had stopped going outside after Najib's death unless necessary, was now enjoying her days off in the immense canyon whenever she had the chance, even if she was usually joined by one of the other members for safety reasons. Today's outing spot had been picked at Ladli's request. Tendai had parked the rover close to the edge of the abyss and the view was breathtaking. He remembered the first time he had awakened on the red planet and seen the gargantuan cliffs in the distance through one of the outpost's small windows. He had seen countless pictures and videos while training back on Earth, but nothing could have prepared him for the majestic grandeur of the site. A few hours silently passed as he and Ladli watched the sun slowly set behind the tall ranges around them from the comfort and safety of the rover. Above, the night quietly turned the orange sky darker and darker, until the starry canopy engulfed everything.

Ladli, sitting next to him, suddenly burst out crying.

"We're not gonna make it, are we?"

"What do you mean?"

"I mean, we're alone now. Earth can't help us, and no one else is coming, so what chance do we have?"

"I know, baby, but we're still here, aren't we?"

"For how long?"

She was looking at him, eyes filled with tears, and Tendai didn't know what to say. She was right, their chances of survival, without Earth re-supplying their small base every couple of years, was slim. He passed his hand on her cheek, drying a few tears, and kissed her lips softly. She abandoned herself in his arms. Looking back at her, he slowly unfastened her harness and lifted her to him, carried her willing body to the back of the rover, and laid her down. Without a word, he unbuttoned her black shirt and freeing one of her breasts, began licking the hard nipple with the tip of his tongue. She moaned as he slowly reached for her secret place with his searching fingers. He then arched up his back, allowing her to release the belt around his pants. Running her hand along his large erected member through the fabric of his briefs, she lifted his shirt and kissed his chest. Tendai gently removed her underwear, pulling it slowly down her legs, revealing her wet treasure. As she bit her own lips in anticipation, he brought his to the sensitive place and worked magic with his tongue, soon causing her body to convulse uncontrollably. When he knew she was ready for him, he opened her legs and penetrated her with one strong thrust of his hard-burning penis. The large member glided effortlessly inside her wet opening, and the two became one. After making love several times throughout the next few hours, they both finally fell asleep.

When Tendai woke up, the thickness of the night was still wrapping its dark scarf around them. Lying on his back on the floor of ARC 2, he stared at the view above in silence. Captivated by the serene darkness, he began to fall into the peaceful realm of wonder as thousands of stars, sparkling against the dark background above, drew him slowly, irresistibly into the unlimited world of his own imagination. Envisioning suns with worlds of their own orbiting in countless arrangements and sizes, some with gigantic gaseous planets, others with smaller, rocky worlds and water worlds, lava spewing infernos and biologically thriving ones, full of life, maybe orbiting a double, even triple star system. He was now on such a world. Three suns, make it four, of various sizes and magnitude, casting strange shadows across an alien world with giant trees and a lush vegetation, bordering a majestic purple ocean. Sharp jagged, ice covered mountain peaks in the distance, partially covering the lower portion of a large Saturn-like gas world slowly rising from the horizon, shot high in the surreal sky. His eyes drawn to movement in the distance, he could see the calm purple ocean beginning to foam. A fantastic being, slowly emerging from the surface, rose far above the water. Almost round in shape, the large creature glided silently towards him, its glossy skin reflecting the light from the suns above. Reaching the shore, the large alien rose its single massive leg and stopped right above him, its four eyes staring at Tendai with intrigue. The creature then suddenly morphed into a ...Black Hole. In the dark background of deep space, gradually overtaken by the growing display of countless stars trapped in a death dance with their host, the lonely traveler was now approaching a disc of swirling gases, a gigantic beast the mass of several billion suns, swallowing ferociously countless stars and planets that had wandered too close. The circular plane of spinning light, coagulated in giant bands of spiraling matter stretched beyond recognition, speeding ever faster to their absolute death, was hard to watch due not only to its overwhelming destruction, but also for its unbelievable brightness. Looking at its very center, Tendai was trying to make out the dark sphere of infinite gravity, an absolute emptiness residing beyond the "event horizon," a hollow space that even light could not escape from. Right above and below the immense disc, perpendicular to the thousands of light years wide secretion plane, the escaping gamma rays and radiation excess were shooting out two columns of plasma, thousands of light years long, rushing in opposite directions at near the speed of light. A distinctive looking object grabbed his attention when it rushed straight past him and dove straight for the giant black monster; an alien spaceship, unlike any he had ever seen. The bulky vessel seemed to invite him irresistibly to follow. All his efforts to resist seemed futile. He could see himself approaching the black hole, in slow motion. He was powerless. His body began to stretch, gradually morphing into a soft rubber-like matter, as it rushed faster and faster toward the infinite gravity of the black abyss. And, as he felt the force sucking him in getting stronger and stronger, his heart began racing faster and faster until-

He abruptly woke up, shaking and sweating. He felt a hand on his arm. Ladli was looking over him with concerned eyes.

"Are you OK?"

"Yes... Just a weird dream..." he replied, panting.

Blobus Viscus

Back in pod 1, Ladli was looking at the video screen.

"So, what do we have?" she asked.

A few miles away, Dedrick was holding a small transparent container.

"It's hard to tell in this light, but it definitely looks bluer than MA 5-23. One obvious difference, however, is how it changes color when I flash a light on it. It's hard to describe. I don't know if you can see that on your screen…" He tried to bring the sample closer to the camera.

"No, not really, but I'm looking forward to seeing it you all get back."

"I'll make sure to get several samples. Meanwhile, François found another passage down to a lower cave. You know how he is. The man can't stay in place. I'm gonna go join him as soon as I'm done here. How's everyone back home?"

"Dedrick! You shouldn't leave him by himself. You know the rules."

"Don't worry about me, Liu Cherie. I appreciate the concern, but I can manage, I assure you," said François who could hear the conversation in his in-ear monitor.

"Yeah, well, don't take unnecessary risks. All is good here otherwise. Tendai is in communication with MF3. He should be done soon. Vera is resting in your pod, Dedrick. She's fine, just tired. I ordered her to get some rest. Anyway... Glad to hear you guys got some samples to bring back. Looking forward to seeing you both when you get here."

"Sounds good. I'm gonna go check on François. I'll call you again in-"

François came bursting out of the tunnel.

"Dedrick! You better come see this!"

He sounded out of breath.

"What is it?"

François didn't reply.

Dedrick knew his French friend too well. From his expression alone, he could tell it was something big. He hurried himself, following the Frenchman down the dark path.

A couple of minutes later, the two were standing in front of an underground water pond several meters wide. The cave's ceiling was low, but a few leveled areas around the body of water allowed enough clearance for the two men to stand on the dry floor.

Dedrick was looking around for a clue to what François wanted him to see.

"Ok, what is it?" he finally asked.

"Check this out!"

Grabbing Dedrick's wrist, he turned off the four flash lights of his suit. As soon as the darkness took over the cave, a greenish light began to glow from deep within the water. The effect seemed almost magical. A few seconds later, the whole pond was shining and glowing from hundreds of small points down below. The light was reflecting everywhere throughout the cave.

Dedrick gasped. "What is that?" he asked, completely baffled, leaning forward. Deep below, he could see small round sources of light. They seem to cover the entire bottom of the deep water-filled depression. He was about to say something when he noticed one of them move.

"Wait, look!! Did you see that?! That one just moved! I just saw it slide. That thing is... alive!!"

"Yep," simply replied François.

"Holy shit! That's incredible! What…what are they?" asked Dedrick completely confused.

"No idea, buddy. But I have named them Blobus Viscus."

"Blobus Viscus? You're serious?"

"Why not? I found them, I can name them whatever I want. It's the privilege of the one who makes the discovery." He grinned. "Check it out. I pulled this one out earlier, and let me tell you, those things are weird."

He was holding the odd thing in his gloved hand. Dedrick had to admit, it did look strange. Some form of gelatinous blob, about twenty centimeters in diameter and half that in thickness. In François' hand, the whole thing wiggled like jelly. Slime was running down François' glove as the creature's body was slowly flexing. The light green hue of its outer skin was contrasting with the dark-brown organ that could be seen in its entrails through the semi-clear body. Dedrick, trying to make sense of the creature he was looking at, realized one could have compared the "Blobus Viscus" to a compressed silicone breast implant with a small potato inside. He laughed at himself for thinking of such an odd comparison.

"Ok, I think you should put it back in the water, now. It doesn't look too happy."

The animal was slowly turning blue, and although they didn't know for sure, it was fair to assume that just as a fish on Earth, the dear Blobus Viscus could not "breathe" out of the water for long. The creature had been in François hand for several minutes now. Realizing the obvious, the Frenchman leaned down and dropped the "fish" in the pond. As expected, the animal slid back down the wall of the pool and disappeared far below the surface emitting its green light as it mingled with its kind.

"Well. Congrats, François. You just found the first life form on another world! I guess you're not so useless after all. Ha ha..."

"Thanks, old pal!" replied François with a smirk.

"Ok, let's get a few containers from ARC 2. We're definitely taking some of these guys home. They are not going to believe this."

Under normal circumstances, a series of steps would have been taken before removing any foreign creature from its environment. At least until it could have been deemed safe for both the life form and the person doing so. But now that they were on their own, certain "protocols" had begun to fall back in the category of "suggestions", rather than guidelines. François had not needed to be told twice. A few minutes later, both men were exiting the crevice, each carrying a small container of Martian water. Inside, several Blobus Viscus were being tossed around as they rejoined the rover. They were soon heading back to base enthusiastically.

#

Everyone was standing around a low table in greenhouse three. In the center of it, François' precious new discovery was slowly sliding against the transparent wall of a small aquarium.

"I haven't found any of the major sensory organs you would normally expect on an animal on Earth. It has no eyes, no ears, no limbs of any kind as a matter of fact. Not even a mouth. I must conclude it's a protist of some sort. It is much larger than any on Earth, though, and substantially more complex. The nucleus, right here, makes out both its nervous system and brain. And for the size of its body, the space the brain occupies is quite substantial too. It may not be what we would call a 'highly intelligent' life form, but it possesses the ability to react to its environment. The fact that it uses bioluminescence is another fascinating wonder of this 'Blobus Viscus', as François so appropriately named it..." she looked at François with disapproving eyes, "…but I still don't know what its source of nutrition is."

"We were wondering about that... We didn't see anything else there. I assume you've analyzed the water?" asked Dedrick.

"Yes, I did. I can tell you it contains several minerals we've never seen on Earth. I need to run more tests to try to isolate their exact composition. But whatever they are, I can't even tell you how those life forms filter it. They have no digestive system, no processing mechanism of any kind that I can see. It's fascinating… One thing for sure, they cannot survive long out of the water." Walking over to a larger aquarium at the back of the room containing three of the creatures, Liu continued, "I've tried to determine if they use any form of communication between themselves. So far, nothing. I have been monitoring for sound waves." She pointed at a screen nearby. "But nothing yet there either. I couldn't find any patterns in their movements. Now, one thing of great interest to me is the light they emit in darkness, but there again, I need more time. They do react to movement from the outside, though. Look!"

Grabbing a small towel on the desk nearby, she waved the piece of cloth vigorously in front of the aquarium. The three Blobs quickly moved to the back of their limited living space, stacking up on top of each other.

"Awe, they're scared," said Ladli fondly.

"Wait, I thought you said they have no eyes. So how do they know you're doing this?" asked Tendai.

"That's the thing. I have no idea... They may possess another sense, unknown to us," replied Liu.

"Some form of radar, maybe? Or maybe they can get a general sense of the amount of light surrounding them? They obviously have some way of sensing the change." suggested Dedrick.

"Obviously... Anyway, I want to run a few more tests but I think these life forms are going to be very helpful to us."

Liu gently tapped the outside of the see-through aquarium. The Blobus passing slowly along the same wall froze.

#

A few days later, the team had come to the conclusion that Blobus Viscus would be a wonderful addition to their diet. Although a few of them had at first been opposed to killing and eating a "Cute Bloby," as Vera called it, it had only taken a few bites of the cooked creature, and one very convincing listing of its nutritional value, to get an anonymous vote of approval. After all, humans were carnivorous by nature. The team now had a new source of food. The Martian outpost living conditions seemed to be looking up. In a few weeks, four new members were going to join them, and Vera would give birth to the first human child ever born on another planet. Although all contact with Earth had ceased, and the small group was now completely on its own, the spirits were high, and soon they would have plenty of reasons to celebrate.

"I know. She just fell asleep a few hours ago. It's gonna be close. Personally, I don't think you're gonna get here in time. She could go into labor at any moment. I wish you guys could be here for it, though."

"I know, Dedrick, us too. We have another eight hours before we enter Mars' atmosphere. Either way, it's bound to be an awesome day."

"*I certainly hope so*," thought Dedrick.

Daniel was looking out the small window of the main cabin in Mars First 3, or MF3 as they all called it. The orange world in the distance was already taking most of the view, leaving only a small corner of black space on the upper right of the porthole opening. In a few hours, he and his three flight mates would step out on the dusty ground of Mars. He knew the world back home wouldn't be watching as he had so often imagined, but the excitement was great, nonetheless.

"*Almost there*," he thought. A big smile appeared on his face.

Ebba leaned forward next to him.

"Wow! Look at that. There's our new home. And there, Valles Marineris. She's so beautiful. Are we filming, Jessie?"

"Yes, both cams are recording. By the way, did you guys notice Phobos back there?"

She was pointing at an object in the distance. The Martian moon was clearly visible against the black background of space. Named after the Greek God, son of Ares and Aphrodite, Phobos was also the personification of horror to the ancient Greeks. Ebba had a fleeting feeling of dread thinking about it but shook the thought off as quickly as it came.

"Hey guys. We're at T-minus two hours, fifty minutes. I think I'd like to do one more check run on the landing module. Ebba, you want to join me in the capsule?" called the commander from the upper level of MF3.

"I'll be right there, Antonio."

A few minutes later, commander Antonio Bardino and medical officer Ebba Andreasson were giving a whole new meaning to the term "Mile High Club."

Phobos passing

"Breathe, Vera, breathe."

"Feww! Feww! Feww! Feww!" was loudly breathing Vera, inhaling and exhaling rapidly.

"Breathe, Vera, breathe," repeated Ladli.

"I am, I AM!" she replied harshly, looking annoyed and obviously in pain.

Vera was lying on her back in the infirmary pod with Ladli, Liu, and Dedrick at her side. She was about to give birth to the first Martian baby. They already knew it was a girl. Her name had already been picked, and to do so, Vera and Dedrick had asked their teammates to help them choose a name they all liked. After a few days of pondering and several close contenders, the expecting parents had finally picked "Chasma," a name François had suggested; a name that came directly from the very valley they called home, Candor Chasma, in the Valles Marineris canyon.

"I can't believe she's having the baby the exact same day the MF3 is landing. Of all times! Talk about coincidence. I hope it's a good omen," said Liu sounding concerned.

"Feww! Feww! Oh, sorry for ruining your day. Feww, Feww, I'm having a baby, here. Do you mind?" replied Vera in pain.

"I'm sorry, Vera, I don't mean it's a bad thing. I just mean it's quite a coincidence, that's all. I think it's great, actually. I'm very happy for you."

The smile on Liu's face was almost genuine, but it also betrayed her longing for Najib. They had talked about having a child, someday. Now, it seemed she would never get to experience that joy. Her eyes slowly drifted out the window towards Mount Shamsi, where Najib was buried. She could not see the spot from there, but tears came running down her cheeks anyway. Two tunnels down, Sabrina, Tendai, and François were looking at several screens displaying graphs full of numbers, and a video of what looked like a bright shooting star in the orange sky. The burning trail behind it attested to its high velocity. MF3 was starting to enter the Martian atmosphere. Sabrina, leaning over to see the sky through the small porthole window in the pod, announced with excitement, pointing at a spot in the sky, "I can see it!

There!"

Tendai got up to join her, and as both watched the ship trace a bright line across the sky on its approach, François, looking at the computer screen, commented on their approach, "Descent looks good. Trajectory angle is perfect. They're right on target. Levels are-"

But he never finished his sentence. A sudden flash brightened the whole screen in front of him, and Tendai and Sabrina, watched helpless, as the ship exploded and disintegrated in front of their eyes, with debris engulfed in flames flying in all directions. At the same instant, all the readings in front of François went blank, and a big red "Complete System Failure" appeared across his screen.

"Oh, my GOD! Oh, my God!" screamed Sabrina, hands to her face.

They could not believe it. Tendai was staring at the scene, silent, in complete shock. François, who had stayed in front of the computer the whole time, turned to them, looking for some explanation of what had just happened out there, when he suddenly realized the ship was gone. They were all dead.

Back at the infirmary, an unfamiliar scream suddenly resounded in the habitat. All seven colonists recognized the sound of a baby crying. The first Human-Martian, Chasma, was born on November 22, 2034 at 16:25 Martian time.

#

The next few days were the most disheartening and strange the group had ever lived since their arrival on the red planet nine years earlier. They had just witnessed the crash of MF3 and the death of its four crew members and welcomed a newborn to the colony the very same day.

They had also never heard again from Lars or anyone from Earth after that last transmission, months earlier. They did not know it, but most of Earth was now lifeless. People had died so fast that entire cities had become ghost towns within hours, all public transportation and air travel had come to a complete stop everywhere in the world within days, and pretty much every continent was by now in a state of desolation. Most life forms, from vegetal to bacterial to large mammals, had already lost the battle, man included. Unless nature's instinct for survival pulled a last second trick out of its sleeve and managed to stop the carnage, the blue planet would soon be a dead world. Once again, a new challenge had entered humanity's already troubled story, but nothing had ever compared or even come close to the magnitude of the global disaster Earth was now dealing with.

François was leaning against the wall of the pod, silent.

Still envisioning the crash they had just witnessed, he suddenly felt a wave of anger.

"Fuck! I don't know what to think anymore," his eyes locked on the small porthole window, scrutinizing the distant landscape as if answers could be found there. "I can't believe they're gone. I mean, the ship made it all the way here. Six months in space without a glitch! What the hell happened? Why did it blow up? Why…?"

As he turned his attention back to Ladli and Tendai behind him, the hatch swung right open.

"It was sabotage!" interjected Dedrick as he entered the room. He was holding a small computer pad in his hand, facing it towards them so they could see the document on it. He had just found a communication from Lars, locked by a program in the main computer and set to be released today.

"Apparently, headquarters had sent this weeks ago, but they had a timer on it, so we wouldn't see it until now. It says that the same group of religious lunatics who had tried to infiltrate the Mars First headquarters back in 25, had sabotaged MF3 before takeoff. Apparently, a magnetic device was hidden on the landing stage of the ship. It was detected too late, weeks after the launch. MF Headquarters was aware of it before the landing, but they chose to say nothing to the crew. They knew they couldn't do anything about it, so they kept quiet. I think that's what Lars tried to tell us in his last message."

"What? I don't understand. You're saying Lars and the corporate guys let the ship take off knowing it would burn?" objected Sabrina.

"No, they didn't learn about it until several weeks after take-off, when they were able to communicate with the affected onboard sensors. They just chose to tell no one, knowing it would have served no other purpose than to terrify the crew… The MF3 team never knew what was coming. Maybe it was better that way..."

"Fuck! I can't believe this… Fanatics and their stupid ideologies! And now they're all dead anyway. What a fucking waste!" Ladli wasn't one to curse usually, but she was still in shock and justifiably upset.

"Well, as Dedrick said, maybe it's better they didn't know. What good would that have done, knowing for certain they were all gonna die, and there was nothing they could do about it…? I don't think I'd want to know that months in advance, especially cramped in a small time bomb like that. You'd go crazy!" said Tendai.

"Yeah, maybe… regardless, those idiots and their pathetic righteousness crap… I hate humans!"

"They're not all bad, François," offered Tendai.

"I know, but the ones who are piss me off!"

"Well, I don't think they can any longer, buddy," added Dedrick.

"Yeah… I guess not…"

"I don't know. I just don't know anymore. I mean, what's the point? Why even bother?" suddenly burst Ladli.

"Well, come on, you can't just give up. Look, we're still here. We've got to take care of each other. Even more so now." replied Dedrick trying to make her feel better.

"But why? What for? I never really thought about it before, but what we were doing made sense because we were part of something bigger. We had people on Earth and friends on that ship. Now that it's just us, I feel empty."

"Just us? Just us? Honey, if everyone on Earth is really gone, we're now the most important people in the history of mankind. If we are really the last survivors of humanity, we have an obligation to do everything we can to survive, and someday grow again into a healthy population," said Tendai.

"Nicely said, but you seriously think we even have the slimmest chances of making it another few years without supplies from Earth? You know as well as I do that the outpost has a shelf life. Some said sixty years with proper maintenance, others ten. But the key words here are 'proper maintenance.' That means as long as we get a proper supply of replacement parts and tools every two years. Now, the first problem we encounter, we're fucked!"

"We haven't had hardly any problems so far, and it's been almost 10 years."

Ladli started crying. Tendai sat next to her, and tried to comfort her best he could, while François shrugged his shoulders at Dedrick.

Realizing he wasn't being much help to anyone, Dedrick chose to quietly walk off to go check on Vera. After the catastrophic events that had taken place on Earth only a few months earlier, this new tragedy was a hard pill to swallow.

The little Martian

Several days had passed, and Dedrick couldn't quite keep his focus on the task at hand. He and Tendai where bringing a new container of minerals to one of the greenhouses when Dedrick checked his wrist clock, again.

"I'd like to go check on Vera and Chasma, if you don't mind."

"What? Oh, yeah, of course, you go do that. I'm OK here. I got this. You go," replied Tendai with a vague hand gesture.

"You're sure you're good?"

"Yeah, yeah, I'm good. Don't worry about me. Seriously," he replied in a reassuring tone that gave Dedrick some sense of confidence he could leave the Zimbabwe man alone. He had recently noticed a change of mood in Tendai that worried him.

Tendai watched the Russian leave the room. He was now alone in greenhouse I. He couldn't help thinking of the absurdity of it all; the entire population of Earth probably gone, and the seven of them stuck on Mars, with a newborn. Ladli was right, what were their odds of survival if the air recycling system failed, or a compartment of the base got punctured or damaged in some way? Their predicament was looking quite desperate, to say the least.

Trying to distract himself from his dreadful thoughts, the Zimbabwean slowly looked around him. A long row of identical rectangular boxes without tops, containing half a dozen plants each, was taking a good portion of the long structure. His eyes landed on a small plant bed at the end of the row, right by the back wall, near his bench bed. A smile came to his lips as he remembered Sabrina telling him once about François' attempt to grow weed in that corner.

"*Ha ha! Leave it to the Frenchman to bring marijuana to Mars,*" he thought, amused.

Sabrina had told him how François had tried to keep his own experiment secret from them, and especially from Mars First, back on Earth. Apparently, the young Frenchman had managed to sneak several seeds with him on board MF1 right before launch. A few months after their landing on Mars, the several experiments ran by the team in the greenhouse had begun to show signs of growth, but most of the plants seemed slow to thrive, except for one tray. Before long,

François had been forced to confess his attempt. That he had managed to keep it a secret for so many months was quite a feat in itself, especially with cameras watching the team's every move. Tendai looked up at the only cam still in place in that corner of the ceiling. At one point, the station had counted sixteen inside and five outside. Of course, most of the ones inside had been turned off months ago when the communication between Earth and Mars had come to an abrupt stop. No one was watching the colonists anymore, and there was no need to waste energy. Some had been added to the five cameras already outside to give the small Martian community a better view of their surroundings. Back when the first four had landed, the world had watched in fascination the daily progress of the astronauts thanks to all the video feeds received directly from the Martian outpost. It was a miracle the Frenchman had never gotten caught by headquarters back then, or worse, by the media.

He giggled at the thought of François having timed his mischievous work during the quiet hours of night when the station was asleep. The ingenuity of the devious French technician had become obvious once caught. He had confessed how he had managed to run a pre-recorded video of the greenhouse through the video feed, allowing him to turn off the cameras when attending to his "secret garden." He had even gone as far as recording a new one each week, so not to raise suspicion, as all the plants and vegetables grew a bit more each day. Nonetheless, they had all had a good laugh at the whole incident, including François after the initial disappointment of the failure of his hopeful project.

After a last check on the greenhouse systems, Tendai walked back to his pod and, feeling truly tired, eventually fell asleep. Later that night, Ladli joined him, after her long day at Vera's side.

"She's feeling much better. She's gonna be fine," she told him quietly as she slowly climbed in bed, next to him.

"That's good. I'm glad," he replied from under the covers.

"*Maybe tomorrow will be a better day*," he thought to himself before slipping back into a deep sleep.

#

The colonists had agreed to explore the area where François believed some debris from MF3 had landed, after analyzing the exact trajectory of the ship right before the crash. Both he and Tendai had offered to go on a reconnaissance mission, to see if anything was salvageable. They didn't expect to find much, but considering their situation, any spare parts for the station would be extremely welcome. It was a strange mix of excitement and sadness when the two had found a portion of the vessel. As mall section from the cargo area, still holding several space suits and bins of various sizes full of supplies, mostly intact.

"What are the chances?" had said François when he had found, untouched in one of the containers, the small spacesuit Mars First had sent especially for Chasma. It was a revolutionary design that offered several customization options, including the possibility to expand the suit itself, to follow the child's physical growth. Expected to fit Chasma from the age of one to at least her early teens, it was a welcome gift to Dedrick and Vera who had already envisioned with dread that Chasma would have no choice but to stay inside the station until her adulthood, when one of their suits would finally fit her. A sad prospect for both child and parents that they were all glad no longer applied. The news had been a wonderful surprise to Vera when François had announced his discovery over his radio. He and Tendai were now about to leave the site.

"No, nothing yet from the cockpit. But we've spotted a few more debris about a quarter of a kilometer to the north. I think Tendai and I have taken everything we could from here. We're gonna go check it out. I'll get back in touch when we get there. François out."

Jumping back in the rover, the two men began to trace across the rocky plateau, toward the second site. The sky was clear, and the sun was shining brightly on the metallic surfaces scattered ahead in the distance. They were less than 200 meters away from their destination when Tendai, who was driving, brought the rover to a sudden halt, making the tires scrape the dry dirt below them. François, jolted in his seat by the abrupt stop, was about to voice his disapproval of Tendai's careless driving when he spotted the reason for his companion's action. About a hundred eighty meters ahead, a section of the cockpit, completely blackened by the intensity of the fire that had enveloped it, was lying on its side, a large portion of its outer shell missing. Near the center of the chamber's floor, now resting at a ninety-degree angle, still attached by their central aluminum leg, two of the seats were hanging a few meters above the ground, their suited occupants still harnessed to them. Most of the wreckage was an unrecognizable mess, with countless wires and fried computer panels hanging everywhere. Amidst the carnage, pieces of burned suits, melted with the shriveled fabric of the chairs, and their charcoaled human remains were a difficult sight to look at. The two men were silent, unable to take their eyes off the gruesome scene. Both knew they would never be able to erase the image now seared in their mind forever. Tendai eventually resumed their approach.

The body on the right, although as black as the rest of the scene, showed an obvious skeletal arm and head, still fairly recognizable.

"*Ebba*!" thought François. "Fuck!" he finally said out loud.

A few hours after their disheartening discovery, the two and their cargo were welcomed back, but not without mixed feelings. The rest of the colonists had seen the video feeds sent by François' and Tendai's camera suits, and although the two had avoided filming much of the heartbreaking scene, their colleagues had viewed enough to wish they had not watched any of it.

The next day, Dedrick and François, along with a courageous Ladli, had volunteered to attend to what was left of their fallen astronaut friends, and without lingering much on the decision, had buried the bodies close to the crash site, right where the ship had originally been expected to land. The area had been nicknamed "Key Largo" long before the fateful accident, and all had quickly agreed to keep the name regardless. After a few days of hard work, four pyramid shaped monuments, each about two meters high, built using rocks found nearby, had been erected across the flat plateau. Dedrick had also asked Tendai to carve a commemorating stone tablet, since he had done such a good job with the one for Najib's grave. Although sculpting a slab of rock with precision using one of the station's forage drills was a challenging task, considering the bulkiness of the equipment, the Zimbabwean had done, once again, a remarkable job. Most of the base's occupants had participated in writing the dedication with the exception of Chasma and Liu, the first due to her young age, the second because she was too emotional to do so. After a few words from Dedrick commemorating their lost friends, the group drove back home, and each couple retreated to their individual rooms, leaving the station strangely silent and ghostly for the rest of the day.

Kardium

A new chapter of their courageous journey was opening, and after the grim events of the past few years, Chasma was a happy change for the members of the station. If having an infant amid seven adults, cramped in a space no larger than a few small rooms, day in and day out, was a difficult challenge, doing so on Mars was a remarkable feat. Regardless, Ladli and Sabrina had been absolute life savers, caring for the baby while Vera, unusually weakened by the birth of her child, had been forced to rest and slowly rebuild her strength. The routine had only been disturbed a few days. Only weeks after the tragic crash of MF3, the small Martian community was refocusing its attention to the well-being and survival of its members. Tendai and Ladli had regained a more positive outlook on their situation. After all, the outpost had been a reliable and safe home for almost ten years now, and unless an unforeseen catastrophe was to jeopardize their dwellings, life at the Mars First base wasn't all that bad. But they all understood, now more than ever, how precarious and precious their small outpost really was. The seven pods and three greenhouses their settlement now counted, would receive no more supplies from Earth. They were quite certain of that. They also knew very well their base required constant monitoring, and anything that happened to any part of their habitat automatically affected the entire base. Station Mars First was their oasis in a desert the size of a planet. They all knew their life depended on keeping their dwellings, computers, and machines performing perfectly. With no possibility of returning to Earth, and the unlikeness Earth would ever make contact again, they were all pretty sure they were on their own.

"So, I think we need to focus our efforts on greenhouse III, right now. Last night's rock slide has weakened anchors five and six. If we use both ARC 1 and 2, one on each side, here and here, we should be able to move the new support in place with ARC 3 without exerting too much pressure on the frame," said Dedrick pointing at a top view diagram of the station.

"Well, what are we waiting for?" asked François.

"I agree. Tendai, you and I take rover 1 and 2. François, you've got ARC 3. You know what to do. Let's go."

Most days on Mars, not even the slightest hint of a breeze would have been felt by anyone walking bare skinned outside, had such a thing been possible. Today was one of those days. The sun, high above the outpost, had brought the outside temperature close to twenty degrees Celsius, a nice change in contrast with the freezing cold of the previous night, which had registered a whopping minus seventy on the outside sensor. Such extreme temperature fluctuations could at times cause so much stress on the Martian geology, that rocks were known to crack and split open, as was the case under greenhouse III. Thanks to a multitude of sensors and check points put in place all over the station to monitor the complex integrity, an alarm had alerted the colonists of the mishap, allowing the team to address the problem quickly the following morning, before the dwelling got compromised any further.

The maneuver had been a success. The greenhouse's stability was no longer an issue, allowing the experiments to resume. But most importantly, their oasis was once again safe. As the weeks continued, it appeared the small human outpost and its eight occupants were doing just fine on their own, after all. Soon the morale of the whole group was rekindled. The search for more water points was back on the schedule. Tomorrow, Tendai was scheduled to go drill a new access in a large pocket that had been discovered a few days before. The newly found deposit was a great candidate for being part of a larger group of underground water pockets, and a few station occupants were very excited at the prospect of finding more crystals, and more Blobus Viscus. Ladli had made Tendai promise he would bring back as many of the minerals as he could, even if he didn't understand why she was so interested in the rocks. But today, he was on his day off, a concept that François had come up with, and presented to the group soon after the crash. Since there were seven of them, it was quite simple. Each one took in turn, a day of the week off, leaving six of the colonists to run the outpost on any given day. Although it augmented, somewhat, the load for everyone, they had all agreed it was worth getting a day a week to goof off and enjoy some personal free time. In truth, most of them still participated when needed, regardless.

Tendai was lying in bed, staring at a small collection of pebbles lined up on the nearby desk, while Ladli, seated in front of a mirror, was tying her hair.

"What are you doing with all these rocks?" he asked.

"I'm starting a collection. Aren't they cool?"

"I guess. I like that one. What is it?" Tendai was pointing at a dark stone sitting to the right of her display, one of the larger specimens in the group. She turned her head to look.

"I named it Kardium. It's from the batch you guys brought back from grid 4-23-A in the Karrad cliff a few days ago. I found several salt deposits in its composition. That's what gives it these thin red veins."

"I see. That's neat. And why are you collecting all these again?"

"Well, first I thought they would be nice to decorate the room with, but then I realized that… Wait, let me show you. Come with me!"

She went through the latch leading to the greenhouse next to their pod, Tendai in tow.

Inside the vegetable garden, Sabrina was taking some measurements from a dark liquid in a container in front of her.

"Hola!" she said without turning around to see who was coming behind her.

"Hey, Sabrina. Mind if I show Tendai the new plants?"

"Sure. Go ahead," she replied, pointing to her right.

They moved across a few vegetable beds and approached a row of tall tomato plants.

"Wow! These are huge! How did you…? Those are tomatoes, right?"

He turned to the two women, speechless. They were both giggling. The five plants were well over two meters tall, and were covered with fruit. Any farmer on Earth would have been proud to get such an abundant yield. Several had already turned red, and Ladli, cutting one right off the closest branch, handed it to Tendai. "Try this and tell me what you think."

"It's fantastic! How did you get them to grow so big? And so fast?!"

"The rocks," offered Ladli. "We're not sure how yet, but by placing some of these stones in the soil, the plants are growing faster than they ever have. This plant was barely a half a meter tall two days ago."

"That's unbelievable! And there's so many of them. Martian rocks, really? Have you tried them on other plants?"

"Yes, some seem to react better than others. Obviously, as you can see, the tomatoes are doing great. So, did the cucumbers. Look!"

She pointed at a box full of them on a table nearby.

"Wow!"

"But it didn't do much for the grapes. We think we haven't found the right mineral yet. I'm hoping you'll find new ones tomorrow, actually."

"Ladli, why don't you show him the algae?" asked her Sabrina with a nod.

"Oh, yeah. You're gonna want to see this. Dedrick got a kick out of this one."

They walked to the back of the greenhouse where two clear water tanks were setup. Bubbles of oxygen were floating forcefully upward in both of them in noisy columns. The tank on the right was filled with small pebbles and sand at its bottom. The rest of the tank was water. But the tank on the left was quite different. Along the seams of its walls, a thick line of greenish grime could easily be seen. Down at the bottom of the tank, a small rock, the size of a tennis ball, was glittering in the churning water.

"What do we have here?" he asked.

"Actually, we don't know. We put this rock in there yesterday morning. I've analyzed it. Its composition is fairly common for a Martian rock. Nothing stood out in the numbers, except for one element the computer did not recognize. But it's in very small quantity compared to the other minerals in it, so I don't know if that has anything to do with it. All I know is that this tank was just as clear as the other one yesterday, and now this. I've taken a sample of that green stuff and started analyzing it. It's a form of algae. Nothing found on Earth, but it's the closest thing I can think of in terms of its biology."

"Algae? That's incredible."

"I know. This tank was clean, but after we laid this rock in water, all this stuff started growing. I'm not done with my report yet, but it seems it's gonna help us grow more food."

"Are you sure it's safe?"

"As I said, I still have some tests to run, but so far, everything has come back positive. Unless one of the last results raises a flag, we should be able to add it to the menu pretty soon. I think we're overdue for a culinary change, don't you?" she finished with a smile.

"You bet!" He tapped on the outside of the glass, trying to make the algae react.

Chapter VI

Rita

Dedrick, leaning on one knee, put another log in the fire. Rita, his beloved dog, had joined him and was lounging on the hardwood floor nearby. Flat on her stomach, her back legs stretched out behind her and her two front paws crossed. Panting, her tongue sticking out lazily on one side of her jaw, she was looking at him, following his every move, seemingly content. Staring at the flames flaring through the crackling logs, Dedrick was day-dreaming when he realized something wasn't right. How could he be in this room? He had not set foot in that house in many years. *When was the last time exactly? It was a day just like this one, to think of it.* Yes, he remembered sitting by the fireplace. He and Vera had made the trip from the Netherlands for a last goodbye. Now it was all coming back. Lars had told them this would be their last trip. Once back at headquarters, they would stay there for good until take off. But wait, that was almost twelve years ago! So, what was he doing here? How could he be back at his uncle's house? No, that was impossible. The Earth had been ravaged by a terrible epidemic. Everyone was gone. He was on Mars. He had been for almost twelve years now. He couldn't be back.

Rita suddenly got up and started barking at the fireplace. As Dedrick watched in disbelief the flames turn purple, a tall figure emerged from the smoke and floated to the center of the room. He was big and strange looking. Humanoid like, but definitely not human. It was hard to see any features on his face, except for his big purple eyes. The rest of his body looked dark and blurry, out of focus. The odd being was so tall, he had to hunch over for his head not to touch the ceiling. His legs looked a lot thicker than normal, and disproportionate to his thin body, and his feet were thick and round, and flared evenly under each leg. The mysterious being slowly leaned towards Dedrick, one hand reaching forward, but before he could touch him, Dedrick bolted out of the room and started running down the corridor. He suddenly realized he was moving in slow motion. Rita, running just ahead, was losing him. She quickly turned down the hall to their right, towards the backyard patio.

"Not that way, Rita. Rita! Come back girl! RITA!!"

He had no choice but to follow her, trying to catch up. But the faster he ran, the faster she did as well. He kept calling her, but she was ignoring him. He finally reached the backdoor. Rita was on her hind legs, frantically clawing at the handle. A quick look behind him told him the menacing figure wasn't in sight yet. He reached for the handle and opened the door. Rushing through the yard, Rita ran straight for the tool shed. Dedrick followed, thinking of the tools he might find there. His uncle enjoyed yard work, and he knew he had an array of saws, picks, axes, and gardening apparatus he might be able to defend himself with. But before he could reach the dwelling, Rita stopped dead on her tracks and slowly turned around. Taken aback, Dedrick stumbled backwards and regained his balance just in time to watch her transform into the tall being he was so frantically trying to get away from. The backyard was fenced and poorly lit, but Dedrick could clearly see the pale blue ray of light that suddenly flashed out of the being's hand and followed it to a group of barrels stacked up next to the shed. But those were not really barrels. No, they looked completely spherical. He had never seen anything like it. They seemed to be glowing from within. He could almost make out a shadow, a darker mass moving inside, pulsing lightly, like a fetus in a translucent white egg.

While Dedrick was staring at the orbs, mesmerized by the scene, the tall being approached so slowly and quietly that he didn't see him until he was almost right on him. The Russian froze. Extending an open hand in front of him, the being presented a smaller sphere to Dedrick. Feeling strangely willed by someone else, he slowly raised his hand to receive the object. Instantly melting into his skin, the sphere quickly disappeared, and Dedrick felt as if he was weightless, a sensation he had experienced many times in zero gravity.

Now hovering toward the shed, he suddenly realized the dwelling had been replaced by a large door. One like he had never seen before. The tall portal was full of strange carvings, lines, and geometric forms Dedrick could not recognize. It was covered in a thick layer of dust that gave the impression it had not been used for hundreds, maybe thousands of years. The strange being waved his hand in front of the door. A light appeared in the center, slowly morphing into a widening ring that rapidly spread across the entire doorway, until it faded to give way to a long, dark tunnel. Completely helpless, Dedrick was now inside, moving along with the stranger next to him, both floating slowly forward in the purple lit corridor. He suddenly realized Rita was with him again, hovering just in front of them. Dedrick felt as if he was being taken through an ancient Egyptian tomb. He also noticed he couldn't taste the air, or smell anything, and the place was eerily quiet. Rita, as if seated on an invisible flying rug, floated calmly ahead. The three of them soon arrived in front of another door. This one looked as if it had been built more recently. It was bright white and free of dirt. The grooves sculpted on it were much easier to see than the first one. Waving again, the alien being made the door slowly vanish and-

... Buzzz... Buzzz... Buzzz...

The sound of his alarm suddenly woke him up. He had been dreaming again. The same dream he had had countless times since his arrival on Mars, more than a decade earlier. The dreams were becoming more frequent lately, and for a moment, he wondered if it had anything to do with the guilt he still harbored for leaving his mother back on Earth.

He shook the thought out of his head, turned off the annoying noise by voice command, and got out of bed. Putting his boots on, he slowly made his way to the dark panel on the far wall of the small habitat and turned on the spotlights outside. The view through the small porthole window was almost completely obstructed by a thick haze of orange dust swirling around in all directions outside the station. Dedrick let out a bored sigh and walked to the pod's small kitchen area. He grabbed a sealed coffee cup and put it in the microwave. A few seconds later, he moved to his computer, coffee in hand, and pressed his finger on the lower right corner of the screen to open his log page.

Monday, June 14, 2037. Today was his mother's birthday, he realized. She was sixty-seven, if she had survived Earth's devastating epidemic, that is. To think of it, he didn't even know if she was still alive or not. It had been almost three years since their last contact with Earth. No one knew what had happened exactly, but they had a pretty good idea. As far as they could tell, a large percentage of Earth's human population was probably gone, but they were unable to even guess the true extent of the tragedy. This unknown had at first given the colonists the feeble hope their loved ones might still be alive. But by now, they knew this much: For the last thirty-five months, the colony's radars and communication devices aimed at Earth had been utterly silent.

Bringing himself out of his dreary thoughts, Dedrick moved to the lounge cove next to his sleeping area and began putting his PLS suit on. He was leaning forward, one boot in his hands, when a single high-pitched whistle suddenly blasted out of the small speaker above his head, followed by the familiar sound of his French colleague's voice.

"Good morning, old man!"

Barely glancing at the monitor screen without stopping what he was doing, Dedrick replied. "Ha! Look who's talking! I think YOU'RE the old one, my friend."

It was true, François was his elder by almost a year.

"Yeah, yeah," said François. "Listen. I was thinking we should take rover 2 this morning. I was checking ARC 1 last night, and I think the left front wheel is still out of whack. We could have problems stirring through Candor.

"Fine with me. You're the expert. See you in the garage in a few," said Dedrick without looking again at the screen.

The high-pitched whistle squealed one more time as the screen turned black, and the speaker went quiet. Dedrick finished putting his suit on, got up to the hatch door, and left the room.

The garage, as they preferred to call it, was a single cylindrical pod barely big enough for two of the rovers it housed. Two small tunnels provided access in and out of it from the rest of their living quarters. On the main wall in front of the rovers, a lengthy porthole window in the middle of the main hatch gate offered a glimpse out onto the flat plateau beyond the station. Dedrick approached the far wall where Sabrina was standing, with her helmet halfway over her head.

"Hey Sabrina!"

"Hi Dedrick. Did you see the storm, earlier? So much for François' weather forecast last night. For a moment, I thought we were gonna have to postpone the excursion until tomorrow."

"You should know better than to trust his 'all-knowing-Majesty.' I knew he was full of it when he announced today would rival a summer day in Florida. You know how much he loves toying with us."

"I know, he can be so immature at times."

After putting their helmets on, both got into ARC 2, and Dedrick turned on the onboard computer and started going down his check list.

"Good morning everyone," said a voice through the rover's intercom.

"Morning, Ladli," replied Dedrick and Sabrina, in unison.

"I just checked the weather conditions at Candor I. Visibility is low but acceptable. You should be able to get a few hours of exploration today. So much for the clear day forecast last night, huh. By the way, where is François?"

"Late, as usual," replied Dedrick.

As if on cue, sliding from under one of the anchoring cables, François reached the passenger side of the rover with a big 2 on it and climbed aboard.

"Well, thanks for joining us, Mr. Menardais," said Sabrina sarcastically.

"Wouldn't miss it for anything, love!" he replied with a wink.

After they were done going through the check list, Dedrick's French co-pilot, looking at Ladli on the console's screen, announced, "Ready when you are, Hun."

"OK, don't forget to lower your visors, I'm opening the door."

Watching them via the visor-viewer from inside the control room, she entered a few commands on the touch screen in front of her, and the garage door slowly began to rise. A thin band of bright orange light appeared under the cracked gate, and sun light soon filled the small shelter with a bright reddish glow. The rising sun was facing them just above the horizon. Dedrick slowly pressed forward on the joystick in his hand and the vehicle began moving.

A few seconds later, the gate was closing behind them, and the team of three began making its thirty-minute trek across the deserted landscape of Candor Chasma to the Candor I site.

#

The ride was quiet. No one seemed to have much to say. François was staring at the giant cliffs in the distance. Below them, the terrain between the cliffs was almost perfectly flat and smooth. Aside from an occasional level drop and a few dried-out riverbeds, the surroundings resembled the flat floor of a dried-up lake, with the immense cliffs stretching far behind the horizon. Several kilometers high in some places, the magnitude of the geology of the Valles Marineris region was absolutely breathtaking. The facade to the left of them was only a few kilometers away and towered far above, as if trying to reach the sky itself. Occasional vertical cracks and crevices in the walls of the rock face revealed long narrow passages into the gigantic feature. François was suddenly jolted out of his seat by a sudden road bump.

"Hey, watch the road, Schumacher!"

"Sorry, I just didn't see that boulder," replied Dedrick, looking a bit startled himself.

"Were you day-dreaming again?" asked François, with a touch of sarcasm in his voice.

"No, I… I was just... Ah, never mind! I'm fine. We're almost there."

Sitting in the back right between the two of them, Sabrina was adjusting her helmet when a bright flash caught the corner of her left eye.

"Hey! What was that? Dedrick! Stop the rover. Dedrick!!"

"What is it?" he replied, while slowing down.

"I saw something. In the cliff. We just passed it."

"What are you talking about?" asked François.

"I'm telling you, I saw a flash."

"A flash?"

"Yes, a flash. We have to go back. Turn around, I'll show you."

Dedrick and François looked at each other. The Frenchman gave the Russian a doubtful smirk, obviously not convinced.

"Maybe it was just the sun reflecting on the window of the rover," suggested Dedrick.

"Or maybe it was a Martian taking pictures," added François with a silly grin on his face.

"I know what I saw, guys. Dedrick, we have to go back."

"OK, Sabrina. Because I like you."

Tracing a big circle, Dedrick drove the rover around a large boulder and back the way they had come. They quickly reached the spot where Sabrina had just seen the light.

"I don't see anything," said François.

"I'm telling you. It was right here, just to the left of that crevice," Sabrina replied assertively, pointing at a wide vertical fissure in the face of the rock.

"Go back again, the other way, like when we passed it the first time."

Executing another grand U-turn, Dedrick drove the rover back in the other direction. This time, all three saw it. A bright flash, as if the sun was reflecting off a mirror, or a very shiny surface of some kind. He stopped the rover dead on its tracks. Slowly backing up, he placed ARC 2 right in the path of the ray.

"See? What did I tell you?" said Sabrina satisfactorily.

The two men were silent for a moment, staring at the brightness in the cliff.

"A piece from MF3?" wondered François out loud.

"No way. We're too far from the crash site," replied the Russian.

"What else?"

"Whatever it is, we didn't put it there," mentioned Sabrina.

"OK... So, what do you think it is then?" asked François.

"I don't know," she replied, shrugging her shoulders. "Maybe some kind of reflective mineral; a gemstone deposit of sorts, perhaps. Obviously, something we haven't come across yet."

"*This could be an interesting,*" thought Dedrick.

"Well, I guess we might as well go see, then," said François.

"I guess we might as well," seconded the female geologist.

Without another word, the team started putting on their suits. After making sure everyone was ready, Dedrick released the door locks, and they stepped out of the vehicle. On closer inspection, it appeared the source of the light was quite far from them, a good hundred plus meters into the passage ahead. The rover was too wide and the terrain too treacherous to enter this narrow crevice. They would have to go explore on foot. They each had enough oxygen for three hours outside the rover. The ground in the fissure was littered with rocks of all sizes, most of them piled up along the sides, as if dropped from above by an earthquake, or in this case a "marsquake" to be exact.

Reaching for the side of his helmet to turn on his radio, Dedrick called the station.

"We have come across an 'item' we want to go check. It's in a trench in sector 42-21. I'm gonna turn my suit camera on to record what we see. The terrain is too rough for ARC 2, so we're going on foot. If we lose you, we'll make sure to stay out of communication range no longer than a few minutes."

"OK Dedrick. But you know how I don't like not having you on my screen when you guys go off the scheduled route, so be quick!"

replied Ladli.

"We'll do."

"I think she just can't stand to be away from me, if you ask me," said François with a silly smirk.

Sabrina simply rolled her eyes at him through her helmet.

For the most part, the path they were walking on, although obstructed in many places by giant boulders, was manageable. Dedrick was ahead of the small group, following the most logical and least demanding path through the messy landscape. Sabrina was right behind him and François, a few meters to their left, was zig-zagging unnecessarily through the obstacles, just because he couldn't do anything like everyone else.

"You're wasting your energy and your oxygen, François," had told him Sabrina a few times already.

"I figured out what we're looking for. It's a Chinese tourist taking pictures. I'm just making sure is not hiding behind a boulder."

"Oh my gosh, you can be SO annoying sometimes!" she had finally said, fed up.

After a few minutes, the small speakers in their helmets emitted a few "cracks" and "buzzes," and a broken voice came through, barely discernible.

"Ded—crack-- I'm starting to los—buzz-buzz. Dedrick, crack--buzz-- hear me?"

"Ladli, I can barely hear you. I guess we're about to lose you. I'll get back in touch in five minutes at most. I promise! Ladli? Did you get that?"

"Dedrick, I –crack—crack—buzz—buzzzzz. OK, don't spend--buzz--time-- crack—need. I'll st—sssssssssshhhhhhhhhhh..."

"Sounds like we've lost her for good," said Sabrina.

"I'm afraid so. We'd better hurry. It looks like we're still a good third of the way from the source. François, come on!"

With renewed determination, the three started walking again. The passage was getting narrower the deeper they went. The sun was now hitting only parts of the cliff above them, and the reflection was gone. Relying on his wrist locator, Dedrick kept moving in the direction of the bulky rock he believed the light had originated from. The trench was hundreds of meters tall. Almost completely vertical, the cliff walls were full of jagged edges and uneven features. Between them, boulders of all sizes were littering the ground. Some as big as a small house. That, in itself, looked strange to Dedrick. Most of the geology in Candor Chasma was ancient and had not changed in millions of years. But this crevice, although in some ways similar to others in the area, looked as if something had happened there in a much more recent past. Could Mars have had seismic activity more recently than planetologists previously thought? Scientists on Earth, Dedrick had learned during his training, believed Mars was a dead planet, and had been so for most of its life. The rocky world had barely changed at all in billions of years. Earthquakes and other major geological changes were believed to have ceased long, long ago. Dedrick had a strange feeling about this small canyon. Something he could not explain.

Most of the landscape surrounding them was the same monotonous reddish hue found everywhere else on Mars. On occasion, a darker stone, or the lighter surface of a broken section, added some welcomed variety. They were walking through a desert of rocks and boulders, occasionally leaving clear foot prints in small ponds of dust scattered across their path. The whole area was in shadows, the sun having already moved high up the cliffs of the canyon behind them. Outside their suits, the temperature had already dropped below minus sixty Celsius, and the ancient landscape seemed completely indifferent to the intruders. A few minutes later, they were right underneath a rocky bulge, protruding out of the otherwise fairly flat cliff face.

"You're sure that's it?" said François. "I don't see anything shinny."

"I know," said Dedrick. "The sun is not on it anymore, but I'm sure that's the spot."

"Well, I don't see how we can possibly get up there without a crane or some giant ladder, two things we do not have. That terrace must be at least a hundred meters above us, maybe more. There's no way we can climb this cliff, it's way too steep."

"There's another way, from above." interjected Sabrina.

"From above? And how do you propose we get there?" replied François amused, pointing at the rock wall. "You expect us to fly up there?"

"Don't be silly. I think we can get there from behind the cliff, with the rover. Hold on… I'm almost positive we've already been to that side in sector…let me see...42-23. Yep, my pad agrees. Sector 42-

23 is right behind that cliff," she said with confidence, looking at a small computer pad in her right hand.

"I think we can make it in less than forty-five minutes if we leave now. It's a big loop, but once there, we should be able to lower ourselves with the tow cable," she added with a touch of excitement in her voice.

"Sounds a bit hazardous, if you ask me. And how long is the cable, anyway? Looks like we're gonna need a good sixty meters of it to reach that terrace from the plateau above," commented Dedrick, looking up awkwardly through his helmet.

"You know what? I think that's a great idea. The rover's tow cable is eighty meters long, just so you know," said François looking at Dedrick. "And we do have a basket in the back. It's just what we need!" Turning his attention back on the cliffs above, he added, "We still have a few hours of daylight, right? I say we go for it. I'd really like to know what's up there…"

Dedrick looked again at the high-perched terrace. "Yeah, w*hat IS up there?"*

"Well?" asked François.

"OK, I guess we have some time left, but only if the terrain on the other side is practical. Any possibility of danger and we turn around."

"Yes captain!" said the Frenchman sarcastically, with a salute.

#

A few minutes later, in the control room of Mars First, the radio started to make sporadic sounds again...

"Shhh--Ladli? Lad—crack--Buzz--Can youshhsh—buzzz--me?--zzz--Crack!"

"Dedrick? Dedrick? Do you copy?"

"Buzz---sssshhhhh----"

"Dedrick? Where are you guys? Are you OK?"

"Crack-buzz-- before we --buzz--come back buzz—"

"Dedrick, I did not get that. Please repeat!"

"Buzz—said we're walking back to the rov—crack-sector 42-23 before we come backrrrack--"

"Dedrick, you are still breaking up. What about sector 42-23?"

"I said we're walking back to the rover now. But there's something we need -sshhh- check before we come back. We're moving to sector 42-23. Did you get that?"

"Ten-four, Dedrick. Loud and clear now. Glad to have you back. I hate not knowing what you guys are doing when you're out there, you know that."

"I know, Ladli. I promise, we'll be careful, and we'll stay in contact at all times. I don't think we'll have a loss of signal in that sector. We'll be high up. Another thing, I'm sending you a few images taken by my camera of the canyon we were just in. Can you upload everything to the main computer and run a complete analysis?"

"You got it. What did you find? And why sector 42-23? You were scheduled to go to sector 50-16 today."

"I know. I'll explain later. We only have so much daylight left. I'll talk to you in a few minutes, when we get to the plateau. Dedrick out."

Climbing in the rover, Sabrina, Dedrick, and François started moving toward the sector 42-23. It was an uneventful drive of just under eight kilometers. Climbing slowly the low grade of the cliff's gentle slope, the rover and its passengers eventually reached the top, near the edge of the plateau they had been looking at from below earlier. Dedrick maneuvered the rover to face the edge of the precipice, leaving a good ten meters between the vehicle and the sheer drop. After putting his helmet back on, he then walked to the back of the rover to get the basket. With François' help, the two attached the carrier to the hook at the end of the cable coming down from the overhead winch. The basket was now dangling in front of the rover, about two meters up in the air.

Sabrina soon joined the two men at the front of the vehicle.

"So, who wants to go first?" asked François.

"Someone has to stay up here to control the winch," Dedrick said.

"I'll stay!" volunteered Sabrina quickly. She was not looking forward to stepping into the abyss, now that she could see it from above.

"I thought this was your idea?!" said François teasingly. He knew very well how she felt about heights.

Turning in the general direction of the station, Dedrick called Ladli on his helmet communicator. Vera, who had now joined Ladli in the control pod, answered.

"Don't worry, love. I promise we're just gonna go down for a quick look, and we won't leave the basket unless it is absolutely safe to do so. I have no intention of missing dinner tonight."

"You better not!" she replied.

After telling her about the shiny object they had spotted earlier, and how they intended to get to it, "very carefully," he had promised, she had reluctantly agreed. She wasn't happy about them taking unnecessary risks, but she knew Dedrick and François too well to argue. No matter what anyone could say, those two always ended up doing what they wanted, anyway.

"Check your feed every five minutes, no matter what. I know your helmet will be constantly sending me images, but I also want to monitor your vital signs. All three of you!" she ordered.

"I knew you cared about me, Vera darling," said François.

"I'm sorry. What was that, François?"

"Don't worry about it. It's just François talking nonsense, as usual," said Sabrina. "I'll stay in visual contact with them. Don't worry," she added.

"OK then, we better get going," said Dedrick.

Following François to the rover's forward crane, Dedrick waited his turn to climb on top of the arm, as the two men made their way carefully into the basket. Securing himself into position, Dedrick gave the OK for Sabrina to start driving the rover closer to the edge, above the cliff. Giving the two one last wave and wishes of good luck, Sabrina engaged the winch motor, and the basket slowly began its descent down into the abyss. Carefully lowering them at a pace of about half a meter per second, Sabrina was following the basket and its cargo on her dashboard screen, thanks to the camera mounted on the crane's arm.

Dedrick was trying to locate the protruding rocky outcrop they had located from below. If there were in the right place, it had to be about fifty meters directly under them. But the view from above was significantly different. It was hard to recognize the cliffs features, and looking down with their suits on was difficult without feeling a bit noxious. They were quite high, and the basket kept rocking, at times dangerously, at any movement the passengers made.

After descending for a couple of minutes, Dedrick told Sabrina to stop the winch.

"Are you there? Did you find the spot? Dedrick?... François?"

A few seconds passed. Vera and Ladli were also listening.

"What's going on Sabrina?" asked Vera. "Why aren't they answering you? Do you have them on your monitor?"

"Yes, they're still in the basket. I've just stopped the winch. They should be able to hear us calling. They're just sitting there, not moving. I can't see their faces, but I think they are staring at the cliff in front of them. Dedrick?" she asked again.

"Dedrick? François? Come on guys, what's going on?" asked Vera as well.

"I know you can hear me," added Sabrina.

Down in the basket, Dedrick and François were dead silent. They dared not even move a centimeter. They were looking at something they could not yet comprehend. Staring at a recess in the face of the cliff directly in front of them, about fifteen meters in depth and just as wide, they were transfixed. The terrace in front of them was perfectly level and smooth, and the flawless shape of the cliff walls around it left no doubt it was not a natural formation. The precision of the perfectly spherical ceiling and back wall was in absolute contrast with the rugged look of the surrounding rock face. But it wasn't the amazing architecture of the place that baffled them the most. On the leveled floor of the encavement, a perfect spherical ball, about two meters in diameter, stood right in the center, partially buried into the ground. Its casing was light in color and appeared to be made of some high-glossy material. Its very top was partially covered by a thin layer of dust.

"That's impossible!" finally said Dedrick, breaking the silence.

"Well, it's right there, so...I'd say it IS possible," replied François pointing at it. "I admit, though…I don't understand what I'm looking at, either. I… I thought we were the first ones on Mars. Do you think the Chinese could've...? No, we would've known about it."

Back in ARC 2, Sabrina could hear both men clearly. "Guys? Guys? What's going on? Talk to me…"

Sixty meters below, Dedrick, still in shock, turned slowly to François.

"No, you don't understand. I've seen this. In my dream! That's what's impossible!"

"Guys! Hello! What are you talking about? Is this another one of your silly routines? This is no time for jokes! Please, talk to me!"

"Sorry Sabrina. I…I hear you. I'm not sure how to describe what we're seeing… There's something down here. It's a... it looks artificial, but we have no idea what it is. I…I've never seen anything like it," François replied.

"What? Right! OK, I see. Dedrick, what is going on down there??" she asked with frustration, guessing François was pulling one of his stupid pranks on her again.

"Sure, but he'll tell you the same thing."

"It's true, Sabrina. We've found something. I can't tell you what. I don't know what we're looking at either. I'm not even sure it's man made. It looks...alien," replied Dedrick.

"I'm sorry, what? Did you say alien?! You mean like little green men? Those kinds of aliens?" She was almost laughing, and had it not been for the fact that she knew Dedrick to well to play along with François on this one, she would have dismissed the whole thing in a heartbeat. But Dedrick sounded very serious and that worried her.

"Sabrina, I'm serious, we've found something, something impossible..." Dedrick added.

"OK, that's it. I'm pulling you guys back up."

Engaging the winch, Sabrina slowly started pulling the basket and its contents back up the cliff. She was watching them on the monitor, waving their arms and babbling something but she wasn't listening. She had already switched her radio to the Mars First station and was talking with Vera.

"I'm telling you. I think it's the altitude or something. They don't make any sense. Anyway, we'll be heading home soon. I'm pulling them up as we speak."

. A few minutes later, the two men were getting inside the rover. Sabrina had already moved to the back seat and relayed to Vera that something was wrong with the guys' suits. Their oxygen mix was probably off, and they were both starting to get delirious, she had told her. Vera was already planning to take the two men under medical observation, as soon as they got back.

Dedrick and François had complained about getting pulled back so soon, but eventually agreed it was time to head back to base anyway. In fact, they needed to regroup and get more supplies before returning to the site. There was some planning to do. For now, the Russian man was thinking while his French teammate was babbling away…

"What was that thing down there? You really think it's alien? And what did you mean when you said you've seen that place before in your dreams? How is that even possible? We've never been to that cliff. We've never even been near it!"

Sabrina listening to them from the back seat said, "OK. Seriously, guys. What is going on?"

Keeping an eye on the terrain in front of him, François tried to answer, "Sabrina, we're serious. We don't know what we've found, but whatever it is, it's like nothing I've ever seen before. There's this circular room and in the middle, there's that big shinny sphere and-"

"François! Stop it! It's not funny anymore. I'm starting to worry. If it's another one of your pranks..." she started saying, but Dedrick cut her off.

"Sabrina, we're telling you the truth. Look!"

Having connected his suit to the rover's computer, he punched in a command on the small keyboard on his left wrist, and a picture appeared on the rover's dashboard.

There it was, not as clear as they had seen it, the camera in Dedrick's helmet wasn't the best at filming in low light, but the circular recess and the orb at its center could clearly be seen. The central object, of an off-white color, definitely looked artificial, but not man-made. Something about it looked out of this world. Sabrina couldn't figure out what. But there it was; whatever it was. She couldn't believe it, yet it was true. She was looking right at it. She kept shaking her head and rubbing her eyes, as if trying to clear the image from her vision.

"I don't believe it. That's...that's impossible!" she finally said dumbfounded.

"I know, that's what we said too, but I'm telling you, it is really down there," assured François, without looking at the screen.

"We need to upload both our suit videos to the main computer as soon as we get back. I guess we're gonna have one hell of a story to tell the others…" added Dedrick.

#

By the time they were back at the base, everyone inside knew something had happened. They just didn't know what. Ladli and Vera had told the small group what they could.

"I don't know. What Dedrick told me didn't make any sense. Sabrina first thought something was wrong with their suits. Then, she started telling me this wild story about an object in the cliffs... Now I'm wondering if her suit isn't acting up as well. All I know is, we need to get them immediately to the infirmary, as soon as they are through the vacuum chamber," finished Vera.

The rover finally arrived in front of the garage. Ladli opened the gate. After driving into the dwelling, the door slowly closed behind them, and François parked the rover in its designated spot. The three passengers stepped out of the vehicle and headed for the pressure hatch. After the light above the hatch had turned green, signaling that they could now breathe without their helmets, they removed their suits, threw them into the sterilizing chamber, and proceeded through another hatch into the station, where they were immediately assaulted and dragged to the infirmary by their colleagues, amid protests and threats, mostly from François.

Two hours later, all eight members were assembled in the main lobby of the station. Dedrick was standing by a desk, looking around the room at his teammates. They were scattered here and there on pillows or kneeled on the floor. Two-and-a-half-year-old Chasma was resting in her mother's arms on the small couch. Everyone was quiet, listening attentively to Dedrick.

"As most of you already know, we have found something in sector 42-21. Earlier this morning, Sabrina, François, and I were on a routine excursion to Candor Chasma. Around 11:20, we spotted a light in the cliff's face, a reflection of sorts about seventy meters up above the floor of the ravine. Unable to reach it from below, we decided to access the location from above, by going around through sector 42-23, right here. He was pointing at a topographic map of the area on the screen behind him. After Sabrina lowered François and me, we came across what looked like a small niche. What really got our attention is how unusually proportionate and flawless the carved recess looks. I think we can rule out a natural formation. And that's not all..."

Turning to the large monitor behind him, Dedrick pressed a few buttons on the computer keypad below. A clear image of the orb appeared on the screen, and those in the group who had not seen the images yet, gasped. Staring, incredulous, they all watched the footage taken by François and Dedrick's helmet cams in silence for several seconds. And then, everyone started asking questions, all at once.

"What is it?"

"Is that-?"

"That's impossible!"

Dedrick waited a few seconds before waving everyone to calm down.

"No, we don't know what it is. The computer has analyzed the footage and came back with nothing. It's obviously nothing we've ever encountered before. I'm not sure what to make of it, but I think we need to go back with the right tools and study the place thoroughly. And we should explore the area around as well. It may not be the only artifact there."

"You think there could be others like it?"

"I don't know. I'm just saying we should check."

"I'm sorry, did I miss something? Are you saying this is some kind of alien machine?" asked Vera, confused.

"Not necessarily, I'm just saying we've found something. I have no idea how it got there, or who put it there, or why. But there it is. And if we want to find answers, I think we need to go back. As Sabrina mentioned to some of you earlier, we believe the object has been partially buried there, untouched, for quite some time, judging by the amount of debris and dirt at its base. It could be thousands of years old for all we know. I propose we put a team together and take two rovers back there tomorrow. A couple of us will need to stay here with Chasma, of course. I think we should figure that out right now, so we can all prepare for tomorrow."

After making plans on who was going, what to bring and what time they would leave, Dedrick finally added: "I suggest we all get some sleep. We have a long day ahead of us. See you all tomorrow. Goodnight."

Much later, lying next to Vera in his pod, Dedrick finally fell asleep, hoping he would not have his nightmare again.

The Sphere

The next day's weather conditions had prevented the group from leaving the base. Several dust storms had rendered the visibility too poor to attempt any outing. The group had stayed put, and shared a few laughs, and tears, watching Charlie Chaplin's The Gold Rush and The Kid. The two black and white movies from the silent movie era had been enthusiastically suggested by François, when he had found the listing in the station's library.

Luckily, today's weather conditions were looking much more promising, and the anxious and impatient explorers couldn't wait to get on their way to the new discovery.

Less than forty-five minutes after sunrise, the two rovers and their five passengers were leaving the garage, in route for sector 42-23. Sabrina and Vera had chosen to stay behind. Someone had to man the station. Vera had preferred to stay with Chasma. Sabrina, having been there the previous day, had opted to do the same, seven if she had not seen the sphere in person yet. There would be a next time.

Rover 2, occupied by Dedrick and François, was leading the way, ARC 3 in tow.

They arrived at the cliff in record time. After securing the basket to the winch, Dedrick and Liu headed down first and sent the carrier back. The next two passengers, Ladli and Tendai, soon followed. François, having already been on the site, had offered to stay up above with the rovers to control the winch. As they reached the site, Dedrick helped Ladli climb out of swinging basket. Liu was too mesmerized by the sight to help. After carefully securing their footing on the level terrace, the four found themselves facing a site like none they had ever seen. For a moment, no one said a word. At the center of the space, the large spherical artifact was mesmerizing. The floor of the shell-shaped niche was surprisingly flat and smooth. Now seeing the enclosure for themselves, the newcomers had no more doubt. It could not have been carved naturally. Liu slowly approached the object in the middle, transfixed.

She kneeled and stared at it for a moment. Its lower portion was partially buried in and surrounded by a thick band of dirt. The surface of the object was perfectly smooth and round, and void of any imperfections.

"Tendai, can you hand me a scanner, please?" she finally asked.

Reaching into the carry-on bag, Tendai grabbed the instrument and handed it to her.

"Thanks."

"Guys, before we do anything…" interjected Dedrick, "I just want to remind you that we really know nothing of this thing, so I suggest we all proceed with extreme caution, at least until we can figure out exactly what we are dealing with here. Just be careful, OK?"

"OK," replied Liu. The other two nodded in their helmets.

The four got to work. Kneeling next to Liu, Tendai pulled a small rod from his tool pocket, and slowly pushed the blunt object in the dirt near the base of the massive sphere. The dirt was dry and cracked in places, but he noticed with surprise that all the cracks appeared to be moving away from the "orb," as Ladli had called it. Something was definitely unique about the ground surrounding the artifact. Meticulously scanning the object with her thermal imaging instrument, Liu was also surprised by the inconsistencies of the readings. The multi-colored picture on the screen was fluctuating widely, registering huge temperatures changes within seconds. Ladli, staring at the rocky wall behind them, was absolutely amazed at its perfect geometry. She ran her gloved hand on the smooth surface, trying to imagine what tool or machine could have created such an even cut, as dust displaced by her fingers fell to the ground. Dedrick, standing a few steps behind her, suddenly noticed something above her head.

"Guys! Look!"

They all turned.

In the sunlight now partially hitting the back of the recess, a shape was starting to emerge. Large geometric lines and grooves were gradually becoming more and more distinct as the rising sun was quickly engulfing the large terrace. Although the large carving and its deep lines were covered by layers of Martian sand and dirt, the entire sculpture was quickly becoming well defined. It had to be a door or gate of sorts.

Dedrick dropped his analyzer to the ground. His mouth half open, he couldn't believe his eyes. There it was, the door in his dream, exactly as he remembered it. The huge feature, covered with strange markings and enigmatic shapes, was standing in front of him, as real and solid as the rocky cliff itself.

"What is that?" asked Tendai.

"Whatever it is, there's absolutely no doubt in my mind it's not man-made," calmly replied Ladli.

"I totally agree... This is amazing!" concurred Liu with excitement.

"I can't believe we are looking at an alien structure. Do you realize what this means? This is definite proof we are not alone in the universe. This is unbelievable!" Tendai couldn't wrap his mind around it.

"I think we should clear the dirt off this door. I want to see what this thing really looks like." finally said Ladli.

"No, wait! You can't just..."

But before Dedrick could do anything, the Irish woman, a brush already in hand, started cleaning away.

"See? Nothing! I'm still alive! Stop worrying and come help," she said with a smile, without looking at him.

Tendai and Liu grabbed a brush and joined her. The three began dusting off all the grooves and crannies they could find. They couldn't easily reach the last meter at the top, but after a few minutes, most of the alien door was standing in front of them, massive and imposing, its intricate markings now clearly defined and visible. Carved right out of the rock face, the door was covered from top to bottom with lines crisscrossing in all directions, making up intricate designs and geometric shapes that all met at a single point in its center. Several centimeters deep in places, a handful of the lines disappeared outside the portal frame, into the floor of the terrace. The outside groove of the large structure appeared to continue deep into the wall, suggesting it was detached from the rock face and had to move in some way.

"What do you think?" asked Liu, looking at the others.

"It's definitely a door of some kind," offered Ladli.

"I agree. Now the question is, how do we open it?"

There was no handle, no lever, no mechanism of any kind, as far as she could tell.

"Whoa! Are we sure we want to do that?" interjected Tendai.

"How else are we supposed to find out where it goes? It's right here, begging for us to."

"Could be dangerous..." Dedrick seconded.

"In the words of François, there's only one way to find out," offered Ladli, as she raised her arm toward it.

"Wait!" But Dedrick's protesting was futile.

Pushing as hard as she could against the doorway, she tried desperately to make the large feature barge, to no avail. Giving up, she began pressing her gloved fingers over a few promising spots, including the central point where all the lines seemed to meet, hoping to find a secret lock, without any success. She stepped back somewhat disappointed and looked again attentively at the impressive frame. It just stood there like a giant puzzle towering over them, and she ached to solve it.

"I don't get it. There's gotta be a way…" she finally said.

"Maybe it doesn't open," suggested Liu.

"What else could it be?

"Actually, Liu has a good point. How do we know for sure it's a door? I mean, it may look like one to us, but maybe it was something else entirely to those who carved it. Maybe it's simply a sculpture of some kind, meant as a display, similar to some of the monuments we have, back on Earth." added Tendai.

"No, it's a door," finally volunteered Dedrick.

"How do you know that?"

"Because, I've seen it in my dreams."

"In your dreams? What do you mean, you've seen it in your dreams?" asked a baffled Tendai.

All three were now staring intensely at Dedrick.

"Well?"

He took a big breath. "I know this is going to sound nuts, but for the past few years now, I've been having this recurring dream… I'm at my uncle's house, back in Russia, and I'm being chased by this odd-looking man. Eventually, we end up in front of the exact same door. The stranger opens it and drags me in," he said, looking at them hesitantly.

Perplexed, Tendai stared at the commander, wondering if he had really understood what Dedrick had just said.

"OK, you're just messing with us, right?"

"No joke. I'm just telling you guys the truth. I don't understand any of it either. I've never been here before, but I have seen this door, many times."

"How come you've never mentioned this before?"

"Not really something I felt like sharing. Only Vera and François know."

"Well…actually… I know about it too," volunteered Liu, in a timid voice.

"What? How?" asked Dedrick, shocked.

"Vera told me. But please don't tell her I told you. She made me promise to never tell anyone. It was a few years ago. She said it was getting worse and she was worried about you."

"Great! That's just great," simply commented Dedrick. "Well, I guess everyone knows now."

After a short silence, Ladli returned to the subject at hand.

"OK then, how do we open this thing, boss?"

"I don't know. In my dream, the man chasing me just waves his hand in front of it, and it just opens."

"I see." Tendai sounded a bit skeptical.

"Ok, then." Facing the gate, Ladli began waving her hands in front of it, drawing different shapes in the air, first slowly, then faster, but nothing happened. "OK, what am I doing wrong?"

"I guess I should've also mentioned that the man has this small object in his hand, a smaller version of the sphere here, and a ray of light comes out and…it's difficult to describe. Anyway, there's a good chance we need that to open it," replied Dedrick.

"I see. So, all we need is a sphere that shoots out a 'magical' ray of light. Well, that shouldn't be too hard to find. I'll just go down to the local store. I'll be right back!" said Tendai sarcastically.

"Ha ha. Very funny," said Ladli, unimpressed.

"Maybe we're supposed to do something with THAT sphere…" Liu was pointing at the large object in the middle of the terrace.

"Maybe, but I don't know what," replied the Russian. "And maybe it's just beyond us. We really don't know what we're doing, here. There's a good chance only those who put it there know."

"Maybe you missed something. What else can you remember from your dream?" asked him Ladli.

"Guys? What's going on down there? Somebody talk to me, please!" a voice came on everyone's earpiece.

"Hey François! Are seeing what we're seeing? Can you believe it? It's just incredible," replied Tendai.

"No, I'm not. I lost signal about ten minutes ago. I've been calling you since then. I was about to come down there myself. All I have is the view on the two baskets from up here. Glad to finally have you back! What happened?"

"Shoot! We had no idea. We thought you were following everything from up there. Aren't you getting the camera feeds?" said Dedrick.

"François? François? I think he's lost us again," he said turning to the small crew.

"No... I'm... I'm here..." he said slowly, in a low voice. He was sitting in the rover, mesmerized by the images he was finally viewing for the first time on the monitor in front of him. Switching randomly from camera to camera between the crew's helmets, he couldn't quite believe what he was looking at.

"I'm looking at the images right now. What is that... thing on the wall?" he finally asked.

"We don't know. We're guessing it's some kind of door."

"It looks so...big." He didn't know what else to say, he was at a complete loss. "And what are all these markings? I've never seen anything like it..."

"We're not sure."

"Oh, look!!" Liu was pointing at the large orb in the middle of the small group. The sun had finally reached the spherical object, and the large orb appeared to be radiating from within. They all took a few steps back.

"Ok, that's new," voiced Ladli.

A thin gas-like substance began to form on the sphere's surface. Gradually spreading over the whole object, the purple haze slowly started churning and glowing. The site was mesmerizing.

"Dedrick?" called out Liu worried.

"What do we do?" asked Tendai, feeling just as uneasy.

They stared a while at the captivating display. Ladli, finally finding the strength to pry her eyes away, glanced again at the door. Still nothing. She suddenly had an idea. "*Maybe it will open now...*" She turned back her attention on the alien door and began waving her hands in front it again. But still nothing happened.

"Liu, what do you have on the infrared scan?" asked Dedrick.

The Korean biochemist raised the analyzer toward the sphere. "Nothing. No heat signature. Apparently, it's completely cold. That's weird..." she puzzled.

"Weird? Of course it's weird. Everything is. Look at this place. I'm really not sure coming down here was such a good idea, after all."

Tendai sounded genuinely concerned, now.

"I don't know what to think, here," continued Liu. "This thing was pegging like crazy earlier. Now, it's like… it's not even there!"

"Dedrick?! What are you doing?" Ladli was watching the tall Russian approach the sphere, his hand extended in front of him.

"It's OK. I just want to check something."

"Dedrick?"

Kneeling next to the large round object, he gently pressed his hand down, and slowly moved it across the smooth surface. His teammates unconsciously held their breath. The purple vapor parted easily around his glove, creating undulating waves all around the object, like ripples in a pond. Checking the Thermal readings again, Liu barely noticed a rise in temperature. Keeping his and on the sphere, Dedrick turned around and stared at the door on the wall behind him with disappointment. He removed his hand, and the glowing gas reclaimed the space his glove had just occupied.

"Well, so much for that idea."

For the next half hour, the group kept observing, and trying to interact with, the alien artifact and its surrounding. But they didn't really learn anything else. The sphere seemed to react to sunlight. That much was established. As for the gas, its purpose was a mystery.

"Guys? I was wondering if one of you would mind heading back up here, so I can take a look down there. I'd love to see that thing up close."

"Sure, François. I'll come up!" offered Tendai right away.

"Thanks, buddy."

A few minutes later, the Frenchman was down in the recess with the others. Tendai was glad to be away from the area. He had suggested to Ladli to follow him up, but she was too enthralled by the alien place to leave yet. Back in ARC 3, Tendai was updating Sabrina on François' whereabouts.

"Yeah, he just went down there to check it out. I'm telling you, the place might be ancient, but that sphere is definitely not. It's like someone put it there yesterday." He was talking to her on the rover's main monitor, while keeping an eye on the small group on the other screen.

"Wow! It's all so surreal…" She was staring at the images as well, from back home.

"Personally, I think we should leave the whole thing alone. We really don't know what we're doing. Who knows what that sphere is for? And if we can't open that door, that...portal, or whatever you want to call it, maybe it's a good thing. Maybe, what's inside is dangerous. Who knows? Either way, I really don't think we should mess around with it. I mean, we're talking about alien technology here. We're way over our heads, here. This is pure madness."

"You have a point, but how else do you want to find out what it is? Aren't you the least bit curious?" replied Sabrina.

"I am, but I'm not sure it's worth the risk."

"Don't worry Tendai, I don't think we're gonna stay much longer," mentioned Dedrick who could hear their conversation in his headset. "OK, let's make sure we have all the footage and pictures we need, and let's pack," he added to his three colleagues down below.

"Hey, Tendai?"

"Yes?"

"Can you ask François to bring back some samples from the enclosure, if he can? A few rocks would be nice."

"Sure. Hey, François? Sabrina would like you to bring back a few rocks."

"You got it."

He carefully approached the edge of the terrace, grabbed a small hammer out of the tool kit and began chiseling away. After getting a few pieces into a small container, he sat a moment on the edge, his feet dangling above the abyss. Across from him, the other side of the narrow canyon was already in the shadows. Far up above, the sun had begun its descent beyond the plateau. Looking down at his feet hanging above the canyon below, he realized it would not be long before the shadow, cast by the facing cliff, had reached them too.

"What are you doing?" asked Dedrick.

"I was just admiring the view." He got back up and rejoined the others.

Within minutes, the sunlight began to move back up the wall of the terrace, and the purple glow around the sphere disappeared.

"I guess we should start heading back soon. We only have an hour left on our tanks, anyway," mentioned Dedrick.

Forty-five minutes later, they were all back in the rovers, leaving a long trail of dust behind them as they zoomed across the reddish landscape. Far in the distance, the sun was now setting behind the tall cliffs of Valles Marineris. Its light gradually shifting from bright yellow to soft orange, the ancient celestial object appeared to be following the racing rovers on their journey back, like a giant eye spying on the intruders. Occasionally reflecting on their windshields, its rays of deep rusty reds and crimsons cut through the canyons from above the immense geological formation, until it finally disappeared behind the high plateau above them.

That night, none of the Martian colonists would be able to sleep.

Chapter VII

Chasma

Crawling through one of the housing tubes between habitat three and its greenhouse, Chasma was holding her favorite doll, Sylvia that Vera had made for her almost four years earlier. Her long blonde hair flowing down her back, she had become quite a beautiful child. Everyone loved her on the base, and she was treated like a little princess everywhere she went. Something she loved, of course. She was turning five today, spoke three languages fluently, and a fourth one quite well. Her French was limited. François didn't like using his French and was a reluctant teacher, when it came to his native language. He always pretended he couldn't remember it very well, but they all knew he simply didn’t like to.

Chasma was of course fluent in English, the primary language of choice for all communication between members of the station, but her natural aptitude to juggling multiple languages showed already. She was also fluent in Russian and Spanish, and her Korean was good. She loved talking to each members of the base in their native tongue. She made a point to do so every day, and they all knew better than to tell her they were too busy, even if they truly were at times. François felt it was useless. They would never go back to Earth, so why bother? Regardless, she was relentless, always wanting to learn more, know more, and would chase them around the small base, asking questions and wanting answers. But her true interest was science. She would ask about the controls in the rover anytime she was allowed in the garage, or want to know how the water recycling systems worked. She was fascinated about the mechanics of the universe, why Mars' atmosphere was almost completely depleted of oxygen, how different gravity was on Jupiter and other planets, and how the universe was created. Another favorite subject was biology and all the different plants in the greenhouses. Every morning, she crawled her way to the lab to go check on the progress of the vegetable gardens, always making to stop by the Blobus Viscus aquariums, and last but not least, have a look at her favorite flowers in greenhouse III: The tomato flowers. The tomato plants made beautiful yellow flowers. It was the only flower growing on the station at the moment.

"Hola, Sabrina!"

"Hola, Chasma! Dormir bien?"

"Si. Y usted."

"Si, gracias! Desea ver las flores?"

"Si, por favor."

Walking through a path between rows of vegetable trays, they soon arrived at the spot where the tomato plants were grown. One plant in particular looked fuller and healthier than all others. There were even more flowers on it than the day before. Chasma loved looking at them, but she loved smelling them even more. Sabrina took Chasma in her arms and raised her up to help her sit on the table, right next to the plant beds, just as she did every morning. The young child leaned over to smell the closest flower to her.

"Ooooo! This one smells good, Sabrina!"

"Yes, it's a nice one; and big too!"

"It's my favorite!"

"Do you want it?"

"Oh, can I? Please, can I?" the girl asked all excited.

In truth, Sabrina had already planned to give her a flower from the batch that morning, for a good reason. Today was Chasma's birthday. In a few hours, the members of the small Martian station would gather in greenhouse II to celebrate her turning five.

A few minutes later, holding her beautiful flower in one hand and her doll, Sylvia, in the other, she burst into her parent's pod.

"Mommy, Mommy! Look!"

"Well, what do we have here? That's a beautiful flower, Chasma. Did Sabrina give it to you?"

"Yes, she said it was because it's my birthday today, Mommy. I'm five now, you know?"

"Yes, you are. You're a big girl, now."

Vera was kneeling in front of her daughter, adjusting the bow in her long blond hair when, coming back from a routine maintenance check, Dedrick entered the room.

Both turned.

"Hey!" he said, happily surprised to see them both there.

"Hi Daddy. Did you see my flower?"

"Very nice, Chasma. Where did you get such a gorgeous

flower?" Of course, he knew where it came from.

"Sabrina gave it to me for my birthday. I'm five now."

"Oh yeah, that's right. I almost forgot," he replied with a teasing smile.

#

When the small group, that now counted eight members, had first settled on Mars, each section of their habitat had been designed for a very specific function and usage by the Mars First engineers and architects. But after the loss of communication with Earth, the group had eventually taken advantage of their newfound freedom, and after relocating some resources, made four of their six pods their new living quarters. Dedrick, Vera, and Chasma, now slept together in pod 3, François and Sabrina were in pod 1, Ladli and Tendai occupied pod 2 and Liu had pod 4 all to herself. The new arrangements seemed to please everyone.

Although the compound counted three more pods, Greenhouse II had become the place of choice for occasional group meetings and special events. The largest of the three by a good meter, it was also the most centralized location in the small outpost. And if that had not been a good enough reason, the astronaut's craving for some well-deserved entertainment had been satisfied when François had pointed out that it was the only greenhouse with its own home theatre. A luxury the Frenchman had managed to setup a few months back.

Today was one of those special occasions. They had all gathered to discuss the possibility of taking Chasma with them on tomorrow's excursion. Not that Dedrick and Vera would have needed their teammates' approval, but they had all agreed years ago to share any decision that could affect the rest of the colony, and in such a small community, pretty much everything did. Although Chasma had been allowed to venture outside many times before, they had never taken her to the "Gate" before. Vera had never been very enthusiastic about letting her daughter go down the cliff side in one of the baskets. She was very protective of Chasma, understandably so considering the countless dangers of the hostile red world. Most of her resistance usually began by pointing out the fact that they had only one suit for her. If anything happened to it, she would never be able to go out on foot again. They knew she was right about that, of course, but as François had argued, what was the point of having it if she wasn't going to allow the child to use it?

Dedrick was looking at Sabrina and her Frenchman. The Guatemalan girl was seated on his lap, her arms around his neck. He had his around her waist.

"Personally, I think the more she knows and experiences, the better. Plus, she's gonna have to go out there, eventually. Why not now?" said François looking at Vera.

"She's been asking a lot about the alien place lately. We can't keep her away from it forever. I think it would be fair to let her come, if that's what she wants," added Sabrina.

"I don't know... She's so young and going down that ravine can be very dangerous. There is no margin for error out there. You all know that. Najib knew that."

She paused, realizing she didn't need to mention his name. She glanced at Liu Xing with a caring smile and turned her attention back to the rest of the group.

"I mean, I know I promised we would take her with us this time but..."

"Love, I understand how you feel. We all care about her, you know that. Chasma has proved how disciplined and attentive to details she can be, countless times. She knows the routine as well as any of us, by now. She's a smart girl, I know she'll be careful, and you know she's not easy to scare."

"That's the part that worries me."

"That's also a quality that can save her life someday."

"I would prefer it if she never had to. Sending her hanging above a precipice is not my idea of an ideal birthday present for our daughter, Dedrick. She's only five, for crying out loud!" she almost cried.

"Come on, Hun, you know how much Chasma wants to go."

"I...I know, you're right, I'm over reacting."

She took another look around the room. No one would ever care for Chasma more than this small group of people, and Vera knew it.

"I know how much you all care about Chasma and only want the best for her, and I love you all for it. Sometimes, my fear of losing her overcomes my sense of adventure and freedom; that same drive that brought us all here on Mars, in the first place. I want Chasma to experience life and its wonders to the fullest, even if our world is a giant desert. And I realize you are right, she deserves to see as much of it as we do. It's also her world."

She paused a moment and then, looking at Dedrick, she added, "You're right, I guess it's time. Let's take her with us tomorrow."

"Well, that settles it, then," finalized Dedrick.

Key Largo

The day was November 21, 2039. All eight of them had left the station in ARC 1 and 3, leaving no one behind. This was a first. Leaving the base unattended had always been a big no-no, especially after the incident with Tendai a few years earlier. Since then, there was always at least one crew member, besides Chasma, who stayed behind to hold the fort, and in most instances two. Since the crash of MF3 had happened on the same day Chasma was born, the team usually commemorated the astronauts' deaths a day earlier. The young girl had never been with them for that. It was time for her to go visit the MF3 memorial. They called the site "Key Largo," and for some reason, she had never wondered why until now.

"Mommy, what's Key Largo?'"

"Well, Key Largo is an island in Florida, one of the states in the US, and-"

"I know about Florida, Mom," cut her off Chasma, somewhat offended her mother thought she didn't.

"Yes, you do. That's right. Anyway, the people we're going to visit really liked that island and that's where they spent their last vacation together before coming to Mars. So, we decided to call the place where they rest now, Key Largo, in their honor."

Chasma knew some of the circumstances surrounding the crew's death, but not all the details. The colonists had told her a malfunction had caused the crash, and that the incident had happened long before her birth. Today, she would get a chance to see where the MF3 crew was buried. It also meant the group was going to take her to "The Gate."

#

"Are you OK, Chasma?"

"Yes, Mom, I'm fine. You don't have to ask me every time."

"I know. I'm just making sure. It's a long trip and the way is a bit bumpy at times."

"I don't mind."

They finally came to a stop at the foot of a slope. Not far away, four small pyramids made of large stacked up rocks were looking back at them. Shoulder high and looking strangely enigmatic, the evenly spaced monuments were hard to miss on the flat Martian landscape. They each featured a small niche, the size of a shoe box, where the colonists had put some of the astronauts' personal belongings they had managed to find after the crash. There was also a picture of each team member taken from the computer archives. Chasma stepped out of the rover holding her mother's hand, and the two began walking to the memorial.

A few minutes later, all eight humans were facing the site. Atop a small boulder in front of the pyramids, a white metallic plaque read the following:

"Here rest the body, spirit, and soul of our friends, brothers, sisters and colleague astronauts Ebba Andreasson, Jessie Bruun, Daniel Patel and Antonio Bardino. May their death not be forgotten, and their life celebrated for the true heroes they were. Pioneers in the conquest of space, they came to Mars and died on this day of November 22, 2034, in the name of all mankind. Stretching the limits of their world, and overcoming the fear of the unknown, they came in peace to explore new frontiers and a world yet unexplored. Mankind is forever in your debt, dear friends."

Dedrick stood in the middle of the small group, facing the fallen colleagues.

"…and we all miss you. We wish you could have seen all this with us. We've finally made good use of the panels we had found from your ship a few years back and managed to build another storage area behind the station. Most of it is built underground, right into the cliff behind the base. So, I guess we have you to thank for that too. Last week, the…"

While Dedrick was addressing the four monuments, the rest of the group had gathered around him in a tight crescent. Chasma was staring silently as the sunlight grazed the side of Jessie Bruun's tombstone. Jessie, team three's mission specialist, had just turned forty-one when the ship had finally left Earth. She was ecstatic and for good reasons. Her passionate love for Mars had inspired more interest in the project, during her astronaut training, than any other candidate ever had. She had the most infatuating personality of her group, and her looks didn't hurt, of course. She had many admirers, to say the least, and François had commented on her feminine charms more than once, which invariably made Sabrina jealous. Jessie Bruun had been the most disappointed of her team when their trip to Mars, originally scheduled for 2030, had been delayed, after the shocking news of Najib's death. She had also found herself quite affected by the astronaut's unexpected passing. But she had worked diligently at helping Mars First convince the powers at play to allow the next ship to launch, eventually getting her wish four years later. Tragically, her dreams of exploring the red planet had died with her when MF3 had crashed on Mars six months later, killing Jessie and her three teammates on board.

"...but that wasn't enough, I guess, so they had to kill everyone! So fucking stupid! We were so close! Leave it to the human race. Makes you wonder how we even got this far, doesn't it?" Dedrick's speeches invariably led to his frustration over Earth's ultimate demise, each time the colonists came to the MF3 site. They were all used to it by now, and no one cared to stop him. After all, he wasn't saying anything they didn't agree with. Although traveling to other stars had seemed a perfectly plausible future for humans to the visionaries of the twenty-first century, that scenario was very unlikely now. With only eight of them left, possibly the very last survivors of their doomed civilization, the universe would forever be left unexplored. And even though Chasma was proof life could go on, even here on Mars, chances were the small outpost would never offer more than a precarious dwelling, destined to eventually breakdown and die, them along with it. The base couldn't be expanded or even repaired, now that they couldn't get any more help from Earth. Eventually, something would need to be replaced, a computer would fail, a door seal would wear out. Whatever the cause, they too would disappear, ending the human saga forever, and they all knew it.

"...yet, somehow, we're still here. Eight small creatures, alone on Mars. That's quite a miracle in itself, isn't it?" He looked up at the sky. "Lars, if you can hear me, I hope you can see us now and are proud of yourself. You made this possible. You and your dream that we were meant for more; that we were explorers and meant to break through the barriers of our own atmosphere, travel millions of kilometers through space and begin anew, on another world. You helped humanity go further than anyone had ever before, and in doing so, as fate would have it, gave humanity a second chance. We will do our best to be worthy. We're going to survive, and we're going to grow. Chasma is the first child of Mars. But there will be more. We will make a better world, a smarter one, a peaceful one. We will make it worth all the efforts and all the losses."

He was staring at the landscape in the distance. The megalithic cliffs ahead letting giant beams of light cut through their plateau's crevices, some casting kilometer deep shadows across the flat plane below, offered a sight rivaling none. On a day like this, occasional dust devils and wind storms were common sights. But, to his surprise, those seemed strangely absent today. As if reading his thoughts, a light wind picked up for a few seconds, as if saying *"we'll see about that."*

Dedrick continued, "Today, we have a new visitor for you. Chasma… Chasma…?"

Only partially listening to her Dad, Chasma was staring at the picture of the dark-haired woman on one of the pyramids.

"Mommy, that's my birthday," she stated, pointing at the date on the inscription.

"You're right, sweetie. The MF3 accident happened the same day you were born. I guess it's time you knew."

"Did you know her, Je…ssie?"

"Yes, sweetie, I knew her. She was a wonderful person. I think you would've liked her very much. And you know what? She loved flowers too. She always had some in her room, back on Earth. And she was funny, gosh she was funny..."

Chasma was listening to her mother, watching her from below, when she noticed a few tears begin to roll down her face.

"I'm sorry, Mommy."

"I know, love, I know. It's OK."

She squatted down to take her daughter in her arms, only to realize how unpractical it was with both their suits on. She looked at Chasma through the glass front of her helmet for a moment, and finally asked with a smile, "Do you want to see something really cool?"

#

Each year since the fatal crash of Mars First 3, the colonists paid their tribute to their dead colleagues at grid C 12-4, aka Key Largo, where the largest portion of the ship had been recovered, and where the colonists had buried their fallen friends. Soon after the alien door's discovery, they had extended that visit to include a stop there as well each year. It was a logical decision since the Gate, as they called it, was less than half a mile away from the crash site.

For all, including the only true Martian on the red planet, today was going to be more special than anyone could have ever imagined. They had just arrived at the top of the plateau in sector 42-23, almost directly above the alien site.

"Chasma? Chasma??"

Everyone turned their attention to Dedrick who was calling his daughter with angst in his voice. The group was finishing setting up the rovers near the edge of the cliff when Dedrick realized the child was missing. After a quick look around, he climbed inside ARC 2 to check if the girl had gone back to the rover. To his disappointment, he only found François, who had beat him to it. She wasn't there. They had no more luck with ARC 1.

"She can't be far. Don't worry, we'll find her," said the Frenchman, trying to reassure Chasma's father. Now, everyone was searching as well.

"Chasma! Chasma!"

Vera, trying to stay focused and poised, was beside herself. Panic was gripping every inch of her body. The slope back down the way they had just driven up was too gentle and wide open for anyone to hide anywhere for several hundred meters, too far a distance for Chasma to have had the time to walk beyond. The other way, there was only the sheer drop of the abyss. Vera, suddenly imagining the worse, met Dedrick's eyes who had just had the same thought. He rushed to the edge of the plateau, praying to God he was wrong. After the initial fright of imagining she could have fallen off the edge, he reassured himself, slowly breathing again, when he saw nothing on the boulders far down below. He simply turned back to Vera and said, "No." He resumed his search, looking in every direction again. "*Where could she be? There's nowhere to go...*" He could clearly see the entire terrace they were standing on. The low south wall nearby was too smooth and even, to offer any nooks for Chasma to hide in, especially in her bright white suit.

"Chasma? CHASMA? Why isn't she responding? Her headset should be on... When was the last time anyone saw her? Vera, I thought she was with you?" he asked.

"I...I don't know. I do remember her next to me, but I was talking to Ladli and..."

"Hey guys, what about here?"

Liu was pointing at a small break to their left, at the edge of the plateau, right where the south wall met the abyss. Dedrick rushed to the area. A small portion of the ledge seemed to wrap around the rock face at that corner, but the ground was missing where a slab of rock had broken off. He couldn't believe he had never noticed it before. To his defense, one had to be just at the right distance and angle from it to see the gap. Still, for a moment, he wondered if the damage could have happened recently. It seemed unlikely, but more importantly, he had to find Chasma. Although the prospect of Chasma having ventured that way seemed highly improbable, it was definitely worth checking. He kneeled down to assess the path better. The passage left by the missing floor was so narrow even her small body would have been partially above the sheer drop. He forced himself to rid his mind of the awful possibility she could have fallen and tried to peek beyond the wall. To his surprise, he could see another terrace beyond the turn that widened further along the cliff.

"Chasma? CHASMA!!" he called out but didn't get any answer. "*Could she have gone that way? Why isn't she answering?*"

"Chasma!" Dedrick tried again.

This time, a crackling sound was heard in all seven helmets.

"Daddy. Crrrrk- I'm here, daddy!" said the small voice.

"Chasma! Thank God. Where are you, baby?" asked Dedrick.

"Where are you, baby?" said Vera, almost in panic.

"I'm OK, Mommy."

"Chas-" Dedrick finally spotted the young girl appear from around a dark corner in the cliff, right behind a small bend on the second terrace. She was walking very carefully along the edge of the shrinking ledge in his direction.

"Chasma, go slow, baby. Be very careful… Give me your hand." He stretched his arm as far as he could around the rocky formation. She slowly reached him and took his gloved hand. With one swift pull, he carefully lifted her up above the protruding rock formation and grabbed her in his arms as he stepped back towards the more leveled open floor of the main terrace, a fairly effortless maneuver thanks to Mars' low gravity. Vera immediately rushed to them.

"Chasma, oh, Chasma, where did you go? Don't you ever do that again, young girl!" she shouted in tears, as she grabbed Chasma and held her tightly in her arms, the girl's helmet resting on her mother's shoulder awkwardly.

"I'm sorry, Mommy. I just wanted to go see the big cloud."

"Chasma, promise me you will never do that again! It's dangerous. You could hurt yourself. What if you… a big cloud? What big cloud?"

"The big cloud, Mommy, down there, in the mountain!" she said, pointing to the area she had just returned from.

"What are you talking about, Chasma?" asked François.

"The big white cloud!" she said sounding a bit annoyed, as she raised her arm and let it fall back down her side with frustration, pointing once more in the same direction.

François and Dedrick looked at each other with puzzled expressions.

"A big white cloud in the mountain…" repeated François, perplex.

"Yes! He said it was OK."

"Who did? The big cloud? He…talks?" asked Dedrick at a loss.

"What is she talking about?" Tendai was genuinely confused, as they all were.

"Yes!" Chasma said, raising both arms up in the air, shaping a big half circle as she let them back down with a big sigh, annoyed that none of them seemed to understand what she was saying. They were all looking at the child, uncertain of what to think, or say.

"He says you should all come, and he will explain everything."

"He's talking to you now? The big white cloud?" asked Sabrina at a complete loss.

"Yes, I just told you!"

"What the hell is she talking about?" finally said François. Vera gave him a disapproving look. "Sorry…I mean, it's just weird."

"Chasma, did you meet the big talking cloud when you went in there?" asked Dedrick.

"No, it was too dark, and I got a bit scared all by myself, so I came back. I didn't go very far."

"I think I'd like to see that big cloud," said François with genuine interest, walking closer to the south corner of the cliff to take a peek at the other terrace beyond.

"Give me a hand, Dedrick, will you?" he said, leaning his arm forward for the Russian to grab.

"Hold on! Where do you think you're…"? Then, thinking about it for a few seconds, Dedrick added, "OK, but be careful!" He grabbed François by his left arm and leaned to his side, securing himself against the rocky formation separating the two terraces. Keeping his feet planted firmly on the ground, Dedrick gave François a slight pull to help him keep his balance as the Frenchman pushed himself over the rocky wall and landed feet first on the other side.

Tapping Dedrick's arm with his free hand, he then said, "Ok, I'm good. You can let go of my arm, now."

"OK," replied Dedrick, as he released his grip.

François carefully moving along the narrow ledge, quickly reached the wider part of the open space. Once he was able to walk freely without steadying himself against the cliff wall, he began to look around. The area was a stretched-out triangle about nine meters wide. The back wall curved up slightly above to form a natural dome over the whole area. Unlike the terrace where they had found the alien gate, this niche appeared to have been carved naturally. He walked closer to the edge and looked far down below at some of the larger boulders that he suspected had broken off from where he was. Turning his attention back to the space behind him, where the terrace met with the rocky protrusion separating the two terraces, François noticed a small fissure that narrowed sharply at the very top. Approaching closer, he noticed the passage seemed quite deep and appeared to continue at a slope, down into the mountain.

"Looks like there's a small cave or tunnel back here, guys," he announced through his helmet microphone.

"Really? Can you see where it goes?" asked Dedrick.

"Well, it's only a few meters wide here, but I think I can fit through. It looks like it widens further in. As for where it goes, I guess there's only one way to find out." François turned his helmet lights on and proceeded into the fissure.

"Wait! François? François?" called out Dedrick.

"Yeah. I'm here. Crr- I'm entrrrr-Crrk- tunnel. It's bigger insss-Crrrrrk-sssssssssssssssshhhh…" and the connection went dead.

"François? François?" called out Dedrick again in vain.

"Crap! I hate when he does that."

"Tendai, give me a boost, will you?"

Already standing by, Tendai secured himself against the rock and the two men locked arms. Dedrick stretched one leg over the wall and lowered himself carefully down the other side.

A few seconds later, he was standing in front of the small tunnel the Frenchman had described. After calling François one more time and receiving no reply, he engaged himself in the narrow passage and disappeared as well.

#

"Can you see anything?" asked Vera seated behind Arc 2's dashboard.

"Nope. I can only see a portion of the terrace," replied Tendai, still standing by the terrace, stretching himself over the rocky outcrop, as far as he could.

"Maybe we should go check on them. It's already been several minutes." Vera was addressing everyone. She looked at Sabrina in the other rover through her window.

Ladli still outside with Tendai felt the need to voice her opinion.

"I don't think going after them is such a good idea, Vera. Dedrick and François are quite resourceful, and I'm sure they'll be fine. Until we hear from them, we should probably stay put."

Ladli was right, she knew it, but her daughter's dad was out there, and she had to summon all her strength to resist running after him. But at least, Chasma was with her. All they could do now was wait. She was too preoccupied to notice it, but the five-year-old girl, seated next to her, was smiling. The big white cloud was talking to her.

#

Inside the dark tunnel, Dedrick's suit lights were only showing him enough down the narrow passage to see about a dozen meters in front of him, at best. Slowly making his way through the corridor, he finally reached an enlargement that seemed perfectly geometric. He quickly estimated that the space was probably a perfect cube. The walls of the chamber were smooth and straight. In its center, François, standing silently, was staring at another sphere, buried halfway in the ground. It looked exactly like the one in the cliff outside.

"Wow!"

"Yeah, check it out! Another sphere. And did you see the rest of the room? Look at the walls!"

"I see that. It's amazing. And look at all those inscriptions. This is incredible!"

"I know."

The geometric lines and shapes covered the entire inner walls of the space. Not a single square meter had been spared. From ceiling to floor, the intricate designs and long grooves were crisscrossing everywhere. Some deep enough to fit someone's entire hand in, others barely visible, the curved lines all seemed to start, or end in the center of the room, where the large spherical object met the floor.

After a few minutes scanning the strangely decorated space, Dedrick turned to François.

"I see the tunnel keeps going over there," pointing beyond the Frenchman.

François agreed with a nod.

"Shall we?"

"After you, Maître," replied the Russian, with an inviting gesture.

Having two sets of lights instead of one didn't seem to help whatsoever. It was almost as if some invisible force was keeping them from probing beyond a certain distance ahead. But they were moving forward, nonetheless. A good fifteen minutes had gone by, most of it spent walking downhill, and the two men were still slowly progressing. Moving deeper and deeper into the mountain, they finally noticed something ahead. The path, widening ahead beyond the tunnel, was offering a glance at some vague but apparently large feature beyond. It wasn't long before they were entering a giant chamber. Their suit lights were too weak to light up clearly the entire place, but they were now able to see much further than they had while in the tunnel. Unlike the previous room, the walls of this new cave did not appear to be decorated with any markings or carvings of any kind, at least as far as they could see. The ceiling towered so high above them that they could not see anything but darkness. It was hard to estimate distances, but the walls stretched several hundred meters before disappearing into the darkness. The floor in front of them sloped down mildly for about a dozen meters before leveling. The two men began walking slowly down the incline until they reached flat ground.

"Now, what do you make of that?" asked François.

The strange oval structure he was pointing at to their left vaguely resembled a partially deflated blimp; a large one. Their lights were too weak to show the massive object in its entirety, but they could tell it was at least the size of a small cruise ship. The uneven bulgy mass was by far the most alien thing they had encountered so far. Like everything in the giant chamber, it was completely covered in a thick layer of dust that made it impossible to tell what it was made of, and aside from its white color, not much else could be seen about it without getting closer. Like a gigantic blob, the "blimp," resting on the floor of the cave seemed to be waiting for its visitors to approach. Both instantly realized they were staring at Chasma's Big Cloud.

"The big white cloud in the mountain! Of course, that's what Chasma was trying to describe," voiced Dedrick.

They both stared at it for a moment.

"What do you think it is? It looks like a giant cocoon to me. I wonder what's in it…You think someone's home?" asked François with a smirk.

"I wouldn't joke about that. I know so far the whole cave looks like it has been abandoned for quite some time, but I keep thinking about Chasma and that 'voice' of hers."

"Come on, you know how kids are. It's not unusual to have imaginary friends at that age."

"Yes, I know, but it's Chasma we're talking about. You know it's not like her to make up stories."

"True. Well, I guess there's only one way to find out."

He walked around Dedrick and headed for the large structure.

Dedrick had to give it to him, if his actions often seemed irresponsible, the French astronaut was rarely scared. He followed his colleague toward the egg-shaped edifice.

By the time he got next to him, François, had already cleared a few square meters of dust on one side of the structure, revealing its off-white surface.

The more they stared at it, the more obvious it became to both men that the strange shaped object, with its large bubble-like protrusions all across its surface, made for a fairly good cloud impersonation. Dedrick, helping François dust off a larger area, suddenly felt the surface give in slightly under the pressure of his gloved hand and stopped. Taking a step back, he shined his light at it again, closer this time, and began to wonder... It almost looked organic to him. He had the feeling he could probably push his arm through its walls if he tried, as if the skin of the object was made of some thick gelatinous material that could flex.

"What is it?" asked François.

"I don't know, but this thing is not as hard as I first thought. Look."

He pressed his hand against it once more, to show the Frenchman.

"Mmmmh… interesting…"

Dedrick took a few steps back again. "I'm not so sure messing with this thing is such a good idea..."

"Come on, don't be such a wuss."

"I'm just saying... I have this eerie feeling this thing is…alive."

"Alive? Pfff! Seriously…" François shrugged his shoulders.

"You can laugh all you want…"

Leaving it be for now, the two men started walking back alongside the big object and followed its contour, until they came all the way back around. There was no way in, at least none they could find. No doors, no windows, no hatch of any kind were visible anywhere. The only two areas they couldn't check were the top of the structure and its bottom. If there was a way in, it had to be through one of those. Eventually, giving up their search for the time being, they began heading for another structure they could see further down the giant cave. As they approached the new edifice, the huge tower stretching from floor to ceiling slowly revealed itself in their spotlights. The even surface of the edifice was broken here and there by oval openings or windows of sorts, placed at random intervals along its entire length. A good three meters in diameter, the two humans were beyond surprised when they realized the openings reflected none of the light from their torches. The oval holes were absolutely dark. On each side of the building, what they figured was an entrance, due its greater size, offered only the same unrevealing darkness, when hit by their searchlights.

"Do you see that? It's like the light stops right there. There's no sense of depth, no shadows, nothing reflecting back. That's really strange. It's like an impenetrable black vacuum."

"An impenetrable black vacuum? How do you come up with that stuff?" asked the Russian chuckling.

"I don't know. It sounded good in my head."

François was once again the first one to touch the new discovery. Passing his gloved hand gently along the structure's wall, he revealed a darker layer under the dust, almost as dark as the "windows" themselves, but this time, the construction did not give under his pressure. He pushed as hard as he could to no avail.

"This one is solid. Like metal."

He hit it once with his wrist and quickly stepped back, as if expecting a reaction, but nothing happened.

"What did you do that for?" asked Dedrick.

"I don't know. I just wanted to see how strong it was."

"Please don't do that again. We don't know what we're dealing with here. I keep worrying we're gonna wake up something."

"Come on, it was just a little tap. This place is dead, anyway. And if you want my opinion, I think it's been like that for quite some time."

"Yeah, well let's try to keep it that way, shall we?"

François simply shrugged his shoulders again.

Continuing on, they finally arrived in front of a portion of the cave that had obviously collapsed. Large boulders, some as big as a small car, were blocking what the two soon realized was probably the main entrance of the cave.

"Well, I guess now we know how Chasma's Big Cloud got in here. Looks like they got trapped."

"Who, they?"

"Who ever built all this," replied Dedrick with a large gesture.

"Well, so far we haven't found anyone, dead or alive. So, hard to say, either way."

"We're gonna have to come back with more equipment; definitely more lights. The others must be wondering what we're doing. We should start heading back."

Turning around, they began walking back towards the tower when François noticed something at the far end of his beam.

"Hold on! I think you may want to see this."

Dedrick turned to see him pointing at a geometric and lengthy object. As both searchlights met and lit up the massive artifact, both men quickly realized they were looking at some sort of machine. It was a good fifteen meters long. In the very center of it, a huge portion of ceiling had collapsed on top of the machine and crushed a significant portion of it. Contrary to the large egg-shaped structure they now referred to as the Big Cloud, this new lengthy object had very sharp angles, and was apparently made of a much darker metallic material.

"That doesn't look good," said François pointing at the big boulder resting right on top.

"Nope. But we really should head back. We'll come back with better equipment. And we're definitely gonna need more lights... What time is it, anyway? Wow! OK, we need to go."

"Lead the way, mon capitaine!"

Slowly moving back towards the tunnel they had come from, the two men walked up the slope and soon disappeared down the passage.

"Wait until we tell the others what we've found!"

Dedrick did not comment back. He was absorbed by a recurring thought. "*What did Chasma mean when she said the big cloud was talking to her?*"

#

"What are they doing? They've been gone for almost an hour, now!" said Sabrina, obviously worried.

"They're OK, Mommy. The big cloud told me so," said Chasma to her mother.

All five of them turned to look at the child.

"What is this big cloud you keep talking about, Chasma? I don't understand," finally asked Liu.

"The big cloud in the mountain! I already told you. He told me he needs to talk to Daddy," replied the little girl.

Now they were all staring at her as if she was speaking a foreign language.

A few moments later, Tendai finally agreeing to go find the two missing astronauts, was struggling to get himself over to the other side of the terrace, when he saw François come out from around the corner.

"They're back!" he announced to the rest of the team.

Sliding back onto firmer ground, he waved at the two men. François and Dedrick soon reached the Zimbabwean, who proceeded to help both men climb back to his side.

"We were worried. You were gone so long. Are you OK?" asked Vera right away to Dedrick.

"Yes, we're fine. We've found a passage into the mountain. Chasma was right. There's something down there. It's hard to explain. I think you all gonna want to see it for yourselves."

"I'm not going over this precipice, if that's what you mean," immediately responded Liu, staring at the treacherous corner.

"Don't worry, Liu, I didn't mean now. But you need to see the footage we took in there. It was quite dark, but I'm sure you'll find it interesting, regardless. I'm also thinking we're gonna need to build a ledge, and set up some kind of safe anchoring, to cross to the other side of that wall. We can get some supplies at the station and come back tomorrow. We should be able to anchor a small bridge across the missing floor between the terraces. Trust me, you're gonna want to go.

It's worth it."

Dedrick was still marveling at what François and he had found down the tunnel. All he wanted was to go back and explore even further. What many more secrets did the place hold? He wondered.

"Good! Because, I'm not going over that hole either," added Sabrina.

"So, what did you find?" asked Tendai.

"Man, wait until you see this! The tunnel goes down for quite a distance. We found another sphere, just like the other one, in a room full of the same kind of carvings on the Gate. But the most amazing part is a much larger cave, full of alien artifacts and structures. There was some intelligent life on Mars at some point, for sure. And they had these machines, and…oh yeah, we found the big cloud Chasma was talking about. Not sure what it is, but it looks pretty wild. I've never seen anything like it," answered François.

"Machines? To do what?" asked Sabrina

"I have no idea, but there's a pretty good layer of dust and dirt on almost everything; so, I doubt anyone has been down there for quite some time. The place could be thousands of years old, for all we know. Either way, I'm pretty confident the aliens who built all that stuff are long gone by now."

"I hope so," said Liu, sounding quite worried.

Dedrick wasn't so sure he shared his French friend's confidence on that last point.

"Ok, let's wrap it up for today. Tomorrow, those who want to can come back with me and François. We'll begin by rigging a safer access to the cave, then, if we have time, we'll do some exploring. Should be interesting..."

After putting all of their gear back into the rovers, the eight passengers climbed aboard and began heading home. Leaving a high cloud of dust behind them, the two rovers were soon zooming along the flank of the tall plateau, on their way back to base.

PART III

Chapter VIII

The big cloud

Vera was the first one to reach the cave, holding Chasma by the hand. Dedrick, François, and Tendai were right behind her, carrying lights and a small generator. Ladli and Liu were the last ones out of the tunnel. Sabrina had opted to stay at the station, since Ladli had done so the day before. They began setting up the equipment in the center of the giant space, and a few minutes later, the cave came to life in the brightness of several powerful projectors.

"Look, Mommy! The big cloud. See?" said Chasma, pointing at the giant white structure.

Vera did not respond. She was slowly taking it all in. They were all mesmerized by the grandeur of everything around them. The chamber was truly gargantuan. Spanning several city blocks, the cave was so large, even their powerful search lights were unable to show it all. They would have to bring more, if they had any left, or move by sections. The videos Dedrick and François had brought back from their initial excursion had not even come close to showing the true magnitude of everything in the chamber. But they now had no more doubt. What they were looking at was definitely ancient and alien.

"*So, there was intelligent life on Mars at some point, after all. This is incredible*," thought Vera.

The "big cloud" was like nothing any of them had ever seen. Now bathed in the powerful flood lights, it looked even bigger than the two men had first thought. Beyond it, the large tower they had discovered the previous day, was in fact only one of six identical structures lined up along the cave wall. Dedrick and François were only now realizing the true magnitude of the site. Vera was about to follow the rest of the group heading for the closest tower when Chasma held her back.

"No, Mommy, this way," she said, pulling her in the direction of the curvy white structure.

"Where are you taking me, Chasma?"

"You'll see."

A few minutes later, the two were standing in front of what Dedrick and François had guessed was the back of the big cloud.

"Help me, Mommy! We need to clean the dirt off."

"Chasma! Don't touch that!" she said as she leaned forward to grab her arm, just in time.

"Don't you want to go inside, Mommy?"

"No and neither do you! I don't want you near that thing, you hear me young lady?"

Vera, taking a step back with Chasma in her grip, was visibly upset and didn't see Dedrick right behind her. She jumped.

"Ah! You scared me!"

"I'm sorry. I didn't mean to startle you. Are you OK?"

"Yes, I'm fine, just a bit on edge. This whole thing with Chasma, and those voices she says she hears…"

"There's only one, Mommy. His name is Jorh."

"Jo…John? He told you his name?" Vera was still unable to truly believe her daughter. Maybe she did not want to.

"No, Jorh, Mommy. He says not to worry. Everything is going to be alright," she replied with a smile. Dedrick kneeled down in front of his daughter.

"I'm sure he's very nice, but we need to stay together as a group. It's for your own safety, Chasma. OK?"

"Yes, I know…" she replied pouting.

Standing back up, he put his hand on Vera's arm.

"Come on, let's rejoin the oth—"

He stopped in mid-sentence. Looking past his wife, he noticed his daughter venturing closer to the white mass next to them.

"Chasma! Come back here, baby."

Vera turned her attention back on the young girl, only in time to see the child reach for the white structure.

"No! Chasma! Don't touch—"

But before she could finish her sentence, Chasma put her hand on the dusty mass, and a purple light appeared under her fingers. It began to grow brighter rapidly.

Vera reached to grab Chasma's arm but realized she could not move. Dedrick tried to say something, but no sound came out of his mouth. He felt just as paralyzed. A few seconds later, the purple glow was too obvious to ignore in the dark cave, and François was the first one to notice it.

"Guys, look!"

The rest of the group turned in the direction of the light and froze. The entire structure was now glowing purple, and the sight was mesmerizing.

"Dedrick, Vera? Are you OK?" François quickly realized they were not. Neither one was moving or answering him. They couldn't.

"What are they doing?" asked Tendai.

"Something's wrong," said Liu.

"Tendai, come on!" called out François as he rushed towards the glowing structure.

Chasma was still standing in front of the large object when François grabbed her in his arms. The glow the structure was projecting suddenly went dark, even quicker than it had appeared, leaving only the small pulsing area where Chasma had laid her hand. An instant later, Dedrick and Vera were coming out of their strange trance. They were all quickly backing off when a loud sound, with a rich deep tone reminiscent of a cruise ship's horn, blasted out of the white structure, and echoed across the entire cave, sending chills down everyone's spine. Ladli and Liu, who had already reached the lower section of the slope, tripped backwards and fell to the ground. Rising up, they all watched in absolute disbelief, as a large oval opening started to take shape at the back of the structure. Now seemingly glowing from within, the purple lit corridor appeared to be inviting them inside.

"What did you guys do?" asked François.

"Nothing!" replied Dedrick. "Chasma just touched the outside of that thing, and then this," he replied, pointing at the new feature.

"We're not staying here another second. Come on Chasma, let's go," said Vera visibly shaken.

The young girl was resisting her mother, pulling in the opposite direction.

"No. Mommy, I want to stay. Let me go!"

"Vera, wait!" Dedrick approached them. "Look, I know this is a bit scary and unnerving, but something tells me it's safe."

"Really? You call what just happened back there safe? I couldn't even move, Dedrick. What is that thing, anyway? I thought you said this place was abandoned. We can't stay here. None of us should; it's not safe."

"I promise, we'll keep our distances. But we have to find out what's in that structure."

"Are you crazy? Tell me you're not seriously thinking of going inside that…that thing!"

"I'm telling you, honey, I don't think it's going to harm us. Isn't it why we came down here, in the first place?"

"That was before that thing came to life!"

"Vera, if we don't explore this thing, we'll always wonder. We have to go in."

"I'm with you on that one. We got this far..." added François.

"François, please stay out of this. Regardless, I don't care what either of you think. I'm not letting Chasma near that thing again."

"But Mommy-"

"I'm not going in there either," interjected Liu as she approached cautiously.

"I second that," said Tendai, already grabbing the containers of analyzing equipment he had brought with him, ready to go.

"None of you need to go inside," said Dedrick. "Until we know what we're dealing with, there's no need to take unnecessary risks. You all stay here, I'll go."

He looked at François, knowing he would not resist coming along. A nod from the Frenchman confirmed he was right, much to his relief.

"It's OK, Daddy. He says we can all go inside," calmly offered Chasma.

Again, taken by surprise, Vera turned to her daughter and kneeled next to her.

"Chasma, who said we can go inside?"

"Jorh! I told you! He said it's OK. He wants to talk to all of you."

Everyone was looking at Chasma, dumbfounded.

"I don't understand, baby. Are you saying this white structure here is talking to you?" asked Vera pointing at the alien object. She was still unable to accept the possibility that Chasma was hearing voices. Yet, deep down, she feared the girl was telling the truth.

"No, Mommy. He's inside. He knows you can't hear him, but I can."

"Can…can you talk to…him too?" asked Liu.

"Uh huh," replied the young girl, nodding her head in positive reinforcement.

"What else did the voice say to you, baby?"

"He says you don't need to worry, Daddy. Nothing bad will happen. He just wants us to go inside."

"Why? Why does he want us to go inside, Chasma?"

"He says he's trapped and he needs our help."

"He's trapped?"

Dedrick looked at François, completely puzzled.

"What do you think?"

"I think we got this far. We might as well see what this is all abou-"

"Wait! What if that…being…what if that thing is trapped in there for a good reason?" interrupted Ladli.

"Like what? Some kinda criminal or monster? Love, we'll never know unless we check," replied François calmly.

"Come on, seriously? Either way, there's only one way to find out."

"Look guys, I don't want anyone to take unnecessary risks, any more than you do. François and I are going to enter that thing. We will do our best to stay in communication, but if you prefer to go back and wait for us by the rovers, I totally understand. I promise, we won't stay gone more than necessary. Ladli, Liu, before you leave, do you mind making sure the generator is on auto? I want to make sure we don't run out of backup power."

"Sure can. But I'm not leaving," replied Ladli.

The two women started walking back to the equipment.

"You're really sure you want to do this?" asked Vera, knowing too well he did.

"I promise, love. We'll be extra cautious," replied her husband.

She let out a heavy sigh and began heading back to the others, her daughter in tow. Any reason to put some distance between them and the white structure was welcome. Dedrick looked at Tendai and gave him a gesture to come closer. Switching to a direct audio on his suit for the Zimbabwean only to hear, "I need you to stay with them. If something happens to us, you will be the only man left. They will need you, for more than one reason. We don't know what we're getting into here. François and I will be extremely cautious but... Anyway, if we're not back within the hour, take everyone back to the station.

Don't try to come after us. The safety of the team may depend on it. Promise me, Tendai."

Tendai knew Dedrick was right. Plus, he was not too keen on venturing in that alien structure anyway.

"You can count on me, my friend. Just don't take any unnecessary risks, and I promise to keep everyone safe, here. We'll follow you on the monitor. Good luck!"

"Dedrick!" called out Vera scared.

"We'll be careful, baby, I promise!" he answered.

He and François then started walking toward the entrance of the "big cloud."

"Wait!" shouted Ladli. "What if it's a trap?"

"There's only one way to find out, love," replied the Frenchman.

As the two men got to the purple opening, they stopped in front of the corridor and tried to peer into the foggy passage. The purple haze wasn't revealing anything. Dedrick turned to look back at the rest of the group at the top of the slope. Tendai had put down his small communication pad on a flat boulder nearby and was checking Dedrick's video feed. The picture was a bit dark, as usual, but of decent quality. He gave the men two thumbs up, while the rest of the team gathered around him to watch their companions enter the opening on the screen. François walked slowly to the edge of the entrance and put one foot on the floor of the structure. He felt a light tug, as if a vacuum was trying to pull him in. Leaning carefully forward, he felt his body becoming lighter. Gradually pulled by an invisible force, he was slowly levitated and floated inward.

"Wooow!" was all he could say, as he drifted away into the depth of the purple fog and disappeared.

"FRANÇOIS!" called out Dedrick, his arm raised toward his friend, but it was too late. The Frenchman had already disappeared in the purple haze.

"I'm OK! I'm OK. It's a bit weird, but it's like floating in zero gravity. Nothing to it. Come on!" came the Frenchman's voice.

Dedrick, somewhat reassured to hear his calm voice after watching him vanish, approached the doorway. After putting a foot on the floor of the entrance, he took a deep breath and followed in.

The others left behind, held their breath as they watched their two colleagues disappear from their screen. Seconds later, the tunnel was slowly closing back on them, leaving no trace of the entrance. Fear suddenly gripped them as they realized they may never see their friends again. A wave of panic rushed through Vera. Holding Chasma's hand more tightly, she stared at the white structure in the distance that had just swallowed her daughter's father. The purple glow was gone. She turned her attention back on the small screen in front of her. Dedrick and François' helmet cams were transmitting good images.

Inside, the wide cylindrical corridor was bathed in an ambient purple light that seemed to come from everywhere around them, but the thick fog they had encountered at the entrance was no longer obstructing their view of the surroundings. The two men were moving slowly but effortlessly, when Vera noticed the thick fog churning above the explorers. Slowly making its way down the smooth curved walls of the tunnel, the purple haze seemed to come from within the ceiling of the—

The screen suddenly went completely black.

"Shit!" said Tendai. "Dedrick? François? Crap, I think we've just lost them."

Inside the big white cloud, unaware their teammates could no longer see their progress, the two intruders were drifting slowly down the long tunnel, hovering a few meters above the floor. The walls were smooth and featureless, and appeared to be made of the same material as the outside of the structure. The curved ceiling above them was covered with a thick fog, slowly floating down the corridor's walls. François tried to move towards one of the walls, only to find he was powerless. Whatever was pulling them through the ship had complete control of their floating bodies.

"Hey, look at your gauges. Notice anything?" asked François.

Dedrick brought his forearm up and read the levels.

"Wait… That's impossible. 79% nitrogen, 21%… There's oxygen in here?"

"Yep, looks like it; and just the right amount, too. Don't you find that interesting?"

And with that, he released his helmet locks and removed the restricting contraption off his head, leaving only enough time for Dedrick to scream, "Wait, what are you DOING?! DON'T-!"

François, looking straight at him, took a deep breath through his nose, and held it for a few seconds, before exhaling loudly through his mouth. A satisfied smile appeared on his face.

"Ahhh, that's much better."

"What the fuck!? Are you out of your mind?"

François looked at his Russian friend with a puzzled look on his face. "What?"

His helmet was now silently floating next to him.

"What is wrong with you? You could have been killed, taking your helmet off like that! What's gotten into you?"

"Oh, come on. You saw the levels just as I did. It's perfectly safe. In fact, the air in here is even more pure than ours at the station."

"Oh yeah? And what if the analyzer was faulty? What if there was some other toxic gas in here? You are completely careless."

"Both of our suits? Defective at the same time? Reading the same numbers? I doubt it."

Dedrick abstained from replying. Instead, he simply stared at François in frustration, the latter floating a few meters ahead of him. The Frenchman's helmet was now hovering next to him, quietly following its owner. The commander finally let out a heavy sigh and began unlocking his.

"I guess now we know what that purple gas is for," said François. Dedrick did not respond.

Several more minutes passed before the two came to a fork. The tunnel split into three passages of equal importance. Although he already knew he could not control where he was going, François was about to ask Dedrick which path he thought they should take, when he felt his body pulled strongly to the right. Something or someone had made the decision for him. Hovering behind him, Dedrick suddenly felt the tug and followed down the new passage. They encountered two more intersections as they progressed through the tunnels, and were pulled in a specific direction each time, obviously guided by an intelligence of some kind along a predetermined path. Dedrick, always planning ahead, made a mental note of each turn for the way back. Of course, he realized there was a good chance they would have no more control coming back than they did going in, but he figured it couldn't hurt.

A few minutes later, the two men arrived in front of a doorway not unlike the Gate they were so familiar with. This one, however, appeared to be made of the same material as the rest of the structure, smooth and white. Countless lines and geometric shapes, similar to the ones found on the Gate, seemed to be glowing randomly, as if lit by an invisible current flowing through the intricate design.

"*The second door in my dream*," thought Dedrick. He had never been beyond it.

As the two kept approaching, the portal began to slowly morph, becoming more and more opaque, until it had completely vanished, leaving a wide opening for the two to gently glide through without ever slowing down. Dedrick turned his head just in time to see the door re-materialize quickly behind them.

They were now in a large oval room, the size of an average movie theater. The walls were featureless, and Dedrick noticed there was no other door visible anywhere, not even the one they had just come through. In the center of the large space, what looked like big long cylindrical containers were arranged in a wide circle. François quickly counted twenty-six. In the middle of them, another white sphere, like the one they were familiar with, was resting on the flat surface of a large round platform. Reaching the center of the room, the two men felt they were slowing down and, to their pleasant surprise, gently brought to the floor where they finally came to a stop, comfortably landing quietly on their feet. They both let out a big breath of relief. François' helmet fell silently to the floor, right next to him. Dedrick was still holding his.

"Feels solid," he said, looking at the floor.

Pointing at one of the twenty-six horizontal capsules, François wondered… "What do you think those are?"

"Not sure, but I have a theory."

"Yeah, me too…"

The room, just as the rest of the structure, radiated the same purple hue, but again, they could not see where the light was coming from. The space had no sharp angles or corners, and the floor, walls, and vaulted ceiling curved into each other flawlessly. Other than the sphere and its twenty-six containers, there was nothing else noticeable. The long capsules, blending with the purple-lit egg-shaped space, were sparking Dedrick's interest, especially due to their shape. Although oversized for a human being, it did not take much imagination to suspect they could hold beings. Dedrick suddenly realized the two of them might be standing in a room full of aliens. He was now questioning their decision to come inside.

"*If there're aliens in those containers, they must be big, very big. And there are twenty-six of them…*" he thought to himself. Another wave of doubt rushed through him. He turned to François, who was already studying the pod next to him. The Frenchman didn't seem the least concerned.

"Man, look at those things! Can you believe how big they are? I'm telling you, there's gotta be aliens in there!"

"Keep it down, will you? We don't know what we're dealing with here. You might wake-up something or someone we should not disturb."

"Come on! Don't be such a wuss. I doubt talking loudly or softly matters. Either way, there's no turning back now. We're here, and something tells me we're supposed to open these things."

"I'm serious, François. We have no idea what we are doing. Half of me is screaming we need to get the hell out of this place, right now!"

"And the other half?"

Dedrick just looked at François without replying. He took another look at the closest capsule. There was no apparent line or break, no feature of any kind on the surface of the pod, and no obvious way of opening it.

"How do you think we open one of these?"

"I don't know, and I don't think we should try to find out."

"And I think we should. Something or someone guided us here just for that. I'm-"

Dedrick turned to his French friend, and with a finger raised in front of his lips, let out a quiet, "Sssshhhh! Listen…"

With a pondering look on his face, François listened attentively for a few seconds, before shrugging his shoulders at Dedrick. He was about to dismiss the Russian, when realized what he was listening to; nothing. His Russian commander was tapping his boot on the floor, but there was absolutely no sound. Or at least, their headsets could not pick up any. He quickly checked that his suit's microphone was on and had confirmation. Even after removing his ear piece, the place was absolutely dead quiet. To think of it, it had been so ever since they had entered the structure. That wasn't necessarily alarming in itself, considering they had made their way inside by floating through it without touching any surface, but now that they were walking on solid ground, they should be able to hear their own footsteps reverberating across the large room, especially without their helmets on. Yet, even the friction of the fabric of their suits was silent.

"That is so weird. How can sound not travel in here?"

"I honestly don't know," replied Dedrick.

François removed his headset completely. "Can you hear me

now?"

The Russian just shrugged his shoulders, with a negative head nod.

That suddenly reminded Dedrick he had been so absorbed, he had failed to communicate with the team ever since they had gone in. His headset still on him, he called, "Vera, can you hear me?... Tendai? Ladli? Anyone?"

No answer came.

François put his earpiece back on. "What is it?"

"I can't reach the team. I had a feeling we would have heard from them already, if our communicators still worked. It's doubtful they are getting any video feed either. We shouldn't stay too long. Let's just get some footage and head back, if we can figure out how..." added Dedrick, looking back at the now featureless wall behind him.

"What about Chasma's voice? What did she call him? John? Jore? I thought we were going to meet an alien…" added François disappointed.

"Well, whoever he is, Chasma mentioned him being trapped, right? So, my guess is he's probably in one of these pods."

"I second that. So why don't we try to figure out how to open one of these things."

Dedrick was about to object, but François was already running his hands over the closest one to him, obviously hoping to mimic the way Chasma had opened the back of the ship earlier. To his great disappointment, nothing happened.

"Well, can we get back, now?"

"Yes, I guess..."

Looking at the invisible entrance, Dedrick asked, "So, what do you think? My guess is we just walk back towards that wall, and hopefully, the door will appear again."

"Well, you know what I always say…There's only one way to find out."

Before Dedrick could add anything, he watched his colleague walk a few steps forward, before being gently lifted up in the air and floated back towards that side of the room. As both men had suspected, the door began to rematerialize in front of his hovering body. François, helmet in hand, glided silently thru the temporary opening and vanished down the corridor beyond. Dedrick, giving himself a push, was instantly lifted as well and was soon following his friend. He looked back briefly. The solid door was already closing behind him.

#

"How long have they been gone, Tendai?" asked Vera, nervously.

"It's been almost fifty-five minutes. They shouldn't be long now..." he replied, trying not to sound concerned.

"Maybe one of us should go check on them?" she asked.

"Don't look at me. I'm not going in there," he said right away. "Dedrick said we should start heading back if they didn't return after an hour."

He looked somewhat embarrassed, but he was not the only one who felt uneasy about staying in the cave this long. It was even more understandable now that they had turned off several of the lights around them to conserve energy. The generator was now only feeding three of the eight projectors they had originally setup around the immense cave. One was near the four members, and the other two were illuminating the back of the ship, where Dedrick and François had disappeared earlier.

"I'm not leaving without Dedrick," replied Vera firmly. "And if Dedrick told you an hour, they still have a good five minutes left."

"Don't worry, Vera, we're not leaving anyone behind," assured her Ladli. She wasn't showing it, but she was getting anxious. "*Come on guys, now would be nice*."

#

Back inside the alien ship, Dedrick and François were silently gliding through the structure's belly. Dedrick was still trying his radio.

"Vera? Vera? Looks like they still can't hear us from here either, but I think we're close to the entrance. Time to get our helmets back on."

Another couple of minutes passed before they were finally in signal range and able to communicate with their companions waiting in the cave.

"Crrrk_ are on... ssshhhhway. Vera? Can... crrrrk ...me?"

"Dedrick...Dedrick? It's Vera. We can hear you, but you're breaking up. Can you hear me?"

"Ssshhhhhsss – I can hear you loud and clear now. We're

alshhhh back, I think. Yes, I see the exit."

At that same moment, Tendai jumped on his feet.

"Look, the passage is opening up again!"

The purple glow of the structure's entrance had appeared as suddenly as it had an hour earlier.

"Here they are! I see them!"

The two men soon emerged and landed effortlessly on the floor of the cave. Behind them, the entrance was already disappearing. Dedrick waved to the group, and the two men began walking their way back to them.

"So? What did you find? What is it like inside?" asked Tendai.

"You guys are not gonna believe this!" answered François.

Dedrick and his French teammate began telling their discovery to the bewildered group who listened attentively.

"I'm telling you, we can't say for sure what's in those pods, but whoever or whatever they are, they're big," replied François.

"And you say there're twenty-six of these things in there?"

"Yes...We tried to figure out, or I should say I tried to figure out a way to open one of them, like Chasma did when she touched the ship. I ran my hands all over one of the pods, but nothing happened."

"The thing is, we really don't know what we're dealing with here," volunteered Dedrick.

"The more I think about it, the more convinced I am that whole structure is a ship of some kind, and we just found its passengers," added François.

"Maybe..." Dedrick was pretty sure he was right.

"Either way, we need to find out. We'll have to come back more prepared and figure out how to wake-up whoever's there."

"I'm not too hot on that idea, François. You guys were in there for almost an hour, and we had no way of knowing if you were OK. It seems quite unsafe to me. If anything happens to one of you in there... And how do you plan to open that thing again, anyway? I'm not letting Chasma near it again." asked Vera.

"Look, I understand your concern, Vera. But it looks like she's the only one who can. I tried to, but nothing happened."

"Even if I agreed to let her touch that thing, how do you expect to open one of these containers?"

François looked briefly at Dedrick before replying. "The same way we got inside the ship."

"What are you saying?" asked Vera, fearful she already knew the answer.

"I'm saying we need to go back in there with Chasma."

There's only one way to find out

Almost two weeks had passed since the team had found the ship and its twenty-six pods. Luckily, they had quickly discovered that the vessel's entrance no longer needed Chasma's touch to open. It simply did anytime one of them approached the back of the white structure, and that was a good thing. Vera had not allowed her daughter to go back after that first day. She categorically refused to put her little girl in any situation she considered dangerous, and taking Chasma back to the cave was on top of her black list; especially now that the "voice" was no longer talking to her daughter. At least, she hoped so.

Unable to convince her, Dedrick and François had gone back with the others in small groups almost every day, hoping to find out more about their incredible discovery. Ladli was almost as enthusiastic and dedicated as the commander and his French friend. The medical officer was by now convinced the "big cloud" was a flying ship, and François couldn't agree more. The two had discovered several recesses on the outside of the white structure, that led them to believe they hid some sort of propulsion system or retractable wings. Dedrick felt they were jumping to conclusions, but he knew there was no point arguing with his engineer on that one. Ladli had also shown more interest in other structures housed in the immense cave, including the "machine" in particular. While surveying the entire perimeter of the cave, she had also discovered three more nodes leading to other small chambers in the mountain. Two of the narrow tunnels had led to dead ends and collapsed roofs, but a third had opened out into another small chamber, similar to the one they passed through every time they came down. Again, another sphere sat at its center. Beyond it, the small corridor continued, until it ended at a flat wall. In the middle of it, the outlines of another door had convinced them they were looking at the back of their Gate outside the cliff.

Inside the giant cave, the towers also beckoned to be explored, but so far, none had been accessible. The tall arched doors at their base were still impenetrable by the colonists' lights. They had even tried using a couple of colored filters to attempt to recreate the purple light from the ship, but that had not helped either. No matter what they did, all they could see past the doorway was absolute darkness. François had dared step a few meters inside before discovering the arch had disappeared behind him as soon as he had turned around. The intense drop in temperature that had followed had been the lowest his suit had ever registered since their arrival on Mars. Staying any longer could have spelled certain death quickly. Luckily, Dedrick had had the good idea of suggesting they attach a cable to his suit, to pull him back out in case of an emergency. Without it, it was doubtful he would have ever found his way back.

A thorough investigation of the "machine" had suggested that the alien contraption had probably been a generator of sorts, maybe a power source for the towers, or as Ladli had theorized, an atmospheric generator, a machine that could have turned the cave into a pressurized and breathable environment. Quite a wild hypothesis, Dedrick had thought, even if an interesting one. Whatever the case, most of it had been severely damaged by a substantial cave-in. There were also several more spheres lying about. Some were almost completely buried under high piles of rubble. Others looked as if they had just been left there that morning. But the largest damage the area had sustained was at the mouth of the cave's entrance. Large boulders, some the size of houses, were permanently obstructing the main passage. If, as François had suggested, the white structure was in fact a ship, the cavern's collapse would explain why the vessel was trapped. And as for the ship itself, it was by far the most interesting structure in the whole place. Soon after their mapping of the cavern, they had eventually turned their attention back on the "big cloud" and begun a new probing. The fog just below the corridor's ceiling had dissipated after a few days and revealed a see-through roof. Even though no one could have known from the outside, especially due to all the dust and dirt on the structure, the explorers could now clearly see the roof of the cave from inside the ship, as if the ship was wide open above them. Even the dirt and small rubbles on the surface weren't there. They had also tried multiple times to figure out a way to take different corridors, wishing to explore other parts of the structure, but nothing they did had any effect on changing their predetermined path. They always ended up back in the same room, with its twenty-six pods.

Dedrick and François had surveyed the large space and its containers from top to bottom. François had even run around the circumference several times, hoping for another corridor to open, without any success. Both Dedrick and he had stood countless times on the circular platform, searching in vain for a recess or definable feature, around the large sphere.

"We're never gonna find out what's in these pods, are we?" asked Ladli with obvious disappointment, looking at Dedrick.

"In all honesty, I still don't know if we should risk it. If there are beings in there, I have a feeling they have been in here for quite some time, maybe for a very good reason."

"What makes you say that?"

"This place. You've seen the far back of the cave. It looks like the whole cavern has been sealed by a large collapse above the original entrance. This ship, or whatever you want to call it, had to have come through that passage, there's no other way in large enough. That collapse didn't happen yesterday, but I keep thinking it was deliberate. Someone wanted this place sealed."

"You really believe that?"

"In all honesty, I don't know what to believe anymore," he paused. "I had another dream, last night."

François looked at him.

"And?"

"It started out the same way, with the fireplace, Rita, and the toolshed in the backyard, but…"

"Still can't get past that second gate? I think that's the strangest part, considering we've been inside the ship several times now, and we know what's behind that door…"

"Actually, it was different, this time."

"What do you mean?"

"This time, the alien brought me and Rita inside the room, and we ended up right here, in front of this very pod," he replied pointing at one of the white containers. "Then, he disappeared, and when I leaned over the pod, I… I could see through it. I could see him, lying inside it, sleeping…"

"Oh, good. So, you finally got further. And then what?"

"Then Rita turned into Chasma, somehow. She was smiling at me… I watched her approach the pod and put her hand on the glass. I tried to stop her, but I couldn't move… and then… the sphere rose to the ceiling, spinning. I don't remember how the pod got there, but it was floating underneath the sphere and…then…there were all these bright colors, and…" he paused, trying to remember. "I think the container just disappeared after that, and the alien was standing in its place, looking at me...blinking."

"Blinking?!" repeated Ladli, perplex.

"OK. So, don't you see? Ever since the discovery of that gate, I've been thinking your dreams have something to do with this whole thing. I'm not sure why or how, but there seems to be a strong connection between you, Chasma, and this place," said François. "I think the same voice that guided her to the cave is asking you to bring her back."

Dedrick looked at François.

"I don't know…"

"Listen, there're only two options. Either we leave them where we found them and forget about the whole thing, or we get Chasma to open those darn things and hope for the best. Personally, I have to know."

François gave a deep probing look at the container in front of him and added, "I wish there was another way... But I think we both know we need to bring Chasma back. Something tells me that's how it's supposed to happen. I don't know why, but she seems to have been…chosen. She says she can hear the alien, right? I know you didn't want to take that seriously, but at this point, I think we should accept the fact that she is more receptive to this place than us. I'm not sure why…Maybe because she was born on Mars…Or maybe because she is young…who knows? Either way, I have a strong feeling she's the key."

"I know. To be honest, I've been thinking the same thing for days now. I just don't like the idea."

"I don't know, guys. She's only five, after all. I seriously doubt Vera is gonna be OK with this. To be honest, I can't blame her. We really don't know how dangerous any of this might be. What if what's in those pods is toxic to us?"

"There's only one way to find out."

#

The three had discussed the idea the entire way back to the station, and the prospect of awakening the aliens had been argued back and forth by the entire group the following day. Vera had again been totally opposed to the idea. Even after Dedrick had told her of his dream, and that he believed only Chasma could awaken the alien. Vera simply refused to let her go. And when her little girl had assured her she knew she would be safe, because the alien named Jorh had told her so, Vera had felt even more opposed to the idea. The voice Chasma was claiming to hear was beginning to frighten her again. Again, Dedrick, and especially François, had worked diligently at convincing the worried mother to let the child come. Her daughter's presence had played a major role in the new discovery. She was the one who had led them to the cave, and it was her who had opened the ship. If Dedrick's dream was more than just a dream, Chasma's presence was essential. How could they ignore the plea for help from another being? They had to open that pod. Their relentless pleading had finally paid off. Vera had eventually capitulated a few days later. Not that the argument alone could have made her change her mind of course, but something in her daughter's voice had. She couldn't quite explain it, but the calm and confidence in Chasma's begging had given her the feeling the young girl would be perfectly safe. There was also the fact that deep down, she was still curious as well.

"Alright, fine. But at the first sign of trouble, we're out of there, right? Promise me, Dedrick!"

"Absolutely, I promise! I have no intention of putting any of us in harm's way. I assure you, love. We'll be ultra-cautious."

They briefly talked about who would stay at the base, and Liu and Tendai had immediately volunteered. If Chasma truly managed to open one of the alien pods, neither one was in a hurry to meet whoever was inside. And so, it was agreed. The rest of the colonist would leave early the next morning.

#

That night, the stars above the small Martian station were particularly bright. François, lying in bed, was staring out the porthole window of his bedroom, when Sabrina appeared.

"What do you think?" she said with a devilish smile.

She was standing in the makeshift doorway of their small bathroom area, wearing a black-lace, two-piece lingerie that left François speechless. He could only smile as his gaze took its time going up and down her sensual curves. She slowly approached their bed in an erotic fashion, licking her parted lips with her tongue and, untying her ponytail, let her long dark hair fall back, partially covering one side of her face. François felt his member get harder under the sheet. She crawled over the bed's edge, pulled the sheets back, and slowly ran her hand up his leg. He felt the sensual energy rush to his erected penis as her hand moved closer. Pulling his briefs down, she grabbed the hard, warm erection. Slowly running her tongue along her lips, she looked at him, her big dark eyes smiling mischievously. Then, as he watched her lean down, aching in anticipation, she finally took his shaft in her mouth, and slowly began the pleasuring motion. He moaned while running his hand through her hair and watched her beautifully arched body move slowly and sensually between his legs. Her large breasts rubbing against his thighs, she kept swallowing his hard member, occasionally running her tongue on its entire length, while pleasuring herself with one of her hands. When she was ready, she slowly kissed her way up his torso, until she reached his mouth. Climbing on top of him, she finally mounted his hard-erected shaft, and brought his hand to one of her breasts. Moaning and breathing heavily, she began moving back and forth on him. Their burning bodies entwined, the two abandoned themselves to the pleasures of their love making, until they both reached climax a few minutes later, almost in unison. She fell back on him, both of them drenched in sweat.

Exhausted, she let her gaze float freely across the tiny room. Through the small round window, she could see the night sky. Thousands of stars shining, glistening through the thin Martian atmosphere, were gazing back at her from the infinite silence of space. In the bottom right corner of her view, Sabrina could just see the top of the nearest cliff, barely visible in the night, if not for the slight contrast its dark shape created against the starry background. She thought again of the alien cave, and the unknowns awaiting them. There was no way to tell what tomorrow would bring, but for the moment, she felt totally content.

Awaken

It was another beautiful morning on Mars. Tendai had tried to convince Ladli to stay behind with him and Liu, but in the end, human curiosity had prevailed, and she had joined the rest of the team. They had just left the outpost and were heading for the alien site. Kicking sand and rocks behind them, the two rovers raced across the deserted landscape with their six passengers, and soon arrived at sector 42-23. After parking by the south wall near the cliff's edge, the colonists left the vehicles and began making their slow descent down to the alien cave.

Twenty minutes later, the team emerged into the giant cavern. The "big cloud" was still there waiting, lying on its grand platform, just as imposing as the first time they had seen it.

It looked even wider than Sabrina remembered.

"Does this thing look bigger to you, or is it just me?"

"I don't know…maybe," vaguely answered Vera without looking, paying attention to her daughter's progress down the slope.

"I agree, I think it looks bigger, and they do say size matters," volunteered François with a mischievous look.

She shook her head at him.

Dedrick was about to say something when Ladli interrupted.

"Come on, you two… Let's go see who's inside that thing…shall we?" she waved at them to follow her, as she made her way to the white vessel. The six explorers were soon gathered in front of the entrance. The purple haze was glowing inside.

"OK, Chasma. You're sure you're up for this? It's OK if you wanna change your mind. You don't have to go inside if you don't want to."

"I know, Daddy. I want to."

Dedrick had the strange feeling she was going to be perfectly comfortable and unafraid, no matter what they would find if they managed to open those containers, and he couldn't explain why. Something was telling him it was all going to be alright.

"Well, shall we?" said François as he proceeded into the opening. As the purple fumes dissipated in front of him, his body began to rise and floated away into the Big Cloud, quickly followed by Sabrina and

Ladli. Vera looked one last time at Chasma, who nodded positively in her helmet, before the two stepped in, Dedrick in tow. Looking at Vera and his daughter hovering hand in hand in front of him, Dedrick was once again lost in thoughts. What surprised him the most was the ease with which his little girl seemed to move about the alien structure. Holding her mother's hand as the two floated slowly through the purple lit corridors, it almost seemed she was the one pulling Vera along with her.

Ever since that faithful day, when the group had decided to bring the young girl along on their visit to the Gate, Chasma had been surprisingly unafraid, and appeared completely comfortable around the alien environment. Her ability to "hear" the guiding voice that had brought them to the ultimate discovery was still puzzling to him but was becoming increasingly difficult to ignore. It seemed obvious something, or someone, was guiding the girl. She was the one who had awakened the alien structure and opened the invisible door, and she had shown no hesitation entering the unfamiliar structure. She seemed to completely trust the voice she was hearing.

"*Let's hope she is right*," he thought.

A few minutes later, they were all standing in the large room. Vera was keeping her distance from the pods, while Chasma was pulling on her hand, trying to get closer.

"Come on, Mommy. I want to say hi to the sleepy people."

"Wait, Chasma. I don't want you to get too close yet. Daddy is going to check a few things first."

Dedrick wasn't checking much. He was standing still near one of the pods, suddenly questioning everything again.

"Well?" asked François. "What are we waiting for?"

Dedrick turned to look at Vera and his daughter. He took a step back, turning to François.

"I'm not so sure this is such a good idea. What if we open those pods, and the creatures inside attack us? Then what? Or what if by doing so, we kill them?"

"Come on. Didn't we just go through all this already? You're not gonna change your mind now, are you? Plus, I doubt seriously whoever is inside wants to hurt us. And if it's not safe for them, why would they try to talk Chasma into it? They're inside their own ship, with a breathable atmosphere which I'm guessing is meant for them, not for us. We're just lucky to breathe the same air they do. I'm quite confident this whole place is safe for them as well. Either way, we've been looking at these pods for over two weeks now, and we've tried everything else we could think of. I don't think we have much of a choice. It's either that, or we will never know who these people are, and what they are doing here," replied François.

"I have to say, I'm a bit concerned too, François. We really don't know anything about this place. I mean, I'm just as curious as you are, but then again, maybe these beings are in these pods for a reason. Maybe they are not supposed to be freed. What if they are criminals from another world, or something worse?" offered Sabrina.

"Criminals? Seriously? What is up with you two? I thought we had all agreed about this already." He paused and looked at Ladli for support. She shrugged her shoulders. He went on.

"Look, I agree, there is an element of risk. But I don't think it's any different from all the other ones we took to come here from Earth, or the risks we take every day by living on this harsh planet. I don't want anything to happen to Chasma anymore than you do. I love you very much, baby, I hope you know that," he added looking at Vera's daughter, "But here we are, in this Martian cave, inside an alien spaceship, and deep down, I feel we're supposed to do this. I'm not sure I can explain it, but I truly believe there are beings trapped in these containers, who managed to guide us here to help them, and I think we should."

"We have to help the sleepy people, Mommy."

They all turned their attention back on Chasma. Vera kneeled next to her daughter. "You're sure this is what you want, Chasma?"

"Yes, Mommy," she replied with a big smile.

"So, tell me, do you know how to wake up the sleeping people?"

"Yes, Mommy, Jorh told me."

"OK then, love. Show Mommy."

The young girl removed her right glove and walked past several containers before stopping in front of one. They all watched her raise her arm and put her bare hand on the glossy surface. Like ripples through water, several multicolored circles started forming where her hand had made contact. She took a quick step back. Within seconds, the outer shell of the pod had become translucent, revealing the giant being inside. He or she was at least twice the size of an average man. Blue skinned and baring disproportionately massive legs, the alien was bathing in a hazy purple gas, churning slowly inside the pod.

"*The alien in my dream,*" thought Dedrick.

A low-pitched vibration followed through the floor of the room, sending shockwaves through all of them. The rotating sphere in the middle of the chamber began to rise toward the ceiling. Dedrick quickly grabbed Chasma in his arms and moved back next to Vera. The transparent pod and its occupant rose a few meters, and slowly glided to the center pad. Lining itself below the spinning sphere, the capsule began to glow. A very bright light suddenly flooded the pod from above. While bathing in the blinding haze, the glassy capsule containing the alien slowly faded away, and the body of the strange being rose out of its sleeping position, while the pod rematerialized in its original place among the other twenty-six below. Staring at the imposing alien, the anthropologist in Liu couldn't help but be mesmerized by the strange being. The alien, floating on his back a few meters above the platform, shared a few similarities with humans. Although of distinctively larger proportions, the being had two legs, two arms, a head, and two eyes, just like humans do. However, the resemblances ended there. The being's cranial features alone were quite different. Its head was significantly larger and curved slightly forward at the top. The closed eyes looked much larger as well, and the mouth was surprisingly small and hard to define. No ears were visible, and two short tentacles dangled below the alien's chin. But one of the strangest things about the alien was at the back of his head. A hollow membrane, resembling a short elephant trunk, hanged down a meter or so below his neck.

Sabrina was enthralled, standing just behind François, holding his hand tightly. Her breathing was heavy.

"He is so big!" she whispered.

"I think he's a she," he replied just as quietly.

The alien slowly floated upright, revealing even more of its massive presence. Male or female, the alien was tall, very tall. "*He's gotta be at least four meters tall,*" guessed Dedrick. The torso, quite small in comparison to the lower portion of the body, was otherwise straight and evenly distributed, but disproportionately thin and short. He suddenly realized the alien had six fingers on each hand, all of equal length. As far as he could see, he had no hair anywhere on him, and aside from four dark wavy lines on the lower part of the neck, the alien's skin bared no visible markings or features, at least none he could see from where he was standing. If she was a female, she had no breasts, or any other significantly curved body lines suggesting so. If the being was a male, he did not appear to possess any visible genital appendage.

Watching the large creature rise further up in the large room, the colonists noticed the sphere up above begin to spin faster and faster, and the bright light shining on the alien starting to pulse, slowly at first, but quickly gaining speed. The alien's blue skin, apparently reacting to the stimulation, began to glow, as if it was being recharged or nourished by the pulsing lights above. The strobe effect, which at times made the alien appear to move, was hard to watch without squinting, but Dedrick and the rest of the group were too captivated to take their eyes off, or move. A swirling gas began to appear around the hovering body and morphed slowly into the alien's clothing. The fabric was soon swaying freely around its inert body, as if softly blown by a gentle breeze. The see-through cloth-like material began to shrink slowly, tightening itself on the alien's bare skin. While doing so, they could see the fabric thickening as well. Strands of cloth began wrapping themselves around the being's arms and legs, in an even-spaced spiral. A few seconds passed before the platform below began to glow as well, a bright neon-purple light, occasionally interrupted by random flashes of colors, creating an impressive display of shadows and light along the entire length of the body. As if reacting to the rhythm of the various colors, the being's entire body was soon convulsing. What felt like minutes passed, until the sphere, after one last elaborate color display, gradually slowed down again, its beam of purple glow finally shining still, as if holding the alien up in the air. The strange being was now hovering, immobile, its large mass bathing in the familiar hazy glow of soft purple, coming from both above and below.

Then, one arm moved.

"Oh!" gasped Sabrina.

"It's OK, it's OK," François tried to reassure her, as she gripped his hand even more tightly. He glanced at Dedrick with an expression that meant, "*OK, here we go.*"

Another wave of tremors shook the ship once again, and the alien suddenly let out a high-pitched growl that sent chills through all of them. Moving back several more steps, Dedrick took a quick glance around him. They were about halfway between the alien and the room's entrance. If needed, they could try to run for it, but judging by the size of the alien's massive legs, their chances of making it beyond that door were probably nonexistent, he quickly realized. Once the alien was fully awake, it would undoubtedly have the upper hand. He shifted his attention to Vera and Chasma. His daughter looked as comfortable and content as she would have been watching TV in her room. His wife, on the other hand, seemed understandably fearful and stressed. But she wasn't panicking; at least not yet. The two were right next to him, and he had no intention of letting anything happen to either one of them, if he could help it. Still keeping an eye on the immobile being hovering in its purple light, he looked to his left. François, the daredevil of the bunch, didn't look that reassured either, but a quick glance back from the Frenchman told Dedrick he was OK. Sabrina was tightly glued to him. Ladli, close to them, appeared to be coping.

The alien had begun to slowly move her arms and legs again, as if loosening the joints and muscles of her imposing body. A strong pulse suddenly shook the being's core once more, and the alien finally came to rest in the middle of the platform, now standing on its massive legs. The being slowly raised her arms out, and began to flex her fingers, its eyes still closed. A moment later, the light show had ended, and it finally stood in front of them, in all its majestic presence, now immobile and utterly silent.

Dedrick, staring intensely at the alien, didn't notice the small buzzing sound until it got louder. He looked around the room, trying to pinpoint its source, but it seemed to be coming from everywhere. By their expression of discomfort, the rest of the team was obviously hearing it too. Fearfully looking around, Vera was about to put Chasma's helmet back on, to protect her daughter from the painful noise, when it abruptly stopped. They all turned their attention back to the alien.

Its eyelids began to flicker. The small group instinctively held their breath. The large eyes, at first struggling to deal with the brightness of the surroundings, having been closed for as long as they probably had, slowly opened on the intruders, and stared in absolute silence. François realized they were about to find out if waking her up was such a good idea after all.

At first, seemingly confused, the alien kept blinking its eyes at them, scanning the room and the strange occupants it obviously did not recognize. Dedrick could not get over the beautiful deep purple of its eyes. The tall being slowly lowered itself off the platform, and after some apparent initial discomfort, took a few steps forward. All six humans stepped back with apprehension, but the alien ignored them and, passing right through the fearful group, simply headed for the circular row of life pods. Leaning over one of them, it appeared to stare through the container for a while, before moving to another pod. Waving its hand over the capsule, it awakened the shell and stepped back. The pod began to vibrate slightly and lit up, quickly becoming translucent, and the swirling gases inside started to change color and dissipate. As the object slowly hovered to the center of the room, the central sphere moved back up to the ceiling, and began to spin again. Soon, the encapsulating container was gone, revealing a second alien, even taller and imposing than the first. A few minutes later, the new giant was opening his eyes on the small group of humans.

Just as the first one had, the alien began scanning the room and its occupants. Its large purple eyes stopped on Chasma. Although the stranger's mouth looked quite different and much smaller than ours, Dedrick could tell without a doubt that the giant was smiling at her. Chasma smiled back. The large purple eyes then turned their gaze on Dedrick. Uncertain of what to do, he attempted a weak smile of his own, which made him feel silly, but appeared to please the tall being. Meanwhile, the first alien was already waking up a third hibernating individual.

A few minutes later, three large aliens were standing in front of the colonists, imposing in their size and unique looks. All present in the room were staring back and forth at each other when Chasma said, "You're welcome," addressing the tallest of the three beings.

"Who are you talkin-" started to ask Vera, when they all heard an unfamiliar voice resonate in their heads.

"*Thank you.*"

The "voice" was deep and clear, with a rich tone that felt strangely soothing. The odd sensation would have been hard to explain for any of them. Completely taken by surprise, Dedrick stared at the giant alien, utterly confused, and yet aware that the voice was telepathically talking to him and his crew…in English.

"*Yes, you are correct. We are communicating with you and your friends telepathically, and we know your language. We can also 'hear' your thoughts,*" added the alien. "*My name is Jorh, and this is Mahhzee, my sister, and Gahneo. We are from Kahnu.*"

Dedrick wasn't the only one in shock. They had all heard the strange telepathic voice. The alien had just introduced himself and his two companions, again in plain English. Before any of them could say anything, the alien named Jorh approached and sat down in front of them, his large flexible legs folded under him. Blinking his big purple eyes at Dedrick, he extended his giant hand, slowly. He slowly opened his six even-length fingers to reveal a small white sphere, the size of a football.

The alien watched him hesitate, and spoke again telepathically, "*This is for you. A Zarfha sphere.*" He then set it on the floor in front of Dedrick.

"*A thank you for your help,*" offered the alien named Mahhzee. "*…For getting us out of Time-Frost. Thank you.*"

Turning to François, Sabrina whispered, "I hear them in my head! This is so weird!"

"I know. Me too. It feels really strange."

Mahhzee was the smaller of the three aliens, but only by a half a meter or so. Two tentacles dangled on each side of her jaw, a feature the other two didn't have. Dedrick also noticed her eyes appeared to blink more often than her companions when she "spoke."

"My…My name is Dedrick. We are from Earth." He realized that last statement probably didn't mean anything to them. "I…I thank you for your gift." He didn't really know what else to say.

"*You are welcome, Dedrick. We are quite familiar with all of you.*"

"I…I see."

Sensing the small group's disconcert, the alien felt he needed to explain himself.

"*Your arrival, years ago, awakened us. We do not know why or how, but it did. Since then, we have been following you. We were unable to free ourselves from the pods, but we could 'hear' you. We are truly sorry about your planet and your people.*"

Dedrick was feeling overwhelmed at the moment. They all did. He had just realized the true magnitude of what was happening. He was engaged in a conversation with beings from another world; another intelligent, and obviously advanced species. They were magnificent in size and stance. They looked proud and confident, and appeared peaceful and mannered. On that last observation, Dedrick truly hoped he was right. After so many centuries wondering if there was life elsewhere in the universe, after so many generations asking if we were alone, they finally had the answer. Life was possible elsewhere.

Earth wasn't the only planet harboring it, after all. So did other worlds, and if these beings were from another star, there was a high probability they were many more out there. But then also came the realization that Earth's population had probably been completely eradicated. To think they were only a few years away from all the answers. A few long seconds passed before he realized everyone was looking at him.

Getting back to the reality of the moment, he quickly assessed that his companions and he didn't seem in immediate danger. The aliens could have easily killed them by now, if such was their intention. But he also thought he would be wise to stay on his guard, nonetheless. There was no way to know yet what the imposing beings wanted, or what they were capable of.

"*You have nothing to fear from us, Dedrick,*" said Jorh.

Suddenly remembering they could read his mind, he tried to stop thinking about anything, only to realize thinking of not thinking was still thinking. Struggling with the idea, he looked up to find the alien female, Mahhzee, smiling at him, somewhat amused. François couldn't wait any longer. He stepped a bit closer.

"Hi, my name is François… I'm… Wow! I'm not even sure where to begin… How do you-?"

The alien named Gahneo didn't let François finish his question.

"We can read your thoughts. It is how we communicate on our world. As Jorh said, we do not know how, but we have been able to listen to all of you, ever since you arrived on Kesra. That is how we learned your language."

"Hearing" the alien's thoughts was getting to all of them, making them a bit confused and disoriented. It all seemed so impossible. And yet, it was really happening. Looking at the intimidating figure, Vera was wondering if they were Martians, or visitors from another world. The alien answered.

"*We are from Kahnu, a planet destroyed long ago. We came to Kesra, this planet you call Mars, to escape. We have been here a very long time. Like you, we are the only ones left of our kind.*"

"We are glad you brought Chasma back with you. Without her help, we would still be in Time-Frost," volunteered the alien named Gahneo.

Although she had a feeling the being already knew her next question, Vera asked it anyway. "Why were you 'talking' to Chasma only, and not to all of us? I mean, before you were out of those things," she added, pointing at the pods. Her voice betrayed her anxiety about the alien's interest in her daughter.

"*Vera, you have nothing to fear from us, I promise you. We have been following your progress for quite some time now, and we have become quite fond of you and your friends.*" The female alien was now seated on her crossed legs, next to Jorh. "*It would appear Chasma is much more receptive to our telepathic call than the rest of you. We think it may be because she was born on Kesra, and is still quite young for your species, although we're not sure why that would make a difference. We tried for years to communicate with Dedrick from time to time, using what you call dreams, but his mind was resisting us. It was an exhausting effort for us while still in Time-Frost. Over time, the connection had weakened, but as Chasma got older, we were able to establish a stronger telepathic bond with her. She was much more receptive than any of you, so we concentrated our efforts on her, hoping she would guide you all to us.*"

"I told you it was OK, Mommy," said Chasma, looking at her mother reassuringly. She was smiling, and the way she did had a soothing effect Vera did not expect. She suddenly felt at peace and safe, looking at her child, so confident and calm. Unable to resist, Vera smiled, passing her hand on Chasma's cheek.

"How long have you been in these pods?" asked François.

"*A very long time, I'm afraid,*" replied Jorh. "*According to your Earth calendar, we believe the destruction of our world took place seventy million years ago.*"

"Se…SEVENTY MILLION YEARS?!" repeated Sabrina loudly, absolutely dumbfounded. She was not the only one taken aback by the alien's statement. The entire group was in shock.

"*Yes. At that time, your planet was still home to large primitive creatures you call dinosaurs, a time when none of the species on your world had yet entered the third stage of evolution, what you call self-awareness. We used to come to your wor-*"

The alien named Mahhzee suddenly wobbled, and barely caught herself at the last moment, before falling on her side. Gahneo, who had not said much since he had been awakened, rushed to her side and grabbed her in his long arms, just before she passed out. Jorh was right next to them, and it was clear the two males were exchanging words telepathically, but none of the five adult humans could hear what was being said.

The larger alien finally turned to Dedrick and his crew, while Gahneo carried the inert female alien back to her pod.

"*My sister, Mahhzee, is still very weak from her long sleep. She needs to rest and so do we. We will have to continue this conversation later. There is so much more to tell you... We will contact you again soon,*" he finished, as he raised his two hands in front of his chest and interlaced his twelve fingers. And for a short instant, the lights and colors that flew through his hands dazzled them. He then turned away and walked a few large steps to his pod and climbed in. Within seconds, the colored gases began refilling the containers, and the three aliens quickly disappeared in their enclosing cocoons. Everyone was quiet for a moment, until François broke the silence.

"That's it? Just like that?" he exclaimed.

"Well, you heard him. They are exhausted," replied Dedrick.

"At a time like this?"

"Jorh said they were in those things for millions of years, right? You can't expect them to jump out and go run a marathon now, can you?" remarked Ladli.

"Millions of years… That's insane…" said Vera out loud.

"Or just another perfectly uneventful day on Mars, I guess," replied François sarcastically.

"Personally, I feel better knowing they're back inside those things," volunteered Sabrina almost too quietly.

"Why are you still whispering?" asked Vera, also whispering.

"I… I don't know…"

"Well, that was quite something, wouldn't you agree?" said the Russian commander.

François just looked at him with a clueless expression, shrugged his shoulders, and glided out into the corridor.

"Unbelievable," commented Dedrick, looking at the Frenchman disappear.

#

Back at the base, the long discussions over the amazing events of the day had finally died out, everyone pretty much exhausted, and the eight colonists had, by now, retreated in their individual sleeping quarters. Outside, the Martian night looked as dark as empty space itself. The world around the lonely outpost was utterly silent and still, if not for a few dust clouds occasionally rising along the nearby cliffs, invisible in the pitch-black night. A few scattered reflections on the low hills beyond the station, caused by the base's own lights, were the only shapes breaking the monotony of the impenetrable scene.

Dedrick, staring quietly at them through the small round

window of his pod, was lost in deep thoughts, still wide awake. His eyes gazed up at the darkness of space above and focused unconsciously their attention on a particularly brilliant star sparkling in shades of white and blue; Earth. As they had countless times before, thoughts of the dangers their small oasis sheltered them from in the immensity of the inhospitable desert beyond, came back to haunt him, stronger than ever.

"*I hope we did the right thing, waking up these aliens.*"

He turned to look at his little family. Chasma was sound asleep in her small bunk bed, and Vera was already under the covers, reading Arthur C. Clark's 2067 on her pad. The Russian commander grabbed the square container at his feet, sat down at his desk, and placed the box right in front of him. He meticulously unlocked the six clamps holding the hermetically sealed top, lifted the cover, and slowly removed the object from inside. Unwrapping the towel surrounding it, he carefully laid each corner out to reveal the alien artifact.

"*A Zarfha sphere. An alien artifact from another world. Wow*!" he thought, staring at the white object. In truth, the artifact belonged to all the colonists, not just Dedrick, but he felt overwhelmed at the moment and for a good reason. How many times had he seen it in his dream? In truth, he had no idea what the object was for, or what it could do, but just looking at it here, as real and solid as any other object in the room, was overwhelming. He delicately grazed its surface with the tip of his fingers. To his surprise, the material felt almost familiar. Had he closed his eyes, he could have sworn he was touching glass. Carefully holding the sphere between his fingers, he placed it directly on the desk and gave it a gentle spin. The object spun freely with ease for a few seconds, before coming to a stop. He stared at it with disappointment.

That night, Dedrick, unable to sleep, spent a good portion of his time trying to make the sphere do something, anything. Ultimately, he was hoping he could make it levitate in some way. The Russian tried many things including talking to it and even rolling it on his forehead at one point, but none of his attempts succeeded at getting any reaction from the enigmatic object. He eventually fell asleep in his chair around 05:00AM, exhausted.

A trip in space and time

The inhabitants of station Mars First were all gathered in greenhouse II. Two days had passed since the first encounter with the beings. As promised by the one named Jorh, the colonists had been contacted telepathically and asked to come back to the cave for another visit.

Chasma was listening to her dad attentively, her doll Sylvia in her arms.

"We have to think about our safety first. Since they asked for Chasma, I have to be there. I know you're all impatient to learn more about-"

"Listen, Dedrick, yes, you're right, we need to be careful," Sabrina cut him off. "But I think I speak for all of us when I say we all want to go. I could hardly sleep last night. We've all chosen to come to Mars knowing the risks. And the reason we did was not because it was safe. It's to discover new things, to go beyond what we know, and live an adventure like no other, right?" She looked around the room, finding approving nods. "Well, this is it! Here we are, in one of the most profound moments in history. Of course, we all want to go!"

Although Liu and Tendai were usually the ones with reservations when it came to dangerous situations, even they appeared to agree with Sabrina.

"Ok, well, if that's how everyone feels..." He scanned the room, meeting only approving eyes and nods. "OK, then, that settles it. I'll see you all in the garage in half an hour."

#

No one had much to say on the way there. They were all absorbed in deep thoughts. There was a mixed feeling of fear and excitement in the vehicles. A few hours earlier, when Dedrick had received a clear telepathic message from the aliens, his first reaction had been one of absolute surprise. After the initial shock, he had wondered how far their telepathic abilities stretched, now that they were awake. They had quickly apologized for their unannounced cerebral intrusion. They had asked if the humans could come back to the ship, stating it would give both species a chance to satisfy their respective curiosity about each other. They had also requested the presence of Chasma. By now, there was no doubt in anybody's mind that the five-year-old possessed an innate ability to communicate with the aliens in a way none of them did or could.

Dedrick wasn't the only one who had not really slept much the night before. The events of the previous day were still mind blowing. Although fascinatingly exciting in many ways, the unknowns of the situation at hand were equally frightening to most of them. Of course, that wasn't the case for Chasma, who appeared simply as happy and relaxed as ever. For François, the whole experience was beyond overwhelming, but his curiosity far outweighed any of his fears. And the more he thought about it, the more incredible it all seemed.

"*Aliens, on Mars, alive after millions of years spent asleep in a spaceship! How is that even possible? And what were they doing in that cave in the first place? If we freed them as they said, that means they couldn't get out of those pods by themselves. So, who put them there, then? Could they be dangerous? What if we released some monsters sent on exile to Mars for a good reason?*" A late seventies Superman movie came back to his mind, where three alien criminals are outcast to wander in space, locked in a glass prison.

"*No, I doubt that's it. These beings could have killed us all already if they had wanted to. Something happened to them after the destruction of their world. And what about the others? We counted twenty-six pods on that ship… Are they all awake now? I didn't think about that until now… Gosh, twenty-six giants, and us… And how far do they come from? What star? How fast can their ship travel?*" he wondered. All questions he was aching to get answers to. Now feeling less intimidated than he did at first, after the initial shock of meeting face to face with the imposing beings, François was determined to ask every question he could this time. He took another look at his wrist display, making sure his camera and audio recorder were functioning perfectly, and his suit batteries were fully charged.

An hour or so later, the colonists were greeted by the three aliens.

"*Welcome back, friends,*" announced Jorh as the group entered what Dedrick guessed was the main deck of the ship. "*You are correct. This is what your people would call the control room, or the cockpit of our vessel. Please, take a seat.*" He pointed, with a sweeping hand motion, at a row of twelve oversized chairs in the center of the room. They were arranged in a semi-circle around a circular platform. The two aliens named Gahneo and Mahhzee were already occupying the two seats at each end of the curved row. Approaching hesitantly, the eight humans each picked one of the chairs, climbed on awkwardly and turned to face the central platform. Just as the hibernating pods had the day before, the seats began hovering in place about a meter above the floor as soon as each person had sat on them. Vera, who had taken her daughter with her on her chair, was asked to let Chasma have her own.

"*Don't worry, I promise she will be fine,*" had said Mahhzee. Chasma had complied with an unworried smile.

The chairs were the most comfortable pieces of furniture the humans had ever experienced. Hovering silently, they felt a slight floating sensation, as if on a very calm body of water. A feeling Sabrina may have described best when she had said out loud it felt like "sitting on a cloud of pillows."

Jorh approached one of the empty chairs, and with a smooth hand wave, made it float to the large gap between Mahhzee and Gahneo. After sitting in it, he addressed them all.

"We know you have a lot of questions for us. We do too, even if we already know a lot about your people, having 'listened' to all these years. There is always more to learn, but all in due time. We know you have reservations about our intentions, and we understand. This is why we thought it would be best if we answered some of your questions first."

His big purple eyes blinked a few times as he looked at the smaller beings around him.

"You mentioned your planet was destroyed and-" began Dedrick.

"That is correct. We told you we are not from Kesra, this world you call Mars, but from Kahnu, a planet orbiting your sun, between Kesra and Dahmes, the one you call Jupiter. Our world was a beautiful and peaceful one. Our population counted almost fifty thousand individuals. Long before your species existed, our people had traveled to other worlds, including yours and this one. Our culture was a flourishing one, and our people were happy. Unfortunately, one day we discovered a rogue planet was on a collision course with ours. Varih-Aru, as it was named, would reach our world within a few years. We tried desperately to save Kahnu but… things did not go as we had hoped."

"What happened?" asked François.

"Our attempt to stop the massive world from colliding with ours failed. You see, on our planet, the council of Elders, our leaders and spiritual guides, was not always willing to listen to the scientists of our world. Every decision, every new discovery, any course of action had to be approved by the council. It took many

months to convince the Elders the rogue planet Varih-Aru would destroy Kahnu if we did nothing. When they finally accepted the seriousness of the danger, the building of a special ship was commissioned, the Ehoran, a vessel capable of diverting Varih-Aru's path. Unfortunately for us, we did not realize the council had a secret agenda. Ultimately, they took the Ehoran to escape our doomed world, leaving us to our fate."

Sensing some confusion among the group, Jorh tried to explain more clearly.

"Our people believed we came from another star, long ago. The first world, Ahtona, was believed to be a planet orbiting a star in what you call the Lyra constellation. We did not know it at the time, but the council actually believed the impending doom was a sign to return. When the time came to stop the danger, the Elders used the vessel meant to meet with Varih-Aru to leave for Ahtona instead. Only a handful of us survived the destruction."

He paused a moment, reflecting.

François couldn't help puzzling over one thing. *"Why would their rulers let their world and its people get destroyed, when they had the means to stop it?"*

"Varih-Aru," specified Gahneo.

François was beginning to find the alien's mind-reading abilities a bit annoying.

Jorh explained, *"Our leaders were resolute believers of the legend of Ferrhem. The ancient legend said that the great Ferrhem, son of the goddess Ahtona, and his female companion Keisha, daughter of the Grand Hallis, grew reckless and undeserving of the mother world, and were banished to Kahnu. There they would stay, until the day they would be allowed to return, having grown wiser and peaceful. Ferrhem and Keisha had many children on Kahnu, spawning several generations. Eventually growing impatient and resentful, Ferrhem traveled back to Ahtona to reclaim his place as ruler of the first world, promising he would soon come back for Keisha and their people, but Ferrhem never returned. Many more eons passed. When the time came for Keisha to leave the world of the living, she appointed her youngest son, Gibhez to rule over Kahnu. In the following centuries, Gibhez created the council of Elders and began teaching the legend of Ferrhem. Kahnu grew strong and peaceful. We began traveling through the solar system, and eventually visited all its planets and moons. Had it not been for Varih-Aru…but Gibhez and the council were convinced the rogue world was a sign; a sign for them, and them only, to return to Ahtona."*

"Sounds like a pretty dramatic way to ask you guys back. I mean, sending an entire planet as an invite? Couldn't a small asteroid have been enough?" François chuckled, but once again, his remark only amused him.

Jorh, apparently trying to explain further, went on. "*Some of us only took the legend for what it was, a legend. But the elders were certain the time had come. We had just created a new Zarfha engine, a technology cable of... Would you like to see?*"

"*See?*" asked Dedrick, attempting to communicate without using his voice.

Jorh's eyes blinked quickly at him several times.

"*Kahnu, our world, and what happened to it,*" he replied. "*We can show you.*"

"You mean like a movie?" asked Sabrina.

"It depends on what you mean by showing us," commented Tendai under his breath, hesitantly.

Dedrick and the rest of them were definitely intrigued.

"*We would love to.*"

"I want to see, I want to see!" rejoiced Chasma, bopping up and down on her seat.

"*Good, but before we begin, we'd like you to join us in an experiment.*"

The faces in the small group turned to each other, somewhat apprehensive.

"*I promise, you have nothing to fear,*" said Mahhzee again, feeling the group's hesitation. Jorh extended his hand forward, and a small Zarfha sphere appeared in his open palm.

Facing Dedrick, Jorh asked, "*Dedrick, I want you to look at this Zarfha and try to move it with your mind.*"

"I'm sorry, you...what? I'm afraid our species doesn't have the ability to do that. On our world, we-"

"*We know. But now that you are here, in this ship, we'd like to know how developed your telepathic abilities really are. I'll explain why soon.*"

Dedrick could sense the urgency in the alien's request. He hesitated a moment... "Ok, I'll try my best." Focusing visually and mentally all his efforts on the white alien object, he tried desperately to make it move, to make it do something, anything. But the Zarfha sphere remained still, resting immobile in the center of the alien's hand. A good minute passed before he finally exhaled heavily. He had not realized it, but by concentrating as much as he had, he had forgotten to breathe.

"Oofff! I can't do it," he let out, feeling a bit dizzy. After regaining his breath, he reclined in his chair, disappointed. *"I'm sorry."*

"*It's alright*," reassured him, Mahhzee.

"Can I try it?" François sounded quite excited, confident he had a better shot at it than his Russian friend.

"*Yes, of course, François*," replied Jorh, moving his extended arm in the Frenchman's direction.

To his grave frustration, François had no more luck than Dedrick at getting any reaction from the sphere. Even after spending almost twice as long as the Russian did at it. To the alien's joyful surprise, the humans each took a turn at the exotic challenge, even combining their efforts as a last resort, to no avail. Only Chasma did not participate. Vera found it odd that her child seemed content to watch only. When all had given up and claimed countless times how impossible the test was, Jorh turned the Zarfha to Chasma, and said telepathically for all to hear, "*Now, Chasma.*"

It took only a second for the sphere to rise above the giant's hand and to begin spinning silently on itself in mid-air. Chasma began giggling joyfully, as the rest of them watched in awe.

"Is that really...? Chasma, are you really the one doing -?" Vera could not believe her own eyes.

"*Your daughter senses things you don't. She has a powerful mind. We have never met another species capable of interacting with Zarfhas. This is most fascinating*," finished Jorh, as he reclaimed the sphere and leaned back on his chair.

The simple test had yielded useful results. To Jorh and his two friends, it meant the young human child could feel, and manipulate, energies no other species but Kahnus could. She could interact at a higher telepathic level than any of the adults. Why? They still could not tell. It also meant a physical connection with the rest of the group would be necessary for what they had in mind, as they had expected.

"What does it mean? What do you want with Chasma?" Vera wasn't so sure her daughter's abilities were such a good thing. The mother in her couldn't help but worry.

"*It is not what we want with your daughter that matters, Vera, it's why she is able to channel universal energies while none of you can. Only Kahnus can connect with a Zarfha. We have studied your kind, and we are baffled as to why she can do so*," volunteered Gahneo.

Vera looked silently at Chasma, pensive.

"Chasma was born here, on Mars. She is the first human ever

born on this planet. Could that have something to do with it?" asked Dedrick.

"*It is possible that helped in some way, but she is still human, regardless. Something else must be at play here…*" He paused before turning his attention back to the platform in front of them. "*I told you we had something to show you…*"

From a delicate swerve of the hand, Jorh pushed the only empty chair to the back of the room and brought everyone closer. They were now all within arm's reach of each other. Another intricate hand movement made a much larger sphere appear in the middle of the seated group, and Jorh reached out for Mahhzee and Gahneo, on each side of him. Their flexible tubular fingers interconnected and began to glow mildly of various colors. Jorh addressed the humans once more.

"*We have 'heard' many of your questions. We believe this will answer most of them, if not all.*"

As they all turned to look at the sphere now spinning faster and brighter, Mahhzee and Gahneo extended their free hands to the two colonists next to them.

"*Please join hands*," asked Mahhzee, looking in turn at all of them.

At first a bit perplexed and hesitant, the eight humans soon complied. For François, who was the one seated closest to the female alien, the hesitation had been quite comprehensible. The long and tentacle like fingers of Mahhzee, each grabbed one of his fingers, as a tubular suction device would have. It instantly reminded him of a milking pump he had seen used on cows back on Earth. The sensation was foreign to say the least, but not unpleasant, he thought to himself. Directly across from him, at the other end of the circle, Liu, seated next to Gahneo, was going through the same odd experience. They both smiled at each other, feeling a bit strange and euphoric, like two drinking buddies sharing one too many drinks. The relaxed sensation soon went across everyone in the circle and was quickly replaced by a strong need to sleep. As the group slowly began to fall under, beautiful light waves of multiple colors began to swirl all around the sphere, extending progressively to the entire space around all of them. Dedrick tried in vain to fight the irresistible feeling of drowsiness, struggling to keep his eyes open on the beautiful light show taking place in front of him. It was a futile effort. Soon they were all asleep, but their minds were not.

Sabrina felt like she was falling in slow motion towards an

invisible bottom, down a giant well surrounded by complete darkness. Although the sensation was unknown, she was surprisingly unafraid. She felt supported in some way, by something or someone. And with her eyes closed, she could "see" in this strange dream state. Soon, she was floating in space, countless stars surrounding her. A strong sensation of forward movement took over her, as if she was racing across the vast emptiness. Comfortably resting in her seat, she could see her colleagues floating along with her, their weightless bodies in their oversized flying chairs, slowly spiraling across the vastness. Flashes of light from stars zooming by appeared to flow right through them at times, giving the explorers a sensation of euphoria. It was an experience no word could describe, a feeling beyond any they had ever felt. And they soon realized something else. Their thoughts were shared as one and heard by all. The connection felt impossible and yet totally natural as well, almost comfortable and reassuring by its familiarity, and they could not help but feel a sense of calm and happiness they could not explain. They also knew they were not really there. It was a dream, a fantasy they were now experiencing in another dimension, occupying the abstract state between time and space. Their minds were adrift in a space they did not know, but felt reassuring and inviting, nonetheless.

Back in the spaceship, Jorh was in control of the ten beings asleep next to him. Mahhzee and Gahneo had the same ability to both be in the present and the past during a viewing, as they called it, but were passive spectators in this instance, sleeping conduits between him and the small human group. Of course, all three were capable of mentally exchanging similar viewing experiences without the need to be connected physically as they were all now, holding hands. They didn't need to be asleep either, but Jorh and his companions had judged correctly that the humans would be telepathically limited to thought exchange only. To show the colonists visual memories or events, the three had to be physically connected to the humans by performing a melting, an ancient practice that had not been used for thousands of Kahnu years but was proving particularly effective in this instance. Jorh slowly opened his eyes and fixed a point on the ceiling above. Within seconds, the light around the room began to dim to a darker shade of purple, and the hovering spinning sphere in the center of the group began to display a light show like no human had ever seen. Unfortunately, none were watching. The group was now in a controlled state of sleep. On the platform in front of them, countless colorful lines, forming in and out of the sphere, flares weaving their vivid and luminous colors in countless shapes, moving like thin scarves flowing in an invisible wind, were now projecting a fantastic color light display across the entire white room.

Jorh, still controlling the sphere in front of him, sent a colorful burst of energy down his arms to his fingers, channeling through Mahhzee and Gahneo, on down to every individual in the room. Shimming through their unified awareness, a thousand small bells rang inside their heads, like countless droplets of water hitting a giant harp, and the blinding light of a million stars exploded in the infinite emptiness in front on them. As if sucked away by a powerful vacuum, their thoughts, feelings, bodies, and minds, helpless witnesses to an incredible experience they could no more control than resist, were now being taken on a ride along universal energies no other human ever knew existed.

Chapter IX

Kahnu

Floating silently into the emptiness of space, stars, and familiar celestial formations were beginning to become recognizable to them. Landmarks like the Orion Belt and the Big Dipper, which would have been better called sky marks, were easy constellations to spot for Dedrick's team, after their countless years training with the Mars First space program. To their left, they could all see a larger body of light, a familiar celestial object they instantly recognized as the sun. They also soon noticed another bright body, far in the distance. They didn't feel the sensation of pull anymore, but they were still floating in space, in their oversized egg-shaped chairs. Liu had just noticed, and so did all, that she could not see her own body; only those around her. Her hands and feet were there, she could feel them move, she could touch her chair with them, but she could not see them. They were completely transparent, as if missing. It was the case for all of them; a very strange realization. They did not dwell long on it. Vera was staring at the rapidly growing round object, when they all realized at the exact same time that they were approaching Kahnu, the alien's home planet. This strange ability to sense and feel together as one was the most profound experience any of them had ever had. Although each individually retained the ability to think and look at what he or she wished, all of them thought and saw the same thing as well. Everything was instantly shared and understood by all, as if they were one entity, one individual, one mind. Within seconds, the large planet was taking most of the view in front of them, revolving slowly on itself, suspended in the darkness of space. If Earth was called the Blue Planet, this one would have deserved the Purple Planet title, without a doubt. Its atmosphere was almost completely free of clouds, giving the observers an unobstructed view of its geology. The alien world was one giant purple ocean, surrounding a single large, and mostly icy, continent.

"*Look, there!*" Everyone's attention had already turned to a smaller body, passing rapidly between them and the purple world below.

"*A moon,*" they all realized.

"*Frohee,*" specified Mahhzee's telepathic voice. "*This was our world, Kahnu and its three moons, Ehoran, Ogg, and Frohee as they looked seventy million of your Earth years ago. Our planet used to orbit Alhis, your sun, between Kesra and Dahmes, the worlds you call Mars and Jupiter.*"

Below, floating majestically in the dark vacuum of space, the large world was quite beautiful. Without a point of reference, it was difficult to estimate its size, but they all felt it was probably comparable to Earth's. Occasionally breaking the otherwise uniformly white surface below, darker patches of land could be seen here and there. Approaching irresistibly closer, they soon stared in awe at the gigantic tree-like features along the shores of the single continent. They were amazed not only by their alien look, but also, and especially, by the enormity of their size.

"*Klomags,*" offered Jorh telepathically. "*We lived in them.*"

The light-brown giants towered over the icy world, their gigantic trunks disappearing down into the hazy distance below. Sporting only a handful of what could have been considered enormous branches, some of them interconnecting between Klomags, the towering trees were several kilometers tall and topped by a very large round space, open to the sky like a giant flower. Its dark shiny petals reminded the observers of the absolute blackness they had encountered in the Martian cave dwellings, but the aliens informed them those were two very different things. All around the perimeter, long protrusions, the size of tall city buildings, hung upside down. Hundreds of spherical objects, as big as small houses, dangled from them, far above the several kilometer-deep abyss below. Coming down further, they began to notice dark spots and cuts along the Klomags' trunk. They soon realized the giant edifices were riddled with tunnels and large cavities. Inside them, hundreds of Kahnu aliens were busy moving about, going through their daily activities, unaware of the travelers. On the upper side of the gigantic tree branches, hovering crafts were orderly flying from Klomag to Klomag. The surreal scene was rendered even more spectacular by the intense contrast between the dark giants and the blinding white of the icy world below. The Kahnus and their giant tree-world rested on top of a high plateau, a good hundred meters above sea level. Still approaching, a thundering noise was building up strength down below. As the group reached the edge of the cliff overlooking the purple waters, they soon understood where the mayhem was coming from. Hundreds of ice columns were breaking off the cliff walls of the plateau, floating away into the calm purple ocean, while others were coming back to reattach themselves to the icy walls, a truly odd geological process. They couldn't help but watch, mesmerized. Most intriguing of all, the blocks were floating standing up. Tall and thin as they were, they should have fallen onto their side or sunk into the ocean waters, yet they miraculously stood in vertically, like giant ice needles. The group could sense the ocean was not the force behind the strange mechanism, and the detaching and reattaching did not appear to follow any kind of logic or rhythm. The obvious randomness of the spectacle made it all the more fascinating. The scene followed the contour of the entire visible coast until it disappeared behind the horizon. From one end to the other, thousands of ice columns were thrashing against the cliffs, while thousands more were breaking away. The noise level was still increasing. By now, the seven human adults were covering their ears. Mahhzee's telepathic voice spoke.

"*We apologize. We just realized this must be quite loud for you. We can hear them as well, but at a much lower level than you. We are used to them.*"

Not wanting to prolong their passengers' discomfort, the aliens moved the group away, and quickly moved on toward a large mountain beyond the plateau. Leaving the ice columns and the Klomags behind, they soon arrived at the top of a tall ice-covered mountain.

"*Nott,*" commented Jorh.

A small cave, its mouth guarded by a large Zarfha, was growing larger as they approached. When they finally entered, the cold icy surroundings gave way to a cathedral-size space. Its walls were covered by countless shiny discs of various sizes, each baring a unique marking at its center. Toward the back of the chamber, large columns covered in large grooves from top to bottom, towered over several Kahnus dressed in colorful clothing. Seated in a semi-circle, the Elders were engaged in a heated conversation with several Kahnus standing a few steps lower in the center of the hall.

François and his friends looked at the aliens hovering over the scene with them. With eyes blinking, Jorh telepathically explained. Yes, the Kahnu arguing with the council was also Jorh, a younger Jorh, trying to save his planet long before its destruction. He and a more seasoned scientist named Ldohar, had discovered the rogue planet would enter Alhis-Ta, the solar system, within a few years, and they were certain about the monster's trajectory. It would collide with

Kahnu.

"You are speculating, Jorh. Varih-Aru is still years away. Why are you so sure it will come for us?"

"And why are you so sure it won't?"

To that last question, the Elders answered as they always did, by first condemning the insolence of the apprentice, still too young in the field of science to present his unwarranted opinion and then scorching him for daring question the council's decision. No real explanation needed be given. Keisha, the ancient mother, had spoken to them, and given her message of truth. No harm would come to Kahnu from the rogue space object. No more was to be said, the council's decision was irreversible.

The observing group suddenly felt a jolt, and soon, their seats were racing. Rushing forward above the giant ice terrain, occasional protruding land masses zooming by, the small humans and their three alien guides finally came to a halt. Still surrounded by the bright white surface, they were now in the middle of a large gathering assembled in an open valley. The flat area was surrounded by a group of icy mountains and two imposing glaciers.

"This was the last great gathering of Darkuj. Look..." pointed Jorh.

Their chairs hovering invisibly through the masses, the sounds and sensations they felt were almost as real as if they had been there. Dedrick's group, fast asleep in their suspended state of unconsciousness, was reliving a moment long lost in time, an event that had taken place seventy million years ago. As the observers watched and listened, they also felt a sense of understanding, a feeling of knowing what was happening beyond mere observation.

The masses had gathered on the icy grounds of Darkuj, the valley where all grand ceremonies and celebrations took place. Thousands of Kahnus had come from all regions for the occasion. Friends and acquaintances were reuniting, seated in small to large circles scattered across the valley, talking about their lives and the impending danger of Varih-Aru that, it had been recently announced, would be soon averted. Some were listening from their hovering vehicles to the beautiful sounds the Ghervz, tall stick-like creatures, were making in the distance. Others were enjoying sharing pleasures with partners, in various group configurations. Young adults, who had only recently left Kahalla, the pool of birth, were joyfully playing imaginary games, one of young Kahnus favorite pastimes. Along the steep mountainside nearest to the large gathering, several niches carved in the ice were reverberating to the deep sounds of Barks, bulky cup-shaped disks, spinning around giant Zarfha spheres. Next to them, several Kahnus were stumping their oversized feet in rhythm, their low-pitched pounding creating a rumbling effect throughout the entire valley, a truly mesmerizing experience.

"*The Shirzu turners. They are the beat keepers of Kahnu and always lead the gatherings with their beautiful rhythms,*" Jorh said telepathically. "*Tonight, the occasion is one of celebration. Soon, the flying ship Ehoran, will meet with the dwarf planet Varih-Aru and force it off its course, saving our world and its fifty thousand inhabitants.*"

Below, large numbers of Kahnus were creating dazzling light shows, colorful displays of love and joy, all bathed in the purple shades cast by Kahnu's three moons, brightly reflecting on the frozen continent. Further down the valley, the same thing was taking place in the Klomags. Bright flashes of various colors were sparkling like stars all along the giant tree trunks. The dark waterways below them adding to the dazzling effect with their own reflections of the fiery display, the visual result was breathtaking. On the horizon, massive alien machines appeared to hover silently above the purple ocean.

"*Vakkehs; transport vessels,*" Jorh told them. From afar, they resembled dark pyramids, cruising above the waters of Mohgvar, displacing powerful undulating waves across the purple ocean below. Although not the fastest vessels, they were capable of transporting cargo loads of up to twenty thousand tons and accommodate several hundred passengers. It was the most common mode of transportation on Kahnu, after individual Voks.

The small group of hovering spectators was transported seamlessly across the ice, toward another group of giant Klomags near the coast. Out of the flat icy terrain bordering the purple ocean, giant protruding roots connected the immense trees to the water. The group approached one of the largest Klomags. At its base, the gargantuan was several hundred meters wide. This was a truly enormous edifice. Tendai looked up. They all did. The massive trunk shot so high up into the sky, they could not see its top. A few kilometers above the spectators, the giant tree vanished in the thick upper atmosphere, as if swallowed higher up by an invisible fog. Liu smiled, and they all did. They had just noticed at the same instant the small filaments of light coming down from far up, falling quietly all around the base like stringy snowflakes. A majestic scene.

"*This was our home, Klomag-Darh. Thousands of Kahnus lived here.*"

They stared in awe as their alien guide slowly led them to the entrance of the towering edifice. They were trying to take it all in. It was odd, and yet so breathtakingly magical. The observers' attention was suddenly drawn to a fast approaching flying vehicle coming straight behind them. The semi-transparent Vok, not much larger than a small bus, passed right in front of the invisible group without a sound, and rushed on into the large tunnel ahead. They all instantly knew the individual at the control was Jorh. Jorh of the past. Vera and her colleagues turned to the alien near her. He blinked at them and turned his attention back to his past self. The Jorh driving the flying vessel was the first to arrive at Harzo, the Grand Entrance Hall of Klomag-Darh, and was quickly rejoined by three others. After parking their vehicles in their gelatinous spots, the three Kahnus rejoined him. The humans recognized Mahhzee and Gahneo instantly. Serm's name was given telepathically to them for the third.

"*Let's go,*" said the young Jorh.

Rushing along corridors and hallways, weaving through groups of Kahnus and a variety of hovering crafts, the team made its way deeper into Harzo, to the secret passage that lead several levels underground. To the humans, watching these large beings running was interesting, to say the least. Their powerful legs gave them an impressive stride. The background noise of festivities above soon vanished, and the determined aliens quickly kept on.

"*What happened?*" asked the one named Serm, while running. "*I don't understand. What did Garnak mean?*" But no one answered.

When they reached the bottom, the small group rushed through a soft gelatinous passage, and hastily made their way to an immense underground pool. Near its icy edge, a structure François and everyone else immediately recognized as Chasma's big white cloud, or one identical to it, was floating in the dark waters. Next to it, another Kahnu, even taller than Jorh, was waiting.

"*Garnak,*" commented Mahhzee.

Garnak, keeper of Darkuj, was one of Jorh's mentors. He wore a long magenta tunic, as all keepers did, which appeared to be floating around his body. The hovering throne he was standing on showed elaborate sculpting and carvings; lines like the ones they had already seen back at the Gate and inside the Martian cave.

The four Kahnus rejoined their elder quickly. Jorh spoke first.

"Garnak, we heard you. What is wrong?"

"My friends, what I have to tell you is tragic, even more than that, it's unfathomable. I wish I had better news, but… The Ehoran will not rendezvous with Varih-Aru."

"What? What do you mean? What happened?"

"I know this is hard to believe, but the Elders have taken the ship and left us to our fate."

"That cannot be! Why would they do such a thing? You are mistaken," interjected the alien named Serm, in disbelief.

"We're doomed. Without the Ehoran, nothing can stop Varih-Aru." Mahhzee was obviously distraught.

Garnak kept on. *"Gihhez lied. He had no intention of saving Kahnu. The Elders left aboard the Ehoran and took twelve of the young ones with them. This is all true, I promise you. I wish it was a lie. They are gone. Without the Ehoran, there is nothing we can do to stop Varih-Aru now. It is only a matter of days before we feel the effects of the dark planet. Kahnu will not survive the destruction fate has placed in its path."*

"We need to tell everyone and-"

"What good would that do, Mahhzee?" he cut her off. *"The end is unavoidable now. Let the people rejoice in these last hours. Only panic and agony will follow if they know. No, my friends, I'm afraid we must keep this somber future to ourselves."*

"I still can't believe the Elders have left us. To go where?" asked the young Gahneo.

"Ahtona."

"Ahtona!?" all four said almost at the same time.

"But, no one can go to Ahtona. It's much too far! I don't understand," said Jorh.

"The Ehoran is a powerful ship. You should know, you created its Zarfha engine. You know how fast that vessel can travel. It is a long journey, but they can make it."

"But, such a trek will take too long, even for the Ehoran!? No one has ever been kept in Time-Frost more than a few months! How can they hope to reach Ahtona?" asked the young Mahhzee in disbelief.

"I'm not sure, but I believe they can. After all, no one knows how long one can stay in Time-Frost. Regardless, the Ehoran is gone. But that's not all..." Garnak paused, looking at the small group hesitantly.

"What is it...? Oh no! Kahalla!" said the young Jorh, who had just

read Garnak's thoughts before the others. He was in shock. They all were. Without Kahalla, the pool of life, no Kahnu could ever be born again, even if they managed to escape the planet's destruction.

"Garnak, is it really true? Are you sure they took the pool of Kahalla?" asked Jorh, incredulous.

"I'm afraid so, my friend."

"Then, we must go after them."

"After the Elders? How?" asked his sister.

"This ship," replied Jorh pointing at the white vessel floating next to them.

"But this Aruk isn't fast enough to catch up to the Eboran. It's a Moon-Traveler. It's not even capable of reaching interstellar space. No ship on Kahnu can catch up to the Eboran," said Serm.

"Yes, I know. At least not like this. That's why we must leave immediately for Kesra.

"Kesra? Why Kesra?" asked Mahhzee.

"Your brother is right," said Garnak. *"You need to get Kesra's Gobhan and Kahjuna's white light. With them, you will be able to catch up to the Eboran. You must stop the Elders and bring back what was stolen from us, before they are out of reach! I have already made arrangements. To save time, Silargh will take another Aruk and go straight to Kahjuna. Once his group has retrieved the white light, they'll come meet you on Kesra, where you'll combine the two and go after the Elders. You cannot save Kahnu, but with Kahalla, you and those with you can survive. I know fifty individuals isn't much to rebuild our civilization, but it will have to be enough."*

"Fifty? Restart our civilization? Garnak, I don't understand. What are you saying?"

"What I am saying, Mahhzee, is that we cannot save Kahnu and its people. There is no time. But what you can do is save as many as two moon travelers can carry; twenty-six passengers each. I know it sounds tragically small, but with the pool of Kahalla, you will be able to survive, even if it's on another world."

"Two ships? I don't understand. We must have at least a dozen more here alone," said a confused Gahneo.

"I wish it was so, but the council had them all destroyed before they left. It's obvious they didn't want anyone to follow."

"But why? Why would they do such a thing?" Mahhzee was truly getting upset and distraught.

"I believe they are following the words of Ferrhem, trying to fulfill the prophecy of Eboran. Now I'm beginning to understand why they wanted the ship

named after him. You all know the words as well as I do."

"But that's only a story, an old legend. How can the Elders be so merciless and leave fifty thousand of us to die for a tale? Gibhez has gone mad!"

"I agree with you on that, Mahhzee. Like you, most of us in this room do not believe in the legend, but I'm afraid some Elders have become blinded by their faith. You must reclaim the Ehoran and its precious cargo. Without it, saving fifty or fifty thousand won't matter. I truly wish you could take everyone with you. But that's impossible. And even if you had more ships, that would still not be enough to save but a fraction of our population. This Aruk and Silargh's are the only ones left now. I know it's not much, but they will have to do. There is no time to waste. You must leave tonight. Those who have been selected to join you are already on their way."

"Garnak, my mother?" she asked.

"She is on the list. Most of your direct family relatives are.

Garnak quickly turned to Jorh.

"Listen, only the four of you can know about this. That is why I asked you to come down here to tell you. We cannot start a panic, or a mad mob may ensue. If anything happens to one of those ships, you know as well as I do, no one will survive. We cannot take that chance."

"Jorh, this ship was never meant to travel such distances. Do you really think we can catch up to the Elders?" asked the young Gahneo.

"Yes. I believe Garnak is correct. But we need the lights. The Elders' ship is fast, but it will not reach full speed for another few months, and they won't expect anyone to follow, so with a bit of luck, we have a chance."

"But you need to act quickly," remarked the Keeper. "The survival of our species depends on it."

Even if facial expressions on the aliens' faces were not easily discernable for the human group, the gloomy feeling around the group was obvious.

"I know it feels hopeless right now, but you'll have to find another world to call home. It will be your decision to make. But I would suggest Jashi-Da." The human observers instantly knew he was speaking of Europa, Jupiter's moon. *"The facilities there will provide shelter and a place to regroup. The poles of Kahjuna would be a good choice as well, but there are many dangers on that wild planet. Either way, you must stop the Ehoran. It's your first priority and only chance."*

"But…Garnak…"

"I know, Mahhzee. Trust me, I know. But if you don't, everyone will perish. I wish there was more we could do here, but we are running out of time. If it's only

fifty that can be saved, then so be it. But even that will be in vain if you don't get the Kahalla back."

"Garnak is right. We have no choice." Jorh turned his attention on Garnak. *"So, where are the others?"*

"They will be here soon. Most were chosen by the Guardians. You know many of them personally. Donjeh will join you too. I'm sure you'll want to-" Garnak paused a moment, as if distracted by a thought.

"Donjeh?" asked Jorh.

He was silent a bit longer, then turned to Mahhzee.

"Mahhzee, you are now the official pilot. Jeggah walked the cliffs of Garhnoj tonight. I was hoping he would not, but… I guess he was unable to face the Elders' betrayal. He was the best pilot we had. You are the next logical choice. You have more experience flying this size ship than anyone else."

"Me? But I…"

"You'll be fine. Jorh will be able to assist you when needed. Jorh, I don't think anyone will have any issue if I leave you in charge. Someone will need to guide them all, someone they can trust and look up to. I know you will be great at it." He paused again and looked up as if distracted by a distant sound. *"Good, Donjeh is on his way with the others. He knows the way to the cave on Kesra. I know you all have reservations about him, but I assure you, you can trust him. He may be eccentric and often obsessive about his work, but he knows more than any of us about the 'Lights.' And he was right about Gibhez and the council. He will be a great asset to your venture. Now, it is time to say goodbye, my friends."*

"Goodbye? Garnak, you're coming with us, aren't you? You have to. We can't leave without you," said a frightened Mahhzee. They all joined her in protests of disapproval.

"That is kind of you my friends, but my place is here, among those who will need me most in these last hours. I am too old now to worry about saving myself. You don't need me. I know you will make it. I can sense it. That is what is most important. And it gives me great joy to know that all will not be lost. Oh, one more thing before I go. Your ship contains the grand library of knowledge. Whatever happens, make sure it is preserved and kept with you, no matter where you go. It will be of great use to you and your descendants in the third world. This will also insure Kahnu and its great history will not be forgotten."

His fingers interlocked, he gave them a quick goodbye, and his hovering throne disappeared down a passage behind him. Before any of them could say or do anything else, Donjeh, followed by a large number of individuals, appeared through another tunnel and approached the small Kahnu group in a hurry. The disproportionate size of their legs gave the strange illusion they were running in slow motion.

"*Jorh! Gahneo, Serm, Mahhzee! Good to see you all here. I have brought everyone with me. We're ready. We need to go now*!" he added, and without waiting for a reply, Donjeh waved his hand over the side of the white Aruk, and a large corridor opened in front of him, its purple hue lighting the way inside. He rushed in, his followers right behind him, Serm included.

Jorh and Mahhzee's mother rushed to them. "I can't believe what is happening. It's so terrible…" Gahneo and the three of them watched the last of the passengers float away and disappear down the ship's entrance. The four were silent for a moment. The young Mahhzee looking up at the ceiling above, imagining the thousands playing, loving and living their last moments on the beautiful world she called home, unaware of the fate awaiting them. Knowing there was no turning back, Gahneo grabbed her arm and pulled her with him into the vessel, Jorh and his mother in tow.

A few minutes later, the ship was departing. Jorh was now in telepathic communication with Silargh, the other ship's leader.

"*We just took off. How much longer do you need?*"

"*Most of us are here. We're just waiting on one more group. Garnak said they should be here any moment,*" replied Silargh.

"*Best of luck on your journey to Kahjuna. I hope Garnak knows what he's doing.*"

"*Me too, Jorh. Have a safe trip to Kesra. See you when we get there.*"

Rushing back out of Kahnu's atmosphere, the observers and their hovering chairs suddenly found themselves racing through space once again, and soon reached the zooming Aruk. In an instant, they were all inside. It was the very same control room they were physically in now, but in a very distant past, and occupied by a dozen aliens. The younger Mahhzee was seated in the center of the group, flying the ship. She looked exhausted. The observers collectively realized some time had passed since the departure from Kahnu. Her purple eyes were so dark from fatigue they almost looked colorless. Yet, seemingly unaffected by her drained body, her twelve fingers, six on each hand, were working busily, weaving shapes in the air at the translucent Zarfha in front of her. A few minutes ago, a cloud of space debris bombarding the ship, had forced the small crew of twenty-six to manually change course and maneuver around the bulkier of the objects, sending the spaceship off track. She was now working on putting it back on course. Like her brother Jorh, she was a scientist, a rational being who rarely lost her temper or her calm, no matter what the situation might be. But after what they had all been through, staying focused and alert was becoming a challenge, even for her. She could feel her long thin arms trembling. Her thick legs were restless and her troubled head heavy, heavy not only from the lack of sleep, but also from doubt and worry as to their true chance of survival in the days to come. She was having a hard time concentrating, constantly thinking about the fate of their doomed planet, the absurdity of their efforts in trying to save a handful of people, when thousands were about to perish. And what if they couldn't reclaim Kahalla? What if they couldn't catch up to the Ehoran? A wave of fear suddenly ran through her body. Sadness started filling her heart again, as it had so many times in the last few days, and for a short moment, her fingers stopped moving. Trembling uncontrollably like a naked child in the cold snow, Mahhzee clinched her fists and closed her eyes. Taking a deep breath, she made a conscious effort to release the unwelcome thoughts.

They were here now, in this vessel, flying through space at more than 400,000 kilometers an hour, on their way to Kesra, the closest planet to theirs. They were among those who had been lucky enough to escape the destruction of their home world. Nothing more could be done but move on. The survival of her species depended on the next few days.

Although quite familiar with the navigation system, having designed most of it himself, Jorh was not the one navigating them out of danger. That task had been given to Mahhzee, his sister, who had managed to steer them clear of the rogue boulders earlier, but not without great effort. Of course, she was the most qualified to pilot a ship this size, the only Guild Elected in fact. Garnak had appointed her as the official pilot. Every member of the crew was capable of flying a Vok, a compact sky vehicle. Those were as common on Kahnu as cars were on Earth in the twenty-first century, but flying this ship in the vacuum of space was as foreign to any of them as it would have been to fly a commercial airliner on Earth for the average person. Mahhzee, having flown several Vakkehs, commercial Kahnu ships, across the vast lakes of Darkuj in her early years as a cargo pilot, had unanimously inherited the position of senior navigator when the assigned pilot had ended his life a few days earlier.

Frantically entering a series of instructions for the ship's artificial brain to follow, using a new landing course she had recalculated four times, "*just to make sure*," Mahhzee finished the command and switched her attention to the view on her left, showing the distance that separated them from their destination. The image of a small reddish planet in the background was easily recognizable. She was more than ever determined to get everyone safely to Kesra, the planet humans would later call Mars. She would also need to land the ship once they reached Kesra. They all had great hopes their destination would bring them some comfort. They needed to re-establish some sort of sense and cohesion in everyone's recently shattered spirit. Being confined to this ship was taking its toll on all of them. She could feel a great deal of telepathic distress and confusion on board. None of them would ever see their home planet again, and the vessel was one of only two that had managed to leave Kahnu in time. Of the thousands that populated their planet, only fifty-two Kahnus had escaped. Twenty-six on each ship. Of course, there were also the elders and those they had taken with them on the Ehoran, but once Kahalla was back in their possession, Jorh and his people had no intension of following the Elders anymore. They would regroup and rebuild their lost world on their own terms. For now, Kesra was their first destination.

Their vessel was about one hundred meters in length at its longest point, and about half that distance at its widest. More or less oval in shape, it resembled a giant egg, with several protuberances of similar rounded shapes all around its hull. Most of them a few meters in diameter or smaller, they appeared in random places on the outside shell of the ship, making for a deformed and odd-looking potato-like vessel. There were no antennas or other attachments, no markings of any kind on the outside, and nothing comparable to wings or jets. Its only distinguishable feature was a solid plasma ring that intercepted the ship at a horizontal plane. Piercing through its hull in four places, two at the front and two at the back, it formed a semi-circle on each side, centered a third of the way down the back of the ship. The glowing halo, no more than ten meters in breadth and less than half that in height, formed a stretched ellipse about a hundred meters in diameter. Inside the ring itself, glowing and pulsing in waves of purple and blue lights, the flowing plasma, running along the length of the loop, was casting random shadows on the hull, accentuating the messy randomness of its curves.

Traveling in total silence through the vacuum of space, the alien ship was on its maiden voyage to another world. It would also be its last. The moon traveler had only gone to Kahnu's moons and never ventured into deep space before.

Mahhzee turned around in her seat and directing her thoughts to Jorh only, said without a word, "*Jorh, I think it's started. I can see something on the aft viewer.*"

"*Thanks, Mahhzee,*" he replied, switching his attention to the view outside. He could see that the brightness of the object at the center of the window had increased since they had last checked. The bright space body in the far distance was Kahnu, their home planet.

The past three and a half days had been excruciatingly long for all. Exhausted, depressed, and on the verge of mental breakdown, the small crew was growing sick of the confinement of the ship, and the relatively small space the twenty-six of them had been sharing since their departure. The living quarters would have seemed adequate in size for any human being, but the Kahnus were over five meters tall on average, dwarfing any man. For them, the individual sleeping compartments of the ship, most not exceeding six meters in height and ten in diameter, were desperately small. The Aruk they were in was a cargo and personnel transport, never meant to travel for more than a few days at a time. Accommodations did not include comfort for such short trips. Only the main control room and cargo bay were of significant size. But even there, when all twenty-six were gathered in the largest open space of their vessel, it still offered hardly any room to move around. But the most difficult thing to surmount had been the feeling of despair they had all felt by leaving their world to its tragic fate, losing everything and everyone they had ever known and loved. Their spirit was lower than ever, and now they were about to witness a sight none would ever be able to forget.

After informing the rest of the crew, Jorh and Mahhzee, along with all the other passengers, turned their attention to the rear window of the ship.

The first visible sign that the carnage had begun came from a flicker of light, far in the starry background. At first no brighter than a small speck in the night sky, it quickly grew in size and brightness, and within seconds became a blinding white and yellow light, as bright as the sun. Even from eighty million kilometers away, they could all visualize the mountains erupting, the icy crust melting, the valleys burning and the oceans boiling. The Kahnus communicated telepathically, and although none were trying to, their combined feelings were compiling on top of each other, causing each and every one of them to sense the entire group's distress. All those they had ever known, their families, friends, loved ones, their homes, the Klomags... The destruction would be complete, they all knew it. For the next few minutes their pain was unbearable... Finally, after a gradual decrease in brightness, a gigantic ring of fire blasted its way across the galactic backdrop, and dissipated into the nothingness of empty space, blinding them all for several seconds.

Everyone remained totally silent and stoic, all eyes wide open, almost unable to accept the horrible reality. They had just watched in agony the destruction of their home planet, unable to do anything, left feeling completely powerless. Kahnu, their beautiful world, full of life, home to thousands of animal species, the grand Klomags, the Shirzu turners, the Tayags…their own Kahnu civilization... It was all gone, scattered into space, in one instant; forever.

As the true realization that none would ever again see their world or their loved ones finally hit them, one by one, they slowly collapsed to their knees in silent cries and moans, fraught, heartbroken, and feeling utterly defeated. Mahhzee, although as stricken as any of them by the tragedy, maybe even more so by the added sense of responsibility now weighing heavily on her, slowly turned her seat back in the forward position, and with great effort, tried to keep herself together, as she returned to the task at hand: Get the ship and its precious cargo safely to Kesra.

An hour later, only a distant smudge of reddish amber, glowing softly and unremarkably, remained where their planet once was. Lost in the crowded starry background that seemed to have already forgotten the incident, the dim glow would soon be hard to spot amid the other stars.

What none of them knew at the time was that the aftermaths of the destruction of their world would also have dire consequences elsewhere. As faith would have it, a few thousand years later, their erratic orbits eventually bringing them into the path of our own world's gravitational pull, several asteroids, leftover debris from the Kahnu catastrophe, would crash on Earth, causing the ultimate demise of the dinosaurs, and changing the course of our planet's natural evolution forever.

Most of the passengers had now made their way back to their sleeping quarters. Mahhzee, refocusing her attention on their destination, brought Kesra in view. The red planet had been in sight for a couple of days already, growing a bit more each hour. Now, its image took most of the forward view. They would be entering its thin atmosphere in less than two days.

"*Jorh, I think I'm gonna go lay down if you don't mind. My eyes are killing me, and the rest of my body doesn't feel that much better.*"

"*Of course, Mahhzee. Go get some sleep, you deserve it. Goodnight!*" he telepathically replied. Looking at his sister walk away, he couldn't help but turn his attention to Gahneo, who was already following her. He realized how different he felt about the two of them, now that they had been together for a few years already, and so much had changed for all of them. Gahneo was a good companion for her, and he was making her happy. That was all that mattered, really. He was glad they had each other. For a moment he thought of himself and Faylah, his lifelong love. She was gone. She had passed away almost two years earlier. A freak accident. She had fallen off the... He shook the image out of his head. After making sure everyone had left the room and the ship was still on course, Jorh left the main deck and made his way to the cargo bay.

The human observers and their three alien companions followed. The younger Jorh entered the large space. In its center, they all recognized the twenty-six hibernating capsules they were now familiar with. The alien checked a few controls and turned his attention to the Zarfha in the middle. He raised his arm and was about to communicate a telepathic command to the sphere when he heard something move in the far corner of the room. The sudden movement was so unexpected, Jorh almost tripped. Knowing everyone should have been back in their respective quarters by now, he finally spotted a dark figure in the shadows.

"*Majhena? Is that you? What are you doing here in the dark? You should be in bed, young lady.*"

"*I'm not sleepy,*" she replied. She was sitting in a fetal position in a corner of the room. Her arms wrapped around her legs, resting her chin on her knees, she was looking at him with a grumpy expression on her face, slowly rocking herself back and forth.

"*You should still go back to your room. This is not a place for a young girl at night, alone.*"

"*I'm fine here!*" she made a very faint grunt.

"*Majhena? Are you OK?*" He could sense she was not.

"*I'm fine. I just want to be alone,*" she replied telepathically.

And then, she started sobbing. Soon, her large purple eyes were crying. Her body, as with any Kahnu who was crying, tuned to a dark gray color. Majhena was now an orphan. Her parents had stayed on Kahnu. She was the only one of her family who had escaped the tragedy, purely by luck, after a set of circumstances had given him no choice but to take her with them, when they had found her hiding in the ship, the night of their departure.

Jorh approached the girl and sat right next to her on the floor. He reached over for her hand and said, "*It's OK to be sad. It's normal to feel pain. You just lost your family, your home, and everyone you ever knew. It's OK to cry Majhena, I know I want to. Cry my child, you'll feel better.*" Putting his arms around her, he pulled her to him and caressed her head, while she abandoned herself in her sorrow.

#

Thirty-six hours later, a blueish streak was scraping the top layer of the thin orange hued atmosphere of Kesra. The long line of light emblazed the cloudy haze over several kilometers, as the ship made its final descent. Entering the lower atmosphere at over 25,000 kilometers an hour, the ship would have been a spectacular scene to watch, had any life form been present on the ground below. But Kesra was, for the most part, a dead world already. Only a few species remained in crevices and underground water holes. But none of them possessed anymore intelligence than that of a starfish on Earth. And within the next few million years, most of them would also disappear. Water on Kesra, evaporating in the thin atmosphere, was slowly killing all life on the planet. Eventually, the once fertile planet would become a global desert, a desolate world, known to man as Mars.

Mahhzee reduced the vessel's speed to 1200 kilometers an hour within seconds. The resulting G-force felt by the crew members was negligible, thanks to the ship's Zarfha controlled artificial gravity field. It was capable of automatically compensating for any change in gravitational force almost instantaneously, allowing it to keep the gravity onboard relatively constant, no matter what the forces exerted on the outside were. This amazing technology was the creation of Jorh. His years spent on Zarfha gravitation engines had made him one of the most celebrated scientists in his field. They were now flying over a region of Kesra man would later call Valles Marineris, an unmistakable planetary feature the Kahnu people had visited many times before. The giant geological trench, over 4000 kilometers in length, and several kilometers deep in some areas, dwarfed most geological features on any world around the sun. The view was majestic. Giant red cliffs to their left were towering over the ship. Their colossal size was an amazing sight. Occasional coves and recesses seemed to invite the intruders to explore them. A desert of dried out river beds, rocky boulders, and flat, vegetationless terrains, made up most of the landscape below. Rocks littered the ground everywhere. Far in the distance, to the right, another cliff could be seen, just as gigantic in size, but hundreds of kilometers away, and stretching far beyond the horizon, where it faded away behind the hazy atmosphere. In the gigantic facade nearest them, smaller canyons branched out from time to time, but the travelers continued forward towards the center of the monumental decor. After a few hundred kilometers, they had come much closer to the cliff, and the speed of the ship was now barely eighty kilometers an hour. They had relied mostly on the Zarfha to bring them to the correct coordinates, but now everyone was paying attention to Mahhzee, who had once again taken over the ship's controls. They were searching the cliffs for the cavern entrance in the rock face, artificially carved by their people many years earlier.

"*I think we're getting close,*" said Donjeh. He was the only passenger who had actually been to the red planet before.

Steering with hands gestures, to face the vertical cliffs, she brought the ship down a few hundred meters above the floor of the canyon, waving commands to the spherical artificial brain of the Aruk. She slowed down the vessel, while pulling back on the nose to level up. Slowly descending vertically while maintaining the ship horizontally, Mahhzee was sweeping the face of the cliff in front of them.

"*There! On the right!*" Donjeh said telepathically, pointing in the direction of a small bulge on the rocky wall.

"*I see it!*" she replied.

Quickly moving the ship to face the location showed by Donjeh, Mahhzee turned the white vessel to face the dome shaped formation. Encased in the cliff's face, the spherical marker meant the entrance was nearby. After hovering around a tall chimney-like rock formation on the right of the marker, a large fissure revealed itself. At first seemingly too narrow to fit, Mahhzee slowly engaged the ship in the tight passage. It was an impressive canyon in its own right. The ship was now getting lower and had slowed down to a crawl. After a few minutes, they were hovering in front of a large gap in the cliff, about sixty meters above ground. It appeared to continue on into a cave-like passage, maybe only twice the girth of the ship. Slowly moving forward, Mahhzee maneuvered the Aruk toward the narrow mouth of the opening, and they entered the dark cavern. The glowing shell of the hovering transport was now illuminating the walls of the tunnel all around them. To everyone's surprise, like stars in the night sky, millions of quartz stones started sparkling, reflecting some of their light back to them. The corridor walls were surprisingly smooth and symmetrical, and many different tunnels branched out here and there, also quite even in their proportions, as if artificially made. In fact, some of them were.

Although the cave was natural in formation, the Kahnus had carved more tunnels into it, like a colony of termites would a beam of wood. Many years ago, when they had first visited the red planet, the council of Elders had agreed to allow a permanent station to be built on Kesra. After almost forty years, it now covered more than five times its original size in length, expanding through the belly of the cliff. Even after Kahnus had visited all the planets and moons of our solar system, and eventually moved on to other type of research, the laboratories and habitats on Kesra had stayed in use for many more years before they were abandoned. Many discoveries were made during those years. Coval salt was one of them; a white powdery substance that had become an important ingredient in their biogenetic Time-Frost hibernation technology. Many leaps were made thanks to research performed in those caverns, especially in the field of biology. The closing of the station, soon after the discovery of Varih-Aru, had been very difficult to accept for some. No one had been allowed back on Kesra since.

None of the passengers on this ship had ever been to the red planet, except for Serm's uncle, Donjeh. He was also the most renown researcher in Time-Frost technology, and one of the few who had fought to keep the laboratories on Kesra operational.

Kesra, the red world

Moving slowly towards the landing site to the left of the cave, Mahhzee aligned the ship and landed effortlessly, after a smooth vertical descent. They were finally there, on solid ground.

Once the back of the ship opened, the passengers started emerging from inside one by one, through the purple gas. They were all wearing a thin suit, providing them with the necessary shielding from the harmful chemical composition of the air, but also giving them the atmospheric pressure their bodies needed to compensate for Kesra's weak gravity. The gigantic cave housed an array of odd looking machines and Zarfha orbs, some serving a similar purpose as computers do on Earth. To the far right, several edifices, almost as tall as the cave itself, revealed the living quarters that would be their new home, at least for now.

The last ones to leave the ship, Jorh and Serm walked to an area of the cave where strange structures and other large objects were lined up in long row against the wall. Below the glassy transparent surface of a wide container, eleven Zarfha spheres were resting partially buried in the floor of the cave. After giving Serm several instructions, Jorh approached one of the machines and held his hands stretched out in front of him, his twelve fingers seemingly probing the air. Pulling out a black saucer shaped device out of a small container, Serm put the instrument on the glass surface just above the closest Zarfha, and raising his open hand above it, started tracing imaginary circles in the air. A column of white plasma slowly emerged from the black device, encircling it and rising towards Jorh's hand. As if shaping it without touching it, both aliens guided the column upward with their hand movements, until it reached the roof of the cave. Then, releasing his invisible grip, Jorh clamped his hands together. A foggy white substance started flowing down, along the outside of the column, while the central pillar, staying in a relatively solid state, began changing colors and pulsing slowly up and down its entire length in waves of blueish-whites and purple-reds. A giant oval plate appeared on the wall of the cave, almost as if it had materialized out of the rock. Eleven red circles, evenly spaced in a row at the bottom of it, began fading in and out, in rhythm. In the middle of the giant oval shape, a big black triangle was slowly moving randomly, as if hovering in an imaginary soft wind. Blue lines soon emerged from it, one by one connecting to the red circles.

After confirming the Zarfhas were receiving the plasma, Jorh left Serm and walked to the living quarters. He was looking forward to taking his suit off. He walked into the dark entrance of the towering edifice and made his way several levels up. After the tight confinement of the ship, staying in an adequately sized space would be a welcome change. He had a few hours to kill while the spheres were charging. It was a great opportunity to rest. He approached a machine near the far wall, and after a few commands, walked to another room. Removing his gelatinous suit, he reached the hovering bed and gladly lied down.

A few doors down, Gahneo and Mahhzee were finally in their new habitat.

"*I think I'm gonna sleep for a week!*" she said, removing her soft suit. The darkness was broken by a small Zarfha spinning slowly in the corner. The reddish glow caused everything to look rusted and old. The ceiling was about ten meters high. The room was circular, and dome shaped. Still small compared to a typical Klomag habitat, it was a great improvement over the tiny cabins of the ship, nonetheless. A corridor at the far end seemed to disappear further down to the right. As they walked on, the walls began to glow dimly. Now, two more doors could be seen on the left. There was an oval shaped screen, straight ahead of them, against the wall. Just below it, an orb was hovering silently, facing a comfortable looking chair.

Gahneo walked toward it and sat down. Mahhzee closed the entrance behind them, and from within the walls, a soft ambient light illuminated the room. There did not appear to be any windows. While Gahneo, waving his hand, made a portion of the wall disappear, offering a view of the large cave, Mahhzee made her way into an adjacent room, just to the left of him. The sleeping quarters were not the largest, but the three hover-beds in the middle looked comfortable and inviting. The Kahnu did not sleep lying down on a flat bed, as humans do. They slept on long hovering lounge seats, comparable to comfortable recliners, padded and molded to the body of the individual lying in it. Mahhzee waved at the wall and another oval window appeared, overlooking a portion of the cave outside. From her vantage point, she could see Serm walking out of the Aruk, pushing in front of him a large container she did not recognize. What puzzled her right away was the similarity in size and shape with a hibernating pod. "*What reason could Serm possibly have to take a Time-Frost pod out of the ship?*" She kept watching. Hovering in front of him, Serm guided the large capsule around the ship, and soon disappeared behind a rocky column at the back of the cave.

"*Looks like everything is in order here!*" Gahneo told her telepathically. "*What about the other rooms? What does it look like in there?*"

Mahhzee was still puzzling over Serm and the strange package. Realizing Gahneo was still waiting for an answer, she finally responded, "*I haven't checked the storage yet, but the bedroom seems fine. The hovers look very comfortable by the way. At least, they didn't forget about comfort when they built this place.*"

"*Well, that's a relief! I'm just about ready for bed. You must be exhausted too! How are you holding up after all this madness?*"

"*I'm OK.*" It was all she could say. Like most of them lately, she was trying to focus on the task at hand, and not think of the destruction of their home planet and the tragic loss of thousands of lives they had witnessed only a few days earlier. Mahhzee was a level-headed person. Her work was her life. It was even surprising she could find time to be in a relationship with Gahneo. The two had become lovers in the last four years of their involvement with the Zarfha Gravitation Engine. Both had been attracted to each other since their first year working together, but it was only after that night in Klomag-Vaha, that they had finally crossed the line that separates friendship and romance. Jorh had been sick that day, and the team had elected to postpone work until the next morning. They were about to test a new gravitation Zarfha, and Jorh's presence was indispensable. It was Mahhzee who had asked Gahneo if he would care to join her on a short trip to Klomag-Vaha. She wanted to visit a girlfriend who had moved there the previous year with her new companion. She did not want to go by herself. She would feel safer if he came with her. Gahneo had not realized it was simply an excuse to be with him alone and go to a place she had thought about for a long time. After a long conversation with her mother the week before, she had made the decision to wait no longer on Gahneo to make the first move, and to seize the first opportunity to tell him how she felt. This was it.

The spring nights on Klomag-Vaha were often spectacular. Klomag-Vaha was on the outskirts of the Varrish Valley and offered one the best unobstructed views of the vast Kahnu Ocean, and its sparkling purple waters. She had even timed their little excursion so to cross the Kah bridge when the sun was starting to set in the west; the most romantic moment of the day. The warm orange-yellows at that time of day had always been Mahhzee's favorite.

"*So, what's your friend's name again?*" asked Gahneo mentally, while keeping an eye on their flyer's trajectory.

They were aboard a Vok, a flying vehicle about eight meters in length, with just enough room for the two of them and a few of their belongings. It was an indispensable form of personal transportation on Kahnu. The vast distances that separated some Klomags could stretch several dozen kilometers; too far to manage on foot regularly. Everyone had a Vok and most used it anywhere they went.

"*Savhina. I told you already,*" she replied. "*You never listen.*"

"*Oh yeah, that's right. Sorry, I forgot. I was thinking about Jorh. I hope he is OK. He's always at the lab. It's strange to hear he is sick, you know? But you know that, you're his sister after all. You know him better than anyone. He is so dedicated to the project… He must be frustrated right now. He knows we can't afford to lose any time. Talking about time, aren't we gonna get to your friend's too late? I mean, most people are having dinner right now, you know? Are you sure that's what she said?*"

Mahhzee wasn't listening anymore. She had blocked out his brain waves. In fact, had he been less absorbed by his current blabbering, he would have been able to sense it. But he was still mentally talking when she spotted an open landing bay on one of the view decks below.

"*There!*" she said pointing at it. "*Take that one. It looks perfect.*"

"*What? What do you wanna stop there for? Is this where we're meeting her? That's a sunset bay!*"

The puzzled look on his face betrayed his naivety. He was still clueless after landing the vehicle and lowering the roof, when Mahhzee started talking about the mountains of Varrish and the beautiful colors the sun created over them, as it slowly came down towards the horizon, displaying its warm shades of reds, oranges, greens, and of course, its breathtaking purples, the color most couples waited for when they docked on a sunset pad.

"*Most first dates happen on bridges such as this one, on nights like this one, all over the region, you know?*" she said.

Gahneo finally realized they were not meeting Mahhzee's friend when she leaned her head on his shoulder and, looking in the distance, asked, "*So, what do you see, Gahneo*?"

Looking down at the top of her head, he replied, "*I see you, Mahhzee...I see you.*"

She looked back at him, smiling, her purple eyes sparkling in the low sunlight, and as they slowly came closer, without a word, they felt each other's body, passionately, savoring the strong attraction they had felt toward each other for years, but had never acted on. Then, sitting in a lotus position in the middle of their semi-translucent Vok and facing each other, they stared into each other's eyes, their fingers interlocking. They were now making love. For the Kahnu, intercourse was a mental experience, first and mostly. The telepathic stimulation they were both engaged in, was complemented by a physical flow of pulses that ran through their bodies, using the sensory channels of the fingers, passing through the arms, and moving all the way to the brains. Like two giant vibrating light bulbs in the night, pulsating irregularly through different shades and intensity of brightness and colors, the two were at times in complete sync, when the light waves going through both bodies would pulse in complete rhythm with one another. The only sound that could be heard was a soft buzzing hum, not unlike the sound bees make when they fly. Sometimes, both humming sounds would sync in exact unison as well. That was when the humming would get the loudest. But Gahneo and Mahhzee were not the only ones indulging in the pleasures of making love in the dim light of Ogg, the largest of Kahnu's three moons, now shinning above them. Nearby, similar displays of passion could be seen and heard all around. And so, like thousands of bees hovering over a field of flowers, the sounds of young Kahnus in love resonated over the vast Mohgvar ocean below. It was common for a couple to perform their love making in plain view of others. Everyone did so. Rare were the love making rituals performed indoors. Being outside and feeling the general euphoria of pleasures they could all telepathically sense, gave the experience a higher level of excitement. Everyone practiced public intimacy. Anything else would have seemed strange to a Kahnu. On Earth, the contrary was true, but on Kahnu, this intellectual sharing of pleasures between different individuals was considered the ultimate experience and was even advocated by the Elders of the great council. When they finally fell asleep inside the Vok's cabin in the early hours of the morning, Mahhzee's skin was still vibrating softly. She slowly fell asleep smiling, Gahneo lying behind with one arm around her.

#

Jorh was the first one in the lab the next morning. He was still upset for having missed the previous day, but also glad he was feeling better. Trying to make up for the lost time, he quickly busied himself setting up the gravity control experiment they had scheduled the day before. Serm walked into the room while he was finishing entering the test parameters in the Zarfha.

"*Good morning Jorh! Glad you're back. Feeling better?*"

"*Hello, Serm. Yes, much better, thank you. I'm almost done with the setup. We should be ready to start in a few minutes. Where are the others?*"

"*Are they not here yet?*"

"*They know we're working today, right?*" asked Jorh, surprised.

"*I thought they were here already," replied Serm. "I woke up late myself. I expected I'd be the last one in. It's not like Gahneo to be late.*"

"*No, and it's not like Mahhzee either. When did you last see them?*"

"*Yesterday, when we all left after you got sick. I went home. I assumed they did the same... Hold on, let me check on Gahneo... mmmmh... I can't connect with him. He must still be sleeping... Did you try Mahhzee?*"

"*Nothing from her either,*" replied her brother. Both of them oversleeping on the same day didn't please him at all, he thought to himself.

Jorh knew Mahhzee liked Gahneo and it was reciprocal, but the two had never done anything about it in the three years they had been working together. He doubted anything was going on now. He always liked Gahneo. After all, Jorh was the one who had insisted with Garnak on having him on the team. But no matter how fond he was of his colleague, Jorh was too protective of his little sister to imagine any male Kahnu touching her.

Finally, Jorh spoke again. "*I can't hear either one! What is going on? We need to find them. I'll go to Mahhzee's. Go check on Gahneo at his place. Drag him out of his hover if you have to. We need to finish this today. We have lost too much time already.*"

While Jorh was talking, both were already walking toward the passage leading back up the twenty-two levels they had just passed on the way down earlier.

Mahhzee lived below their mother, on level six of Klomag-Darh, close to the top. It took Jorh a good thirty minutes to reach his mother's doorsteps. He was already mentally connected with her when he entered through the front door.

"*No, I'm telling you, she is not here. I haven't seen her since yesterday afternoon. She left right after lunch. She was talking about going to visit her friend Savhina in Klomag-Vaha. She mentioned Gahneo might be going with her. I thought that was a good idea. I don't like your sister going there by herself.*"

"*Why didn't you tell me?*" said a frustrated Jorh.

"*Since when do I need to tell you what your sister does? She's an adult, isn't she? And I was told you were sick yesterday anyway. You can't keep telling her what to do. She won't listen anyway. She's like your father, stubborn as a Klomag. I'm sure they're fine. They probably slept at Savhina's.*"

"*What do you mean, slept? Are you saying...? Are they...?*"

Suddenly Jorh realized his mother was right. Mahhzee wasn't a little girl anymore, she was a Kahnu woman, her body showed that clearly, and she was at an age when young Kahnus longed for a companion. She was attractive, he knew it. And her social position was a big plus for any potential suitor. Mahhzee was a pilot, as good as many of the males at the school of flights, and a great scientist. And she did not just pilot Voks. She was trained to fly commercial Vakkehs, dark pyramid-shaped carriers a hundred meters high, used for public and cargo transportation between coastal colonies. Mahhzee was also one of only six on a team trying to save their civilization, a task that required a maturity beyond that of the average Kahnu. She was an accomplished individual in her own right and didn't need his permission to love who she pleased.

"*Still...*" thought Jorh, "*maybe it's just a coincidence. Serm? Serm?*"

"*Yes, Jorh I'm almost there. I still can't connect with him. Did you find Mahhzee?*"

"*No, she's not home. Looks like she slept at a friend's house in Klomag-Vaha. Let me know the moment you get to Gahneo.*"

"*I will.*"

#

"*Mahhzee! Mahhzee! Wake up!*" Gahneo was shaking her, trying to get her to respond.

"*Mmmh? What?... Leave me alone. I'm sleeping...*"

"*Mahhzee, we're late. We overslept!*"

"*What? What time is it?*" she said. "*Gahneo? The sun... Oh no, we're late! Come on, we've gotta go!*"

She was already grabbing her things and getting in the driver's seat.

Gahneo was still moving around the Vok, looking for his clothes, when Mahhzee started lifting off the ground and quickly made a sharp turn that sent Gahneo flying to the back of the aircraft. Landing on a large container, he didn't hear Mahhzee say, "*Oops, sorry!*" with a giggle.

No one was at the lab when the two of them got there. They had both disconnected from receiving any telepathic communication, to avoid any possible distraction on the way, until they got inside. Hoping they would not have to explain themselves, they came in separately, Gahneo first, followed by Mahhzee, a minute or so later. But even before she had joined him, Gahneo could clearly see that a grueling interrogation would be unavoidable. He released his mental block first. Within seconds, Serm was asking him questions.

"*I overslept, that's all. I stayed up late last night, catching up on some work, and I guess I slept too late. Sorry.*"

"*Where are you?*" said Serm. "*I went to your house. You weren't there.*"

"*You probably just missed me. I'm at the lab.*"

"*Well, Jorh is going crazy trying to find Mahhzee, now. Let me tell him I found you at least. Maybe he's found her by now.*"

"*I'm here, Serm. I'm at the lab with Gahneo,*" said Mahhzee.

"*Hey Mahhzee! Well, that's lucky. Did you oversleep too?*" he said with a laugh.

"*Hem... Yeah... I did... I just arrived soon after Gahneo. We're both here.*"

"*You better tell Jorh, then. He went looking for you at your mom's*"

"*Crap!*" thought Mahhzee to herself.

"*Mahhzee? Mahhzee, where are you?*" she heard Jorh's voice in her head.

"*I'm at the lab, Jorh. Gahneo is with me. We're ready to work. I'm sorry for being late. How are you feeling? Better?*"

"*Yes, I'm fine, I'm fine. Never mind me. What about you? Where were you last night?*"

"*I went to see my friend Savhina in Klomag-Vaha.*"

"*Really? And how is your friend?*" said Jorh with a suspicious undertone.

"*She's... fine,*" she replied, not wanting to say any more than she had to, in case he had talked to her mother.

"*I went to mom's house looking for you. She said you went with Gahneo?*"

"*Hem... Yes, I didn't want to fly all the way there by myself. I thought it would be safer if someone came with me...*" she replied, as Jorh stormed into the lab, looking frustrated and upset. He was staring at her and Gahneo intensely.

"*Hi Jorh,*" said the young lab assistant a bit uncomfortable. "*It's all my fault. I—*"

Jorh, still staring at his sister, lifted his hand for Gahneo to stop talking. After a few awkward moments, Mahhzee broke the mental silence.

"*OK, fine! Gahneo and I went to the Kah-bridge. We—*"

"*I don't want to know about it!*" interjected Jorh. "*Don't need to know.*"

"*But, I just want you to underst—*"

"*No! I'm not interested. Don't want to know. Let's get to work. We've wasted enough time.*" And with that, Jorh walked right up to the Zarfha and initialized the Mahkiar matrix.

The human group was briefly informed by their guide, Jorh, that the Mahkiar was a three-dimensional access point matrix, used by his people to tap into specific universal energies. Something quite advanced that he would attempt to explain some other time.

Meanwhile, disappointed by her brother's reprimanding attitude, Mahhzee turned to Gahneo.

"*Why can't he be happy that I am happy?*"

"*Are you happy, Mahhzee?*" asked Gahneo.

"*Yes, very!*" she replied, looking at him with love in her eyes.

The first portion of the day was just as rough as it had started. The team had kept their thoughts to the task at hand, staying off the Mahhzee-Gahneo subject, but the tension between the four was obvious. Although managing to produce some promising results, the experiments had so far yielded negative results. But no one was willing to give up, especially so close to the goal. Jorh and Gahneo had conferred several times, as each experiment was being reset and readjusted. By the early evening, Jorh was feeling quite optimistic. The preview test had given him a false moment of excitement, when the Zarfha in the containment chamber had begun to show some reaction.

"*Here is the last chart, Jorh. I have increased the seventh elemental to thirty-eight cubic parts. Two more than the last test, just as you asked.*"

"*Good. Energize the Zarfha and make sure to keep an eye on the plasma fluctuations. Don't let the rotation fall under two hundred revolutions per cycle. Serm, Mahhzee, are we ready to initiate the countdown?*" he asked, without looking at either.

"*Yes, all systems are a go,*" replied Serm.

Mahhzee was watching the flux oscillator on the oval screen above the fusion chamber. In the small window, a bright blue light could now be seen, shining in the middle of the empty chamber.

"*Ready when you are, Jorh,*" she said.

"*OK, Serm, ready? Now!*"

Immediately engaging the counter, Serm started relaying the numbers telepathically to the rest of the team. "*Twenty, nineteen, eighteen…*"

They knew they were on the verge of a breakthrough, but none of them could really concentrate on the task at hand. Gahneo, looking at Jorh inconspicuously, was still trying to gauge how upset he was. The Zarfha in the corner of the isolation chamber began to rise, its spin rate increasing.

"*Fourteen, thirteen, twelve...*"

Jorh, unaware of the eyes on him, couldn't stop thinking about his sister in the arms of Gahneo, an unpleasant thought he was trying very hard to get rid of. Small bursts of multi-colored lights were now starting to emerge out of the sphere.

"*Nine, eight, seven...*"

Mahhzee, staring at the small window, kept thinking about the previous night, and Gahneo's pulsing waves of passion flowing through her entire body. Serm seemed to be the only one actually paying close attention to the experiment, for once. The Zarfha sphere was now just below the ceiling of the sealed room, and bright flashes were reflecting all over the chamber.

"*Five, four, three…*"

"*Get ready to drop the plasma sphere, Gahneo!*" said Jorh.

"*Two, one, zero,*" finished Serm.

"*Now!*"

Gahneo immediately engaged the glowing blue ball of plasma in the tubular receiver of the pod, by a simple wave of the hand. The bright sphere dropped straight down inside the egg-shaped chamber. Its molecules mixing with the Zarfha rays, it progressively turned from blue to red, to purple and then blue again for another few seconds, before exploding all across the room in a bright display of blinding sparks, like thousands of mini fireworks. Quickly spinning a few meters above it, the Zarfha expanded, then retracted, and finally contracted back onto itself until it had become a small ball of fire, floating silently in the center of the containment field. A few more bursts of plasma continued to escape from its surface, before vanishing into a cloud of purple gas that quickly dissipated. After some adjustments by Gahneo and Jorh, the plasma flux was soon stabilized in the chamber.

For a moment, they all forgot what had transpired earlier. They were now completely absorbed by the object in front of them. Mahhzee, finally prying her eyes off the colorful scene, turned her attention back on the readings in front of her, and conveyed the new numbers back to Jorh. Gahneo was now checking the Mahkiar matrix. After double checking everything, he gave Jorh the anticipated confirmation.

"*It's sustaining itself. Amplitude at eighty-four percent, ray-loads engaged and stable.*"

"*We did it!*" announced Jorh with a feeling of victory." *My friends, we have finally created a stable, self-sustainable, multi-level gravitation engine; the first Flexor Zarfha capable of displacing twenty-eight Kahs! This is fantastic. Now, all we have to do is get it inside the Ehoran.*" That last part, he knew would be easy.

The rest of the evening had been spent running tests and checking lists of analysis, trying to account for every contingency. Like all gravitation flexors, the new Zarfha had to maintain a constant gravity aboard the ship, but also be able to compensate for the size, mass, and composition of Varih-Aru. This new success was a major breakthrough for the success of the mission. Equipped with it, the Ehoran, the grand ship the Elders had ordered to be built, would be able to divert Varih-Aru from its destructive path, using the ship's enormous artificial gravity to pull the rogue planet off course. For the moment being, Jorh was only thinking about the success of the day. He felt proud of the team's progress. Regardless of the situation they were all in, he had true respect and fondness for his team. He just wished they could have all worked under more comfortable circumstances. The utter destruction of their home planet looming above them was getting heavier every day and taking its toll on everyone's morale. All they could do now was to stay focused on the work at hand. They were almost there.

After a few signs of congratulations between colleagues, Jorh wished them all goodnight and spent a few more minutes cataloging the experiment's results. He would have to give a complete report to

Garnak the next morning. He had already put his sister's romantic outing with Gahneo behind him and didn't appear the least concerned at the moment. The two could not have been more pleased, not having to explain themselves after all.

After shutting down the lab, Jorh resealed the entrance behind him with a hand gesture and began the trek back home up the tunnel. Serm was already half way up Klomag-Darh when Jorh reached the Main Hall. He watched Gahneo and his sister climb in their Vok and disappear. He was not really upset anymore. He was just glad the day had ended on such a good note and could not wait to get in his hovering bed. Truthfully, they were all exhausted and glad to go home. In particular, two of them, whose previous night had been all but restful.

Chapter X

Varih-Aru

Mahhzee was jolted back to reality, when Gahneo entered the room to see why she wasn't answering him.

"*Mahhzee?*" He touched her shoulder when she still did not respond.

"*Hmmm? Hey...*" she said looking at him with melancholy in her eyes and a loving smile.

"*Everything OK?*" asked Gahneo, a bit at a loss.

"*Yes, Gahneo, everything is fine.*" The feeble smile stayed on her face for several more seconds. Most of the other passengers had already moved their belongings to the new living area in the big towering edifice, each one hurrying to pick a desirable location, preferably high above ground. The good news was there were more choices than there were travelers, so everyone was fairly satisfied with their living arrangements, when all was said and done.

The Kahnu were used to living thousands of meters above ground. Back on their home planet, they lived in well-designed dwellings of comfortably arranged coves and shell-shaped habitats, interconnected by a maze of tunnels and shafts carved in all directions, right into the giant Klomags. The corridors and hallways connecting the different dwellings could at times protrude on the outside of the gigantic structures and form outdoor towers that usually reconnected further up. Those outside also housed more luxurious private living quarters, with breathtaking views, while the ones inside Klomags were more common or reserved for public structures such as libraries, city halls, recreational areas, and other functional facilities. The lack of natural light in some of the indoor dwellings was in no way a problem for Kahnus, whose purple eyes were able to adjust to the dimmest of luminosity. Like major highways connecting cities on Earth, the branches of the giant looking trees allowed Kahnus to travel from Klomag to Klomag easily. A Klomag's outer bark was covered entirely by a smooth layer of vertical vines, hanging straight down along the body of the structure. Several dozen meters in length, and colored in dark browns and deep reds, they swung like giant hair strands along a furry mammoth leg, slowly changing colors in giant waves of wind orchestrated dances. At its top, thousands of pockets, hanging under the massive flower-like head of the Klomag, released thin strings of bright lights that made their long journey straight down to the far ground below. When the time of day was right, light flakes slowly sprinkled the entire length of the structure, as they fell from above, offering a dazzling spectacle. From a great distance, even a small group of Klomags offered an impressive sight. Taller than anything on the planet, they could reach high into the upper atmosphere of Kahnu, where they collected more sunlight. Gigantic in circumference as well, Klomags grew close to waters of the planet's single ocean and had enormous blue roots that allow them to move along coastal regions, just not very fast of course. A Klomag could take the best part of a year to move a few hundred meters, but through its life span of ten thousand years or so, it could travel substantial distances. As it did, the ice around the roots of the massive tree helped its progress, replenishing the ground below, keeping the integrity of the coast intact. Since Klomags usually lived in groups, they rarely ever traveled the entire perimeter of their single icy continent. Even as old as they could live, their slow zig-zagging progression meant they almost never came back to their original birth place.

The two species, Kahnu and Klomag, lived in total symbiosis. The Klomags provided Kahnus with shelter and support for their complex, multi-leveled cities, and in return, Kahnus gave the giants something they could no longer provide for themselves; Fioo. An algae-like life form, found in the deep coastal regions of Mohgvar, the great Kahnu ocean. Over the millenniums, the Klomags roots had gradually lost their ability to reach for their food, after the Kahnus had started mining it for themselves. The aliens, harvesting huge quantities of the purple plant, had eventually rendered the giants completely dependent on their own supply.

The alien colonies were an intricate maze of passages, hallways, and tunnels bored right through Klomags. Like termites in a wood post, Kahnus drilled passages, chambers, tunnels, ramps, hallways, and bridges in every direction. They carved shelters and habitats, caves and towers, chimneys and pools. On Earth, as perforated and drilled as the Klomags were, trees would have never been able to survive such a treatment, but the peculiar nature of the symbiotic living arrangement between the aliens and the Klomags had long be part of both species' evolution, thus resulting in their perfectly harmonious, and beneficial, joint venture. Overtime, the air passages in their trunks had allowed the gigantic structures to grow even taller and healthier. And as generations of both species learned to live together in a peaceful and harmonious cohabitation, they also eventually learned to communicate with each other, when the Klomags had begun developing a simple form of telepathic ability of their own. Of course, the council of Elders was partially responsible for that, having spent countless years and ceremonies trying to manifest the giants' aptitude. And so, when diving deep in the great Mohgvar ocean to collect needed supplies and minerals, the Kahnus would also harvest Fioo algae for their gigantic friends.

For Jorh and the small group of castaways, the unfamiliar surroundings of the immense Martian cave were making the survivors feel sadly homesick.

Back in the cave dwelling, Jorh, who couldn't really fall asleep after the difficult past few weeks, was starting to wonder where Serm had gone. He was just about to search for him telepathically when he spotted his colleague talking with Donjeh near the back of the ship. Serm, sensing eyes on him, immediately walked away from his uncle. The older Kahnu lingered a few seconds before heading back to the towering dwelling.

Jorh pondered a moment, founding it odd, but not enough to dwell on it. He was too busy to linger on the thought, anyway. Getting off his hovering bed, he called, "*Gahneo?*"

"*Yes, Jorh. I see you've chosen a space. How are your quarters?*"

"*Not bad. Definitely more spacious than the ones on the Aruk. What about you?*"

"*Good. I've checked all the systems in our rooms. Everything seems to be in perfect working condition. Mahhzee is checking on everyone else right now. By the way, I think you'll like the hover beds. They are really comfortable. Such a nice change from those crappy ones we had to sleep on those past ten days.*"

"*I Come on, they were not that bad. But I must admit, the ones in here look definitely inviting. Almost as comfortable as mine back home...*" The thought gave Jorh a knot in his stomach. His home was no more. His entire world was forever gone. Once again, he made a conscientious effort to focus on the present task.

"*I know, but you must admit, the ship was everything but comfortable. Anyway, we're only waiting on you guys now. How are the atmospheric generators coming along?*"

"*Almost online. I'm waiting on the fusion Zarfhas to finish charging. Serm should be back any moment to give me a hand with the alignment of the matrix.*"

"*Actually, where is he?*" Jorh thought to himself again. He and Donjeh had disappeared, again...

This time, he didn't hesitate to telepathically call him.

"*Serm? SERM? Where are you? I need you to finish the matrix alignment.*"

But no response came. Jorh couldn't sense Serm anywhere in the cave. That, in itself, was very strange. The recent conversation he had just witnessed between him and his uncle seemed odd, the more he thought about it. What were the two up to? It was true, Donjeh was a strange character after all, and Serm had his moments as well. Maybe the two were planning a surprise for Ldohar's birthday. Gahneo's dad would be 321 next month. A middle-aged Kahnu, and a well-loved researcher himself, he had been one of the first to work on the new Time-Frost technology. It was he and Donjeh who, almost twenty-eight years earlier, had theorized that the containment chamber of hibernating capsules could be subdivided into multi-level Zarfha zones, and cumulatively inter-connect, using the Mahkiar mapping system. By coating the walls of the containers with Coval salt and Gohhan extract, the Zarfha could increase the plasma's efficiency, multiplying their hibernating time capacity to unknown limits. Unfortunately, it was also thanks to the improved Time-Frost properties of the new hibernating pods that the Ehoran was now on its way to another star. Because of it, Jorh's group had come to Kesra to collect more Gohhan, the "Dark Light". Once Silargh and his crew had found the "White Light" on Kahjuna, the two vessels would regroup, and attempt to race after the Elder's ship to reclaim Kahalla, the Pool of Life.

Lost in thoughts, Jorh had left his room, heading down to the atmospheric Zarfhas. He walked past one of the towers filled with Gohhan. The impenetrable blackness had been collected decades ago, in the depth of Kesra's polar ice cap. The substance's origin was a mystery, even to the Kahnus. They had found it while exploring the red world, and quickly discovered its potent energy, almost by pure luck. Its extreme mass and unbearably cold temperature made it very impractical to carry or move, except in very small quantity, but its capacity to increase the power of a Zarfha engine was worth the years it took to collect. Able to quarry no more than a few kilos at the time, the Kahnus had collected it gradually and stocked great quantities in the towers of the Martian cave. From time to time, small quantities were brought to Kahnu, but the extreme characteristics of the dangerous energy it contained, had made the Kahnus very selective in their need for it. Jorh stared a few seconds at the absolute darkness beyond the tower's entrance. As soon as the cave's atmospheric conditioning was complete, they would transfer the needed amount of Gohhan, no more than a few kilograms, to the ship. That thought reminded him the Zarfhas were probably charged by now.

He was almost back at the atmospheric machine, when a voice jolted him out of his reveries.

"*Jorh, the Zarfhas are at full charge, and I have engaged the orbs on the launching ramp. Ready to align the matrix when you are.*"

Serm was only a few meters behind him. Surprised by his sudden presence, Jorh turned around to face him. He had not felt him approach, and he could sense a general discomfort and nervousness when he looked at Serm's elusive eyes. He wanted to ask him what he was up to but refrained. After a short awkward moment, Jorh turned without a word to the Zarfha behind him and started creating intricate patterns with his hands. Serm moved next to him and began to do the same thing. Within a few seconds, all eleven Zarfhas were hovering a few meters off the ground, arcs of colored light occasionally flashing between them. Above the two aliens, a pipe about two meters in diameter slowly emerged out of the cave's wall, progressively extending horizontally until it had reached a good fifty meters out toward the center of the cavern, hanging far above the ground. A small white orb of churning plasma slowly appeared out from the large pipe and hovered its way down to the two Kahnus. Without paying much attention to it, they kept waving directives at the larger spheres below.

"*Ready?*" said Jorh.

"*Ready!*" replied Serm.

With perfect timing, the two placed their hands over the plasma orb hovering between them. The gaseous ball, spinning faster and faster, while quickly changing from blue to purple, to fire red, to burning yellow, became so white and bright that it was almost unbearable to look at directly. Finally, it suddenly turned completely black and came to a rest. The two, commanding the final step of the procedure, watched eight more orbs fly out of the overhanging pipe, and move to the middle of the cave, where they started hovering in a circle, evenly spaced, just below the ceiling of the cavern. Jorh and Serm let their arms down, and the orbs started spewing a dark looking gas that engulfed most of the cave's higher portion.

The atmosphere was now being slowly transformed in the cavern. The resulting effects of the chemical morphing would soon allow them to breathe without their suits. Now, they just had to wait another two hours or so for the cave to completely be conditioned. The temporary visitors would soon have the essential necessities to survive their staying on Kesra. They all hoped it wouldn't be a long one.

François and his human companions, still watching with fascination events that had taken place so long ago, were momentarily distracted by a strange fog that began to engulf them. The surprised observers also noticed the surroundings wrapping around them. The three aliens knew immediately what was happening. Their human friends were beginning to feel the strain of the experience. Passing through each one like a sleeping spell cast by an invisible magic wand, a strong sensation of fatigue quickly enveloped them. They needed a break. So did Jorh and his two companions, still weak from their long hibernating sleep. Realizing the time had come for everyone to recharge their own batteries, so to speak, Jorh began to bring them all back to present reality.

A moment later, the group was waking up, the Zarfha sphere in front of them quietly coming to a rest on its platform. They were back in the big white cloud, on their Mars.

#

The odd viewing experience had been quite exhausting for all, but not so much to deter any of them from going back the very next day. And as the sessions succeeded one another, the humans had begun to learn how to interact telepathically with the three aliens and had a better understanding of the Kahnu world and its lost civilization.

The alien population had counted just over 49,700 individuals when the planet had been destroyed; a number that had seemed quite small to the colonists for such an advanced people. As Sabrina had pointed out, back when Earth's human population had counted only that many, man still had a long way to go before he would venture out into space. The main reason for their small population, had explained

Mahhzee, was that the birth of a Kahnu was a rare event. Unlike humans, Kahnus were not the direct result of intercourse between male and female individuals. Procreation was only possible during Kahalla, the birth ceremony, and required the council's approval and guidance. Once every twenty-six Kahnu years, large groups gathered for the great circle of birth, where the council of Elders chose twenty-six lucky couples out of hundreds. During a long and elaborate ceremony that took several days, the chosen individuals were bathed in the "Pool of Life," where they coupled for an entire day, while others, spread out across the plains of Kahalla, joined the celebration in their own way. The next day, the exhausted couples were pulled out of the birth pool and brought back to their home, where they usually spent the next few days recuperating.

The colonists had also learned that the infant's gestation period was four Kahnu years, spent in a Sharfoo, a cocoon-like egg, and left in the Elders' care. The child was then formed by the council until he turned twenty-six, when he was finally released to the care of his biological parents. By then, the young Kahnu was a full fledge adult. Kahnus did not change much physically during their adulthood. Unlike for humans, getting old was a foreign concept to the aliens. Signs that a Kahnu's life was coming to an end were rarely witnessed. When an individual reached the age of knowledge, four hundred years old, he was expected to choose the time of his parting. Some individuals had been known to take as many as fifty years to make that final decision. But when he did, a Kahnu did so willingly and proudly. All Kahnus eventually walked the path of Nott to the cliffs of Garhnoj, where they released themselves from the physical bonds of their own body. and plunged into the depths of Mohgvar, the grand Kahnu ocean, never to be seen again. Once below the cold purple waters, it was said they journeyed to the Grand Hallis, the entrance to the first world, where all living things came from. Only the Elders of the council, who counted twelve members, did not. For them, time was on a different scale. In fact, no one truly knew how old they were. Some had said that Gihhez, the patriarch, was born before the time of Harzo, the great librarian. If that was true, he was at least 3000 years old; Kahnu years, that is.

Mahhzee had given Dedrick and his colleagues a few numbers regarding their own ages. In Kahnu time, Jorh was 149. Gahneo had just celebrated his ninety-eighth birth year, and Mahhzee was still a fairly young forty-two-year-old. Of course, that was only true if one didn't consider the seventy million years they had just spent in hibernation, as François had been quick to point out. But when the colonists did the math, taking into consideration that a year on Kahnu was equivalent to almost four Earth years, they realized Mahhzee was in fact closer to 170, Gahneo was about 392, and Jorh was almost 600 years old. And if the oldest Elder was truly 3000 years old on their world, that would have made him 12,000 years old on Earth.

Rock the Casbah!

"Happy Birthday to you, happy birthday to you, happy birthday dear old man, happy birthday to yoooouuuu!" sang everyone, with François strumming wildly his guitar on the last chord of the song, a big smirk on his face. They all clapped cheerfully at the frowning Russian.

"Happy birthday, Dedrick!"

"Happy birthday, Dad."

"Yes, happy forty-ninth, buddy!"

"Thanks guys, I could've done without the reminder."

"Come on, love, you're not that old," teased him Vera.

It was true, Dedrick was the oldest of the group, but the years had been kind to him. He barely looked forty. François attributed it to his "cold Russian blood" as he had put it, which always frustrated Dedrick, the main reason François loved saying it. That night, everyone had agreed to put on a little show for him and the aliens. After their viewing that day, the Martian colonists had decorated the cargo area of the alien ship, and a few hours into the festivities, the conversation between Dedrick and Jorh had turned to the subject of the three aliens and their hibernating pods.

"*There's one question I've been meaning to ask. What happened to your friends, the ones that came with you to Mars? We only found the three of you in the hibernating chambers.*"

Jorh blinked at Dedrick a few times. "*That is not a story we like to think about.*" The alien paused, as if looking for words. "*You remember us telling you about Silargh's ship, the one that left for Kahjuna, your Earth?*"

Dedrick nodded.

"*Well, as you know, we waited for them to come to Kesra, but they never did. By the time we realized something was wrong, several weeks had passed. It was too late to go after the Ehoran. The Elder's vessel was too far out into space, and our Kaballa was gone forever. We knew we would never catch up to them. It was hard on all of us. Without the pool of life, we would never have children again.*

Even so, we had to go try to find Silargh's ship. While most of us agreed going to Kahjuna was the right thing to do, Donjeh and Serm were strongly opposed to it. They kept insisting that something had happened to Silargh and his passengers, and we could not take the risk of losing any more lives. At the time, we did not realize how determined they were about it. I knew Serm and his uncle were up to something from the very first day of our landing on Kesra, but I never thought they would go as far as they did to get their way. It happened fast. A few of us were here on the ship preparing for the long journey to your Earth. Mahhzee, Gahneo, and I were in the Aruk, checking the Time-Frost pods, when Serm disabled the Zarfhas that controlled the air and atmospheric pressure in the cavern. Outside the ship, no one had time to get to their suits. We lost most of our people within seconds.

By the time we knew what was happening, Donjeh had already taken over the ship's main controls. He trapped us in the Time-Frost room. We tried to reason with him, but it was in vain. We barely had time to get into the pods. It saved our lives, but it was also how we got trapped in them. Donjeh locked us in them and put us in Time-Frost. The rest, we know only from what the Zarfha witnessed."

He paused. Looking now at the humans in this room with him and his two alien colleagues, the events he was recounting seemed so ancient. And yet, it felt like they had happened only days earlier to him. Jorh seemed momentarily distracted. He wrapped his long tubular fingers around the small Zarfha hovering silently in front of him.

"*Outside the ship, Serm was on his way back to his uncle, when he was confronted by Lodlar, Gahneo's father, who had managed to get to his suit just in time. The two fought and-*"

His recount was interrupted by a telepathic message from Mahhzee. Jorh turned to the Russian commander. "*Maybe I'll tell you more some other time. I hope you don't mind.*"

Dedrick realized she had asked him to change the subject and wondered why, but he figured she had her reasons.

"*Of course, I understand,*" replied the human.

The alien blinked again rapidly. He turned back his attention on his sister. She was leaning against Gahneo, and the two were watching the rest of the humans dancing joyfully to the old rock classic, "Rock the Casbah," by the Clash. Both aliens looked quite entertained by it.

"*Jorh, I am very sorry about your people...*" Dedrick did not know what else to say. He was looking at his feet, thinking about his parents and his dog, Rita.

"*I know, thank you. I am sorry about yours as well.*"

The two were silent for a long while, looking at their friends celebrating Dedrick's special day. At least, they all had their health, and life wasn't so bad after all; at least, for now.

Chapter XI

Status report

"I'll have the prime-rib," finally decided François, giving the menu back to the waiter.

"And how would you like that cooked, sir?" asked the young man.

"Medium-rare, please."

"Certainly," he replied, as he turned and walked away.

"I always feel uncomfortable when someone calls me sir. It makes me feel old or something. Don't you?"

"No, I can't say I do," replied Sabrina.

"Yeah, of course, I know. But I mean…Ok, it's like calling you Mam. Doesn't that make you feel older? I think we should all use names. We know his name, so why shouldn't he know ours. I think it would make things more comfortable for all. Don't you?"

"Yeah, OK. Whatever," replied Sabrina. "So, where are Vera and Dedrick, anyway?"

"Well, I know I said they were coming, but I only said that because I didn't think you would have, if I had told you it was just gonna be you and me."

"François! I already told you, I'm not interested. You're not my type! I find you obnoxious, egocentric, and you don't respect women!" she said upset, slapping her napkin on the table.

"Give me a chance. Just this one time, please. I promise, I can be really nice. And look, I got us a table at your favorite restaurant."

She had to admit, he appeared genuinely honest about wanting her to stay. And, truth be told, she did not find him so unlikable. On the contrary, although she would have never admitted it, she found the Frenchman quite charming and lovable, at times.

"I admit, you did good on the place," she finally said with a sweet grin, seating back down." I didn't expect that from you," she added looking around the room.

"Thanks!" he replied a bit sarcastically.

"See what I mean… No, I'm sorry. I gotta go."

François caught her wrist.

"Please, stay… Please…"

After some hesitation, she sat back down.

"OK. But the first sign of-"

"Yes, yes, absolutely," he smiled at her. She looked particularly beautiful tonight. She was wearing a stylish, shoulderless evening dress, and her dark curvy hair fell perfectly to one side of her face. She looked gorgeous. Prying his eyes away, he raised his hand and called the waiter.

"Garcon? Garcon? Jean-Luc?"

#

A half hour later, both laughing hysterically, Sabrina casually touched his hand.

"Do you wanna dance?"

"Dance? No, I'm a terrible dancer. Trust me, you don't want to see me dance."

"Oh, come on. You can't be that bad. Come on, let's dance," she repeated, pulling him off his chair.

"No, I'm serious, I can't dance."

"Come on, François! You said you would do whatever I asked, remember?"

"No, wat I meant was-"

He finally gave up and let her pull him up. On the stage, the band introduced their new song. "Hi, everyone. My name is Corinne Bailey Ray. This song is called "Like A Star." I hope you'll like it."

"*Shoot! A slow one,*" he thought. And then, it dawned on him. "*That's odd…What is Corinne Bailey Rae doing here?*"

A few songs later, François was holding Sabrina in her arms, her head resting on his shoulder. Seizing the moment, he whispered something in her ear. To his pleasant surprise, Sabrina's usual rejection of his clumsy advances was replaced by a longing look. Her lips met his.

The two had just returned to their table, when François, staring through the large bay window behind Sabrina, noticed a very bright star in the dark distance. He couldn't tell what, but something about it looked odd. Suddenly, an alarm began screaming, and people began running in all directions. Above them, a red light was now flashing brightly. Unable to pry his eyes away, he stared, as the star grew rapidly. It was heading straight for them. Grabbing Sabrina's hand, he tried in vain to run, but his legs felt too heavy and slow. Helpless, he could only listen to the tremendous roar of the speeding inferno, helpless as it crashed onto the building, sending him and Sabrina flying into the air. Their bodies were about to get crushed by the collapsing ceiling, when he woke up, drenched in sweat.

"Fff! Fff! Fff!..." He was still breathing heavily, when he noticed the alarm in his pod had gone off. A red light was flashing on the panel in front of him. Rushing to his feet, he quickly entered a few commands on the keyboard. A graph appeared on the screen, partially covered with the word "WARNING!" After pressing a few more keys, the message changed to "AIR COMPOSITION INCORRECT!"

"Merde!"

#

"And that's France. That's where Uncle François is from."

Chasma was looking at the map on the screen with dedicated attention. Seated on Dedrick's lap, she asked her dad another question. "Where were you born, Daddy?"

"You know that, Chasma. I've shown you many times."

"I know," she said with a smile. "Show me again."

Suddenly, a loud voice came through the intercom above them.

"Dedrick! Dedrick!" François sounded out of breath.

"What?"

"We have a serious problem. You need to come to pod two, right now!"

Dedrick could hear the gravity in his friend's voice, and that immediately worried him. Whatever it was, it wasn't good.

"On my way!"

"Sorry, baby, I have to see what uncle François wants. Be a good girl. I'll be back soon."

Dedrick put his daughter down and grabbed his tool belt. He rarely went anywhere without it. Jumping through the adjoining tunnel, he rushed past Vera and rushed down the next passage, before she could ask him where he was going in such a hurry. She turned her attention back to her work. She knew François was in the next pod. "*What did he do this time?*" she thought to herself.

François was seated in front of the main monitor when Dedrick entered the room. He spoke immediately, without looking at him.

"This is bad. Real bad."

Dedrick leaned over François' shoulder, and stared at the monitor.

"What am I looking at? What is it?"

"You don't see that? The venting, there!" replied François, putting his finger right on the screen. Dedrick finally saw the blurry line.

"Crap! What is it?"

A small column of clear gas was escaping from one of the pipes. It was barely visible, was it not for the wobble effect it was causing on the display, as it spewed quickly from a joint in the tubing system. It was already causing the readouts on the panel to their right to rise rapidly.

"Looks like we're leaking CO2, or carbon monoxide. The readings are conflicting. Maybe the sensor is defective too. I don't know. Anyway, it's in pod one, in the back of the west panel where all the support lines meet. I've already sealed the room and rerouted some of the feeds. But this is not good. Not good at all. We need to fix that leak pronto."

"Fuck! FUCK!"

"Yep, exactly! I don't even know what caused it."

"You think a small meteorite could have come through the outer shell?"

"I thought about that as well, but the sensors didn't detect any outside damage."

"I was able to reroute most of the oxygen lines, and I shut down the electric ones, but the real problem remains. If we're leaking CO2, it's workable, but if it's carbon monoxide, the slightest spark, and the whole thing will light up like it's the fourth of July."

"Carbon monoxide?" asked Dedrick obviously surprised.

"Yeah, it's part of the air recycling system. Those gas pipes go through all the pods. Right now, the leak is contained to pod one, but… Either way, better hope it's not what we're leaking, or we're screwed!"

"Don't even say that. Can the air system function like that?"

"For now. But we need to patch this leak soon. And I think we should tell the others," added François.

"Yes, of course. I'll ask Vera to gather everyone in the main room."

"No, I mean the 'others.' The aliens."

"The Kahnus?"

"Well, maybe they can help. They are technically more advanced than us, right? I mean, they have a spaceship, and technologies we can't even comprehend. Maybe they can help us fix this. I think it's worth trying. You know me, I don't worry easily. But I'm telling you, if it's what I think it is, this is bad."

"Hmm... I guess you have a point..."

But Dedrick didn't look very enthusiastic about it. The Kahnus had not left their ship since the team had awakened them. He wasn't sure of the reason, but he had wondered if it was because they couldn't. Then again, as François had pointed out, they were definitely more advanced. Maybe they could still do something, even from there.

"*Well, it's worth a shot,*" he thought.

Vera was sitting in front of the console, with Chasma standing next to her, when Dedrick entered the pod.

"Hi Daddy! Look! Isn't she beautiful?" Chasma was holding a yellow flower between her fingers, her hand raised towards him.

"Wow! That is a pretty flower, Chasma. Where did you get it?"

"It's a potato flower, Daddy. There are lots of them in the greenhouse right now. They are so pretty. Don't you think?"

"Yes, very pretty. Listen, I need to talk to Mommy. Why don't you go see what Liu is doing? I think she's in pod four. You can show her your beautiful flower. I'm sure she would love to see it."

"Ok Daddy," and off she went through the small corridor, carefully holding her flower.

Vera turned to Dedrick.

"What is it?" She could tell something was wrong.

"We have a problem. There's a gas leak in pod one. Don't panic, we should be able to fix it, but I need you to get everyone to greenhouse three. I'll explain everything."

"What do you mean a leak? How serious is it?"

"Just call everyone in the main room, will you? I'll explain everything. I need to check something. I'll be right there."

"Right now?"

Dedrick was already sliding feet first through the passage, when he replied "Yes!"

A few minutes later, Vera and five other team members were sitting in the conference area of their station, talking and trying to figure out what this leak story was all about, when Dedrick entered the pod.

"Where is François?"

"He said he would be here as soon as he could," replied Vera.

"Dedrick, what's going on?" asked Tendai.

"Hold on, we need François." Then, moving to the console near him, he pressed the intercom control.

"Hey, you're coming?"

"Yeah, I'll be right there. I was gathering some data."

"Ok. We're all here in the main room. We're waiting for you."

"I know."

Dedrick turned off the mic and turned to the small group gathered around the "coffee table", as they liked to refer to it, in the center of the room. The circular desk housed a library of digital backup drives, full of informative documentation on pretty much anything and everything. It included a large number of videos, movies and games, as well as references on a wide variety of subjects, from medical procedures, to Martian geology and planetary data to safety protocols.

Most importantly, it also included all the blue prints and maintenance information on the entire station and its inner workings; a section François was glad to have at hand at the moment.

"So, you wanna tell us what this is all about?"

Dedrick grabbed the seat next to him and sat down. Facing everyone, he was about to say something, when François entered the room, holding a small digital pad in his right hand. The Russian commander immediately sensed things were even worse than they had hoped.

"Well?" asked Vera again.

François took a seat and looked around the room before answering. He scratched the back of his head and began.

"We have a situation in pod one… A gas leak in the air recycling system."

All gasped at once.

"How bad is it?"

The Frenchman, shifting position to try to make himself more comfortable, rolled his eyes at the ceiling, obviously searching for words. Finally, after inhaling somewhat loudly, he answered, "Well... It's not good." He clinched his teeth together.

They all knew François too well by now. After almost fifteen years spent together in the confinement of the small station, he had never looked this concerned in any situation. And much less at a loss for words. He had always found a way to make fun of almost anything. Aside from the war on Earth, Najib's death, and the crash of MF3, nothing had ever fazed him much. But this time was different. He looked like he had just been told he had a fatal illness and had only a few days left to live. They were all staring at François, and panic was starting to build up in some of them. Taking another big breath, François slowly began again.

"Well, about half an hour ago, a sensor went off on the central console. It woke me up. I checked the readings immediately. It was registering a leak in our room. I moved Sabrina to the greenhouse and closed off the pod. It took me a few minutes, but I eventually found the problem. There is a leak in the west wall. What looks like a cracked pipe. Now, we don't have much in terms of replacements parts on the station, as you all know, but I figured we would be able to patch it, and hopefully, find a way to bypass the defective section later. Anyway, I showed the problem to Dedrick, and we both agreed you all needed to know."

Next to him, Dedrick nodded, and François continued, "After he left, I decided to run an analysis report through the main computer..." François paused.

Everyone was listening quietly, but he could tell, occasionally glancing at their faces, that some of them were starting to really worry. Even Dedrick, looking at his friend, was sensing something much worse than the leak the two men had discussed earlier was troubling him.

"The thing is..." he continued, "It's not CO2 that is leaking, as I had first presumed. It's carbon monoxide."

"Carbon monoxide? Is that bad?" interjected Sabrina.

"I'm afraid so. You see, if it was CO2, we'd be OK, as long as we can patch the leak. It's not a flammable gas. But carbon monoxide, on the other hand..."

"What?" asked Vera

"Well, one small spark and… Any flame, any electrical short, or high heat source can spell disaster for us." Again, François paused, looking for the right words. "But that's not the worst part…"

The room was now dead silent, and a thick feeling of dread was growing in all of them.

"Here's the thing…when Dedrick and I were looking at this

problem about a half hour ago, we didn't know what caused the pipe to crack, but my first guess was a defective part had finally gone bad, obviously sooner than was expected… But at least, it was localized to one area. With a little luck, we would be able to bring the problem under control, even if it required some MacGyver work." His feeble attempt at humor, a nervous reaction on his part, was completely missed by the group.

He went on, "Here's the real problem. The analysis report says the pipe cracked because it's not up to specs."

Dedrick frowned. Sabrina was about to say something, but François continued, "In other words, it broke because it's not the one that's supposed to be in there to begin with. It's almost an eighth of a centimeter thinner than it should be, and it's not even made of the right material.

"What do you mean? Not up to specs?" asked Dedrick.

"I'm saying someone decided to cut corners and installed an inadequate pipe in that section. Probably to save a few bucks. I'm just amazed it made it through quality control."

"If it's just that section, can't we find a way to bypass it?" asked Tendai.

"Well, that's the thing… It's not just in that section. This pipe goes through every pod, and it's only a matter of time before leaks start to spring everywhere."

"What are you saying?" Liu suddenly blurted, shaking, as she realized the seriousness of what François was telling them.

"I'm saying we don't have sixty years, as was predicted, before this whole place starts to fall apart. If the air system starts to leak now, the station will soon become inhabitable."

"Oh, my God... How long do we have?" asked Vera, eyes wide open in absolute shock.

"Hard to tell... A few months? Weeks? I honestly don't know," replied François.

Looking at the floor, Dedrick let a quiet "Crap!" under his breath.

"Shit!" said Tendai out loud. "What do we do?" He looked completely lost. They all did.

"I'm afraid there isn't much we can do, guys. We don't have anything to replace these pipes with. There's too many of them."

"What about the aliens? Maybe they can help!" suddenly asked

Tendai hopeful.

"That's what I said to Dedrick earlier. We don't know if they can do anything, but it's worth asking."

"Yes. That's also why we wanted to talk to you all," added Chasma's father. "I didn't realize the severity of our situation, but François had already suggested talking to them about the leak. Now, I definitely agree. We don't have any other choice. And if they can't help us repair the station, we need to ask if we can move to their ship, and the sooner the better."

"The ship? You mean the alien ship?" asked Sabrina.

"Yes, love. Think about it," replied François, "If other parts of the station start to leak, we won't be able to maintain the integrity of the station for very long. Losing one pod for a few days is already a huge problem, but if this gets worse... The only other place I can think of, that can provide us with shelter, is the alien ship. Dedrick and I spent countless days in there without needing to use our suits, and you've all been there. It may not be ideal, but it sure beats the alternative."

"I agree with François," added Dedrick. "I don't see too many other options. If we lose our habitat, we have nowhere else to go. I suggest we start thinking about packing some of our survival equipment. Just in case. Anything you can think of that we may need. Extra suits, clothes, computers, lab equipment, food! Prioritize. Only gather what is essential. We need to find a way to take as much food as we can, if we end up having to leave the station."

"Shoot! That means the greenhouses won't survive either," said Ladli looking at him.

"You're right, we need to think about that as well. See if you can transfer some of the plants and vegetables to portable containers. And water! Damn it! What do we do about water?"

Everyone in the room started to realize the true magnitude of their predicament. Even Dedrick, who had always seemed calm and in control when faced with difficult situations in the past, was now struggling to not let his emotions take over him. They all felt the weight of the Martian world on them. Unless the aliens could help them, the station was dying, and they would die with it. And unless they were able to transfer the water recycling system to the Kahnus' cave, moving there would not help either. It all seemed pointless. Sabrina started crying. Her head in her hands, she let out a wailing, "I don't wanna die!" and doubled up on her cries, sobbing and hyperventilating.

"No one is going to die," said Dedrick firmly. Realizing he might have scared Chasma, he turned to look at his daughter. To his surprise, she did not appear the least affected by the situation. Vera, on the other hand, looked like she was about to cry as well. Tears began rolling down her face.

"No one is going to die!" repeated Dedrick. "We didn't fly a hundred million kilometers through space and managed to survive on Mars by ourselves for the past fifteen years, to give up now. We've accomplished too much, been through too many challenges. We've discovered more than anyone had ever hoped we would and proven we can do the impossible; survive on another world. I'm not willing to just give up like that! I'm telling you, we're going to figure this out. We have to! The more I think about it, the more I'm convinced the aliens can help us. After all, they owe us for getting them out of those pods, don't they?"

He wasn't truly convinced of that himself, but his words had the wanted effect. The colonists seemed to perk up from their sad demeanor. Maybe all was not lost after all. "François, I think you need to stay here and work on fixing that leak as best you can. Tendai, you can help him. Vera, take Ladli and Sabrina with you, and start packing everything you think is essential. The things we just talked about. Use your best judgment."

Gathering around the table, they began organizing themselves, and were soon off to their individual chores. All except Liu, who seemed completely disconnected from the situation, staring at her feet.

"OK, so one of you should come with me," continued Dedrick looking at her.

He had noticed how distraught she looked earlier, and thought going to see the aliens with him might distract her. He needed someone anyway. No one was supposed to leave the station alone, for obvious safety reasons. Plus, she had an interesting connection with Jorh. She did not respond, seemingly lost in thoughts. He could see the glaze in her eyes. The memory came back from years earlier, when she had plunged into a deep depression after the death of Najib, the man she loved.

"I wanna go, Daddy!" offered Chasma with excitement.

"You better stay with Mommy, sweetie. She needs you to help her pack. I promise to take you next time."

"But that's what you said last time," replied Chasma frowning.

"I know, baby. Next time. I promise."

"Fine," she said, crossing her arms on her chest, and tapping her foot on the floor. She then turned her back to him. Vera grabbed her hand.

"Come Chasma, Daddy has something very important to do. You and I are going to pack our clothes together. You wanna help me?"

Still frowning, Chasma replied loudly, "I don't care!"

"Come on, it'll be fun." They then walked to the pod three tunnel. Vera lifted Chasma into the corridor and followed in. Dedrick turned his attention back to Liu still looking at the floor. He approached her and held his hand out.

"Liu, you want to come? Come on Liu, I need you for this. Jorh likes talking to you and I know you enjoy it too. Liu...?"

She slowly raised her head and gave him a weak smile. The tears were still rolling down her face…

"Come on. It's gonna be OK. I promise." He slowly helped her up to her feet, and both headed for the suit room.

A new home

Liu was standing a few steps back behind Dedrick who was in a mental conversation with the tall beings.

"*We cannot survive long if we don't manage to repair this damage. Our air supply depends on it.*"

Jorh, seated in his hovering chair, had been listening attentively. He spoke, "*We know about your situation. We heard your distress. I wish we could help you repair your home my friend, but your technology is incompatible with ours. I can sense your fear; for yourself and those you love. From what I can tell, it is unlikely that your habitat will survive this malfunction for long. However, it does not have to be the end of your journey. We agree your best bet is to move here. We heard your conversation with your people. We had already planned to offer you to move to our ship before you got here. As you know, it offers enough room for all. Gather what you need, and we will gladly provide your people shelter.*"

"*That would be most appreciated, Jorh.*" Dedrick was slightly surprised, not having expected the alien to offer them refuge so easily, but he was certainly glad.

"*Yes. You are the last surviving descendants of your species, just like we are of ours. We ought to help each other.*"

The reassuring deep, soft tone of Jorh's mental voice brought peace and warmth to Dedrick. He felt a genuine sense of safety around the aliens. This was their best option.

Liu slowly approached and lowered her head in reverence toward Jorh.

"*Thank you, Jorh-San! You are most generous.*" She crossed her hands on her heart and took a bow. Holding one of his large fingers below her chin, he raised her head to look into her eyes.

"*You are welcome, Liu-San!*"

Then, slowly rising, he walked majestically toward one of the pods, and passing his hand over a panel, stood still as the pod opened, and Mahhzee slowly emerged from the foggy fumes escaping the regenerating pod. She approached the two humans. Standing next to her, they looked more like small children than adults. Blinking at Dedrick and Liu with her large purple eyes, Mahhzee addressed them telepathically, "*Bring your friends and family here. They are no longer safe in your habitat. We will adjust our rooms to accommodate your needs. Go now, while you still can.*"

Her smooth mental voice was like honey to Dedrick. He was once again mesmerized by the alien. His mind drifted off for an instant.

"Are you ready, Dedrick? We should go."

"Yes, of course…"

#

Two hours later, the eight Martian colonists were busy packing all they could into the three rovers and their respective trailers, which they had only rarely used since their arrival on Mars. They had wasted no time debating how long the station had before it became unsafe. As soon as Dedrick and Liu had returned, the transferring of supplies had begun. They had estimated it would take at least two trips to get the bare essentials. More importantly, they were going to need to transfer some of the greenhouse's content to the cave. They knew they could only transport a portion of the plants and vegetables, but François had an idea. He believed he could modify the trailers, originally designed to transport the landing pods, into one big towing platform, that would allow them to relocate at least one greenhouse to the cave.

"We better hurry, then. We have no idea how long we have before the whole habitat gets affected," said Dedrick.

"Mommy, where is Sylvia?" asked Chasma looking for her doll.

"I don't know, baby. I'm sure Sylvia is in our luggage, somewhere," she replied while packing.

"We have to find her, Mommy! I can't leave her behind!" Chasma was almost in tears.

'We don't have time, baby. I'm sure she's in your blue bag."

"No, I checked. I can't find her anywhere! We can't go. We have to find Sylvia!" she screamed.

"Ok, baby, calm down. We're gonna find her. Let me look."

"You guys ready?" asked François, who had just popped into the pod.

"We can't find Sylvia!" replied Vera, frantically lifting up bags and clothes.

"There! Is that it?" asked François, pointing at the doll lying under Chasma's bed.

"Sylvia! There you are," rejoiced the girl, grabbing the toy to her chest.

"Ok, good. Come on baby, it's time to go!"

The three exited the pod through the small corridor, and were soon in the garage, adding a few more bags to the already over-packed rover trunk of ARC 1.

"Where is Liu?" asked Dedrick.

"Right here!" replied the Korean. She climbed on board and sat in the front passenger seat next to him. Vera was already setting herself in behind them with Chasma. Near by, François and Sabrina were waiting in ARC 2. Both rovers were packed to capacity, waiting. Dedrick pressed a few keys on the dashboard screen. The garage door opened, and the two vehicles started making their way to ARC 3, already waiting outside with Tendai and Ladli. Chasma turned her head back, looking at the only habitat she had ever known.

"Mommy, are we going to a new home?"

"Yes, Chasma, we're going to a new home," replied her mother, stroking her blond hair softly.

"Are we coming back?"

"I don't know, baby. I don't think so..."

As Chasma watched through the rear windshield of the vehicle, the station kept shrinking until it finally disappeared in the dust behind them.

#

"*We can extend the ship's primary resources to the immediate surroundings of the cave but no further. If you can bring your greenhouse here, we should be able to provide you with air and an acceptable atmosphere. There is a large platform behind the ship, near the back of the cave where you will be able to secure it. We will do the rest.*"

Jorh's words had greatly reassured Dedrick and his teammates. After unloading the supplies and its passengers, Dedrick, François, Tendai, and Ladli were off on one last trip, to get one of the greenhouses. They knew only one could be taken back to the cave. They had already taken most of the living essentials on the last three trips. Now they would try to transfer as many plants and vegetables as possible to greenhouse two.

François' idea of using the three trailers to transport the greenhouse had proven an excellent one. A few hours later, the small party was returning with a full greenhouse, hauled behind the two rovers. A few tubes and wires hung unplugged to one side of the cargo.

Using the crane they had installed a few weeks earlier above the cliff, the team began pulling up the big container from down below to the cave's level, about fifty meters higher.

"Tendai, can you hear me?"

"Ten-four, François. I receive you loud and clear."

"Ok. We're ready. You can start lifting the package."

"Ok."

Down below, Dedrick, Sabrina, and François watched as the cables started rising, slowly forming a large pyramid above the greenhouse. Finally, the four corners stretched tight, and the platform was jolted slightly, and began its ascent to the cave's entrance.

"Looking good, Tendai. It's coming up nice and straight," informed him Dedrick.

A few minutes later, the platform and its cargo were slowly swinging fifty meters above the ground. In no time, Vera and Ladli, standing at the cave's mouth, secured the anchors and slowly pulled the package in. After a bit of manual coordination between the two rovers and the cave's team, the container was resting on its bottom, in front of the large alien passage. Jorh, Mahhzee, and Gahneo were ready to help as well. They had joined the human team, wearing their gelatinous suits. François wondered why the aliens had not ventured out before in those suits. If the aliens heard his thoughts, they did not offer an explanation. Instead, with hand gestures, Jorh and his companions commanded the large Zarfha they had brought with them. The object began to hover. After going through its spectacular light show, the sphere came to a rest, floating just above the greenhouse. Then, as if pulling it with invisible force, the white Zarfha levitated the dwelling a couple of meters above the ground. The three aliens then proceeded to walk back to their ship, Zarfha and greenhouse in tow.

A few hours later, one more trip to the Mars First station was made to grab some overlooked items, but by early evening, everyone had safely moved into the alien vessel.

"*Thank you!*" said Dedrick to Jorh again, while everyone was busy relocating all the plants that had been moved separately to the greenhouse behind the ship.

"*You are welcome*," he blinked.

The first night on the alien vessel was a bit strange to the new tenants. They had never spent a single night away from the station in fifteen years, except for rare rover excursions. It was not for lack of comfort. They had brought their bedding with them, and the aliens had allocated four of their twelve rooms to house the colonists, although Dedrick's team would have been just as grateful with one. It was the unfamiliar surroundings that made it hard for most to fall asleep. Aside from Chasma, none of them slept much that first night. The next morning the humans were up long before the aliens. Quickly realizing their range inside the ship had been widened, they took the opportunity to explore a few new rooms, transported at will by the alien fog throughout the purple corridors.

Eventually reaching the Time-Frost room, they were greeted by their three hosts. Jorh and his companions had slept in their hibernation pods. They still preferred those over the rooms' hovering beds, at least for now; especially for their nourishing and reinvigorating properties. They were not weak from their long hibernation anymore, but they had gotten used to the pods. They didn't know it yet but soon, everyone on board would be glad the pods were so nurturing.

Chapter XII

Kahjuna, the brown world

Dedrick recognized the familiar feeling right away. It was the one he always got when Mahhzee was about to speak to him in his head. Similar to the light electric jolt one gets as he puts his tongue on a small battery; uncomfortable, yet slightly arousing.

"*Hello Dedrick. How are you feeling? Did you and your friends sleep well?*"

"*Hi Mahhzee. I'm well. Thank you. How...are you?*"

"*I am well. Thank you.*"

Her voice was low and thick and had a soothing effect on Dedrick. The Russian commander was by now quite familiar with it.

"*We would like you to join us in the main room. We wish to show you something,*" she added.

"*Sure, I'll be right there.*"

By now, he was quite used to thinking back to the aliens, instead of talking out loud, but the feeling was still foreign and slightly unnerving.

He leaned above Vera still in bed and kissed her forehead. She moaned a bit in her sleep.

"I'll be back, love," he said quietly as he got up and made his way to the other end of the room. A few minutes later, he was floating slowly down the ship's main corridor. The door opened as his body approached, and he slowly glided inside. Mahhzee, Jorh, and Gahneo were standing in the middle of the large white space, encircling the central sphere hovering a meter or so above its low pedestal. Dedrick slowly approached the tall aliens.

"*Welcome, Dedrick!*" said Jorh. "*We want to show you something.*"

Jorh raised his arm and pointed at the sphere. The round object started spinning and glowing. Drastically changing colors from white to yellow to green to blue, the object eventually morphed into a familiar shape.

"Earth!" said Dedrick out loud.

"*Yes! This is your world. We call it Kahjuna.*" Jorh approached the sphere with his hand, almost touching it, and pointed at the African continent.

"Many millions of your Earth's years ago, one of our sister vessels also escaped the destruction of our world and traveled to your planet, Earth. We believe Silargh's ship and his passengers landed somewhere on this side of your home world. We never heard from them again and presumed they had either crashed or become stranded. The events that took place, here on Kesra, prevented us from going to their rescue, as you know. But if there is a chance the ship made it there, and they were able to retrieve the white light, we may be able to get to it. We could definitely use some of the ship's systems as well. If anything, we may be able to retrieve the Zarfha engine."

"Earth! You can go to Earth? With this ship? Wait, does that mean you can take us with you?" Dedrick's excitement was obvious.

"Yes, Dedrick. We plan to take you back with us to your world. We cannot leave you here, anyway. The three of us have no reason to stay on Kesra any longer. Some questions need answers. We wish to go to Earth and wish you all to come with us," replied Jorh. In truthfulness, Jorh knew as well as Dedrick, that the humans were now totally dependent on the alien's ship and bound to go wherever the vessel went.

"That's fantastic! I had no idea this vessel was still able to fly. This is the best news I've heard since the..." an uneasy feeling suddenly came over Dedrick. The excitement of the moment had almost made him forget the sad reality of Earth's state. He started thinking about the chemical war that had ravaged Earth years ago. They had absolutely no idea of the extent of the devastation.

"We know. We have followed you for many years. Unfortunately, we cannot tell from here how bad your planet has suffered, we do not have that capability. But some of your people may have survived. More importantly, it may be your best chance for a new home. We know this ship is not ideal for your kind."

Mahhzee looked at the Russian. "Don't you want to find out what happened to your world?"

"Of course, I do! But I must tell you, humans are not always the friendliest. They usually fear the unknown, and I don't know how well they will receive you. They've never met aliens before, you know?"

"You can talk for us," offered Mahhzee.

Looking up at her big blinking eyes, he realized how ridiculous his concern was. He could hardly contain his excitement.

"How soon are you leaving? I need to tell the others."

"We are ready to leave when you are, Dedrick. Go tell your people," replied Jorh.

Blinking a few times, unconsciously, Dedrick smiled and

thanked the aliens before heading back for the purple corridor. Floating away, he soon disappeared down the hall, overwhelmed by the news, and a few minutes later, Vera was awakened by his voice.

"Vera. Vera... Wake up. I just talked to the Kahnus. They are taking us back to Earth."

"Hun... What? Did you say Earth?" she jumped up in her bed, and stared at him for a few seconds, rubbing her sleepy eyes.

"What are you saying?"

He could see the emotion building up in her.

"We're going back to Earth."

"What?! Really? Are you sure? But how?" she was almost tearing up from the joy and excitement.

"Their ship. They said they can take us back. All of us."

She turned her head in the direction of Chasma's bed. The young girl was still sleeping peacefully. Smiling, crying, and laughing all at the same time, Vera brought a hand to her mouth.

"Our baby girl is going to see Earth."

"I know," he replied almost as emotional.

#

François and Tendai were sitting in one of the rooms they had requisitioned. It had been turned into the colonists' main supply storage area. Lifting a long green box containing plants, Tendai looked troubled. He put his load down and sat next to it.

"So, you really think this is a good idea? I mean, I'm excited to go back to Earth and all, but I'm not thrilled about losing the greenhouse. Everything we've worked for these last fifteen years, gone, just like that."

"I understand, but there's not much we can do. We'll take everything we can with us. This ship is substantially faster than ours. We should be there in a couple of weeks," replied François.

"Don't you forget something? What about that chemical war in 2034? Remember? Better hope we can still find food on Earth," said Tendai, looking unconvinced.

"Come on, don't be so pessimistic."

Sabrina entered and gracefully landed on her feet, as if she had done so all her life. "I know this amazing restaurant in Sanarate; the food is out of this world! And I can't wait to have a cold Margarita!"

Tendai just walked passed her unimpressed and left the room.

"What's up with him?"

"Oh, I don't know. I think it's that time of the month."

"That's not funny, François."

"I know. I'm sorry. Come here," he said smiling at her.

She approached and stood right in front of him. He was sitting on a tall stool. He extended his legs on each side of her and grabbed her waist in his hand to pull her closer. Slowly bringing her chest to him, he kissed her cleavage.

"We're going to Earth, baby."

"I know. I can't believe it." She kissed his forehead.

Then, grabbing his head with both hands, she kissed his mouth passionately. He grabbed her thighs and pulled her on him. Sitting on his lap, facing him, she felt his hands open her suit and rush down her bare back. The sensation sent a wave of goose bumps all over her body.

"François. What are you doing? Not in here."

"Why not? It's our last night on Mars. Let's make it a special one."

#

The group, gliding effortlessly through the corridors, was following Jorh and Mahhzee. As they approached the door at the end of the passage, the entrance slowly dematerialized, and they all entered the main cockpit of the vessel. The glossy black wall facing them was even larger than François remembered. In the center of the room, the Zarfha sphere was hovering just above its platform. Landing on his feet, Dedrick could see everyone's image on the glossy wall acting like a mirror. One by one, they came down silently and stood next to him. Mahhzee approached one of the large seats and sat. Raising her arm, she executed a few hand waves, and the Zarfha's rotation began to change direction and speed.

"*Please, you can sit down if you wish,*" Jorh told them, pointing at the chairs. They all did. Within seconds, the black wall in front of them morphed, until it became completely transparent. The dark cave outside the ship appeared, brightened and enhanced by the clear window. The large window, almost as tall as the aliens, took most of the wall in front of them. Several strange markings were flickering on its outer edges. François assumed they were readings of the outside surroundings, or navigational information of some kind.

"*You must have an amazing view of space when you travel.*" commented

François.

"*We do. All of our ships do. But they are times when it's preferable not to. If traveling to Alhis, the sun. In that case, we can lower the light sensibility of the opening, or close it. We can also view in any direction around the ship,*" replied Jorh.

"*You've been to the sun?*" asked Liu amazed.

"*Our people have traveled to all the major planets and moons of your solar system, many times over, the sun included. But Gahneo, Jorh, and I have only been to Kesra. Only a selected few have traveled to other worlds. We've never been to Kahjuna either. We are looking forward to seeing your beautiful Earth,*" replied Mahhzee.

Refocusing her attention on the Zarfha, she went through another elaborate movement of hand, something the human group was now quite used to, and brought the sphere to an even faster spin. As the colorful light waves began their beautiful show, the spectators realized the outside view was changing gradually. The ship was slowly rising above the cavern's floor, but the transition was so smooth, had they not seen the walls of the cavern move, they would have never known. They could not feel a thing. There were no vibrations or sensation of movement whatsoever. The ship began to turn slowly onto itself, until it faced the entrance of the cavern. Gahneo entered the room.

"*The path has been cleared,*" he confirmed, as he sat next to Jorh.

Through the large translucent wall of the cabin, they all watched the ship approach the mouth of the cave, hovering effortlessly under Mahhzee's hand commands. The large boulders, that had until recently blocked the tunnel's entrance, had been removed. Dedrick wondered how the aliens had managed to do so so quickly. Something he would have to asked, but later. For now, he was too captivated with the maneuver. The walls of the dark passage ahead, made clearly visible by the accentuated contrast and colors of the front window, appeared just wide enough for the vessel to move through without touching on either side, but barely. Gliding seamlessly along the corridor, the ship and its occupants eventually made their way to the other end of the tunnel. As they emerged far above the sheer drop of the cliff face, the large front window of the cabin adjusted accordingly, bringing the bright daylight down to a comfortable level for everyone's eyes. The vessel began to rise vertically and a few seconds later, the travelers were racing above the plateau, quickly climbing towards the upper atmosphere of Mars, in absolute silence. Mahhzee waved another command, and the view changed to show the small Martian outpost, now visible in the distance, as they gained altitude.

"Mommy, look! The station," said Chasma, pointing at the quickly shrinking dwellings. They all watched in silence. The small Mars First outpost had been their only home ever since their first landing. A strange feeling of sadness ran through them; a sense of loss. They would never come back, and they all knew it. As the ship began to reach space, the orange world Dedrick and his friends had called home for so many years began to move away. The Martian planet and its grand crater looked just as impressive as it had when they had first seen it from space, so many years ago. In the next few days, it would gradually shrink until becoming just another bright star.

"I'm gonna miss it, you know?" Sabrina said quietly to François.

"I know, me too, love."

They stared a bit longer at the red planet slowly moving away, until Mahhzee returned to the view in front of the ship. Ahead, the amazing expanse of space was offering a starry spectacle like they had never experienced before. Beyond the large clear wall of the vessel, enhanced by the alien window, the stars appeared more dazzling than ever, their sparkling light accentuated by the ship's view. Too small to make out yet, a pale blue dot was flickering far in the distance. They were on their way to Earth.

#

The next several weeks were long and quite frankly boring to most of the passengers. Nonetheless, Dedrick and his friends had learned to adapt to their new living quarters quite well by now. But there was nothing much to do on the ship, except attend to the small makeshift greenhouse they had managed to recreate in one of the ship's cargo areas. If they took care of it, the temporary food storage would supply them adequately for a good month. Luckily, the trip to Earth was much faster on the Kahnu ship than any manmade rocket. The small human group was certainly looking forward to their home planet's abundant supply of food and water, even if they knew Earth had been severely damaged by the last chemical war. No matter the situation back on the blue planet, their return would certainly be a cause for celebration. And if that wasn't enough to get the attention of the powers at play, coming back with aliens and their amazing ship would undoubtedly do so, and force all human differences aside, resetting human values and our place in the universe in a big way. At least, that's what Ladli was quite confident about, as she had mentioned to the team several times already.

Her Russian commander wasn't so sure of it. He remembered too well the gut feeling he had experienced, during the last transmissions from Earth, almost six years ago. Things had not looked good for the blue planet, when Lars Bruininck had told them of the global destruction taking place, and the rate at which everything on Earth was dying. The more he had thought about it, the more he had realized the gravity of the situation. If anything, he knew for sure the situation on Earth had been catastrophic. Simple logic dictated that Lars would have tried to avoid panic in the small Martian station, at least for moral and psychological support for the team. Alone on a desert planet, almost a hundred million kilometers from their families, they knew better than to tell them everything. Then there was also the protocol. Dedrick remembered vividly the last transmission they had received. Lars himself had admitted he didn't think Earth would "make it through this one," as he had put it. The words were still ringing clearly in the commander's mind. "*Every form of life on Earth is being affected. Even animals and plants are dying by the millions. Life is resilient, and the human race has survived countless catastrophes before, but this one… I don't know.*"

The group had heard it just as he had, but it seemed to Dedrick that only he had really understood the true extent of the devastation. Now, on their way to Earth, he hoped with all his heart he was wrong. He shook his head and cleared the thought out of his mind.

"*Come on! What am I doing? This is no way to spend my time in this amazing ship. Look at this view!*"

He slowly got up from his hovering bed and walked to the giant window at the end of his room. Outside, the darkness of space was littered with the sparkling light of countless stars. The void was immense, yet, it was overpopulated with the startling beauty of a million solar systems. Each and every one of them was so distant from its closest neighbor that its light took anywhere from a few to thousands of years, to get from one to the other. But their source was so gigantic and powerful that they could be seen across thousands of light years in the emptiness of space.

"*What a magical sight! And here we are, traveling through this incomparably beautiful vista.*" Lost in thoughts, Dedrick had not felt Mahhzee's presence.

"Oh, I… I didn't see you there."

"*I know, Dedrick. I didn't mean to startle you. I was listening to your beautiful thoughts. I hope you don't mind.*"

He smiled timidly. Even after so many weeks since their first encounter, he was still in awe of her majestic presence. She was truly an impressive being not only in size, but also in the way she moved and talked to his mind. He realized again that she was probably listening to that thought as well. Of course, she was. But she made sure not to show it.

"*I came to show you something. Look!*"

She gracefully walked to the window and placed her hand on the glassy material. With a lateral movement, she dragged the view and pointed at a small object outside. A quick zooming effect brought it right in front of them, and Dedrick instantly recognized what he was looking at.

"Earth!" he said out loud.

"*Yes, your home planet. We will be there in a few days. I thought you might want to have a better look at it as we approach.*"

"*Thank you, Mahhzee,*" he replied mentally, while transfixed on the three-dimensional image. He noted the pale bluish planet didn't look as bright and colorful as he remembered it. That immediately worried him, especially after his morose thoughts moments earlier. He pushed the thought away again and looked at the view. It was Earth regardless and it was still a beautiful sight.

As promised, for the next two days, Earth grew larger on the visioning window of the ship's cockpit and soon, they would enter Kahjuna's atmosphere. The one thing that began to really worry Dedrick and his crew as they approached the blue planet, was the dullness and washed out colors of the continents and oceans. The closer they got, the more obvious it became that things didn't look right. Even Chasma, who had only seen Earth in photos and videos, expected much more vivid tints of blues and greens. As for the cloud cover over Earth's mass, it was giving them by far the strangest feeling of all. From pole to pole, the once bright white swirly features now appeared doll and gray, giving the world ahead a lugubrious look.

"I don't understand. It looks like another planet. What happened here?" finally said Tendai, breaking the silence.

"*Mahhzee, can you show us a close up of this?*" asked Vera telepathically, while pointing at the island of Manhattan, on the New York coast of the American continent.

Mahhzee reached out and moved her six fingers across the Zarfha.

"Where is everybody? I... I can't believe it! It all looks abandoned, like no one has been there in years. Where are the people?" She did not want to face the truth yet. "How can that be? I mean, the buildings are still standing, right? So where is everybody? They couldn't all be gone?!"

Mahhzee brought the view even closer until... they finally saw them; human bodies, laying everywhere in the streets. Most still partially clothed, their skeleton remains confirming their worst nightmare. They had been dead for years, and no one had been there since. Vera stopped talking and brought her hands to her face. All eyes in the room were transfixed. It was a scene from a true holocaust.

"*I am afraid you will find the same thing all over your world,*" telepathically said Jorh as Mahhzee pulled back the display to a general view of Earth. The aliens could feel the distress in all of them. Even Chasma, who had always seemed so comfortable and happy in any situation, looked upset. Liu slowly approached the window.

"*Mahhzee, can you let me see this place, please?*"

Mahhzee obliged.

The city of Seoul, in South Korea, quickly appeared. As they all feared, it looked just as devastated. Dead carcasses, trash, abandoned vehicles, and all sorts of debris littered the once buzzing avenues. The mess all around was a testimony to the rapidity at which everything had happened. Boxes, bags, furniture, food stands, advertisement signs, bicycles, store canvasses, broken glass, machines, TVs, and so much more were piled up all over, as if a giant flood had dragged everything out of the buildings and strewn it all about. More evident that whatever had taken place there had happened in complete chaos.

The next few minutes were enough to let them discover thousands more corpses in the streets of others around the world. They had flown over dozens of large metropolises and witnessed the exact same scenes. Not a single sign of life, human or animal alike. Only scattered skeletons, pet carcasses and trash, littering the roads and highways. All had died years ago. And now, even the most cherished manmade structures, humanity had proudly congratulated itself to have created, were crumbling away all across the globe. It was hard to believe, but in time, no trace of them or mankind would remain.

They had all expected to find a battered Earth, aware of some of the tragic events that had taken place years ago, but none had truly thought the planet would have become too hostile for them to survive there.

The spaceship was now flying just a few dozen meters above the ground. By now, all of them knew Earth was no longer a possible home for them. Nothing green had survived. Grass, plants, flowers, crops did not exist anymore. The only visible remnants of the once thriving vegetation were dead tree trunks and dried out bushes and plants, a sad reminder of the once beautiful and lavish forests of Earth. Parks in urban meccas and residential areas had become dirt covered lots. Eventually flying over more rural parts of the world, the true magnitude of Earth's predicament became evident. Everywhere they went, they found only desolation and death.

"*I'm afraid your world has become uninhabitable as well, my friends. We are truly sorry*," said Jorh to the group, as they passed over Australia.

"I can't believe they managed to destroy everything," Tendai said out loud. "I mean, we've had wars before but this...It's…" he couldn't finish.

In the back of the room, Liu was crying, curled up in a ball. Mahhzee was seated next to her.

"*I am truly sorry that your world is gone, Liu. I can tell it must have been a wonderful home for you and your people. I had seen Zarfha recreations from the Grand Halis Library, but seeing it now, I can only imagine its true beauty, with the vibrant colors and life I remember from our library of knowledge. Our world was beautiful as well, and when we lost it, I lost a part of myself. It was a long time ago, but for me it was yesterday. I miss the Klomags and their majesty. I miss our Mohgvar Ocean…I miss my home…my mother...*"

Liu was now listening attentively to Mahhzee, feeling less alone, knowing she had experienced a similar tragedy. She had stopped crying.

Back at the other end of the room…

"Crap. So, what now?" asked Tendai.

Dedrick was about to ask Jorh a question but the alien, reading his mind, answered it before he could.

"*It's toxic. The ship's probes indicate that the air is unbreathable for your people. It can no longer support your life as you know it. You and your friends would need your suits to breathe. You would not survive long. I am truly sorry.*"

"Are you sure it is so everywhere? What about the poles?"

"*Even at the poles. Nothing there has survived either but a few scattered small life forms that barely register on our probe. Not enough to sustain you and your friends.*"

"So, what do we do? Return to Mars?" asked Tendai.

"We just left Mars because we could no longer survive there, remember? Earth is all we have left now. There has to be a way…" Ladli was visibly upset.

"*What about the oceans? Could there still be life there*?" asked François.

Jorh turned his attention to the Zarfha…

"*Your oceans still harbor some life forms, but they are too few and deep-down remote regions of the oceans. Most are small creatures living near volcanic vents and deep trenches. All fish and mammals are gone.*"

While Jorh was telepathically talking to Dedrick and his crew, the images of Earth's desolated cities and land masses were replaced by deep ocean views, void of any colors. Small ghostly looking creatures crawled on a desolate oceanic floor, floating slowly above heated chimneys of hot gas, clearly visible in the dark murky waters. Some resembled small crabs and shrimps, and others even looked completely alien to the human crew. But all were relatively small, no more than a few centimeters long.

"*Not all life is gone but your planet will take many centuries, possibly thousands of years, to replenish its former abundance of life, if it ever does. Some worlds have come back from such dramatic change. Yours was one of them, many eons ago. Our archive speaks of several documented world changing events that had re-written Kahjuna's history.*"

Chasma, seated on Vera's lap, was pointing at the giant forward screen, fascinated by the exotic images of dinosaurs and giant tropical forests that were being projected by the ship's Zarfha.

"*…but it is hard to say how it will fare this time. Only time itself will tell.*"

Jorh paused and turned his attention to Gahneo and Mahhzee.

After the three had seemed to exchange thoughts the small human group could not hear, Mahhzee got up and moved toward the forward view. Pointing at a point in an overhead view of the African continent and its surrounding oceans, she spoke warmly to the small passengers.

"*Silargh and his crew landed here on your world. We were hoping they had managed to use their Time-Frost pods and survived, but we would have felt them by now...*"

"The other ship? In South Africa?" asked François out loud, as surprised as the rest of them. "*I know that's why you wanted to come here, but I didn't think you were really expecting to find much. That was seventy million years ago! I know Mars' geology has not changed much during that time, but Earth has been very active, even in the recent past, and I doubt you'll find anything but fossils from that era. Plus, I'm sure someone would have found it, if there was an alien ship in the jungles of Africa*," he finished telepathically.

"*We know the Aruk is still there. Our own ship has detected its signal.*"

A small yellow dot was now flickering in the center of the image, as the view zoomed to a remote area of the big continent.

"I'm assuming that's where we're going next, but that doesn't change our own problem. What do we do now that we can't live on Earth? How long can we survive on this ship? We only have enough supplies for a month, if that!" suddenly said Sabrina out loud. Her voice was shaking.

"Exactly! What now? Earth was our only chance. We're screwed. We're all gonna die!" Tendai screamed, looking at Dedrick, hysterical.

"I don't wanna die!" started crying Liu from the back of the room.

"Calm down, calm down! Nobody is going to die," interjected Dedrick, looking at Chasma and his wife, trying to reassure them. "We didn't come this far to give up now, right?"

"*There goes Mr. Positive, again*," thought François to himself, unconvinced.

Africa

Outside, the southern tip of Africa was slowly rotating under the ship orbiting a few kilometers above. From that distance, the once lavish green land now looked mostly bare and desolated. The ship was soon flying along the coast, a mere few meters above the water. The dark murky ocean added to the gloomy of scene. A few dark clouds were scattered in the distance. Occasional wave surges were creating white foamy tops below. Ahead, a protruding land mass was approaching. The sun was shining brightly in the early afternoon sky as the vessel reached the shore. It slowed to a mere few kilometers an hour. Again, all they could see was the bare ground, stripped of its vegetation and left naked, dead trees and dried out bushes scattered about. A few minutes later, they were landing softly at the foot of a large hill.

"*We are very close to the place where the ship is. Gahneo and I need to go get what we came for. You are welcome to join us, but don't forget you'll need your suits. Earth's atmosphere is toxic now,*" told them Jorh, looking at the small humans.

Dedrick briefly glanced at François.

"*Actually, François and I would like to come with you, if you don't mind.*"

"*I'd like to come as well,*" added Ladli.

"*Of course, you are welcome to join us.*"

"Personally, I think I'll stay here," said Tendai.

Liu wasn't in the mood to join either.

"It's probably better if you stay here with them. I'm sure we'll be safe with Jorh and Gahneo, but I don't want you to take unnecessary risks," told François to Sabrina."

"Honestly, you don't have to convince me. I'm not really feeling like taking a stroll at the moment," she replied, sounding justifiably depressed.

"We'll be back before you know it," said Dedrick, looking at his wife.

"I know, be careful," she replied as she kissed him.

Stepping out of the room, Jorh and Gahneo traveled to the end of the ship, dragging a large container with them. They were both wearing a form fitted suit that covered their entire body, their head and face included. Except for a dark section in front of their large eyes, the gelatinous looking suit was mostly see-thru. After having suited up as well, Dedrick, Ladli and François soon rejoined the two aliens.

The two aliens stepped out of the white vessel and began walking toward the hill ahead, when they heard their troubled human friends behind them.

As soon as François landed softly on the ground, the strong gravity of Earth reminded him immediately how much the lower gravity of Mars had weakened his body. Fifteen years spent on the red planet had noticeably atrophied his muscles. Dedrick and Ladli realized quickly what was happening as well.

"Shoot! I forgot. We've been on Mars for so long, Earth is making everything feel much heavier, especially our suits."

Jorh walked back to them. Extending his arm, he released a small Zarfha from his tubular fingers, and the white sphere hovered to François. The Frenchman felt instantly relieved from the uncomfortable weight. Two more Zarfhas came resting in mid-air next to Ladli and the Russian commander.

"*These will help counter the effect of your planet's pull.*"

"*Thank you, Jorh,*" replied Dedrick.

Leaving the vessel, the tall beings and their three human companions walked up the rough terrain and soon disappeared behind the hill.

"Ok, so I guess we'll be waiting right here, then…" said Tendai a bit sarcastically, as the five vanished from the giant screen.

#

Almost an hour had gone by the time the explorers finally got back.

"So? Did you guys get what you were looking for?" asked Vera to Dedrick.

"Did we ever?! Let me show you."

Inside the main cabin, the small group gathered around him and Dedrick turned his suit pad on. Near the Zarfha, Mahhzee was getting some details on the excursion, from Jorh and Gahneo.

Dedrick's screen was only twenty centimeters wide, resting in the middle of his torso, but for once, the picture was bright and of high quality. He took the device off his chest and put it on the table, so he could watch as well.

"*Let me give this to our Zarfha. You will see more comfortably,*" came Jorh's mental voice. He did not wait for them to respond. Grabbing the small video tablet, he brought the object to the sphere next to him, and the pad disappeared into the Zarfha's white surface, as if swallowed by quicksand. Within seconds, a three-dimensional view of the trail Jorh and the others had taken, formed around the sphere. A large three-dimensional image, projecting all around them, soon filled the ship's entire cabin.

"That's the entrance to the cave!" said François out loud.

"I can see that," replied Sabrina.

Aside from the strange ghostly look of the five explorers in the video, everyone could clearly see from their large hovering chairs.

After a bit of effort getting the container through the tight passage, the five explorers began their slow journey down the cavern tunnel, Dedrick and François' helmet spotlights lighting the way. Fifteen minutes later, the narrow path opened into a large cavern. Gahneo opened the container he and Jorh had brought with them, and a small Zarfha rose out of it, slowly spinning on itself. With a wave of the hand, the alien sent the sphere toward the center of the cave, and the Zarfha instantly illuminated the large underground space. Near the back, the alien vessel was now clearly in view. A portion of the ceiling of the cavern had caved in from above and damaged it substantially.

"*We found out from the vessel's records that the collapse happened twelve million years ago, your years, during an Earthquake,*" mentioned Gahneo to the three humans in the group. As they approached the ship, it was easy to see the large agape hole caused by the crushing roof. The two suited aliens made their way through the rubble and entered the vessel, followed by their human companions. The inside of Silargh's ship was a mess. From large boulders to small mounts of debris, dead over grown plants, and broken artifacts were littering the floor of hallways and rooms everywhere. The small party kept on, making their way through the rubble, toward the main cockpit. The large room appeared intact, but was covered in a fine layer of dirt and dust. Gahneo approached the Zarfha, and after an elaborate display of hand gestures, awakened the large white sphere. Some of the chairs, lying on their side on the floor of the ancient vessel automatically reset themselves, hovering in their upright position. Jorh and Gahneo sat down and began an intricate hand dance, focusing again on the Zarfha. The following light show, now quite familiar to all, began and a beautiful three-dimensional view of an ancient valley began to form all around the five explorers.

"*That's quite interesting,*" thought François. "*So, we're all in the ship outside, right now, in this three-dimensional projection, experiencing what Dedrick, Ladli and I witnessed about an hour ago, as we relived what happened to the ship in the cave, seventy million years ago. Talk about messing with your head.*"

"*I have to admit, it's pretty weird. It feels like a strange dream,*" agreed Sabrina.

"If you think of it, it's like seeing yourself on TV watching an old movie." Dedrick was correct, but the three-dimensional projection made the whole experience confusing, especially due to the three time events occupying the same space. Those in the present found some of the objects and beings moving around them, to pass through their bodies, like ghosts. The sensation was quite eerie to Vera.

"*We never found out what happened to Silargh and his passengers. Now, the ship's Zarfha can finally tell us.*"

These were the events that had followed the difficult landing of the ship; a story that even Jorh and his companions had never been able to see until now. They knew Silargh's ship had never made it back to Mars, but what had happened to him and his people had only been speculations. The Kahnu's telepathic abilities could be used across vast distances, but not from one planet to another.

The valley of giants

The valley was silent. The sun was almost gone by now, and the evening sky was slowly laying its soft blanket of dusk over the quiet landscape. As the last crimson rays of sunlight filtering through the mountain tops were slowly fading, the quiet sounds of the jungle below were making their entrance, one by one, on the stage of another beautiful cretaceous night. Coastal winds still had enough energy to make their song heard among the trees and bushes, and here and there, strange sounds could now be heard. A few chirps, up a giant tree at the foot of a hill to the right; a big splash in a lake to the west. Gliding above a cliff to the east, a few enigmatic looking birds, several times the size of the largest condors ever recorded in modern human history, were screaming their prowling "quacks." The rummage of animals passing through bushes down below, would randomly stop, and then start again. An occasional roar from a Rapetosaurus reverberated in the distance.

Nearby, two Masiakasaurus were scoping the area. Their eyes scrutinizing the grounds, searching for food, they were making loud snorting sounds. Walking swiftly through the bushes with agility, they were soon focusing their attention on the mayhem ahead. They had been drawn to the place when, a few hours earlier, they had witnessed a giant fire ball zooming across the sky, followed by a devastating thundering crash. Now, in the calm of the early evening, animals were starting to show themselves, curious and drawn by others. If anything, they were seeking a potential meal. At the bottom of the hill, a wide path had been forced through the jungle. Trees and vegetation had been crushed and ripped out of the ground in a long straight line that revealed a tortured landscape full of debris. The path left by the scraping and dragging of the huge alien ship, when it had force-landed, was obvious. The terrain was bare in places, accentuated by deep parallel trenches, dug through rocks and earth, over several kilometers. Smoke and fumes, still rising from fires burning here and there, could be seen all along the mowed corridor the ship had carved. The entire scene was attesting to the violence of the crash. At the end of the giant runway, a gigantic white mass, unrecognizable and definitely not of this world, rested, partially buried at an uncomfortable angle, its front-end stuck in the ground under a pile of rocks, dirt, and vegetation. The vessel was leaning on its right side, and its back was rising above the floor of the landscape substantially. Purple gases were escaping from beneath the wreck. Even five hours after the event, the heat emanating from the spacecraft was still preventing animals from venturing too close.

Slowly making passes above the wreckage, a young Pterosaur, intrigued by the oddity, was attempting to land on top of the strange structure, when a side panel suddenly moved, releasing a column of smoke with a loud whooshing sound, sending the animal back in the sky, its large wings flopping away as he screamed a treacherous "croaaak", and disappeared in the night. Inside the Aruk cockpit, Silargh was trying to get his bearings. At first disoriented through the haze of colors and shadows moving about, he started to regain his vision. Bathed in purple light, the confusion of crackling noises, passengers shuffling around, and occasional vibrations, made him realize where he was. He was in the ship, alive and seemingly uninjured. He was still secured to his seat thanks to the magnetic harness in the back of his suit. The purple hue of the walls around him told Silargh the atmospheric controls inside the ship had not been compromised by the rough landing. Any malfunctioning of the life support systems, or any hull breach, would have caused the ship's internal walls to turn to green. As long as they stayed purple, they were safe; at least as far as that was concerned.

He had no idea how long he had been unconscious, but he knew it had been a while. He could hear some of the passengers' thoughts and feelings. A few were already moving about the ship. Most were scared, disoriented, and worried about their own situation. He needed to assess the damages to the vessel, and everyone's state of health. He knew Tehe had not returned to her seat before the crash. He attempted to locate her.

"*Tehe? Tehe? Are you OK? Where are you?*"

But Tehe did not respond. Still a bit disoriented, he got up and began looking for her. He soon could sense that most of the passengers with him in the cockpit, ten or so, were OK. A few were still coming out of their groggy state, but no one appeared physically injured. He moved on into the belly of the vessel. Those still in their own quarters, seemed to have fared the best. He checked the Time-Frost room before reaching the cargo bay. She was nowhere to be found. He finally got to the infirmary. He instantly knew something was wrong. Someone was badly hurt. He entered the room to find Tehe lying on top of Berhis' body, clutching to him, her face buried in his chest, moaning.

Lishieru noticed Silargh the moment he entered the room.

"*He was thrown out against a wall when we first decelerated so violently, right before landing. He was trying to secure two containers in the cargo bay...*"

Tehe suddenly felt his presence in the room and got up from Berhis' body. She turned and looked at Silargh with such anger and despair, that for a moment, he feared what she might do. But she just kept looking at him with rage until she exploded.

"*It's all your fault! Why did you have to do that? He would still be alive if it wasn't for you! You killed him! He was...*" her emotions turned from anger to hate and then, as the tears started rolling down her face again, she turned back and collapsed by Berhis, sobbing. She was holding her face in her hands, looking at the love of her life. He was gone. And in truth, she knew it wasn't Silargh's fault.

"*I'm sorry, Tehe... I am so sorry... I had no choice. I had to stop the ship before it crashed, or we would all have died... I am truly sorry...*" There was nothing else he could say. He was genuinely distraught as well. Berhis was his friend. He could feel her pain, and it only added to his own. Tehe knew he had done the only thing he could have to save them. They would all have perished without Silargh's quick maneuver. She just wanted Berhis to still be alive with all her heart... She wanted it so much… But she knew blaming Silargh wouldn't bring him back. As she slowly started to calm down, and eventually managed to hold back the tears, Silargh repeated "*I am sorry.*"

She looked up at him and mustered to say, "*I know,*" with crushing sadness in her eyes, "*I know...*"

#

By the time Silargh was back in the cockpit and opened the ship's window to take a look at their situation, the night had turned pitch black. And apart from a weak moon crescent, dimly lighting general shapes around the ship, the outside surroundings did not look very inviting. Scanning the immediate area, Silargh noticed the bare earth and dirt in the small crater left by the ship. A thick perimeter of trees and vegetation were also surrounding them, all alien things he had never witnessed in person, or touched, and only seen in the Zarfha books of the Grand Hallis library. Up above, the thin slice of moon visible was much smaller than he had expected. His home world counted three large satellites of comparable size, but orbiting closer to Kahnu, they appeared noticeably larger. Straight ahead in the distance rose a majestic mountain. Its peak was covered in a white layer of ice, clearly visible in the pale moon light. Silargh's attention was suddenly diverted by a moving shadow in the night sky. Hovering in uneven circles far above the ship, the flying creature the crash had attracted earlier was now keeping its distance, screaming an occasional croak. Down below, a few small rodents and other creatures could barely be discerned, rummaging about in the vegetation. Already feeling bold enough to approach within a few meters of the ship, a larger predator let out a loud growl that would have scared a good number of spectators.

Suddenly, Silargh noticed movement in the trees ahead. An even larger creature appeared from behind the thick vegetation, immediately followed by another. Although of a relatively small size compared to a Kahnu, those were not beings to tangle with, and Silargh already knew some species inhabiting this planet to be very aggressive. The two creatures were definitely on that list. He did not know it but Silargh was staring at two Masiakasaurus, fierce carnivores from Earth's Jurassic period.

"*What are they?*" asked a young Kahnu girl who had just entered the messy room.

"*Dahhize! How are you, child? Were you hurt at all during landing?*" he asked, surprised to see her out of her room.

"*No, I'm OK. Thanks. But what is that?*" she asked, pointing at the two predators outside.

"*I don't remember their names, but I remember learning about them in training class. They are very dangerous. They hunt in packs of two or more.*"

"*I think they look cute,*" she said smiling.

"*They may look small and cute, but they can kill you. Don't forget that,*" he replied with a firm voice.

Unexpectedly, a massive dark figure crossed in front of the large window and rushed towards the two Masiakasaurus. Fleeing for his life, one of them sprinted back into the thick vegetation a few meters away, but the other wasn't so lucky. Taken by surprise, the animal reacted too late, and the giant's jaws came down swiftly, and grabbed its back in a clenching bite. The large Majungasaurus, measuring a good twenty-five meters in length, lifted the doomed Masiakasaurus up in the air and, crushing several of its ribs in the process, and shook the animal furiously from side to side. The small raptor screamed loudly for a few seconds, before the massive jaws finally crushed its spine, killing it instantly. The proud predator then turned around and calmly walked away, the limp body of its next meal hanging off the sides of its lower jaw.

Both Silargh and Dahhize kept silent for a moment, staring at the window, in shock. They were not used to such a graphic display of violence. In fact, most life forms on Kahnu were non-predatory. It was hard for them to watch what they had just witnessed. The Kahnus were a peaceful people who fed on different forms of algae, found in abundance in their big ocean, and so did most animals on their planets. Only a very few did, but even those were rarely witnessed. But what they had just witnessed was truly shocking and mortifying to both of them. Dahhize's smile was gone, and Silargh realized the precarious reality of their situation, having crash landed several thousand kilometers from their intended destination.

"*Why did the gravitation generator raise the outside weight of the ship so drastically on our descent? Only a few of us can control the Zarfha engine...*" Silargh was thinking out loud, and the young girl was listening attentively.

"*You think someone is responsible for the crash?*" she asked.

"*I'm not sure. But I intend to find out...*"

Inside the crushed ship in the Madagascar cave, Jorh had waved at the Zarfha and the scene around everyone changed quickly to show Silargh seated in front of the clear window. The new view now showed the landscape in a bright sunny day.

"*Silargh, we are at the cave. Everything is ready,*" informed him a telepathic voice.

"*OK, great! On our way,*" he replied.

Turning to his crew, he announced preparations for the maneuver. They had been working on restoring main power to the ship for the past few days now. Most of the ship's systems were functional. But the Mahkiar matrix controlling the Zarfha engine was unusable. The other major damage the ship had suffered was a hull breach near the nose of the vessel; an impossible repair without more Kehoas, a substance only found on their home world. That meant they were stuck on Kahjuna for good. There would be no way for them to get the light they had come for, and they would not be able to rendezvous with Jorh and the others on Kesra. All they could do now was to do their best to survive and adapt to the harsh environment of Kahjuna, their new home. Although the ship could no longer travel through the vacuum of space due to the damage its shell had sustained, flying in Earth's atmosphere would have been no problem, had the gravitation engine not been damaged. The ship was now flyable solely on limited power and going to the blue planet's South Pole, their original destination, was no longer an option. The power left in the Zarfha would have to be preserved if they intended to survive.

Silargh, seated in the center of the group, raised his arm and gestured the necessary commands to the hovering orb. Soon, the ship was lifting itself off the ground, in the mix of debris and earth falling off its surface, with trees and rocks crashing loudly to the ground behind the alien vessel. Wild animals watched the large foreign object rise slowly above the tree canopy from a distance. The spectacle was the center of attention for the next several minutes, as the ship made its way quietly to the large opening that had just been artificially created in the mountain's face. Maneuvering the vessel through the dark passage, Silargh eventually brought the ship down to its final resting place. Meanwhile, the gigantic entrance gap was already being resealed by the crew using several Zarfhas to levitate the giant boulders back in place.

The next few weeks would prove to be difficult, to say the least. The breathable atmosphere on Earth was not that different from the one on their home planet. And although Kahnu's gravity was about one and a half time that of Earth's, both worlds could have been considered compatible for both species. But without the Flex-pod source of power, making their present location a safe and sustainable home was greatly jeopardized. The real challenge for them now was to survive in the foreign and harsh environment outside. In fact, the castaways would have had a better chance, if they had landed on Earth during one of the planet's many ice ages. They would have felt right at home when Earth's temperatures were substantially closer to that of their world, and wild life would have been much less threatening a few million years later. But their present was now, the end of the Jurassic era, and wanted or not, they were here to stay.

For the next few months, the planetary castaways would work diligently at resolving their gravitation engine issues while trying to survive the treacherous wilderness around them, but in vain. Eventually, one by one, they would succumb, either from animal attacks or for some, from sickness contracted on the alien planet. Earth's numerous viruses had no equal on their planet, an ice world devoid of such pests. The Kahnu immune system did not stand a chance. But that story, Jorh and his companion felt was unwarranted to show to the human group. Instead, they opted to move forward with the rest of their findings.

From Ape to Man

The three-dimensional projection took them back inside Silargh's abandoned ship and the five explorers that had visited it earlier.

"Jorh said this was the lab," whispered Dedrick to Vera, when the images got to a room filled with odd looking containers and rows of storage compartments half open or broken. It was obvious the damage had been caused by something else than an earthquake. Not something necessarily more powerful, but of an intelligent doing. Some of the items in the room had most definitely been hung by someone. Countless lines of an unrecognizable material were connecting several pillars and tall objects as if deliberately placed in an intricate order. An intelligent design meant to display something important, or maybe a message. At least, for a moment the idea lingered in Sabrina's mind until Mahhzee corrected her.

"*Actually, we can tell you what those are. The cargo inside the ship was transporting a large sample of our planet's living library; several dozen species, at least those that could survive the transfer. Along with them, what your people called DNA strands were also gathered in the hope to save what could be. We didn't know where we would eventually relocate, but Jashi-Da, the moon you call Europa, was our preferred choice. We had, until then, kept from interfering with the evolution of any planet in Alhis-Ta, your solar system. Your planet and ours were not the only ones harboring life. So did Jashi-Da. At the time, the life forms on the small icy moon were still quite primitive, but several large marine creatures, as well as countless small ones, thrived in its iced ocean. When it was certain we had to abandon Kahnu, Garnak, our loyal Keeper, had made sure the two ships had on board everything that could be saved. Kahnu's rare eco-system had to be preserved at all cost. Each ship had a large cargo, covering not only our culture's knowledge but also, and most importantly, life; living representatives of our world. Our DNA was also kept safely on the ship's labs. Let me show you something.*"

Mahhzee turned again her attention to the sphere, and with a quick hand gesture, brought another view of the lab. The place was the same but appeared much less messy. The lines were gone and most of the machines, large container columns and display cases seemed fairly intact. The place looked old, obviously abandoned, and covered in dust, but most instruments and containers appeared well organized and orderly laid.

"*That's obviously not what I filmed...*" thought Dedrick.

The difference in quality was incomparable. The three-dimensional world they were now in seemed so real, it was hard to believe they were in an artificial projection. The space changed seamlessly to a view of the outside of the cavern, where countless creatures were slowly making their way to the cave, through the same fissure the four visitors had used earlier to reach the cavern. They were so great in number, that a traffic jam was taking place at the crevice's entrance. Something was attracting the animals by hordes. Several species, including some large birds, had also chosen to enter the passage. Following their progression, they were soon at the cave, where the strangest gathering was taking place. More tortoises than any human had ever seen before in one place were blanketing the ground of the cave, along with countless rodents. Several dozen large saber-tooth cats were grouped to the far left, forming walking circles within circles, pacing behind one another, as if engaged in an elaborate ritual. To the right, along the far wall of the cavern, over fifty giant hyaenas were resting on the floor, all posed like sphinxes, facing the damaged vessel, surprisingly uninterested in the other preys around them. Above, circling slowly the ceiling of the cave, a myriad of birds, some as small as canaries, others larger than eagles, were flying orderly in countless circles and directions around the perimeter of the space. On any other day, an absolute carnage would have taken place in such a situation. Yet, for some unknown reason, the various species were at peace with each other. The predators and the preys, as if gathered in some sanctuary where the laws of nature did not apply, a common ground where some invisible force was countering the natural impulse of their wild instinct, were cohabiting effortlessly.

Only one species seemed at unrest; the chimpanzees. They were getting more and more agitated. Their skittish behavior was as much due to the presence of the other predators as it was to the ship. Somehow, the calming power of the vessel did not seem to have the soothing effect on them it did on the other species. Fearful and hesitant at first, it wasn't long before several of the chimps found their way through the belly of the ship. Tossing and breaking almost everything they came in contact with, most likely looking for food, some eventually made their way into the Kahnu lab. One of the apes, of a smaller stature than most of his group, approached a small glossy object another chimp had just thrown violently to the floor. He grabbed it with one hand and brought it to his face, taking a deep short sniff from it. Proceeding to turn the artifact upside down above him, he began to drink the liquid running down from it until it was dry. Seconds later, the driven animal was frantically going through every container it could find, drinking everything he came across. He finally found a container he could not break, not easily at least. After several attempts at hitting the jar on the ground, the object finally burst open and the small chimp rushed to collect his prize. Grabbing several of the gelatinous eggs released from the broken container with one swift swoop, he rushed them to his mouth and managed to cut himself in the process, fingers, lips and throat alike. Suddenly feeling the pain caused by the sharp pieces, he dropped everything, and ran out of the room screaming and moaning. But the damage was done, and the animal had forever altered the future of his species. Mahhzee made another movement with her hand, and the surroundings disappeared, as if engulfed slowly by a fog. The sphere glowed a second longer, and then landed quietly to rest in front of the human observers, its three-dimensional light show coming to an end.

"Did we just witness what I think we did?" asked François out loud.

"What?" asked Sabrina.

"*When was this?*" asked Dedrick mentally.

"*About two million Earth years ago,*" replied Jorh. "*We are as surprised as you are. We had not anticipated something like this could take place. But now, it explains many things. It would appear your species and ours have more in common than sharing the same sun. A part of us is in you. That would explain why we are able to communicate telepathically with your kind. You can hear us because part of our DNA has morphed with yours.*"

Jorh turned to look at Gahneo and Mahhzee and went on, "*The three of us had been wondering about that. You see, back when our people used to visit your planet, we had tried many times to establish some form of telepathic connection with the animals of your world but had never succeeded. I was at a loss for the reason your landing on Kesra had triggered a reaction in our ship's systems and had awakened me.*"

"*Now, we understand,*" concurred Mahhzee with a caring smile that betrayed her feelings for the small group of Earthlings.

"You mean we're... You're the reason?" The biochemist in Liu was completely baffled. "But...you can't transfer DNA like that. It would take countless generations over several millennia to take place. How can this be the...?" She was now speaking out loud, too distracted by the puzzling discovery to care to think only.

"*We are fairly certain. The blue liquid you saw the creature drink was a genetic compound our scientists used to cure diseases on my planet. And the Tayags, the small eggs of Ghervz, provided everything our body needed to cure itself from anything we had ever encountered over the millennia. We know its genetic signature, and we know what it can do. There is no doubt. Your current human DNA was genetically spawned that day by the combination of those two elements. The Zarfha records show the animal's intelligence grew substantially over the next few hundred years. It took many more generations to develop what you call self-awareness, but the seed was planted.*"

"No way! That's the missing link?" Tendai was just as dumbfounded as the rest of them. "You're saying that's how we branched off and went from ape to man? I think most of our scientists would have disagreed with you on this, Jorh."

"*I am sorry to disagree, Tendai, but we are confident this is how and when your kind began its journey to become human. Although some apes on your planet began walking on two legs long before this event, the ship's archive never recorded any sign of intelligence beyond that of your primates, until this. The Zarfha archives don't lie. It is a shame that none of the other creatures on your world had a chance to get to that evolution step, be glad you did. You are the last representatives of an amazing, wonderful and unique race, a hybrid in a way, combining the genes of two worlds, and it pleases us greatly to know some of us is in you.*"

"*It's so hard to believe... We look so...different from you...* Vera was looking at the aliens in a different way, she realized. They were all looking at each other a bit differently. The events of the last few weeks had brought them closer, but this new information was quite different. There was a sense of belonging, a new level of understanding and connection; a feeling of inner peace.

A long silence followed. The aliens listened quietly to all the thoughts floating in the room while their human companions, unable to shield their mind from them, tried to make sense of it all. It was quite a revelation. Most anthropologists back on Earth would have been amazed. Some would have been crushed, all their confident theories proved wrong, but finally knowing what had set man apart from the rest of the animal kingdom would have been one of the most profound answers of all time. And for many religious entities around the world, such a revelation would have caused quite a stir in their beliefs. François, looking at his alien ancestors in their hovering chairs, thought about the many God's mankind had venerated throughout history. Every supreme being, every Deity who had been imagined, coming down from the heavens above or the Earth below to create man, were standing right in front of them. And as amazing at it may seem, Francois realized man had finally met his maker, or at the very least, one who had played a major role in its evolution.

#

The following day, the ship was resting on a large plateau of ice, on the continent of Antarctica. Jorh and Gahneo had left before the human passengers had gotten up to go find the "White Light," the power source Silargh and his crew had originally come to Earth to collect.

"*They are back*," announced Mahhzee to Dedrick's group.

Outside, the two aliens and their hovering container were approaching on the white ground below. Dedrick wondered what the "White Light" the aliens so desperately needed was. The Kahnus had mentioned that the "Light" was only found on Earth. But what was it? He would have to ask. After entering the purple back gate, Mahhzee's two companions soon reached the cargo bay and secured the precious item. She was already taking the ship back into space when the two aliens entered the cockpit and sat among their human passengers.

"*The light is secured*," told Jorh to his sister.

"*Everything here is ready*," she replied.

The vessel was now stationary fifty kilometers above Earth. The outside view was breathtaking, even if the planet looked sadly dark. François, staring at the continents slowly shifting as the Earth revolved below, was momentarily distracted by a small object flying towards them. It took him a few seconds to make out the satellite. There were still countless of them orbiting the planet. Although several had crashed back on Earth over the years, following the great chemical war, many were still flying blindly on their preset loop around the globe, sending their data to no one. It flew by at several thousand kilometers an hour, only a few meters from the vessel. He jerked back instinctively. He was still trying to get use to that. Jorh had assured him the ship would automatically move out of the way, if one of them was to come too close. There was absolutely no reason to worry. Still, it was unnerving. He turned his attention back to the conversation at hand. Tendai was still trying to find a solution to their food problem.

"*Maybe we could start replanting some of the seeds we have with us from our greenhouse and with your help—*"

"*You will run out of food and water long before you can rebuild anything on your planet. Earth's air and waters are polluted. And you won't have anything left to drink soon,*" replied Jorh, looking at the small group.

"Fuck! So, what do we do?" blurted Tendai out loud, looking at the Russian.

As usual, all eyes turned to Dedrick. In consequence, as he often did, the Russian commander felt compelled to find a solution to their dire predicament. He briefly looked at them, then paused on Vera and his little girl for several seconds, before looking back at Jorh. For the first time since they had landed on Mars, over fifteen years ago, he was at a loss. He didn't know what to do. He couldn't think of a way to survive on Earth or Mars. The greenhouse they had left behind in the alien's cave was certainly lost by now. Unattended for weeks, they all knew it would not have survive. No matter where they went, or what they did, they were doomed.

"*No, you can still survive. Come with us,*" objected Mahhzee, having listened to Dedrick's thoughts.

"*What do you mean? Where?*" he replied puzzled.

"*Yes, I'm curious too. Where can we possibly go? Back to Mars? Our station is gone. Earth? Same thing. So, what's left? Europa?*" asked Tendai sarcastically.

"*No, there.*"

They all turned their attention to Mahhzee. She slowly waved her hand in front of the viewing window, revealing a dark starry sky. As the image zoomed in closer and closer, one particular star in the center of the view began to shine brighter than all others. Soon, a planet was in view, and Mahhzee dropped her hand back.

"*This is Ahtona; the First World.*"

"*Ahtona? The planet you told us your Elders escaped to? But, I thought you said your ship couldn't fly that far?*" asked a surprised François.

"*That is correct. Aruks are moon travelers. They are not designed to travel outside the solar system. However, now that we have the white light, and enough Gobhan, we believe we can reach Ahtona. It will just take some time. About six thousand of your Earth years,*" she said casually.

"Six thousand years?!" exclaimed Tendai and Liu in unison.

"I'm sorry, did you say six thousand years?" Sabrina was just as baffled.

"You will sleep during the flight. Like us. We have already made plans to leave this system and go to Ahtona. We see no other choice for you. We do not know if the Ehoran and its crew made it to Ahtona, but if they did, we hope to reunite with our kind," replied Jorh.

"Huh, I don't know if you realize it, but your people left for that planet, about seventy million years ago, right? Assuming they made it there, and assuming they survived, and again, assuming they didn't kill themselves at some point like we did, they must have evolved so much that they may not even look like you or recognize you. You may not even be able to communicate with them. Their language may have changed, even their ways, and how will we fit in a civilization of aliens, millions of years ahead of our own?" asked Ladli.

"It is true, we may appear primitive to them. After seventy million years, they will have evolved in many ways. But I'm afraid are choices are limited. Dedrick, my friends, like us, you and your people have nowhere else to go. Your Earth can no longer support life, and you cannot go back to Mars. So, we offer you the only option we have. Come with us. The pods can be recalibrated to keep you in Time-Frost during the journey to Ahtona."

"I think it's the craziest idea I've ever heard in whole my life. I mean, how can you be sure these pods can work on us the way they do on you? And what guarantees do you have that your Ahtona is still a livable world, anyway? A lot can happen in seventy million years…" asked a reserved Tendai.

"Tendai! Use your mind to talk. Stop talking out loud, that's not polite!" finally objected Sabrina, tired of noticing his reluctance in joining the telepathic conversation.

"I know. I'm sorry! I keep forgetting. *I mean, I will,"* he answered.

"It's alright, Tendai. And you are correct. We do not know for sure what we'll find there. And we can't predict how the planet has evolved during all that time. There are too many unknowns and variables. But we believe this is the best option, for all of us."

#

Later that night, the group was addressing their situation once again.

"There is no way I'm gonna let them put my little girl in one of those pods!"

"It's the only way, love. We can't stay on Earth, and we won't survive long on Mars. What Jorh offers makes sense. It's our only option, Vera."

"But Dedrick, it's crazy; asleep for six thousand years? And how do we know their hibernating pods will work on us? What if sleeping in those things kills us? What if-"

"Vera, Vera. I understand how you feel, believe me. I would never want anything to happen to either you or Chasma. You know that. But we have no choice. Earth is gone, and the Mars First station isn't safe anymore. We will run out of food and water soon if we stay on this ship awake. Jorh's plan is our only chance."

"Hey guys, I found some three-dimensional maps of the Ahtona region in our database, strangely enough," announced François, as he glided silently into the room. "It's a multiple star system about fifty parsec, or 160 light years away in the constellation of Lyra. The night skies of any world there must look incredible. Jorh's description of their first world makes me believe we're in for quite a spectacle. Personally, I can't wait."

"You're both insane!"

"Vera, come on. What else do you suggest we do?" Dedrick was holding her shoulders, looking straight at her. She seemed to be searching for an answer, but quickly gave up in frustration. "I don't know. I don't know what we should do. I'm scared," she replied tearing up.

"We are all scared," said Ladli. "I can't even imagine what it really means to be in hibernation for 6000 years?! I think we're all overwhelmed by the idea. But the reality is that we have nowhere else to go. This is it, Vera. It's all or nothing. But I tell you what, if the aliens are correct and we all make it there, we're in for an amazing journey. We'll be in another star system, exploring an alien planet. And imagine what we might find? If the Kahnu Elders made it there millions of years ago and managed to rebuild a new civilization, imagine how advanced they must be now? They must have amazing cities and spaceships, and knowledge beyond what any of us can even imagine..."

"Look, they were in those pods for millions of years and they made it just fine," added François.

"Of course! They're aliens. What makes you think it will work on us?" replied Vera sharply.

"I don't know... Somehow, I believe they know what they are doing. And I think it sounds like a pretty amazing adventure, if you ask me," he replied with a big smile.

"Amazing? Amazing?! It's crazy! That's what it is," suddenly shouted Tendai. "I've been biting my tongue, listening to all of you and I can't believe you are seriously entertaining the idea of following this crazy plan!"

"Hey, take it easy! I'm just trying to find some positive in this whole mess. I know as much as you do that our situation is pretty bleak, but I also believe we're here for a reason. We've all dreamed of exploring other worlds, to go beyond that horizon and discover new things. Well, here's the perfect opportunity. We've come this far. The aliens are offering us a ride, and I think we should take it."

"Tendai, they are right," added Liu in a low voice. "I am scared too but… I don't wanna die here."

"Me neither. I remember why I joined Mars First. I wanted to live an adventure. I wanted to do something nobody could take from me; something special. I used to dream of traveling to distant stars when I was a little girl, to discover new worlds and alien life forms no one had ever seen before. We've all had those dreams. Think about it… The more I think about it, the more I am convinced this is going to be unbelievable! I say we go to Ahtona!" finished Sabrina with confidence.

Tendai sat down, feeling defeated. He knew they were right. He was just scared to death at the idea of getting stuck in one of those containers. He wanted desperately to find another way, but he knew there was none. Ladli looked at him and smiled tenderly. "I know how you feel, hun. But I have to agree. I say we go on. Who knows? We might actually make it. After all, what's a few thousand years?" she added with a sneer.

#

The next morning came early for the group, gathered in the make-shift greenhouse to say their last farewell before the crazy interstellar voyage.

"So, we're sure we want to do this?" asked Vera.

"Yes, it's the only way." Dedrick was holding her in his arms.

They were all looking at each other, nervous and worried, but also somewhat excited.

"Remember what Jorh said. We will not realize how much time has passed when we wake up. It will be like going to bed and waking up the next morning, as if only a few hours had passed. I'm sure it won't be a pleasant one, especially after being immobile for so long, but I've had plenty of hangovers in my days. How worse can it be?" François had a smirk on his face, as usual.

"So, this is it guys, our last moments before the deep sleep." Dedrick looked at the few plants gathered around the room. For a moment, he contemplated telling them that the aliens were planning to eject the make-shift greenhouse before take-off. Mahhzee had explained to him that it would begin to decompose soon and would only cause a lot of rotten bacteria to infest the ship. She wasn't too concerned for the vessel, none of those simple organisms would survive the long trip, but there was no point on keeping them onboard. What could be kept had already been stored in the remaining fifteen Time-Frost pods. It wouldn't be enough to sustain them long once there, but with a little luck, they might manage to plant some on the new world, allowing them to regrow food again. In the end, Dedrick chose not to tell the rest of the group. It would only make their precarious situation feel even dire.

For a long moment, they all stared at the outside view of their home planet. Mahhzee had zoomed in close enough for them to see the murky waters of the Indian Ocean crashing its foamy waves along a deserted coast. Not the most beautiful visual of Earth to remember, but this was what it had become. The planet they had all cherished and grown to love, the world of countless life forms and beauty, of so many generations before them, with their great human achievements and all their love stories, this world of amazing triumphs and tragedies, transformation and rebirth, was no longer the paradise they remembered and probably would never be again.

Vera put her hand on her daughter's hair and brushed her fingers gently through it.

"I wish you could've seen it the way it was, baby. It was so beautiful. There were colorful plants and trees, birds and animals of all sorts, and big cities. People sang and danced, you could swim in the ocean, and there were dolphins, and whales, and horses! You would've loved horses. We had some wonderful things on Earth..."

Tears began to roll down Vera's cheeks again.

"Mommy, don't cry. It's gonna be OK. Wait until you see Ahtona. You're gonna love it. It's beautiful!"

Vera turned to look at her little girl. The smile on her face gave her the strange sensation Chasma had been to the alien planet already. "*How could that be?*"

A very strange feeling came over her, something deep and ominous; an inner voice telling her how special Chasma really was. She hugged her daughter tightly as if never wanting to let go. After what seemed like countless hugs from everyone, the seven friends and their little Martian girl floated slowly together to the main hibernating chamber, where Gahneo and Mahhzee were already getting things ready for them.

A million dreams

Dedrick was watching Vera entering her pod naked. Jorh had told them their clothes would not survive the long trek, and only they could be put in Time-Frost. At first voicing some reservations, everyone had eventually capitulated and removed their clothing and jewelry. Staring at Sabrina with her arms crossed over her naked chest, François was sitting in his capsule, his bare torso strangely poking through the clear shell of the alien pod. Not far, Chasma was already lying in hers, a big smile on her young face. The Russian commander scanned quickly the rest of the team, trying not to linger on the females any longer than necessary. Sabrina caught his furtive gaze and winked at him. He quickly looked elsewhere, feeling quite embarrassed. François, who had just witnessed the exchange, smiled as he leaned back in his pod. Ladli had to comfort Tendai, who was once again uncertain about the whole idea. The Zimbabwean finally entered his Time-Frost pod. Nearby, Liu was clumsily getting situated with one arm while trying to hide her breasts with the other.

When everyone was finally settled, Gahneo and Mahhzee waved an intricate series of hand movements to the Zarfha, and each pod began closing on the human voyagers. The aliens had promised them the experience would be a pleasant one, but Jorh had also told them not to panic once the pods were closed. He had explained in detail that the purple gases inside would quickly put them to sleep once the capsules were sealed, and that they might experience a feeling of euphoria before passing out.

The Zarfha at the center of the room was now rising toward the ceiling of the large space, spinning faster and faster. Mahhzee approached Dedrick while he gazed one last time at Chasma's face disappearing in the purple haze of her capsule.

"*It is time, Dedrick. Everyone is safely secured in their individual pods. We will monitor your Time-Frost signs until we are sure you are all set for the voyage. We wish you a good and restful journey.*"

Behind her, the Time-Frost pods and their eight human passengers were now hovering silently in their respective places above the platform. Directly above them, the spinning Zarfha had begun its dazzling light show. Gahneo walked gracefully back to the entrance and glided out of the room. Mahhzee was about to follow when Dedrick had a thought.

"Wait, Mahhzee. If we had not been there to get you out of these pods, you'd still be in them, right? So how will we get out when we get to our destination?"

"This is different. We were locked in from the outside. We do not have time now for me to explain, but you do not need to worry about that now. I promise, the Aruk will wake us when we get there."

As the alien ship gained altitude over the Antarctic ice, Dedrick felt his fingers get heavy, then his feet and legs. Soon, his entire body was completely relaxed and engulfed in the churning purple haze of gas that was filling his pod. A growing sense of joy slowly came over him, increasing quickly into an uncontrollable feeling of pleasure that made him want to laugh out loud. The purple gas soon became so thick, he could no longer see anything but darkness, and as his eyes started to close and his breathing slowed, he had one last thought. Would he dream during the voyage? Slowly but irrevocably falling under in a deep sleep, he vaguely heard a telepathic reply from Mahhzee who had heard his thoughts.

"*Yes, Dedrick, you will all dream a million dreams. Safe journey, my friends, See you on Ahtona.*"

After checking that all eight were in a perfect state of hibernation, Mahhzee rejoined Jorh and Gahneo in the vessel's navigation center, where the three of them would go over the final preparations for the lengthy journey. And soon, they too would climb into their own pods and go to sleep for a very, very long time.

To be continued...

ABOUT THE AUTHOR

Yves LF Giraud was born in France. He moved to the US in the late 80s to pursue a career in music. Since then, Yves has written over 200 songs and poems. In 2014, Yves began writing his first novel, Kahnu, after moving to the small town of Burnsville, North Carolina.
In order to pursue both his passions as a novelist and a singer-songwriter, Yves moved to Nashville, Tennessee in 2018, with his friend, agent and manager, Misty Huffman, and his dog, Rio.

For more info on Yves' books and music, please visit Yves LF Giraud's official website at: WWW.YVESGIRAUD.COM

Made in the USA
Lexington, KY
25 September 2018